OUR SINS IN BLOOD

COVEN OF SIN BOOK 1

AIDEN PIERCE

D1522450

Editing: Killing it Write Editing

Cover Design: Addictive Covers

CONTENTS

A Word of Warning   VII

1. A Bump in the Night   I

2. "Hello, Ruby"   6

3. No Princess Should Live in a Cage   II

4. A Man so Dark and Deadly   15

5. Brainwashed Princess   20

6. The Devil's Spawn   28

7. Vincent Feral is an Asshole   35

8. The Feral King   40

9. The Youngblood   48

10. A Bite for a Bite   55

11. A Bloody Kiss and a Brutal Vow   63

12. Death Drives a Rolls-Royce   69

13. An Unhealthy Obsession   76

14. A Dark Addiction 84

15. The Silver Prince 92

16. Vampire Monarchies Suck 99

17. It's a Date 108

18. Bastards, Lies, and Green Eyes 116

19. Pretzels, Zombies, and a Kiss 127

20. Just Like the Rest of Them 137

21. Questions and Answers 145

22. The Man on the Flyer 152

23. The Monster Inside 161

24. Dirty Deal with the Youngblood 170

25. Bitter Goodbyes and Bloody Bargains 177

26. Fangs in the Thigh, Knife in the Back 184

27. Good Little Monster 189

28. Aphrodisiac 196

29. His Bidding 202

30. A Stupid Idea 208

31. Girl Talk 216

32. A Death Wish 226

33. Time to Play 233

34. A Choice in Blood 244

35. Mercy 251

36. Blood, Lace, and a Touch of Disgrace 259

37. A Dangerous Game   265

38. Once Bitten   275

39. Sibling Rivalry   284

40. Lies, Seduction, and a Plan   292

41. Miss Lavinia Sharpe   299

42. The Half-Blood and the Prince   310

43. Pheromone   320

44. Sterling   326

45. Reborn with a Silver Spoon   339

46. Golden Gift from a Silver Prince   351

47. Lesson in Blood   360

48. Sate the Monster   368

49. Crashing the Party   373

50. Skeletons in the Attic   381

51. Magic   390

52. Sins in Blood   398

53. Precipice   407

54. Filthy Mouths and Favorite Sins   414

55. An Offering   420

56. Bloody Union   428

57. Rude Awakening   435

58. An Unexpected Moment   445

59. Showdown   453

60. What in the Hell is Vincent Feral?   462

61. A Dangerous Deal   470

62. Dark Pledge   482

63. Midnight Snack   492

64. Night with the Youngblood   501

65. A Promise   513

66. Bathroom Break   522

67. What's His   534

68. Confrontation   540

69. Queen Psychopath   546

70. Monster   554

71. Dance with the Beast   562

72. Rescue   571

73. Rain of Silver   583

74. Revelations and a Sordid Promise   592

A Note from the Author   606

A Word of Warning

This book contains graphic sex, violence, and dark themes such as kidnapping, bullying, bloodplay, cutting, chokeplay, bondage, violence, gore, and scenes recounting sexual trauma. Reader discretion is advised.

CHAPTER ONE

A BUMP IN THE NIGHT

E ver since I could remember, I'd been a prisoner.

When most people thought about prison, they probably imagined steel bars and orange uniforms. They didn't think of a little girl's room with painted pink walls and stuffed unicorns arranged on a frilly pink bedspread in a three-bedroom suburban home in Quincy, Massachusetts.

But it'd been my prison for twenty-three years.

It wasn't anybody's fault that I was a prisoner in my mother's house. I didn't believe in God, so I couldn't blame him for giving me a weak heart. But some days I'd pretend I still believed in a higher power just so I could have someone to blame, someone to get angry at.

Because it wasn't my mom's fault that I was sick.

Now that I was older, I'd moved past a lot of the resentment I had for her when I was a teenager. Puberty's a bitch behind bars. But I get it. She's just trying to protect me.

Were the bars on the window and the half dozen locks on the door necessary? Maybe if I was she-hulk or something. I understood where her paranoia was coming from. The slightest startle, a bump in the night, a trip, even a scary movie could make my heart rate skyrocket, and then I would fall down dead, and it would all be over.

According to my doctor, I had the worst case of Tachycardia he'd ever seen. If my heart rate rose too high, it could result in a stroke, cardiac arrest, or death.

Not that dying seemed like that bad of an alternative most days. In my darkest and weakest moments, I'd tried to sneak out because experiencing even just one night of the outside world seemed more exciting than rotting inside these pink walls of hell for the rest of my life.

But, after a few failed escape attempts, the bars on the window and the locks on the door were installed.

"'For your own good,'" Mom always said. *For your own good.*

Those words once made my blood boil every time I thought about them. Sometimes they still made me mad. She was just trying to protect me, I remind myself. But I couldn't shake the feeling that she's trying to keep me away from the rest of the world, not trying to keep the rest of the world away from me.

It wasn't fair.

I'd been condemned to this life in prison for as far back as I could remember. And it didn't matter if my walls were pink or that I had a comfortable twin bed and TV with cable and movies and hundreds of books lined up on my bookcases, filling an entire wall. The distractions had never been enough to make me forget that I was still a prisoner. Nothing could make me forget the bars, the locks, or the flap on the door where Mom passed my meals on a plastic tray.

Being homeschooled had been the best distraction from it all. I loved to study, to learn about the world outside of my walls. But now that was done and over with. With every year that passed inside this room, it got harder and harder not to get caught up in my own mind; a prison within a prison.

Maybe I wanted to die after all.

Such a dark thought. But hey, it's one I'd had a lot. Who in my position wouldn't? There were only so many times I could reread the same books. Only so many times I could watch the same shitty re-runs on TV.

Mom typically brought me new books and magazines every month, but I blew through those in a few days. Boredom was killing me. At least, I wished it was.

Dying had to come with some benefits, right? Mom said Hell was real, and all the bad people were there. At least bad people were interesting. Even if my personal purgatory was these pink walls, the screams of my next-door neighbors getting tortured in their own hell would at least remind me I wasn't alone.

The metal flap at the bottom of my bedroom door swung open, the creak of its hinges announcing dinner.

"Hope you're hungry, honey," Mom's muffled voice sounded from the other side of the door. "I made meatloaf."

It was a stupid thing to say. She knew I was always hungry. Always starving. But no amount of meatloaf, my favorite dish, could curb my hunger.

My bedroom and the bathroom attached to it were my whole world. So when the dark-haired man with pale skin and beady eyes came to visit, it was like Christmas. Dr. Sharpe was never much of a talker, but at least he was a flesh and blood person. Other than him, I *never* had visitors. Even my mom never came into my room.

Dr. Sharpe wasn't exactly big on small talk, but he'd always been informative on my condition. According to him, my hunger was a common side effect of Tachycardia. I'm not sure how an insatiable hunger relates to a weak heart, but hey, I'm not the doctor.

A tray pushed through the flap, bearing several generous slabs of fragrant meat, a glass of cranberry juice, mashed potatoes, and beside the plate a new romance novel.

"You got me the sequel to the series I've been reading!"

I scrambled off my bed and reached for the book, then settled down with my back against the door, shoveling mounds of potatoes into my mouth with one hand and holding my book open with the other.

I freaking *loved* werewolf romance. I'd basically been in love with all the men in pretty much every romance book Mom had brought me because I knew they were the only men in my life that I would ever have.

Except for Dr. Sharpe, but obviously, he didn't count.

I liked pretty much all romance sub-genres, but the supernatural men in paranormal romances fascinated me the most. There was something sexy about shifters. Wolves and dragons were my favorite. I liked vampires too, but Mom seemed to avoid bringing me many of those.

"Vampires are Satan's creatures," she'd admonish me whenever I asked for a particular title I'd find in the back matter in one of my werewolf novels and would instead bring me yet another werewolf romance. Which was fine.

Bad boys, bullies, heroes with hearts of gold, anti-heroes, hell, even villains. I liked them all because my lonely ass needed the company, even if none of them were real.

"Goodnight, honey. Don't stay up too late," Mom said, the old stairs to our historic Massachusetts home creaking as she went back downstairs.

"Fine," I called down to her, though it was a lie. I loved staying up late. Nighttime was when everything went dark in the house, all the noises from the street outside that seemed to bleed into my room died down, and my imagination came alive.

I stayed up well into the night reading and drifted to sleep next to my door with my book still in hand, dreaming about the worlds in my books and the characters within them.

But I was foisted from my dreams with a sound that jerked me awake. My eyes flew open, and I froze as I listened. I'd always had exceptional hearing. I could even make out the steady rush of Mom's breathing in the room next to mine.

So I knew the creak I heard wasn't coming from her.

Creak.

My heart pulsed loudly as I realized someone, or something, was coming up the stairs.

Chapter Two
"Hello, Ruby"

My heart pounded hard in my chest.

Creak.

Another step closer by whoever was in the house. A stranger! A burglar? My heart began to pick up pace as my mind splintered with panic. What if they hurt my mom?

Creak.

With every step, my heart rate accelerated. For healthy people, that was normal. For me, it could be lethal. This home invader could be the death of me before he even found out I was here.

"Bloody hell," I whispered, a phrase I'd picked up from Harry Potter. Was this really how I was going to die? By being scared to death?

That was no fun. No way. I couldn't go out like this. If I was going to die, it would be because I finally managed to sneak out of here and maybe stole my mom's car keys and got into a street race or robbed a bank with the entirety of the Quincy Police Force shouting on a megaphone 'We have you surrounded.' Or maybe have an orgy with the main male cast of Supernatural. Going out with a bang, literally.

If I was going to die young, it had to be doing something adventurous. Even if it was something that normal people wouldn't find a super unique death. Compared to the rest of my snooze fest of a life, at least it would be *something*. Something that would be the one interesting thing to have ever happened to me in my short, sad life.

My stupid, pathetic, weak heart. Why did I have to be built like this? Maybe reincarnation was real. Maybe I'd done something horrible in a past life to earn this karmic payback.

My weak body didn't match the way I felt inside. I wanted adrenaline. I wanted to be shocked and surprised and thrilled and maybe even a little bad, without worrying about my heart just crapping out on me.

Creak.

Whoever was coming up the steps, they were getting closer. With each step, my heart lurched almost as if it were in sync with the intruder's footsteps.

What did they want? Why were they here? Mom worked at an assisted living facility. She wasn't rich. We had nothing. She was a single mom who went to church and work. That was basically it, so it wasn't like she had enemies.

But what about my dad? I'd never known him. Mom never talked about him, not even once. I had stopped asking about him a long time ago. Sometimes I fantasized about him being some billionaire and how he'd come for me and take me to some huge mansion where there were no bars on the windows and no flaps on my door to slip food in.

But that was just fantasy, right?

Because in reality, if he did come for me, would I forgive him for abandoning my mom and me? If it meant rescuing me from this princess-themed bedroom from hell, maybe.

The guy coming up the stairs was probably just a nobody burglar. He would leave when he found nothing worth stealing. That's what I told myself, again and again as my heart pounded harder and harder. I held my breath as another creak met my ear.

My mom had come up and down those stairs so many times I'd come to know the groans and moan of each antique step. So I knew he was standing on the very last step before my door.

He was on the second floor.

There was a long pause. I swear I could smell him on the other side of the door, so he couldn't have been more than a few steps away. His scent was so strange yet almost... familiar. I loved thunderstorms. On stormy nights I would slide my window open between the bars and just smell the electricity in the air, the rain-soaked asphalt, the salty tang of the storm-ravaged ocean that sat just out of sight from my bedroom window. He smelled like a dark and dangerous storm, and it sent a charge of energy down my spine like a clap of lightning, making the little hairs on my neck stand straight.

The whine of hinges sailed through my senses, and my heart went into another frenzy of potentially lethal beats. *He's going into my mom's room!*

Crouching down beside my door, I pressed my cheek to my carpet and lifted the food flap to peer into the hall. I lifted it oh-so-slowly so as not to make it creak. By the time I had a clear view of the bottom half of her door, he had opened it and gone inside.

No, no, *no.* This couldn't be happening. What was he planning to do?

I had to warn her!

So I screamed.

I screamed as loud as I could, shrill and ragged. My mom's voice, incoherent and hazy from sleep, began to call for me. "Ruby? What's going on—"

But it was too late. She never finished her words. A muffled cry, silenced by maybe a hand, was smothered and died out as a male's voice whispered something I couldn't make out.

What was he saying to her?

Tears warped my vision.

No more sounds came save for his footsteps approaching. Large combat boots appeared in her doorway a second later. I slapped a hand over my mouth to keep any noise from leaking out, which was stupid since he already knew I was here, thanks to my scream.

And that's when my heart monitor went off.

Beep, beep, beep!

The black band I wore around my wrist to alert me when my heart rate went too high blared like a warning. My heart thudded so hard I could feel it in my throat. My skin prickled in dread. So much stimulation, so many emotions, I could barely sort out what was going on.

I fumbled at the monitor and pressed the button to silence its shrill cries.

When I looked back at the flap, my heart nearly gave out right then and there. Through the square hole at the bottom of my door, two eyes filled the space.

Blood red eyes.

Strands of raven hair framed the sanguine orbs that ran me through, making my chest squeeze and my stomach flip with new levels of terror.

"*Hello, Ruby,*" the owner of the eyes cooed in a voice as dark as night and as deep as hell. "I was going to ask you to let me in, but it looks like someone so conveniently decided to install the locks on the wrong side of the door. So I'll be letting myself in now."

CHAPTER THREE

NO PRINCESS SHOULD LIVE IN A CAGE

T he man's voice was startling, not because of its deep timbre that could rival the Allstate man, but because of the way it immediately sank straight through my core, heating me in ways only fictional werewolves had accomplished up until now.

Which was completely stupid. This was an intruder. For all I knew, he could be a serial killer. Oh God, *oh God*. Was he going to kill my mom?

With my heart in my mouth, I backed away from the door. My hands searched for something in my room, anything to use as a weapon, while my attention remained anchored to the red eyes staring at me through the door flap.

Why couldn't I look away from him?

My heart beat so fast, it rattled my skull and blurred my vision. Any moment it would give out. It was too weak for this. *Too weak.*

The last thing I'd ever see would be those *eyes* staring into my soul and setting it on fire.

My heart condition was stressful enough without having to worry about a freaking house invader with eyes as red as the devil's.

He slowly stood, his heavy combat boots now the only part of him I could see through the hole in the door. The clicks of a half dozen locks struck me like a slap, and I flinched with every one he unfastened.

Weapon! My brain screamed at me to find something, anything to protect myself.

Fuck, fuck, *fuck.*

In my panic, a power I never felt before slammed through my veins. Was this adrenaline? My attention clamped down on one of my bedposts. Before I could take a moment to think, my hands were already wrapping around the wood, and with strength I didn't know I had, I ripped the post free with my bare hands like it was made of balsa wood.

I gaped at the splintered piece of wood in my hand, my mouth wide open in a dazed shock. The post was so thick my fingers didn't even meet around its girth.

What the actual hell?

I shouldn't have been able to do that.

But there was no time to question these weird fight or flight instincts.

Every muscle in my body flinched as my bedroom door flung open on its hinges, kicked in by a big boot.

When my eyes settled on the male in the doorway, my erratic pulse immediately stilled, like it had frozen in my chest.

He was tall, his head almost scraping against the top door jam. Bloody hell, I didn't even know they made humans that tall.

Because he's not human. How could he be?

It's not like I was an expert on guys, but humans didn't have eyes the color of blood, didn't have skin so pale you could see their dark, bulging arm veins... And his *arms!* Damn. His thick forearms were covered in an elaborate network of veins so dark they looked like they were filled with ink.

The rest of his build was nothing but slabs of tapered muscle wrapped in moon-pale skin, covered in a tight-fitting white-shirt and dark denim jeans. He had a thick neck that would look right at home between the shoulders of a football player or a wrestler. Neck tattoos depicting ravens covered his throat, stretching up to his broad jawline. His nose looked like it had been broken one too many times, and his thick brows were pulled together into a scowl that made my mouth go dry.

He was brutally handsome and perfectly terrifying.

Swallowing hard, I held up the broken post, splintered side up like I'd seen in action movies.

For a long heartbeat, the man didn't even look at me. His gaze roved over the room, taking in all its floral details, the unicorn pillows, the pink walls, all the things that would indicate this room belonged to a five-year-old. Then he looked at the bars on the windows, and his upper lip curled in disgust.

His gaze flicked back to me, causing my heart to leap into my mouth. His attention dropped to the makeshift weapon clutched in my hand, and a dark scoff rolled past his lips as he licked them.

"What are you going to do with that, Princess? Stake me?"

He took a step forward, and I jabbed it in the air at him. "Don't come any closer!" I spat, my voice more warble than menace.

To my amazement, he halted, took another look at my room, then twisted to inspect the door with its almost hilarious collection of deadbolts and chain locks.

These days I could find the humor in how overboard Mom had gone with making sure I couldn't sneak out. But this guy didn't find it so cute, judging by the guttural growl rumbling from his chest. It slithered over my skin, covering me in goosebumps.

"This is how the human has forced the princess to live? Like an animal in a fucking pen?"

Princess? Was that supposed to be me? And was the human supposed to be my mother?

He would only call her that if he wasn't...

I gaped at the male. "You *aren't* human?"

His lips curved into a humorless smile as he slowly shook his head. "No, and neither are you. Half-blood or not, no princess should live in a cage."

Chapter Four

A MAN SO DARK AND DEADLY

P rincess? Why did he keep calling me that?

"Who are you?" I demanded, the hand holding my splintered bedpost beginning to tremble. His gaze slid to my shaking hand, and a smug as fuck smile slid across those infuriatingly perfect lips.

"That's a question you should be asking yourself. Who are you really, Ruby? Because you don't seem to know."

For the second time tonight, he said my name. He knew me. How did he know me? How could anyone like him know anything about the shut-in with a weak heart?

"How do you know my name?" I demanded. "What else do you know about me?"

"I know a lot about you, Ruby Renada Baxter. I know *all* about you." He swept another pointed look around my room. "Except for your living conditions."

"What did you do to my mom? Did you hurt her?"

His blood-red gaze darkened, causing me to shiver involuntarily.

"I didn't hurt her, but from where I'm standing, she deserves to feel a little pain."

My heart rate jumped again, fear clawing my spine with its icy nails. Then in the next instant, that fear turned to red-hot anger. I held my weapon in front of me, glaring daggers at the deadly male.

"Leave her alone."

He canted his head, and his red eyes narrowed, glittering with interest. "You care for this human?"

There was that word again. *Human.* Why was I getting the feeling this was a jailbreak from his eyes? A monster, busting out another freak. Only, he'd gotten the wrong house, the wrong prison. I was just a sick girl, locked up for my own good.

"Of course, I care for her. She's my mom."

He let out a wicked chuckle like I'd just told a joke. "How precious. Stockholm Syndrome's almost cute on you, Princess. But it's time to kiss Mummy goodbye."

My stomach cartwheeled, and my nerves began to split. Was he threatening to kill her?

Of course, he was. He wasn't human. He'd probably kill me too when he learned I wasn't the person he'd come for.

Not that death really scared me. Hell was where all the fun people were, after all. But Mom didn't deserve to die.

"Don't you dare put a fucking finger on her."

His gaze narrowed, something close to amusement making his eyes flash. "What are you going to do to stop me?"

My nostrils flared as my heart slammed against my ribcage. What could I do? Nothing. Absolutely, bum-fuck, nothing. I was all talk, and he seemed amused at calling my bluff. Which sent a zap of adrenaline through my veins.

This guy was all sinew and strength. A body like that didn't come to anyone who wasn't comfortable in a fight. Not only that, he was accustomed to winning. And who was I? Nobody. I hadn't even hugged anyone, let alone thrown a punch.

"You've got some nerve, asshole. Breaking into a sick girl's room."

He laughed, a tattooed raven's wing twitching with the bob of his throat. "You're not sick."

My heart dropped to my stomach. "What are you talking about? Yes, I am."

I *was* sick. It has a shit reality, one I had trouble accepting all the time. I'd spent so many nights imagining a different reality, imagining some alternate life where I was healthy and normal and well-adjusted. Where I could go to school, make friends, date, fuck. But I wasn't allowed to do any of that because ever since I could remember, I was told I would die if I went outside. So better to stay locked up inside where it was safe.

Suddenly, I wasn't so scared of this monster of a man, whatever he was. Who the hell was he, breaking in here and suggesting my life was a cruel lie?

My fingers curled tighter around the broken bedpost. "You're a liar."

The man arched a mocking brow. Ugh. Why was he so sexy when he scowled like that? *Come on, Ruby, so you're a little sex-starved, but this one isn't even human.*

Despite my internal chastising, my vagina wasn't listening. It throbbed and ached in the same way it did when I read the steamy parts of my novels. It was almost like the intruder knew how much his voice affected me. And by the way his nostrils flexed and his red eyes glinted with irritation, I knew he did.

"A liar, am I?" He looked down at the forgotten tray of meatloaf and the romance novel beside it. "Seems you don't know a lie even though your mommy serves you a big fat heaping pile of shit along with your dinner and your smut every night. She tried to keep you fed, stupid little human, thinking she could sate the appetites of a monster with fictional cock and meatloaf."

My cheeks burned red in a heady cocktail of embarrassment and rage. What was he trying to say?

"I'm not a monster."

"You are."

"Prove it," I spat, daring him.

It was a dangerous thing to demand. But I had no experience with danger, especially when it was rolled up in a sexy, masculine package that radiated violence and secrets from an unknown world beyond my cell door.

His lips spread into a wolfish grin devoid of all kindness. He took a step forward, shrinking the precious little distance between us. My heart rate had gone from a steady canter to a full-blown, wild gallop. Maybe I would just drop dead before he could prove whatever it was he was trying to feed me.

God, I hope not. As crazy and terrifying as this all was, it was *interesting*.

"You're strong. Sick or not, human girls can't break their beds with their bare hands." He chuckled, his glare harsh and his words mocking. "Well, not without the help of a lover."

Another move forward, and he stepped into the square of moonlight that filtered through my single window, the steel bars painting his face in strips of shadow and silver light. His upper lip peeled back, and he tongued a needle-sharp canine that glinted in the moonlight.

Fangs.

CHAPTER FIVE
BRAINWASHED PRINCESS

All the blood in my veins crystallized. I stumbled back, my butt bumping into my now lopsided bed frame. I fell back onto the mattress and glared at the intruder defiantly; despite how hard my heart pulsated in my chest, each beat possibly its last.

He stalked toward me, looking all too pleased with my invitation to *prove it*. If I died now, the last thing I'd ever see was a man looming over my bed with his crimson eyes gleaming from the shadows, banked with disdain and desire all at once. Or maybe that was just wishful thinking on behalf of my traitorous vagina.

I gave another quick internal scolding to my hormones and forced myself to think about what he'd just said. Sure, most people couldn't rip off bed legs with their bare hands, but I had a TV. I saw the news. Stranger things had happened. Right?

"I've heard on TV about a woman who lifted a car off her toddler in a rush of adrenaline. It's the same thing."

His chest rumbled with a mocking chuckle. "Is it the same thing?"

"Yes." My voice was shaky, and I hated how weak it sounded. I couldn't even convince myself of the lie. Somehow I knew it wasn't really the same thing at all. But my brain didn't want to comprehend the reality of what he was trying to say.

Maybe this was just a dream. Yeah, that's what this was! I had fallen asleep and forgotten to take my medication.

I was so stupid for not realizing it earlier. This was just a dream or a hallucination.

"My pills," I cried, choking out my revelation.

He cocked his head. "What about them?"

"I didn't take my medication for my heart. I'm just imagining you. That's how you know my name. You're just a figment of my own mind, one of my book boyfriends. That's why you have fangs!"

He blinked at me, regarding me like I was speaking gibberish. "Book boyfriend?" The corner of his mouth lifted into a sardonic sneer. "Am I anything like the males you fantasize about, Princess?"

My throat tightened. No, not anything close. He was somehow better and worse all at the same time.

Another step forward. The floorboards groaned beneath his weight. I could practically feel his aura charging the air with dark and deadly energy that licked at my body in places only my hand had ever explored.

No, this couldn't be a dream or a hallucination because I didn't ache and throb like *that* in my sleep.

"Those pills you take aren't for your heart. They're to quell your thirst. But they don't do much good. You're thirsty all the time, aren't you? Hungry too. Our little princess has a raging appetite..." He glanced down at my forgotten tray of food which contained a half-eaten slab of meatloaf and the dirty werewolf novel. "For more than just meat, I see, at least of the loaf variety."

My blush deepened. He now stood over me, so close that his knees were nearly touching mine. He smirked down at me, where I was slumped over my bed, my back flat against the mattress and my unicorn plushies in a chaotic array around my head, like a childish crown for a childish princess. I hated the derisive amusement lighting up his shadow-shrouded gaze as if he was thinking the same exact thing.

His spine slowly arched as he descended on me like a seductive predator. The mattress dipped under the new weight as his hands pressed down on either side of my head.

Any sane girl in my position would scream and fight. But I couldn't bring myself to move. I completely froze beneath him, transfixed by the bloody depths of those hypnotic eyes. Besides, I was trapped. Trapped beneath the second man I had ever met. The first being Dr. Sharpe. And Dr. Sharpe was an older man, with salt and pepper black air, formal mannerisms, and had a clinical touch.

This hellish man was different. He was young, or at least he appeared that way. He wore sex and arrogance like freaking fashion accessories to complement his white t-shirt. The shirt struggled to contain his powerful, muscular torso, and the cotton fabric was so thin I could make out his perfectly sculpted pectorals and the dark circles of his nipples. The outline of his raven tattoos could also be seen, stretching from his defined jawline all the way down to the ripple of his abs and disappearing beneath his belt line into a world I couldn't help but imagine.

He was male and death incarnate. And what did a shut-in know about death? Only what I had seen on TV from crime shows and action flicks. But somehow, I knew he wasn't alive. I couldn't hear the throb of his heart like I could with Mom's when I pressed my ear to my door.

With quaking fingers, I reached out to stroke his cheek. He purred a growl, the sound scraping over my flesh and making it sting.

He was as cold as death.

My brain fumbled with all the pieces of the puzzle, and I knew I now had the complete picture, at least much of it.

The word was on the tip of my tongue, but I couldn't bring myself to say it. "Y–you're..." My tongue was heavy in my mouth like I'd been drugged by this gorgeous monster with just a grazing touch.

"I don't have all night, Princess," he snarled low. "The sun will be up before too long. So fucking say it already. What am I?"

I gulped and shivered as a rush of adrenaline coursed through me.

"You're a vampire."

"That's right, little princess," he said through a devilish grin.

"But... Vampires don't exist."

"And what does someone like you know about the world and the monsters within it?" It could have been a trick of the shadows, but I could see something close to pity in those bloody red pools. "Though I guess you know a thing or two about the monstrosity that is mankind, seeing how your own mother has kept you caged like an animal."

A vein pounded in my temple, and my fingers tightened around the broken bedpost that had slipped from his attention. "My mom isn't a monster. I don't know what you're trying to tell me with your lies about my pills and my adrenaline, but I'm just a girl with a medical condition. The locks are for my own good."

"For your own good?" he gritted out, his tone razor sharp. "You're fucking brainwashed."

"I'm not like you! Get out of here!" I'd had enough. I didn't like what he was implying, and it terrified me that I was even considering everything he was telling me.

I swung my weapon with as much force as I could muster. He was just inches away, so I should have been able to hit him. But he moved so fast, his hand was a blur. I blinked, and when I opened my eyes, his fingers were curled around my wrist in a crushing grip that made me wince. He gave a vicious jerk of my wrist, and the piece of wood fell to the mattress beside us.

"My patience is running out," he snarled, yanking me close to him, so his breath feathered my skin. It smelled metallic, like blood. "You don't have a fucking *heart problem*. You're perfectly healthy. People with weak hearts don't have strength like yours. They don't have senses like yours."

"I'm not like you," I balked, my protest weaker than the first. "I'm a human with a beating heart. When I stand by my window, the sun doesn't burn. I can see my reflection in the mirror."

"That's because you're only half-vampire. You're more like me than you think. My maker was the vampire king. A cruel and miserable fuckhead of a master, let me tell you. He created four vampires in his long life. And you know what else he made? A biological daughter."

My mind reeled at this impossibly. "No..."

"Yes." The monster before me nodded, his fingers still wrapped like a vice around my wrist, so tight there was no way he wouldn't leave a bruise. "So in a weird fucked up kind of way, we're step-siblings."

"I don't want anything to do with you! My father wasn't a vampire! Now let me go, you fucking monster!"

He didn't let go. He only sneered, an expression so cruel it froze the blood in my veins. 'Your father was a vampire. He was my father, too, at least the closest I ever had to one. You think I'm fucked? You better thank whatever god you believe in that you were never unfortunate enough to meet him. And I don't want anything to do with you either, little girl. But vampire law states that on the king's death bed, he pick a progeny to take his throne. And the real shit-kicker is he picked *you* as his heir with his final breath."

The monster's fingers clenched tighter on my wrist, making me yelp in pain, but the sound was drowned out by his heated growl.

"He picked *you* over his four, full-blooded vampire sons. And I'm not serving some halfling queen who doesn't know shit about the outside world, let alone vampire kind. Our coven would eat you alive, Princess. So you're coming with me to tell the Elders that you don't want anything to do with us so they can gain some sense and make me or one of my brothers king. Got it? Then you can come back to your precious cage and rot here forever for all I care."

I could barely hear what he was saying anymore. None of the words were making sense. Half-vampire? I never knew my dad. He could be a circus clown for all I knew. But a *vampire?*

That would mean my mom hadn't locked me up for my own safety.

She had done it for everyone else's.

And Dr. Sharpe. His skin was as pale as a ghost's... Could he be one of them? Were the pills he'd prescribed really to sate my thirst? Was it blood I lusted for? Every time I took those pills, my appetites seemed to die down.

My entire existence has always been kind of sad. But before, it was due to sad circumstances, a twist of fate no one could have prevented. But if what this monster said was true, it meant my life had been stolen from me.

A sham.

A lie.

No. No, that couldn't be it. I refused to believe it. It hurt too much to believe. My mom loved me. She was a good person, who took care of the elderly for a living, and in her free time, she went to bible study and sung in the church choir.

She kept me here for my own good. *For my own good.*

The more I told myself that, the less I believed it.

"You're lying. I'm not anything like you. I'm not. I don't need blood to survive."

"For fucks sakes, Princess. As a half-vampire, you don't need blood to survive. But you crave it all the same, don't you? Even more, now that you skipped your pills..."

"No, I'm not—"

His patience had apparently run out because he didn't let me finish. A rattle of a growl slid from his throat, making my skin prickle. With his free hand, he grabbed a handful of the blonde hair at my nape and gave a savage tug, yanking me off the bed toward the door.

He was going to make me go with him whether I was willing to or not.

CHAPTER SIX
THE DEVIL'S SPAWN

"Let me go!" I screeched, thrashing as he dragged me across the carpet of my bedroom toward the door.

My heart lurched in my chest as my focus settled on the wooden bedpost. I managed to grab it just in time before he pulled me out of arm's reach, and I drove it into his ankle with as much force as I could summon.

He howled in pain, the sound splitting my skull and causing my vision to blur for a second as it sounded more like a raven's screech instead of a man in pain.

Seething, he kicked the weapon out of my hand and hauled me to my feet with a snarl.

Wrenching my head back, so I was forced to look at him, I met his glare with one of my own.

Apparently, this vampire did know who I was. He knew my father. Whatever else he knew about me, it was enough to decide that he hated me. Because that hatred burned in his eyes with as much heat as a raging fire, and he was content to let those flames devour me.

"You let yourself be caged like this your entire life, and *now* you find your fight? It's too late for that, Princess. Why don't you just lay down and let other people make decisions for you like you're used to? And if you're a good little monster, I'll return you to your precious cage where I found you."

His words scorched me like a brand because they were true. I had let things happen to me, accepting everything told to me at face value. My mom had been content to let me rot in here, and I had done fuck-all about it.

And that pissed me off.

Anger was something I was pretty familiar with. I'd always lusted for more, adventure, relationships, a normal life. But that anger had never lasted because I thought I was a victim to circumstance. Turns out...maybe I wasn't. Maybe I was just a victim of lies and fear-fueled abuse that had been disguised as love.

Nope.

I was done being anyone's victim.

So I punched the vampire who held me like I belonged to him. Because I didn't belong to fucking anyone.

Not anymore.

Slamming my tiny fist into his nose with that same inhuman strength I used to rip off my bedpost, I was rewarded with a satisfying crunch beneath my knuckles.

The vampire released his grip on my hair and reeled backward. He stepped back into the square of moonlight that poured in through my single window, painting his masculine features in silver and stripes of shadow. Blood as black as night poured from his nose, dribbling over his lips and down his chin in inky strands that blotted his white shirt.

His lips stretched into a wicked grin, and his fangs glinted in the moonlight.

"You're strong. Stronger than any human I've ever fought."

"Touch me again, and I'll break something else, fucker."

"Are you going to behave yourself and come with me?"

"Go fuck yourself!"

Heaving a sigh, he started to advance on me, consuming the distance between us with long-legged strides. "Then I am going to have to touch you again, Princess. And you're not going to like it."

He lunged at me.

I dodged out of the way, quicker than I thought I could ever move, because I'd never tried before. My heart slammed into my ribs with a force that should have already had me dead on the floor. But I was beginning to believe everything this asshole was telling me. How could I not? The evidence was too strong, and I wasn't fucking stupid. Naive maybe. But not stupid.

My body moved at an impressive speed, but he was still faster, stronger. He caught my forearm and wrenched it behind my back so hard my eyes watered. Thrashing against him, I slammed back into his chest, and a satisfying rush of his breath left his lungs, feathered my neck.

We stumbled into my dresser.

Drawers rattled, and the vanity mirror mounted to the dresser toppled to the ground, cracking.

He wrestled me to the ground like we were on the set of WrestleMania. He was using moves I recognized from

ESPN, and I realized that the vampire had to be some kind of trained fighter because he had me pinned to the carpet in a rear-naked chokehold.

"Calm the *fuck* down," he hissed in my ear.

And I did. Not because I cared at all to obey a single command this asshole gave me, but because of what I saw in the mirror laying on the ground beside us.

In the cracked glass, my blonde hair had come undone from its bun and lay across my face in a tangled mess. My brown eyes burned with a fury that felt good to unleash for the first time ever. My breasts heaved in the thin, white cami I wore.

If I knew to expect company, I would have put on a bra, at least.

I felt something hard press into my leg. The apex between my thighs heated, knowing what it was.

"Do you always get off on holding down weak, defenseless girls, you sick fuck?"

"I'm getting *really* tired of you calling yourself weak," he hissed in my ear.

I lifted my gaze in the mirror, looking over my shoulder to meet his. My heart stilled as I was met with only my own reflection.

"You're not real," I gasped.

"Not real? You mean like one of your 'book boyfriends?'" He let out a mocking chuckle as he reached around and pinched one of my nipples.

Biting my lip, I smothered the hot moan that burned in my throat. I didn't want him to know how much I liked the touch when all it should have done was make me mad.

My nipple pebbled, straining against the cotton fabric of my top.

He chuckled again. "See how your body reacts to me? I'm very real, Princess. You can't see me in your mirror because I'm a fucking vampire."

"Then I'm not like you because I can see myself."

"You're a halfling. How many times do I have to repeat myself? You can also stand in the sun. You can probably even touch silver. You bleed red, and you've got a delicious pulse." His nose pressed against my jugular, and my skin became stained with his black blood in the mirror.

"But you still thirst for blood, and you can feed on humans just like the rest of us. Only you don't need it for survival. You will live a long time, but one day you'll die of old age."

"No..." I screwed my eyes tight as if this entire nightmare would fade away, and I would wake up back in the normalcy that was my life, where I was still just a girl with a heart condition and nothing else.

That was the less complicated reality. Because in this one, I was a monster. A monster who'd had everything taken away from me, and I hadn't even known it.

Gathering my hair, he wrapped it around his wrist like a freaking leash and hauled me to my feet. He dragged me from the room and being too tired to fight anymore, I let him.

He dragged me into my mom's room.

Every cell in my body froze as I saw her form slumped on her bed. She was still breathing, her chest rising and falling in a gentle rhythm.

"What did you do to her?" I whispered, my voice sounding small and weak.

"I mesmerized her."

As he brought me closer, I frantically scanned her throat for any signs of bite marks, but to my relief, there were none. He pushed me onto the bed and held my nose to her throat.

"Do you smell that, Princess?"

I hadn't been this close to my own mother since I was a baby. She smelled like the old person's home she worked at and cheap shampoo. It wasn't a smell anyone else would have found comforting, but so many nights when she'd bring me my meals, I'd catch the scent of her and imagine it as strong as it was now, simply because she'd open the door and asked for a hug.

The lump in my throat swelled, making it hard to swallow, and thick tears burned my eyes. I'd lost count of how many times I wondered why she didn't want to be near me. Turns out, she'd been afraid of me.

I wasn't the sick daughter she'd locked up to keep me safe from the world. I was her monstrous daughter she'd locked away to keep the rest of the world safe.

My heart hitched in my chest, and all my muscles clenched as a new scent met me, making my mouth water. The thirst was something I was no stranger to, but it wasn't ever this bad before.

I hadn't taken my pills. On top of that, I was now certain Dr. Sharpe was one of *them*. A vampire. Because he hadn't smelled anything like my mother.

"Tell me what you smell."

A whine leaked from my throat as if some creature was trapped inside me, clawing to be released so it could feast on my mother.

Mom smelled absolutely divine. Like food. Like something that should be eaten. I could practically taste her blood already, even though it was something I'd never sampled before. It was like my body needed it, lusted for it like it had never lusted for anything else.

My teeth ached with a sharp pain I'd never experienced, maybe because I'd never been this close to her. I could practically feel them growing in my gums, elongating.

No, no, no. She was my mom, not something to be eaten. This couldn't be happening. I was a person, not a feral animal.

As if he could sense my thoughts, the vampire leaned closer from behind me until his mouth was practically pressing against my ear. "She locks your door, bars your window…" He jerked my head so that my gaze rested on the cross mounted above her bed.

"And she hides behind her crucifixes not because she cares about your safety, but because she cares only of her own. You terrify her. And do you know why? Because she knows what you are. She thinks you're the devil's spawn."

He pulled on my hair and positioned my head so that I was forced to look at him. He licked his smirking lips. "And take it from me, Princess. You are."

Chapter Seven
VINCENT FERAL IS AN ASSHOLE

The cold night air hit me like a slap in the face.

I hadn't been outside since I was a toddler, and I barely remembered that. To normal people, it wasn't anything special. Normal people went outside every day.

For me, being out of my room was like being on a different planet.

I had dreamed about going outside pretty much every day of my life. But now that it was actually happening, my dream had turned into a twisted nightmare, one that I couldn't wake up from.

"Ow! You don't have to manhandle me, asshole." I jerked my wrist out of his hand as my *rescuer* tried to pull me to a car across the street.

To my surprise, he let me go and whirled on me, baring his teeth in warning.

"Fine. But if you try to run from me, I will catch you, Princess."

A shiver darted through me, and I pulled my hoodie tighter around my body. It was cold outside, colder than I thought it would be. At least he'd let me change. Wherever he intended on dragging me, I wasn't super down to go anywhere dressed like I was previously. It's not like I had tons of clothes for going out. Most of my wardrobe consisted of ratty band t-shirts and sweatpants. For tonight, I put on my favorite outfit—a Ramones' hoodie and yoga pants.

"You don't treat me like a princess, so how about you stop addressing me as one, okay?"

"After we make our appearance in front of the Elders tonight, I'll be the new king, so I can call you whatever the fuck I want." He jabbed a finger at the shiny black car across the street. Thanks to car commercial ads, I recognized it as some kind of Rolls-Royce.

"Wow," I rolled my eyes. "So the prince of the night is loaded. Did our daddy's money pay for this?"

"Don't call me that," he snapped.

Propping a hand on my hip, I flung him a dagger-sharp glare. "Then what do I call you? Asshole? Kidnapper? Woman-beater?"

"I didn't beat you." He glanced back over his shoulder, his thin smirk catching in the moonlight. "Don't pretend you didn't like me manhandling you, Princess. Your body is desperate for the touch of a male. Too bad for you that yours is too stupid to know the difference between man and monster."

My feet froze where I stood in the middle of the deserted street. This late in the night, there were no cars. All the houses were dark, and the only light was from the streetlights as the moon dipped behind a swath of clouds.

So he thought he was a monster. Glad we agreed on something.

Approaching the car, he opened the driver's side door and shot me a thoroughly irritated scowl. The way his dark brows pulled together when he looked at me like that was pretty damn sexy.

Bloody hell, why did I have to have a thing for alpha jerks like him? The difference between him and the alpha-holes in the books I read was this one would probably end up killing me.

"Vincent Feral."

I blinked. "What?"

"That's my name." He opened the back door of the car. "Now get the fuck in before the sun comes up."

He didn't wait for me to get inside before he slipped into the driver's seat and slammed the door behind him.

I stood in the street, glowering at him through the tinted glass. "I think 'Asshole' is more suiting to you," I mumbled.

For a few moments, I stood there alone in the street, staring back at my house. Looking up at my window from this side was completely surreal, like being in a dream. I wasn't really sure yet if this was all a nightmare or if I'd died and gone to heaven.

On the one hand, I'd gotten what I'd always wanted. Freedom. But at what cost? I'd just learned that my entire life, as small and pathetic as it had been, was one big fat lie. And that had me wondering if my mom really even loved me.

Maybe a little. Why else would she go out of her way to buy me all the books, movies, and music I could ever want, all to keep me entertained? Why had she gone out of her way to make the kind of food I loved?

Still didn't make me resent her any less. She'd lied.

What would happen when she woke up from the weird hypno-vampire-magic Vincent had cast? Probably nothing. She had to know Dr. Sharpe was a vampire. He was in on the lie too, and it had been he who'd given me those pills to curb my thirst. She probably knew my father was a vampire too. How could she not? A lump swelled in my throat, and I tried to swallow it down. No wonder she hadn't said a thing about him.

As crap as this all was, I was no longer her prisoner. Maybe the locks, the bars, maybe all that had been more than just an effort to protect herself and others from me. Maybe Mom had been trying to protect me from my father and his coven.

Because wherever Vincent Feral was taking me, it was going to be a lot more dangerous than my bedroom. But the bright side in all this? There was a zero percent chance I'd die of boredom in the clutches of this coven.

And that's about as far as my shut-in dreams had dared to reach. So wish granted, I guess.

In some fucked up way, Vincent Feral was my hero, though I would never tell the prick that to his face. Because he was not some shining white knight, that was for fucking sure.

The car honked, making me jump.

Vincent rolled the window down and propped his arm on the door, which looked a bit out of place in the luxury car with his unkempt black hair and blood-streaked white shirt.

There was movement in the passenger's side, telling me that he was with someone.

"Are you going to get in, Princess? Or am I going to have to drag you all the way home?"

Snorting, I opened the car's back door.

Vincent Feral, huh? Yeah. Asshole definitely seemed more fitting for this broody vampire, who had a pension for antagonizing me. What the hell did I ever do to him?

Sliding into the lush, white leather interior, my attention settled on the stranger in the passenger seat.

"Jesus Christ, Vin," the new voice said. "What the fuck did you do to her? That better be your blood all over her."

"Halfling's don't bleed black, Corry."

Eyes of the deepest blue found me, their owner sliding me a heart-melting smile that had me turning into a puddle in the backseat of the Rolls-Royce.

"Whoa." The guy called Corry leaned closer to me, his nostrils flaring and his pupils dilating until his whole irises were black. "You're beautiful. And you smell *good.*"

One moment his eyes were blue, and the next, they turned the deepest crimson, just like Vincent's. They glinted with a deep hunger that filled me with fire.

"Vin, why does she smell *so damn good?*"

CHAPTER EIGHT
THE FERAL KING

The man in the front seat that Vincent had referred to as Corry looked young, younger than me even by a year or two. Vincent was broad-shouldered and square-jawed, with mouth-watering sexy raven tattoos and ink-black hair that spilled over his blood-red eyes. While Corry was more slight, with an athletic build and a straight nose. His brown hair with bleached tips was gelled up in the front, and when he flashed me a smooth smile, a dimple dotted his left cheek. He was cute, in an adorable frat-boy, jock sort of way.

Hell, he almost looked normal. Nice even, which was a welcomed breath of fresh air after the introduction I had with Vincent. But his cocky, heartthrob smile and his good looks were a bit overshadowed by the way he was looking at me like I was smothered in gravy and he hadn't eaten in a week.

But damn, maybe I'd just let him eat me because he was a slice of blue-eyed heaven. Or at least he had been up until a second ago when his eyes turned red. I assumed that happened when they were either hungry or smelled human blood. Or both.

"Don't make me regret bringing you, Youngblood. You can't eat her." Vincent's crimson glare locked with mine in the visor mirror. "At least not until after she tells the Elders she isn't interested in being queen."

"Yeah, like the council is going to do her bidding over Master's." Corry chuckled with an airy lilt to his voice that was refreshing in contrast to Vincent's gravelly baritone. "It was his dying wish for her to take the throne, and you know how those old shits kissed his wrinkly ass."

"They aren't going to make some half-blood shut-in the vampire queen."

"I don't know, bro. It would be Master's last laugh. You know how he loved suffering, especially ours." Corry inhaled again, licking his lips. "Whoa. She smells human, but like one of us at the same time... And shit, her scent alone is making me hard. What *is* that?"

Vincent's gaze flicked from Corry back to me in the mirror, irritation and accusation carving his handsome features as if Corry's question was somehow my fault.

"That's the scent of a virgin, Cor. No surprise you've never scented it. You've been confined to the mansion since you were turned, and all the over-used pussy there doesn't smell anything like that. Now stop smelling her, or I'll make you walk back to Provincetown."

Provincetown? Wasn't that all the way north on Cape Cod?

Clearing my throat, I slid to the middle seat and leaned my elbows on my knees so I could be in a position to glare at both of them.

"Excuse me? Um, yeah, so I'm going to pretend like you didn't just imply that you can smell my hymen because *gross*. Can we please stop pretending like I'm not right the fuck here? And I think someone better tell me what in the bloody hell is going on? Why are you taking me to Provincetown?"

Vincent snorted. "'Bloody hell?' Where did you learn that, Princess? The BBC?"

My cheeks flamed. I didn't answer him because telling him I'd picked up the phrase from Ron Weasley, my crush from the *Harry Potter* series, would probably just give Vincent more ammunition to ridicule me.

Corry's light brown, almost blond brows scrunched. "Wait. You didn't even tell her who she is or where we're taking her? Jeez, bro, she's gonna think we're kidnappers." He turned to answer my question. "Provincetown is where our coven is."

My lips tilted into a too-sweet smile. "You *are* kidnappers, for the record. But I guess I'm crazy enough to half believe your wild-ass story about me being a half-vampire princess because I'm so damn bored out of my mind I would probably get into a white van for a piece of candy. But don't mistake the boredom of a housebound girl as stupidity. If this ends up being some fucking lie to mess with me, I'll—"

Vincent twisted in his seat so fast, the sneer on his face so callous and cold, I swallowed the rest of my words in an involuntary gulp.

"You'll *what?*" he challenged. "What are you going to do, little monster?"

"I'll break your nose again."

Corry let out a light laugh, like none of this suffocating tension between his vampire pal and me affected him in the slightest. "Vincent is an MMA fighter, a pretty famous one in these parts. They call him the Feral King. He's used to a broken nose, so best just aim for his junk next time. But knowing you socked him in the face is pretty fucking hot." The friendlier vampire's eyes glittered, still red. "Can you do it again?"

Vincent's jaw could be seen tightening in the rearview mirror. "Shut up, Corry."

I'm not sure why, since I had literally just met this Corry guy, but seeing the way Vincent talked to him pissed me off. In fact, everything about Vincent Feral pissed me off.

The way he had just kind of burst into my house and turned my life on its head, uncovering all these lies and secrets like it was no big freaking deal, without so much as an apology or a second to let me process.

"You know what, Feral? I can't say I'm really into this big dick energy you're giving off."

The male twisted in his seat, shooting me a venom-dipped glare. There was something banked in his red eyes, something I couldn't easily put a name to like I could with the need in Corry's gaze. Whatever it was, it sent a shiver skittering down my spine and sunk straight into my core.

"What the fuck would you know about my dick, Princess?"

"Maybe I can sense it with my vampire senses or whatever. Like how you can apparently sense out my virginity. I can sense that you're a dick."

"Real fucking cute, Princess. Now, how about you shut that pretty little mouth like the good prisoner you've always been until we get home."

Corry let out a whistle. "Wow... You could cut the sexual tension in here with a knife. I'd say get a room, but if you're anything like our master, you would beat the fuck out of—"

"Shut the fuck up, Cor!" Vincent seethed.

For a second, I just stared at both of them, noting, in particular, the way Vincent exploded when their master was mentioned.

"Wait. My father... He was your master, right? Your... maker?"

It was Corry who gave a nod. "Yeah."

"Did he..." I swallowed hard, knowing my next question was a dangerous one. "Did he hurt you guys?"

A barbed silence settled inside the car. Vincent turned on the engine, and the luxury car purred to life as he guided the car off my street and away from my prison.

"Your father, the vampire king, was not a good man if that's what you're asking. He was a cruel master, especially to his progeny. You'll find that all four of us are glad that he's dead."

Well, there went all my fantasies about him being a good guy and about meeting him one day.

My stomach turned over with a sour taste that spread up my throat, leaving my tongue bitter and cottony. So dear old dad had been an evil prick.

I didn't bother asking for more details about his personality or his relationship with his progeny. Besides, I was sure I'd find out more later.

"What I want to know is why he had me here, locked up with my mom? She lied to me. She made me believe I was sick. She told me I had a weak heart. But you two already knew that, don't you? Because Dr. Sharpe is one of you."

The two vampires shared a look. Corry looked back at me, frowning. "Sharpe is an Elder."

"And who are the Elders?"

"A council of the oldest vampires in Massachusetts. Most of them are a part of the Cape Cod Coven."

"The Cape Cod Coven?"

"Yeah, that's us. The oldest coven in America. Founded by your father when he came over from England on the Mayflower."

"My dad was on the Mayflower?"

"Yeah, but he's a lot older than that. He came over to America with Sterling, who was turned in the twelfth century or something like that, right Vin?"

Vincent said nothing, his silence confirmation enough. He didn't seem too pleased by his brother spilling all this information, but I was thankful that didn't stop Corry from talking.

"And who's Sterling?"

"Our master's first progeny. He was a priest or something like that. He's the only one of us four brothers who's on the council of Elders. You'll probably meet him tonight."

"My dad turned a priest from the middle ages into a vampire?"

"Yeah, Master always had a sick sense of humor. Kinda got off on other people's pain, and torturing a devout Catholic with eternal damnation was right up his alley."

The meatloaf I'd had for dinner wasn't sitting so well with me anymore. I was so naive to have actually believed my father was some rich, benevolent man who'd one day come for me. But I wouldn't have ever guessed the reality. Turns out he was just an evil fuck. Sure, he was rich, and it was his sons who'd come for me. But none of that made me feel any better.

"So my dad was a twisted sadist, huh?" I forced a sadistically sweet smile in Vincent's direction. "That explains you, I guess."

My face nearly slammed into the middle console as the car came to a screeching halt.

"What the fuck, Feral?" I barked at the vampire, who unfastened his belt and stepped out of the car.

"Uh-oh," Corry breathed.

A second later, my door was torn open, and the male vampire standing there glared down at me with death in his bloody gaze. He oozed sex and violence and pure fury that had the human instincts inside me withering away from him, wanting to put distance between the predator and us.

But something else inside me, something I hadn't discovered until tonight, was dying to get closer to this monster. It was like the beast inside me, the very same that my mother had feared and locked up, wanted more of this male.

Like it didn't care if he devoured us whole.

Vincent arched down and grabbed my throat in his crushing grip. I sputtered from shock and lack of air.

"Come on, man, let her go," Corry said, looking at me with pity. "The Elders will have you staked if you hurt her."

"Fuck the Elders," Vincent snarled at his younger brother, his veins bulging in his neck, making the raven wings tattooed into his pale flesh twitch like they were trying to fly.

"And you," he gritted, clamping his gaze back down on me. It was a look so terrifying, it could make a grown man shit his backbone. But I only met his glare, refusing to show any fear.

"Never compare me to your father again. Got that, Princess? You didn't know him, and you're a lucky bitch for never having to know his reign of terror. You were kept with your mother for your safety. I'm sorry she locked you up like an animal, but what you endured in that house was fucking paradise compared to what my brothers and I have been made to endure for decades and in Sterling's case, centuries under your father's brutality and savagery. So excuse me if you don't get any sympathy from me because you should be on your knees thanking me for keeping you away from him."

"I'll thank you for one thing, Feral," I sputtered against his choking grip. "By freeing me from my cage, I realized I can never go back. Meaning I won't be anyone's bitch ever again. So sorry, but I'm not going to get on my knees for anyone. *Especially* you."

His full lips spread into a brittle smile, and his eyes burned into me like he could see every freaking inch of my soul. His fingers squeezed my windpipe in a way that shouldn't have been pleasurable... but it was. And I hated my traitorous body for wanting more of him and his ruthless attention.

"We'll see about that, Princess. We'll see about that."

CHAPTER NINE
THE YOUNGBLOOD

A million thoughts flew around in my head as I watched the blur of Quincy's streetlights streak past my window.

I had a lot to think about.

Like what Mom would do when she woke from that trance Vincent had put her in. Probably nothing. If she knew about the vampires and the coven, she knew where they were taking me. It's not like she could call the cops or anything. Now that the coven wanted me, there would be no getting me back.

Would she even want me back? My stomach curdled at the thought. She was all I had in the world and tonight felt like a bitter betrayal.

Now I had nobody but these pricks in the front seat. Not only were they strangers, but they were also dangerous strangers. Lethally dangerous. Vampires. And if I was really half-vampire, where did I stand with them? Was I prey or princess?

It didn't sound like they were huge fans of my dad. Corry didn't seem to carry any animosity toward me, though. In fact, with the heated glances he kept shooting over his shoulder, he was full of curiosity. And standing at the opposite end of that spectrum was Vincent Feral, who I was convinced might be compelled to smile if I somehow randomly combusted in the backseat.

He had told me in my room that vampire law was for the king to select a progeny to take his place, and in doing so, he had named me as his successor on his deathbed.

Why?

Did he really hate his adoptive sons so much that he would make a sheltered half-blood girl his heir instead, just to rile them?

Thanks, Dad. On TV, most estranged relatives left their beneficiaries furniture, jewelry, money, or their taxidermy collections. Not entire, monstrous cults.

Guess all I was to him was a tool to make everyone else suffer. I didn't exactly agree with the way the prick went about it, but maybe Vincent had the right idea by bringing me to the Elders so I could tell them I wasn't interested in being queen. I didn't know the first thing about being outside, let alone being the ruler of some ancient vampire coven.

I couldn't go back to Quincy after all this. No, Human Ruby was getting left behind in this town, and I guess Vampire Princess Ruby was waiting for me in Provincetown. The question was, who was that person?

Not a sheltered girl with a heart problem. No, I had to be the person I'd always dreamed I would be. An adrenaline-seeking badass who wasn't afraid to cause a little trouble. I had never dreamed of that tougher, wilder Ruby being a vampire, but hey, I could roll with the punches. I certainly wasn't cut out to be some vampire queen, but I could at least do my best to rock the fangs.

"Stop the car," I said, spotting a sign for a pharmacy up ahead.

Vincent's brows pulled together in the rearview mirror, scowling. "We're not stopping until we get back to the coven."

I tapped on his heavily muscled shoulder and gave him a honied smile in the rearview mirror. "Stop the damn car, asshole, or I'll be pissing all over your fancy leather upholstery."

Corry snickered.

"Real cute, Princess," Vincent growled but pulled the car over into the pharmacy parking lot and cut the engine. "Make it quick. Don't try running either, because I will find you."

Scoffing, I slammed the car door behind me and went into the pharmacy.

A little bell sounded as the electronic door of the building slid open for me, causing me to jump. Seeing things on TV was different than actually experiencing things, so even though all this looked familiar, it still felt like I was on an alien planet.

Before I had left the house with Vincent, he'd allowed me to say goodbye to my mom even though she was still in a trance from his weird vampire hypnosis. It was a bitter goodbye because I was angry at her. So I hadn't felt too bad for swiping her wallet from her dresser. Thankfully it had a handful of cash in it.

Walking to the hair care section, I found what I was looking for.

Bright red hair dye.

Mom never let me dye my hair. And it's not like I had the luxury of the teenage rebellion phase because she kept me locked in my room.

I stared at the model on the box for a second, glaring at the beautiful woman on the front with cherry-red hair.

I knew exactly who I wanted to be, who I should be. But the bars and the locks and the fear of a nonexistent heart disease had kept me from being that person.

So today, I would be reborn. And it started with some dumb gesture because, hey, I knew it would make me feel better. Tonight was the start of a new life for me, one of freedom. And I'd mark the occasion with a new kick-ass hair color that my mother would have never allowed.

"That will be $16.98," the cashier at the front counter said with an unenthused smile.

My gaze fell to the shelf behind her, and my curiosity piqued. "Can I also get a bottle of that?" I pointed to one of the bottom shelf vodkas.

Okay, so I didn't want to be a stereotypical twenty-three-year-old buying cheap liquor when I definitely shouldn't be getting drunk, not when I was in the company of strangers being taken to who the fuck knew where. But it was a night for firsts, and tonight I wanted to try booze.

The cashier asked for my ID, and I showed her my mom's. Luckily it was an older picture where mom was a lot younger. We looked similar enough for the lady to hesitate.

"You don't seem old enough to have been born in 1980."

"Yeah, well, good genes."

"Uh-huh..." The cashier's line of sight shifted to someone in line behind me. Her eyes lit up, and her bored expression disintegrated instantly. "Hi! Can I help you?"

"Um, I was here first. Can I at least buy the—"

"I'll get these things for her," a familiar voice said behind me. "Also, this."

Corry stepped up to the counter beside me, flashing the cashier a dimpled smile as he laid down a box, his ID and some cash.

"Oh um, sure!" she said, giving him a flirtatious smile as she rang him up. I rolled my eyes at her as she looked at his ID a little too long.

"Wow, you live in Provincetown? Do you know The Feral King?" she gushed.

"Yeah, I know him. We're practically brothers."

"No way!" She held the ID like it was Brad Pitt's ID she had been handed and not some random guy's from Provincetown. "You live at the old Knight Mansion? You live with him?"

"Okay, time to go," I grumbled, snatching the plastic bag with the hair stuff and the vodka from the counter. "I'll be in the bathroom."

"Hey, wait up!" Corry left the girl behind, jogging behind me. "I bought the booze. At least share."

"Can vampires even get drunk?"

"Yeah, but it would work better if we drink the blood of an intoxicated human. More fun that way too."

"Cool. Well, that cashier seemed pretty willing to let you take whatever you wanted from her, so while you go do that, I'll be dying my hair."

"Nah. Vincent would kill me. I'm not really allowed to be around humans yet since I'm still a youngblood. I was only turned about six months ago. Can't control myself too well when feeding."

"You know, I almost thought you weren't a vampire when I first saw you. Since you didn't have red eyes like your brother."

"Oh yeah, we get the creepy red eyes when we're hungry." His grin stretched wide, and he winked. "Or horny. Or both. Older vampires can control it. Funny Vin couldn't earlier. He's around blood all the time, so he's normally better at reigning in his thirst. He even fed before we got to your house."

We stopped right outside the ladies' room. I turned on Corry. "So you knew my dad?"

His smile slipped, and he scrubbed the back of his skull with his hand. "Um, kinda. Oh yeah, look what I got you!"

He dug around in the bag, extracting what he had bought alongside the vodka. It was obviously a distraction, and damn, it worked when I saw what it was.

"Oh, a cell phone!"

"Haha, yeah. Just a cheap pre-paid thing, but it will do for now until we get you on the coven's family plan. Vin is doing a pretty shit job at showing you how you're not a prisoner anymore. So I thought this would be a good start."

I looked down at the phone, a mix of emotions filling me. "Um, thanks. This is nice, Corry." My cheeks warmed. "But uh...I don't know who I'd call. I don't know anyone."

His grin returned, and while Vincent's radiated arrogance and hostility that seemed to fill me with fire, Corry's only warmed me, making me feel at ease. "You know me. Here." He took the phone, entered his contact information and handed it back to me with a wink.

"That will fill up fast, Princess. Need help with your hair?"

"Aren't you supposed to be a dangerous youngblood or whatever you called it? Also, you commented earlier on my virginity... Should I be inviting you into the bathroom with me?"

Corry let out a laugh that reached his eyes, making his eyes sparkle with mirth. "I said Vincent probably can't handle you, Princess. If Vincent can't handle you, you'll freaking destroy me, so I'd be an idiot for trying anything."

I gave him a glare of warning then pushed open the bathroom door. "Fine."

He stayed where he was, surprised that I had actually agreed. "Okay, but full disclosure, I am kind of an idiot."

Laughing, I disappeared inside the restroom and left the door open in invitation. Okay, so was it a bad idea to be alone with a baby vampire unsupervised? Probably. But he seemed a hell of a lot less dangerous than his counterpart.

"Come on, Corry."

CHAPTER TEN

A BITE FOR A BITE

I t only took a few minutes to apply the dye. Luckily my hair was light enough that I didn't need bleach. I sat in one of the stalls with the lid down and the stall door open, so I had a view of Corry, who sat on the sink.

I froze when I realized I could see his reflection in the mirror. "I can see you in the mirror."

He blinked in confusion, so I continued. "I couldn't see Vincent in the mirror back at home."

Corry's expression stretched with understanding. "Ah. Yeah, it must have been an old mirror."

"Probably. A lot of the furniture came with the house when my mom bought it, and that was before I was born."

"That explains it. A long time ago, mirrors were backed in silver, so it's only in old mirrors that we can't see ourselves. Course that probably doesn't apply to you since you're only half-vampire."

"So silver really can hurt you?"

"Yeah. It can hurt a lot. It can't kill us with simple contact, but it'll burn like a bitch." He shifted on the sink and cast the restroom door a nervous glance. "You know, Vin's gonna come looking for us soon. He's gonna be pissed."

Snorting, I took another swig of the vodka. The liquid burned as it went down, and I winced, not quite sure what the big deal was about alcohol. It tasted disgusting.

"Let him. I'm not scared of him."

"You know he once almost killed a man with his bare fists on live television," Corry said, grinning. "So maybe you should be scared of him."

"I'd be scared of him if I was afraid of things like death. But I'm not. Probably because I was isolated for so long, death seemed like the only way out a lot of the time."

"Whoa... That's heavy shit, Ruby. But I bet you not giving a shit about death comes from your dad. You are the daughter of the vampire king, after all. He wasn't afraid of anything either."

There was a heavy sensation in my belly like I had swallowed a rock. Hearing about my dad was weird, partly because I had gone so long not thinking about him and partly because I had learned that he was not only a vampire but the king of them.

It was a lot to swallow.

On top of it all, I was quickly gathering that maybe it was a good thing I hadn't ever gotten to know him while he was alive. There were questions I wanted answered, but maybe it was better that his adopted sons filled in all the missing pieces I had tried to fill for years.

"So, how did you meet him? My dad, I mean."

"Eh. My story isn't as interesting as Sterling's, Vincent's, and Deathwish's."

I nearly choked on my next swig of vodka. "Did you say Deathwish? What kind of name is that?"

"It's not his real name. His real name is Eros. Deathwish was his fighter name. He was an MMA fighter just like Vincent. He's retired now, but everyone still calls him Deathwish."

I crinkled my nose. "Why?"

Corry looked a little uncomfortable. "Fits him better than Eros, I guess. He does the dirty work for the coven. Travels all over. I would say that you'll meet him soon, but something tells me Vincent and Sterling won't want you around him."

Frowning, I decided it was best not to linger on this Deathwish. "So, how did you meet my dad?"

"Oh right. I was out riding on my bike, and I got hit by another car going like fifty over the speed limit. It was a miracle it didn't kill me instantly. Your dad saved me by turning me."

"So he saved your life?"

"Kinda. He was the one who hit me, so I guess he thought he owed me. The other three were turned pretty much exclusively for the suffering of others."

"Oh... I'm trying really hard to find any reason to believe that maybe my dad wasn't a complete piece of shit, but you and Vincent are making that really hard."

"Eh." Corry shrugged. "I'd lie to you and tell you he was an okay guy, just to make you feel better. But something tells me you're pretty sick of lies."

"I am."

"Right." Corry heaved a sigh and picked up the box of dye, pretending to be enthralled by the directions on the back of the packaging. "He was a complete piece of shit in most cases, kind of sadistic. But in his defense, he did protect his family. The Cape Cod Coven wouldn't be what it is today without him."

He flashed me a heart-melting grin as he tossed the dye box into the wastebasket beside the door. "Anyway. I think you'll like the coven. Even with all the assholes in it."

For several minutes, Corry and I sat in silence. It wasn't like it was uncomfortable. In fact, it was kind of nice. I had made a friend, someone pretty much right around my age. He seemed pretty chill, for technically being dead, so maybe being a half-vampire wasn't really so bad.

"Help me rinse out my hair?" I stood up a little too fast and regretted it. The restroom spun, and I stumbled.

Corry hopped down from the sink and was standing beside me, having moved so quick my eyes weren't able to follow the movement.

"I'm okay. I think it's just the vodka. Now I understand why people drink this crap. I feel...hungry."

Corry's brow wrinkled with concern. "Uh-oh. Well, maybe we should grab you some food."

"No. No, I don't want food. Even after I eat, I'm still hungry. What the fuck is up with that?"

"Because you need blood to sate the thirst. As a human, you don't need it to survive, but I bet it's uncomfortable to go without it all the same. You wouldn't happen to have any of those pills Sharpe prescribed on you, would you?"

My heart felt heavy in my chest. My stomach rumbled, and my throat went dry. "No... Am I always going to have to take those, or do I have to start biting people?"

The prospect of actually biting another person should have been revolting, but now that it was actually on the table as something normal my kind did to sustain themselves, it was hard to think about it as anything but natural. Maybe that was my monstrous instincts talking, and the alcohol wasn't helping slake that urge at all. It was making it worse.

"You don't have to, no. But the coven Elders will teach you how to do so safely and discreetly, eventually."

I frowned. "That girl at the front seemed to like you. Maybe you could go and do that hypnosis shit that Vincent used on my mom."

"Ruby, that isn't a good idea. Besides, I don't know how to do that yet. The ability to mesmerize humans comes with time and practice."

I shook my head, trying to knock some sense into it. What was I thinking? Had I actually just suggested that we go attack that poor girl?

Walking to the sink, I turned on the faucet and stuck my head under the water to wash out the red coloring. Corry stepped up behind me to help. For a vampire, he was surprisingly warm. He was so close, his heat seeped through my clothing and warmed me all over.

There was something about his presence that was comforting, safe. And he somehow made me feel more human. Which was weird since he wasn't human at all. I felt his fingers in my hair, massaging my scalp and coaxing the dye from my roots. His touch was strong but gentle.

His breathing turned heavy and labored behind me. Shutting the faucet off, I wrung out my now cherry-red hair and looked at his reflection in the mirror.

"You okay?"

Corry jerked a nod, his Adam's apple bobbing with a gulp. "Yeah... You just smell really good. Better than anyone I've ever smelled before."

A smile curved my lips, and I saw in the mirror that my cheeks had blotted with twin stains of pink. "You normally go around sniffing girls?"

He let out a nervous laugh. "No. As a youngblood, I'm pretty much confined to the coven these days, and the women there don't smell anything like you. You don't really smell like a human either."

He leaned closer, burying his nose in my mane of red. He inhaled, his eyes growing half-mast and a sultry grin sliding across his lips. He lifted a hand and coiled one of my freshly colored locks around his finger.

"Ruby-Red. Soon to be queen of the dead. Your scent smells like something sent from the gods."

I arched a brow at him. "You're a religious vampire?"

"No. But your scent is enough to make me believe in something holy. That's for fucking sure."

His voice had dropped to a husky, wanton timbre. The tip of his nose nuzzled the sensitive skin beneath my ear, and his breath tickled my skin, causing me to shiver despite his heat that enveloped me like a blanket.

I caught his gaze in the mirror and swallowed a gasp. His eyes had turned crimson again, and his fangs had dropped. They were so close to my neck, if he decided to bite me now, there would be no getting away.

But he didn't, and it seemed to be taking all of his control not to sink his teeth into me.

"What happens when a vampire bites another vampire?"

His cheeks burned to a hue of red that almost matched my hair. "A vampire biting another vampire is something completely different than a vampire biting a human. It's more...intimate."

"What? Really?"

He gave a slow nod. "We get all the nourishment we need from human and animal blood. It's deliciously satisfying, but when we feed from our own, it's another kind of hunger that awakens."

"Have you ever done it?"

He closed his eyes, shaking his head. "Never."

I swallowed, gathering my courage. "Can you teach me how to bite?"

His eyes snapped open, and his jaw practically dropped open into an expression of shock, his thick, deadly sharp fangs glinting in the bathroom's fluorescent lighting. "I shouldn't. Not yet. The Elders wouldn't want me to."

"You can bite me in exchange," I offered.

Shit, what was I doing?

Was I actually inviting a vampire to suck my blood?

Bloody hell. Hours ago, I was curled up on my bedroom floor with a werewolf romance and a slice of meatloaf. Now here I was in a public restroom somewhere on the outskirts of Quincy with a strange guy telling him to bite me.

Fuck. And I was here for it. But that might have just been the booze talking.

Whatever. Some people did drugs. And all things considered, letting myself get bitten by a pretty nice vampire was a much better idea. Right? Especially if I was going to be returning the favor. Because he smelled freaking good too, and sinking my teeth into him was a much better alternative than hunting down that poor cashier.

I pulled back my red hair in invitation and grinned at Corry in the mirror. "Go ahead, Youngblood. Bite me."

CHAPTER ELEVEN

A BLOODY KISS AND A BRUTAL VOW

"I shouldn't," Corry breathed against me, his hot breath feathering my throat where the needle-sharp tips of his fangs scraped.

Shouldn't. But he wanted to. Something deeply instinctual wanted him to bite me too. It stretched much deeper than a drunken curiosity.

My body throbbed for his penetration... And not just from his fangs. The blood in my veins hummed for him like a siren's song and stretched to much more intimate places than where his lips were currently pressed.

"Why not?" I asked in a ragged whisper.

"Because you're not my mate. No one's claimed you yet."

"Mate? Claim? You mean like werewolves?"

He nodded, his nostrils flaring as if my scent was too much for him to resist much longer. "Pretty much the same, yeah. Vampires deliver a claiming bite to our chosen mates, which serves as a warning to all others of our kind to stay away. By letting me bite you, you're giving me way more than your blood, Ruby."

The corners of my mouth lifted. "And what would I be giving you?"

His tongue snaked out from between his fangs and slid over my jugular, tasting me. The growl that slipped from his lips was the most erotic thing I'd ever heard. It was sensual, masculine, and completely predatory. A throbbing, hot hunger pooled low in my belly, and I pressed back into him.

His arms curled around me, drawing me in. "You'd be giving me your submission. My scent would be on you, telling every other male you're mine."

I bit my lip so hard a drop of ruby-red blood slipped down my chin. I belonged to no one. I spent too long locked up to ever let anyone control me again. So if I wanted to fool around with this vampire, with any of them for that matter, it wouldn't be with fangs.

Just as I was about to push him away, the door to the restroom ripped open and there stood Vincent Feral, looking pissed as fuck.

Great. Here came the big growly dick energy to spoil the mood.

"Get the fuck away from her, Corry," Vincent snarled. Corry did not let go. His eyes were two obsidian disks with thin rings of red around them. His fangs were still dropped, dripping with saliva and so dangerously close to that delicate juncture between my neck and shoulder.

"She wants me."

"She's basically a brand new vampire, and on top of that, she's a sheltered kid. She doesn't know what she wants."

"I'm not a kid," I argued. "If I decide to let Corry bite me, isn't that my prerogative?"

"You don't know what it is you're asking."

"Why do you care?"

"Because you don't belong with us. You may have the blood of the vampire king in your veins, but that doesn't mean you're cut out to live among us, let alone be our queen. You don't belong, Princess. After tonight you can go your own way and take a human mate, or do whatever the fuck it is you want to do. As long as it's not Corry."

Vincent lifted his murderous glare to his brother, and his eyes turned to slits as he noted the way the youngblood held me possessively.

The older vampire came into the room and let the door close behind him. "Step away from her," he ordered, a low rattle rumbling up from his chest, warning the other male to back down. "Don't make me fight you, Corry. You know I'll win."

Several tense seconds of silence crawled by on their hands and knees as the two vampires stared each other down.

Fuck, what have I done? I didn't mean to start this battle of male dominance shit in the pharmacy bathroom. All I wanted was red hair.

Finally, Corry dropped his hold over me and reluctantly stepped away.

"Go wait in the car," Vincent commanded.

The younger vampire glanced my way, clearly not wanting to leave me alone with his brother.

"It's okay." I gave him a reassuring smile that was shakier than I would have liked. "We'll be out in just a second."

Corry stormed out, leaving me alone with his big angry asshole of a brother.

"Wow, you really have some anger issues, you know that? You can't just come in here flexing your muscles, throwing around your orders like I give a shit about what you—"

I didn't finish my sentence because before I realized what was happening, Vincent had closed the distance between us, and his mouth was on mine in a bruising kiss. I had never been kissed before, and like most little girls, I used to dream about my first. Of course, I wasn't so naive to think that my first kiss would be anything like I had imagined. But I hadn't imagined this. Because I deserved better than a brutal demonstration of dominance delivered by an infuriating dickhead in a Walgreen's restroom.

What I hated most about the whole thing?

I fucking liked it. With the Feral King's lips on mine, something exotic and powerful and carnal within me roared to life. Every nerve ending was set on fire, and I wanted nothing more than to burn to ash and be born anew.

He kissed me until my lungs were screaming for breath, pushing me away with a rough shove only after I'd beat on his chest, battling against him so I could fucking breathe.

Gasping, my back slammed into the concrete wall, and I doubled over with my hands braced on my knees.

"What the fuck, Feral?" I peered up at him through my stringy, still-wet crimson tresses.

He was smirking down at me with his head cocked to one side, licking his grinning lips. His eyes had turned reddish-black like Corry's had when he'd come close to biting me. And that's when I saw the smear of blood on his lips.

I had bit myself when Corry had been in here, spilling a few drops of my blood.

Feral had kissed me for the taste of it.

I straightened, glaring at him. "You're a fucking monster, you know that?"

"Yeah. I do know that. And where we're going, you'll find a lot more monsters just like me. So do yourself a favor, Princess. Keep your fluids to yourself while we're there. Especially your blood."

He licked his lips clean, and he uttered a gravelly purr like it was the most delicious thing he'd ever tasted. "Take it from someone who knows. Wars are waged over blood like yours. And vampires like Corry don't end up winning fights with monsters like me."

"What are you saying? That you would fight others for my blood?"

"That's exactly what I'm saying. There isn't a male or female, for that matter, who wouldn't tear open your pretty lips to see what spills out. And I'm not just talking about the set on your face, Princess. So if you know what's good for you, you'll come with me to the coven, stand before the Elders and tell them you have no wish to be our queen, and then you'll leave."

My cheeks flamed. "And if I don't?"

"If you don't, there will be males vying for your submission so that they might rise as the vampire king. You're a sweet prize, Ruby Renada Baxter. Know why?"

All I could do was shake my head stupidly.

"Because you have the strength of a vampire, the blood of a human, and you have the reproductive capabilities of a mortal. By taking you as their mate, a male will not only become the vampire king, but he'll have a steady supply of blood as sweet as ambrosia. And by breeding you, he could have biological sons. That's something that can usually only be achieved by bedding a female human, and most don't live through the pregnancy."

"I don't get it. If I'm such a great catch, why do you want me to go in front of your Elders to tell them I don't want to be queen?"

"Because I *will* be king of the vampires. I endured too much of your father's torture to take anything less. I have done my fucking time. It's my turn to rule our kind into a new era. By vampire law, I should be king, but it was your father's dying wish that you be queen. It's a wish the Elders will respect. So if you accept the position, know this, Ruby. I will be king one way or another, and if I have to claim you as my own for that right..." He stepped toward me, bringing his face so close our noses nearly touched. "I will."

Chapter Twelve

DEATH DRIVES A ROLLS-ROYCE

"You're going to stay away from her, you got that?" Vincent snarled at Corry the second we were back in the car.

The youngblood snapped his attention on his brother, his eyes—back to blue—widened, and his brow contorted into a furious scowl. "What? "

"Because you were about to bite her."

The anger on Corry's face almost looked out of place, but damn, I have to admit it was pretty freaking hot seeing him so furious with the older vampire. His vein throbbing with rage had a way of making a fucked-up girl like me all warm and fuzzy on the inside. Not because I wanted to see two hot vampire guys with their hands wrapped around the other's throat—but because Corry was getting so upset over the notion of staying away from me.

Vincent's glare turned lethal, its bloody burn so intense I caught a little of its heat despite the fact that it was, for the first time tonight, not directed toward me.

"You were about to bite her," Vincent repeated. "After all the work we've done in getting you out of this damn bloodthirst phase. You want to repeat that little incident of yours from last month?"

I perked up a little in the backseat. What incident?

Corry's cheeks flushed red. Damn, I didn't even know a vampire could blush. His gaze flicked quickly to me, then back to his brother. Whatever Vincent was talking about, Corry did not want me to know.

"Bro, this isn't the same thing."

"No, you're right. It won't be the same because this bitch isn't some random, cracked-out street whore that no one will care enough about to come looking for. She's the biological daughter of the vampire king, and the Elders will notice if you kill her, Corry, all because you can't keep your blood boner in your goddamn gums. Sterling and I can't keep cleaning up your damn messes."

"Oh, fuck off. Sterling's an Elder."

"You think you're safe because he's an Elder? You're acting like a six-month-old vampire who doesn't know shit."

"I am a six-month vampire, asshole. I never asked for this. I never asked for you to babysit me like you're my daddy."

"I babysit you because Daddy is dead, and Sterling is too busy kissing up to those geriatric fucks to keep tabs on you."

"I don't need you to watch my every damn move."

"Yeah? I probably still have bloodstains in the trunk's upholstery that says otherwise. I'm watching you to keep your body count to a minimum. Otherwise, the Elders won't make any of Master's progeny his heir."

"So that brutal fuck who blinded Sterling was their perfect leader, but I kill a couple of worthless humans, and suddenly I'm the monster?"

"That's the thing about the vampire king's brutality, Little Brother. Thomas Knight tortured his own. He kept his demons within his own halls where there was no chance for the human world to catch onto his nature. He was evil, but he was tidy about it. Nothing evil about you, Cor. You're just a dipshit, and you're going to expose the coven if you aren't careful."

For a second, a tense silence so thick I thought I might choke settled over the car's interior. Vincent's red-hot glower shifted to me and back to Corry as if to say, *"look what you made me say."*

I got the impression they both had let out a lot they hadn't meant to. This little spat between brothers was of epic proportions. They were putting on a show so insane I almost wished I had popcorn, if it wasn't over the fact that Vincent was basically letting on that Corry had murdered at least one innocent person. Probably more.

I wasn't so naive to think these vampires didn't hurt people, but...Corry? He seemed so sweet, so innocent. I would have put bets down on Vincent being the dangerous wild card, not Corry.

And for some reason, Vincent had let the youngblood follow me into the pharmacy. Then again, he probably hadn't guessed we'd barricade ourselves in the women's restroom with boxed dye and cheap vodka. It sounded innocent enough, but throw in Corry's bloodlust and some late-blooming hormones on my end, and yeah, it could have been an epic disaster.

And what was that shit about my father blinding Sterling? Sterling was the oldest of the four, the one who'd come over on the Mayflower with Thomas Knight.

It was the first time I'd heard my dad's full name, and despite how basic of a name it was for an ancient vampire king, it still sent an icy shiver scraping down my spine. He was dead. Gone. But even the mention of him charged the air with intense, ominous energy.

My guts twisted, thinking about Sterling.

Even though he was only mentioned a couple of times, it didn't take a detective to figure out that Sterling was respected by his younger brood mates.

I couldn't help but wonder what kind of person he was to earn their respect and tolerate Thomas Knight for almost an entire millennia.

My stomach clenched, thinking on what kind of man my father had to have been to blind his own progeny.

I don't know what made me feel sicker, the fact that I was descended from that monster or that Corry maybe hadn't fallen so far from the tree if he was going around killing innocent women and brushing them off like they were nothing.

"I wasn't going to expose the coven by giving the princess what she asked for," Corry spit out a moment later.

"You have no right to mark her. She's not yours."

"She's gonna be queen. She can pick whoever the hell she wants as a mate."

"No, she isn't, and no, she can't."

"You gonna look me in the eye and tell me you'd say no to a female like her asking for your mark?"

Vincent's gaze flashed red, his glower red hot and terrifying. All the while, he refused to meet my stare in the car's rearview mirror. "She didn't know what she was asking for."

"Whatever, bro. You're just jealous. Maybe try not being such a raging dickhead, and she'd be begging for your bite too."

"Hold up," I interjected. "First of all, I didn't beg. Second, it would be *great* if you two shitheads stopped talking about me like I'm not here. I don't want either of you. This circus is getting too creepy for my tastes, so can we just get going already so I can tell your Elders that I don't want any part of this?"

I wish there had been enough time to pull out the phone Corry bought me to snap a picture of Vincent's face. His jaw was practically in his lap.

Maybe he hadn't expected me to give in that easily. But the thing that happened in the bathroom between the three of us wasn't some basic bad-boy drama.

These were predators. They were dangerous.

Vincent was right. I didn't have any business even pretending for a second that I had any right to the vampire throne. Shit, I didn't have a right to anything. I was homeless.

I had nothing, nothing except my freedom and my beating heart.

But something told me if I hung out with this crew for much longer, I wouldn't even have those.

"Good," Vincent ground out, recovering from his surprise by my announcement a second later.

"What? No!" Corry snarled. "That's bullshit. She has nowhere else to go."

"She can figure it out. You don't get to keep the human just because you have a hard-on for her."

"She's only half-human. And stop pretending like you don't want her as much as I do. It's really starting to piss me off, Feral."

A tendon in Vincent's jaw ticked. His fists clenched tight around the steering wheel to the point I thought it might disintegrate. "I don't want her. I don't give a fuck about her."

It was no secret we weren't exactly hitting it off, but hearing his blatant opinion of me and how little he cared what happened to me was like salt in a very fresh wound. The stark reality was, no one gave a shit about me. Corry just wanted my blood, my virginity, or both.

And all Vincent cared about was getting the throne.

Treacherous flames lapped at my core as I dwelled on what he'd said in the restroom.

He'd claim me if it meant securing the throne. What did that mean exactly? Was it anything like how it worked in the romance novels? My whole body grew hot and the juncture between my thighs wet, thinking about the way he'd manhandled me in my room. Jeez, I was one fucked up girl. I'd spent my entire life thinking I was some weakling, and in one single night, I discovered that I was half-vampire and the daughter of the vampire king. I also had some infuriating attraction to my...

Shit, what even were Corry and Vincent to me? Stepbrothers? No, that was weird. Whatever they were, my traitorous vagina was all for this whole kidnapping and whisking me off to whatever creepy castle they lived in plan.

And that's exactly why I had to get away from these men.

No matter how much my body burned to let them bite and fuck me into oblivion, I knew they would be the death of me.

Before, I hadn't been afraid of death. But that was before when I'd thought death to be an escape, a definite end to pink walls and barred windows.

But tonight, I'd learned death wasn't some skeleton decked out in robes with a scythe. He was a gorgeous monster with pale skin, red eyes, and raven tattoos all over his body.

With him, death wouldn't be an escape.

It would be a life sentence.

Chapter Thirteen
An Unhealthy Obsession

A little ding sounded in my pocket, causing me to jump when I realized it was the phone Corry had gifted me. Digging it out, I found a text from him. I almost smiled when I saw he'd entered himself as Corry (the hot one) in my contacts, but that slipped away when I read the text.

Corry: Hey... ur not gonna actually leave, right?

It took me longer than it probably should have to type out an answer. These days kids got their first cell phone when they were five, and here I was, twenty-three freaking years old, and I was just now tapping out my first text. Several minutes later, there was a beep from Corry's pocket. He pulled out his phone, and the front cab lit up from the white screen. Vincent gave us both a side-eyed glare but said nothing.

Ruby: Yeah, I'm leaving as soon as I talk to your Elders

Corry: Where u gonna go?

Where was I going to go? I didn't exactly have a plan, but sleeping on a park bench seemed a touch less dangerous than sleeping in a strange house filled with vampires. For a sliver of a second, my mind dwelled on the possibility of going back to my mom's, but I immediately shoved it away with a shudder.

I couldn't go back, not after knowing all the lies she'd fed me over the years. The bars on the windows, the locks, the fucking heart monitor wristband that was all for show. No hugs, no birthday parties, no contact with the outside world whatsoever. My own mother passed me my meals on a cafeteria tray through a metal flap on my door.

A fucking *flap*. They reserved that for the worst kind of criminals in high-security prisons.

She was never trying to protect me. She was just trying to protect herself.

So yeah, going back was way out of the question.

Ruby: Don't know.

Corry: Stay with us till u figure it out.

Ruby: Vincent won't like that.

Corry: So wut? He's not in charge even tho he acts like it.

When I didn't reply, he sent a second text a few minutes later.

Corry: Does he scare you?

I bristled as I read the question, pounding at the keys of my phone a little too hard.

Ruby: Nope ;) I just hate his guts.

Corry: What happened between you two in the restroom when I went back to the car?

What was I supposed to say? That he'd threatened to forcibly take me as his mate if it meant being king? Okay, so he didn't exactly imply that it would be by force, but there was no way his game was strong enough for me to go along with it. It's not like I was into this broody badass vibe he was throwing down.

Okay, so I was into it. And it was that fact that scared the crap out of me. I was learning all sorts of things about myself today. I didn't have a heart condition, I was perfectly healthy except for the whole vampirism thing. Also, turns out I have a thing for mannerless, undead pricks.

Ruby: Nothing happened.

Corry: So that blood on the corner of his mouth isn't urs?

Shit. Part of me wondered if Vincent hadn't licked it off intentionally just so he could rub it in Corry's face.

Ruby: Must be some random hooker's blood since apparently, it's okay to kill those, right? Since they're just humans?

My final text shut him up.

With a heated sigh, I folded my arms over my chest and foisted my attention out the window.

I hated how hungry, horny, and confused I was.

I'd only met Corry a couple hours ago, yet I already felt betrayed. But mostly, that was my fault. I'd let those blue eyes and the cool, dimpled smile trick me into thinking he was normal.

And Vincent? Well, he wore the fact that he was a monster on his sleeve. But I was pissed more at myself that my dark and dangerous knight was having this kind of effect on my body.

I thought back again on what went down in the bathroom with both of them.

I had asked Corry to bite me, and apparently, vampires biting other vampires was kind of like shifters marking a mate. And the youngblood had been happy to oblige the request until Feral had barged in with his big-dick energy, threatening to do the exact same thing if I dared to challenge him for the throne.

I squirmed in my seat, annoyed with the barrage of heated tickles that licked between my thighs, and my cheeks flared red when my gaze locked with Feral's in the Rolls-Royce's rearview mirror, his blood-red gaze banked with a heady mixture of violence, fury, and hunger.

I decided to momentarily shove aside my irritation with Corry and picked up my phone, tapping out a question.

Ruby: So why does Vincent still have red eyes? Yours went back to normal.

Corry: Means he's either hungry or horny. Or both.

That's when it dawned on me that Corry had been right.

On some predatory level, Vincent wanted me. And that fact probably pissed him off more than the potential of me making a grab for the throne.

I typed out my next question and read it at least five times. I contemplated deleting it and asking a more appropriate question but to hell with that. Nothing about this situation was appropriate, and I wasn't going to get all shy now.

Ruby: So what's with the whole claiming bite thing?

Corry: It's a mark a vampire places on his mate to show other males she's taken.

Ruby: Well, what if a male bites a female against her will?

The energy in the cab immediately shifted. I could practically feel the heat rolling off of Corry's body in front of me, his neck muscles bunching up and the cords of his neck tightening.

Corry: Is that what he did in the bathroom? Did he bite you? After he told me off? That asshole.

Ruby: No, that's not what happened.

Vincent Feral hadn't bit me.

He'd kissed me. If that bullshit power move could even have been called a kiss.

My lips still throbbed, phantom sensations of his mouth on mine lighting up my nerves.

He'd kissed me like he was trying to crawl into my body, to tear me apart from the inside.

It wasn't like any kiss I'd seen on TV or read about, either. It was better. And that's how it had been with The Feral King tonight.

My mind recoiled from the monster with mean eyes and cruel words, but for some reason, it just sprang back, seeking more. It was a confusing coalescence of desire and disgust.

As we drove deeper into Cape Cod, my thoughts eventually drifted away from vampires, dark secrets, and red eyes when something glinted in the corner of my vision, pulling my gaze to the passing world beyond the window. My heart lurched when I realized what I was looking at was the moon's reflection on the ocean's surface.

The ocean.

I'd seen it on TV, read about it in books. Hell, I could even smell it from between the bars of my bedroom window. If the house had been facing the other way, I would have had an ocean view. Of course, as the universe seemed to have some kind of vendetta against me, my bedroom faced inland.

Everything inside me turned cold as my throat grew thick with emotion. Would it have been so hard for my mom to have unlocked the door so I could look at the ocean from the hallway window?

Anger blurred my view of the silvery ocean, my fists clenching on my thighs.

I wasn't ready to confront her yet. But eventually, I'd make her pay for the life she'd stolen from me.

All dreams of revenge slipped to the back of my mind when the car rolled up to an iron gate that looked like a copy of the one from *The Haunted Mansion*. The driver's side window rolled down, and Vincent leaned out to stab a code into the security pad attached to a post. A second later, the gate peeled open, allowing the car to pass through.

"Welcome to the Knight estate, Red." Corry grinned back at me, his gaze glittering with amusement as he watched me take everything in with a gaping jaw.

The Knight Mansion was absolutely massive. It sat on a cliff overlooking the sea, the moon sitting just above its roof, bathing the structure in a kiss of silver light. I half expected a gothic mansion made of stone, with tall peaks and stone gargoyles. Instead, the mansion had been built in the boxy, colonial-style like many others its age in the area. It reminded me of the Corwin house in Salem that I'd seen in a history book on Massachusetts. Only this place had to be five times the size, with at least a dozen windows on the front, a gable roof and thin wooden slats for the siding where the salty wind had long since stripped the paint.

Other than its gargantuan size, it almost seemed too ordinary of a place to house a vampire coven. Then again, if my dad had arrived here on the Mayflower with the intention of making this place home to him and his brood, he would have gone out of his way to fit in among the witch-crazed, overly superstitious colonizers of the time.

The grounds were well groomed, filled with beautiful gardens, a barn with a fenced-in pasture that contained sheep and goats, and a giant hanger on the opposite end of the grounds. Vincent pulled the car into the structure, and I couldn't bite back my gasp. It was packed with dozens of luxury and vintage cars, from Lamborghinis and G-Wagons all the way to Model Ts.

Vincent parked alongside a collection of motorcycles. "Who do all these belong to?"

"The coven," Corry answered. "Although most of the bikes are mine," he grinned back at me. "Want me to take you for a ride sometime?"

I wasn't sure when we were going to take a "ride" since I'd already told him I was planning to bail after tonight, but I found myself nodding, the idea of being on the back of a motorcycle sending a thrill down my spine. "Maybe, yeah."

Vincent cut the engine, barked at us to "get out," and left the car, slamming the door behind him. Corry and I exchanged an uneasy glance before exiting the Rolls-Royce.

I started to follow Corry's lead out of the hanger toward the mansion, but strong fingers gripped my wrist, holding me back. I spun around, glaring daggers into Vincent. "Let go of me, asshole."

Corry turned, his brow arching as he registered the way Vincent was holding me. "Dude, what the fuck?"

Vincent's brow cut his scowl so deep, the look had me shivering in his grip. "Go inside, gather the Elders and tell them the princess has arrived. We'll be there in a few minutes."

The youngblood's gaze connected with mine, and I could see the conflict banked in his oceanic eyes. He wanted to protect me from his brother, but Vincent was his superior, and as the older vampire, he was stronger.

A lot stronger.

"It's okay, Corry. We'll be inside in a few minutes," I reassured him through a shaky smile, repeating what Vincent said. The young vampire gave a slight nod, flinging his brother a nasty glare of warning as if to say, "*be nice.*" Then he slipped from the hanger into the night, leaving me alone with the vampire whose nose I'd broken, authority I challenged, and rightful place as king I threatened.

And fuck me, I'd loved every potentially lethal second of it.

There was something so intriguing in the way this Feral King regarded me, something that made my entire body burn with curiosity. Maybe it was the way his sanguine eyes blazed with dark and brutal promises if I dared stick around and try to take the throne from him.

And fuck, I was almost half tempted to.

But a brute like him could swiftly turn into a dark and unhealthy obsession. But hey, I'd never been afraid of death. Not while locked up in my pink prison in Quincy and certainly not pinned under the deliciously wicked gaze of Vincent Feral, my dark and damned knight.

CHAPTER FOURTEEN
A DARK ADDICTION

My heart pounded so hard in my throat, it was still embedded in my brain to instinctively check my heart monitor. But I couldn't move. Vincent's cool fingers gripped my wrist, making the plastic bite into my flesh.

"What do you want, Feral?" I bit out, my words sharp and deadly like shrapnel.

"I need to know exactly what you're planning on telling the Elders before I let you go in there."

I shot him a sour glare and yanked my arm out of his grip, rubbing the bruised skin. "I told you. I don't want anything to do with you or your creepy little cult. Have your throne, play the cruel king. Knock yourself out."

He straightened, his dark gaze falling into shadows as he contemplated the authenticity of my conviction.

It was almost like he could see straight through me. Like he knew a small part of me wanted to stay.

"You don't belong here."

"Look, I'm not the one who told you to come bust me out of my suburban prison. You forcibly dragged me here.

Remember?"

"You should be thanking me, Princess."

I scoffed. "For *what?*"

"For setting you free. You think busting you out of that house was the end all, be all? Please. Your mother wasn't your only jailer. It was the wish of your father and the Elders that you stay there, locked away from the world. Only so you could be set free when you could be useful to anyone."

My heart beat like a roaring engine in my ears.

This fact shouldn't have come as a surprise. Dr. Sharpe was in on it, after all. All he really did was lie and give me pills to make sure I didn't go ape-shit on my mom whenever she pushed meatloaf and cranberry juice through my food flap instead of human blood.

Maybe I wanted to rise up to the throne of vampire queen just to make them all pay for treating me like an animal up until I was useful.

If only I was strong enough, I'd make them all pay.

"So what do you want, Feral? A big fat fucking thank you for springing me? *Thanks.*" My voice was clipped, and I propped my fists on my hips while flinging him an indignant glare. "I'd offer some kind of payment, but oh, wait. You stole my first kiss. So let's just call us even, alright?"

The vampire's nostrils flared, and his brows pulled together in a scathing grimace. "Oh, please. I get you're a shut-in and all but stop acting like a petulant teenager. What, you gonna go write an angsty diary entry about how mad you are at the big angry vampire now that you can't give your first kiss away to the prom king?"

Angry, hot tears burned my eyes, but I refused to let them spill. Vincent had a special way of making me feel stupid, and I hated him for it.

This wasn't about my first kiss. Not really. It was about having the power to choose taken away from me. All my life, the choice to choose my own path had been taken away from me. I'd just let myself get swept away in the tide of lies.

Bile burned in my throat as I thought about how much I hated him, how I hated all of them. My mom, my dad, Dr. Sharpe, Vincent Feral. Corry was trying a different angle, but he was an asshole for trying to fool me into thinking he was a nice guy. So I hated him too.

And I knew I'd hate this Sterling person just as much.

"Look, I don't know why you have such a hate boner for me, Feral. I already told you I don't give a shit about your throne. Was my daddy really so horrible to you that you feel like you can get back at him for being a raging dickbag to me?"

The vampire prince's lip peeled back, and my heart lurched in my chest, seeing he'd dropped his fangs. They were now glinting in the slice of moonlight leaking in from the hanger's cracked door. "He was the biggest fucking monster in this country, Princess. He was my own personal Lucifer. He ended my life, and unfortunately for our kind, that isn't any kind of reprieve. So yeah, tearing open his untouched, sheltered, halfling daughter seems like a damn good way of getting back at him."

Vincent's menacing voice was so low and guttural it scraped over my skin like sandpaper. He looked so imposing, standing there with the slash of silver painting his muscular frame, lighting up his bloodied shirt, his smashed nose, his bulging, inky veins.

Vincent Feral was an absolute monster.

But the only thing about him that scared me was how much he made me crave the fire he set inside me whenever he looked at me like *that*. It was like some animalistic instinct inside him was telling him to eat me, and the fact that he couldn't because I was the princess pissed him off. My cheeks flared with heat as I glared up at him defiantly.

"Then why don't you? Why don't you 'tear me open' then if you're so hard up for it? Why so adamant that I walk away from the coven if you actually want me to stay and be your new little toy, all in some sad attempt at getting back at my father?"

I hated how hard my heart pounded with him this close to me. By the arrogant lift of his mouth, the smug prick probably thought it was because I was scared of him, not because he was driving my lady bits crazy. Despite how much I hated to have him think I was afraid of him, it was better than him knowing the actual depths to which he was affecting me. Maybe if I just ignored all the messages my vagina was sending me, it would let go of the idea that Vincent Feral was at all a good idea.

"Because, like you, I have two sides, Princess. I have the side that wants to protect you from the monsters inside that house. Brutal males who would give anything to taste that virgin blood and your virgin pussy." His expression hardened, blood-red eyes glinting in a way that made my breath hitch. "Myself among them."

"I—I'm not like you," I balked, throat thickening with an unknown emotion. "I don't have two sides."

"Bullshit. You've got the human side that wants to heed my warning and run away from here and never look back. Then there is your other side, the side that wants to be eaten."

"I don't want to be eaten, asshole."

Vincent's head tilted, and his lips stretched wide into a challenging smirk. His eyes were still blood-red, but his pupils had blown up, leaving a thin ring of crimson around obsidian disks, just like Corry's had in the pharmacy restroom.

Vincent leaned close, his huge, muscular body draped over me, caging me against the Rolls-Royce. He brought his mouth to my ear, dark hair tickling my cheek and his breath feathering over the delicate skin of my throat.

"So you're telling me, if I were to bite you right now... you'd say no?" He let the question hang in the air for a moment before pressing closer to me, brushing so slightly against me that I could feel the hardness of arousal against my thigh. His hands dropped to hover over my hips, barely touching me. "Or maybe you'd like me to tear you open on a different part of my body."

His voice had dropped an octave, gravely and as deep as Hell.

My heart rate thundered, my head pounded. Then my damn heart monitor went off. I'd almost forgotten I still wore the stupid thing. Ripping it off my wrist, I flung it to the ground in a hiss of disgust, its existence a sour reminder of all the lies. I returned my attention to Vincent to see his eyes glittering in triumph.

"You're a fucking asshole, Feral. You got your wish. I'm going to tell your Elders to all fuck off. Then I'm out of here forever. Are you happy?"

His head canted, an arrogant smirk on his lips. "Is that really what you plan on doing?"

"Why can't you believe me?"

"Because I can scent how badly you want me. You want to stay. Maybe I made a mistake in telling you I'd claim you as mine if it was the only way to get the throne. It was supposed to scare you. Not turn you on."

My entire body flushed with heat, and my gaze turned venomous, storming with hatred. Not just because I hated him. But because I hated that he was right. Being locked up in that room for years on end, I fantasized about a life of thrill and danger. And now, the promise of one loomed over me in the form of a dangerous, terrifyingly enticing monster. If books had taught me anything, it was normal for a locked-up princess to dream of a life with her knight in shining armor. But Vincent Feral wasn't exactly a white knight, and this wasn't a fairytale. If I made the decision to stay here, our tale would be a twisted one for sure.

And, of course, that made my fucked up heart pound even harder.

"I don't want you."

He shrugged, the shadow of a triumphant smirk tugging at the corner of his mouth. "Lie to yourself if it makes you feel better, Princess. But I can scent your lies, curling up between your legs."

His Adam's apple twitched with a swallow of his own, and by the dark hunger banked his eclipsed gaze, I couldn't bluff my way out of this one.

He knew the truth.

And I knew his.

"Your eyes are red. They haven't gone back to their normal color since you first laid eyes on me. So how about you stop pretending like this is one-sided, hmm? You want me too, cupcake." I flashed him a terse smirk, trying to look more confident than I felt.

"Maybe I do. But that isn't good news for you. You're my master's daughter. You can't even begin to grasp the sort of torture he put me through. You think I'm evil? I'm a fucking fairy princess compared to that sick bastard."

Vincent's hand came up as if to caress my cheek. His cool fingertips grazed so softly against my skin as they drifted down to trace the hollow of my throat. Then they began to curve around my throat, squeezing. He applied just enough pressure for me to breathe, but each wheeze of air struggled to make it up my windpipe past the force of his palm. I became light-headed, and my belly fluttered.

"So, yeah," he snarled. "Sinking myself into you seems like a great way to stick it to the dead fucker, and get my throne. So your choice, Princess." He gave a half-shouldered shrug as if he were laying out my choices for something mundane like where to eat for dinner. "You can stay and be my mate and queen, or leave and save yourself the pain I'll inflict. By the time I'm done with you, you'll wish I'd never let you loose from your room back in Quincy. For your own good, Princess, go before the Elders and tell them you decline the throne and that you don't want anything to do with the coven."

With that, his hand dropped from my throat, and he made his exit from the hanger.

My eyes narrowed on the muscular expanse of his back. "And if I don't?"

I had already decided that dealing with Vincent while trying to figure out how to be a vampire queen wasn't worth any of the trouble. But shit, antagonizing the vampire was becoming a swift addiction.

He froze in the doorway and slowly turned, his features awash with moonlight. Then his mouth stretched into that rare, brutally handsome grin. "Then don't. See what happens. Either way, I'll get what I want."

CHAPTER FIFTEEN
THE SILVER PRINCE

T he interior of the Knight Mansion was decorated in a way that screamed decadence. There was no question this was the home of a wealthy, ancient and powerful family. The filigree wallpaper was like something out of the Victorian era, old and faded. Countless oval portraits, framed in gold, lined long corridors. Thick, wax encrusted chandeliers hung from the high ceilings with sputtering candles chasing away the shadows to the far corners of the hall, painting everything in an orange, eerie glow.

Seeing homes like this was one thing on TV. Being inside any type of space that wasn't my own bedroom was like being on an alien planet. But standing here in the foyer of this mansion that was the home to a four-hundred-year-old vampire coven was like being in some kind of drug-induced nightmare.

There was no question I would need some hard-core therapy after all this.

When I'd first followed Vincent through the mansion's double doors, we were completely alone. But it was almost like they could smell my presence because only a handful of beats later, doors opened, and heads poked out to get a peek at the guest.

A handful of vampires floated down the stairs and several more down the corridor, stretching past the grand staircase. They were all tall, thin, and ghostly, their eyes watching me with a combination of curiosity and hunger. Nostrils flared. Some pulled close and whispered as I followed Vincent's gesture to follow him through the mansion's main corridor. The words "Princess" and "half-blood" flitted from the mouths of the gossips as we hurried past.

They knew exactly who I was.

I shivered as I felt a dozen pairs of eyes cutting into my back, a sweep of warm relief rushing through my limbs when Corry came into view, standing beside another set of double doors. In a sea of cold distrust, his was the only face that bore even a shred of kindness.

"The Elders are ready for us, bro." Corry's attention darted over Vincent's shoulder to me. "You ready, Red?"

"I'm ready," I lied with a gulp.

I shuffled, looking down at my hoodie and yoga pants. From the few examples of vampire governments I'd seen on TV, people never sought an audience with them in their pajamas. Then again, none of those people had been pulled from their beds in the middle of the damn night.

Corry's brows bunched with concern as his gaze swept over my skin, which now layered with a cool sheen of sweat.

"You sure you're ready? You kinda look like you're freaking out."

Damn his perception. My fingers curled around the hem of my hoodie, gripping it tightly with white knuckles. "Yeah, I'm fine. I just want to get this over with."

The sooner I met with the Elders, the sooner I could get out of here. This place was intense. I could still feel every cold eye in the place on my back.

Vincent apparently noticed how the coven vampires were watching us, too, because he snapped his severe glower on them, making everyone stiffen. Good to know it wasn't just me he had that effect on.

"All of you need to get to sleep. The sun will be up soon."

A woman with dark brown hair and sharp midnight eyes stepped out from the dozen or so vampires gathered. She was achingly beautiful, with a small nose and soft, plump lips that seemed to hide a secret by the way they were twisted. "We have a right to know if the Elders are actually fool enough to make this half-blood the new queen."

Vincent's mouth slashed with a hard line as he regarded the woman with cool indifference. "Fuck off, Lexi."

Her lips contorted into an icy smirk. "I see you've gotten too comfortable with telling me where to fuck, Vincent."

The vampire brushed her off with a scathing scoff and gestured to Corry, who opened the double doors while shooting a warning glare at the small crowd. The youngblood might have been the youngest of the brothers, but by the way everyone took a step back, the title of prince still seemed to carry weight no matter how young.

It was when Vincent pushed inside with me in tow that Corry stepped in and closed the doors behind us, baring out the looky-loos with a definite *thud*.

The room was huge, with large windows giving us a stunning ocean view, heavy velvet drapes framing either side. In front of the windows were seven thrones all lined up, side by side. They were all the same size except for the middle throne, which was slightly more elaborate than the rest. It was also the only throne that was empty, which meant it was a safe bet that this seat belonged to none other than the vampire king. Or at least, it had.

Before I shifted my attention to the other six filled thrones, I took in the details of my father's empty one. It was old, made of wood so dark it was almost black. The legs and arms were thick, crafted to support a sizable body, and the back was elaborately carved. Squinting through the dimly lit space, I could just make out the screaming face of a woman, her mouth filled with needle-sharp teeth. The wood that sharped her teeth was stained with a liquid all the way down her neck and to the velvet padding of the chair, which also formed her dress.

Real blood.

It looked like the woman was wearing a string of sharpened pearls or maybe shards of moonstone, but I realized a second later that her necklace was made with real fangs.

My stomach churned.

The throne was a gothic treasure of terrifying proportions and an unsettling tribute to the kind of man who once sat on it.

How perfectly at home Vincent Feral would look in it.

At that bitter thought, I swept my line of sight down the row of thrones, taking in the details of each Elder one by one.

I wasn't sure what I'd expected from an ancient vampire council, but it wasn't this.

In movies and TV shows, they always wore matching red robes, maybe with a sexy human girl captive in one arm, squirming sexually as her captor preyed on her slender neck. And maybe there would be some ominous chanting in the background while the coven leader approached an altar at the center of the room where a virgin was tied.

Instead, they were all wearing normal clothes. No robes, no chanting, no altars, no virgin. Well, except for me.

There were five men and one woman. The woman and four of the men were dressed in suits.

The man at the far left of the room I immediately recognized. Every muscle in my body tensed as I took in Dr. Sharpe sitting there, regarding me coolly as if he'd done nothing wrong.

My fists balled at my sides as I slowly took up a standing position in the middle of the room, with Corry and Vincent coming to flank either side of me.

I should have felt small sandwiched between the stature of these two, who were easily the two fittest people in the room. Instead, I felt like I actually belonged here with them, on the same side of the coin, looking at the Elders with resentment palpable in the air.

"Good evening, Ms. Baxter. It's good to see you released from your room."

My chest swelled with anger as I registered that it was Dr. Sharpe speaking to me. "Yeah, no thanks to you. You lied to me."

His expression remained completely blank. "I did what your father asked of me, Ms. Baxter. The important thing was that you were kept safe."

"You mean locked in a cage until you needed me?"

Corry and Vincent were both stone stiff beside me. Vincent looked pissed, the cords of his neck taut with barely-reigned irritation. And Corry looked both amused and anxious as fuck.

I was ready to fire off another spiked comment in Sharpe's direction, but another of the Elder caught my attention. He was sitting at the far right of the room and was the only one not wearing expensive clothes.

The instant I registered the details of the new face, all the pent-up rage I was getting ready to lob in Sharpe's direction evaporated.

For a second, my mouth remained completely open, the words I was about to say completely robbed by the male, who wasn't doing anything but sitting in his seat, watching me with quiet curiosity.

Even sitting, I could tell he was incredibly tall, taller than Vincent and Corry, and lither than both. He wore a thick knit, charcoal gray sweater and dark wash jeans. Clothes that looked a bit out of place against the rest of his features.

His chin-length hair fell in silvery waves around his sharp features, his locks as white as snow, washed in moonlight. His skin was the palest in the room, almost translucent. He had a long, thin nose, a sharp jawline, and high cheekbones. Dark shadows encircled his milky white eyes.

Cataracts.

This was the person Corry and Vincent had mentioned a handful of times in the car, the one my father had blinded.

He was incredibly handsome but definitely not in the same way as his brothers. Something about his beauty was off-putting, monstrous even but it wasn't like Vincent's inky veins and bulging muscles. This man had an aura about him that suggested he was absolutely ancient, wise, and possibly the deadliest being in the room even though he'd the form of a dancer.

It was haunting.

"You must be Sterling," I said after several tense moments of silence.

There was a shift behind the haze of his eyes and a twitch of his lips, almost like he was holding back a smile. "Yes, that's me. It's a pleasure to make your acquaintance, Miss Baxter. Truly."

Chapter Sixteen

Vampire Monarchies Suck

B y his tone, I actually believed he was being genuine.
"You're not anything like your brothers," was all I
could manage to say.

His smile broke free, softening his sharp edges. "No, we
count our blessings, as few and far between as they may
be."

Was that a... joke?

By Vincent's scowl in my periphery, it had been, and
there I decided that Sterling was already my favorite out of
the trio.

Oh, the stories I bet this guy could tell. Not that I was
sure I was going to stick around long enough to hear any of
them. I snuck a sideways glance at Corry, then the other
way at Vincent.

It was hard to admit, but a part of me didn't want to
leave. Mostly because Corry was the closest thing I'd call a
friend. And riling Vincent excited me in ways only steamy
books and late-night HBO had managed to do before.

And now, here was Sterling, with his eerily penetrating gaze and weighty presence, which was as caustic as it was kind.

But all those were probably questions I'd never get answers to. I couldn't stay here. Even if I was half-vampire, I was still half-human too. To these creatures, humans were prey. And I was in a den of predators. Beautiful predators. And as much as I wanted to stay and play with these lethally gorgeous sons to the vampire king, it would be an incredibly stupid move.

Sure, I wanted to sleep with Corry, I wanted to crawl deeper under Vincent's skin, and I wanted to sit down with Sterling and unload all of my questions... And wasn't there supposed to be a fourth brother? Where was he?

But none of those things were exactly safe for humans.

Corry had been ready to bite me and had visibly struggled to let me go when his brother had ordered him down. Vincent wanted to eat me, clearly, probably just so he could get the satisfaction of watching me squirm and beg for mercy.

And Sterling looked so ancient and wise he could probably kill me with a snap of his fingers.

So despite the fact that my heart ached at the idea of leaving, deep-seated survival instincts were screaming at me to run far away from this place as soon as possible. Because no matter how incredibly drop-dead gorgeous these men were, they were still monsters.

"I trust, Ms. Baxer, that my brothers were delicate with the situation in informing you of the situation and position."

Vincent's shoulders wound so tight I thought his head might pop. Dark, smothering energy rolled off him.

I didn't bother reigning in a dry laugh. The Elders exchanged confused glances, all except for Sterling, that is, who glared in Vincent's direction, almost like he could see his broken nose and the bloodstains on his shirt.

Sterling's jaw ticked, and oh God, his demeanor darkened. "What did you do?"

"I did as you asked. I went, and I got her. I didn't want to fucking do it, but she's here in one piece."

"I should have gone," Sterling muttered to himself but loud enough for the rest of us to hear. And no doubt, this night would have gone incredibly different if Sterling had been the one to break me out.

I could feel Vincent's pointed glare drilling into the side of my skull like it was somehow my fault he'd been a dick and gotten caught.

"She's alive, isn't she? I even kept Corry from biting her."

"Way to throw me under the bus, bro," Corry gritted beneath his breath on the other side of me.

Sharpe cleared his throat. "Regardless of how the princess was recovered, she's here now. I trust you know your purpose here, Ms. Baxter?"

"Oh, yeah. Apparently, I'm the biological daughter to the vampire king, and as a way to stick it to his progeny, he named me, a sheltered, half-human who's never ruled anything in her sad life, his heir." There was a sharp suck of breath from everyone in the room, but I kept going. I stuck a hand on my hip, curling my lips at Sharpe. "Of course, that would have been a really neat thing for you to mention all those times you came over for a 'check-up' Dr. Sharpe. Are you even a doctor?"

The tension in the room was hard enough to chip a tooth on. Everyone was looking at Sharpe with bated breath as if waiting for him to snap. But the doctor was as emotionless as always. He'd have to be to lie to me like he did. Instead, it was Sterling who spoke next.

"Indeed, he did name you his heir, Ms. Baxter. Which came as a surprise to all four of his progeny, as none of us knew of your existence. He kept you a secret from everyone, save for his most trusted council, Sharpe among them."

Was that supposed to make me feel better? I guess, in a way, it did. For some reason, I was under the impression Corry and Vincent had known about me all this time, that maybe my existence came up as talk of the pathetic little halfling locked up in her bedroom, and everyone would have a good laugh about it. But now that I was thinking about it, Vincent had been surprised to find me in the living conditions that I was in. Meaning Sharpe and Thomas Knight had kept it secret from the princes.

Suddenly it made more sense why Vincent had been so worked up. He'd spent all this time thinking he would be the next king, then news of me was dropped on him like a bomb. And when he went to spring the princess from her tower, he found me. A sheltered little nobody.

"You can't possibly be considering making me the vampire queen. Everything I know I learned from TV or a book. Tonight was the first time I've stepped into a pharmacy even. Hell, the first night I went anywhere. The first night I tried alcohol, the first night a guy made a pass at me."

Corry and Vincent exchanged scathing glares at one another, but I kept going.

"Dr. Sharpe, you know all this. I don't know how to do basic human stuff like operate a microwave or drive a car, or pay bills. I don't know how to be a freaking vampire! How could you even begin to consider letting me rule? That's like slapping a toddler into the oval office."

It was the woman who spoke next. She looked to be the oldest among them, with silver hair like Sterling's but countless lines etched her papery skin. "Believe me, Princess, this is not our tradition. In all my years, I've never heard of a mortal ruling the vampires. It's highly irregular and, if you ask me, inappropriate."

The disapproval in her aged tone was evident, but it was weird hearing me addressed as "Princess" without the layers of cynicism whenever Vincent called me that.

"Yes, but this was the parting wish of our long-time leader and my friend," Sharpe interjected. "Mrs. Murta is right. Traditionally the honor is bestowed to the eldest of the king's progeny. Seeing as Sterling has declined the honor, the throne would have gone next to Vincent. But instead, he named—"

"I don't want it," I blurted.

The room went eerily still. The other Elders shifted uncomfortably. Sharpe's expression shifted into a stony glare, and Sterling's ghostly physiognomy was unreadable. Vincent looked at me, almost like he was stunned that I had told the truth when I said I wouldn't be sticking around.

"You don't...want it," Sharpe repeated slowly, blanching.

"I. Don't. Want. It."

More silence. Jeez, did these people have hearing problems? Thankfully, Vincent came to my aid.

"There you have it. She isn't qualified in the slightest. She'd have too much to learn, not to mention it's too dangerous for someone like her to even be here. Making her queen would make this coven a laughing stock among our kind, and we've spent too many years trying to improve our image. On top of that, she doesn't want it."

I shuffled awkwardly where I stood, my eyes dropping to the floor. Why did his words hurt so much? They had only been the truth.

Sharpe made an irritated clicking sound with his tongue. "I understand your argument, Mr. Feral, and you do make an excellent point. But we are an old coven. Our traditions run deeper than the roots of the oldest trees. And it is tradition to honor the wishes of a good king, should he have had the fortune of expressing them before one passes. And in your case, your king and master. Regardless of his intentions, he wanted her to take the throne. She does not need to be crowned tonight. First, she will be taught how to feed, how to mesmer, how to—"

A flurry of angry voices rose up from Vincent and all the Elders. I looked at Corry, who just shrugged helplessly.

After several seconds of furious arguing, Sterling cleared his throat, and everyone fell silent. "Very well, we'll put it to vote. Who among the Elders believes the biological daughter of Thomas Knight should be allowed to take up the throne as vampire queen?"

Three raised their hands, Sharpe among them.

"And who is of the opinion that one of the king's sons should take up his legacy?"

Sterling and two others raised their hands.

Clearly, Vincent and Corry weren't allowed to vote, so that made it a tie.

My breathing was coming in short and heavy, to the point where I was growing light-headed. My fate was being determined for me, and apparently, I had absolutely no say in it.

Were they really going to force me to stay here and learn to be a vampire queen? What would happen when I inevitably bombed at the whole queen thing? They'd probably eat me.

Oh God.

I swayed on my feet, my knees threatening to buckle. Corry placed a hand on the small of my back, steadying me. "It's going to be okay," he whispered in my ear. Even though I could hear the uncertainty in his voice, it was still nice he was trying to comfort me.

When I foisted my attention back to the Elders, they had now gathered together in a small circle before their thrones, whispering among them. Their heads were bowed, six strangers determining my own fate for me.

I felt like I might be sick.

They debated for what felt like hours, but it couldn't have been that long by the position of the moon, still suspended just over the ocean, barely kissing the horizon.

Finally, they parted, and all of them resumed their seats.

Sharpe cleared his throat, his voice as cool as moonstone. "A decision has been made, Ms. Baxter."

My heart plummeted to the deepest pits of my being. Whatever the decision, it hadn't gone in my favor, by the emotions nestled in the slash between Sterling's snow white brows.

Vincent must have gathered that, too, by the way he tensed beside me.

"There is a way to honor both Thomas Knight's dying wishes and our age-old tradition," Sterling edged.

There was a suck of breath in my ear from Vincent and a soft gasp from Corry in my other. "How?" we all said at once.

"You be queen. But before you are crowned, you must select a mate for yourself to serve as your king. Seeing as you don't seem to get along well with Mr. Feral, the court has decided that you may choose your king among all four of Thomas Knight's progeny. You will have four months to make your decision."

My head was a hurricane of thoughts. My entire body went hot and cold.

"Four months? And what happens if I don't pick anyone by the end of those four months?"

Whatever cool mask of indifference Sterling was trying his best to keep up, it was crumbling. Sharpe spoke for him.

"As a member of vampire kind and a soon-to-be representative of the Cape Cod Coven, you are governed by this council, Ms. Baxter. You are under strict orders to choose a king for yourself in four months' time. During the decision process, all four princes will assist in teaching you the ways of our kind. Four months will be plenty of time to know who among them will be best suited to rule alongside you."

My fists clenched so tight at my sides my knuckles hurt. Ice filled my chest, and all the blood in my body seemed to rush into my cheeks.

These people weren't listening. Then again, it was becoming abundantly clear that my opinion wasn't valued in the slightest here.

"You didn't answer my question. What if I don't pick any of them to be king? What if I refuse?"

By the lethal, glass sharp glares of the Elders, I almost regretted the insinuation of rebellion.

But these assholes had to know if they were going to force me to do something I didn't want to do, that I wasn't going to just lay down and let it happen to me.

Sharpe's nostrils flared, and for the first time ever, anger banked his eyes. "It will be in your best interest to choose, Princess. If you do not, this council will allow the princes to do the choosing."

The ice in my chest rapidly spread through my entire body. "What does that mean, they do the choosing?"

"The males will fight amongst themselves, and the strongest among them will earn the right to be your king. To avoid unnecessary bloodshed, I strongly advise that you make a decision beforehand."

Chapter Seventeen
IT'S A DATE

This had to be some kind of dream. Any minute I would wake up in my room, and all this would have been some wild nightmare. I'd still have a weak heart, which would suck, but at least I wouldn't be a half-freaking vampire, being forced to choose a mate like I was some hunk of meat.

Although, this stupid meeting made it clear that's pretty much all I was to them. A blood heir to the old king's throne, so the Elders can feel good about honoring his dying wishes while giving all the real responsibility to one of his progeny.

My entire body went cold, hot, then cold again. I wanted to defend myself, but I couldn't summon the words that were swirling around in my head, like chunks in a blender. Not only was I being forced to stay, but I was being ordered to choose a mate.

And if I didn't, there would be a straight-on cockfight for me.

Bloody hell.

"This is fucking bullshit," Vincent snarled, his tone dripping with lethal malice. He stepped forward so that he was right before the thrones. He looked each and every one of them in the eye. "By vampire law, it's Sterling's right to the throne. Since he's declined that right passes to me."

If Sharpe was intimidated by the violent energy rolling off of Vincent in suffocating waves, he didn't show it. "In four months, a king and queen will be crowned. If you want the throne so desperately, Mr. Feral, you'll need to take it up with Ms. Baxter."

"Why does she fucking get to choose?" Vincent continued to snarl. "If you're going to force her to be here when she doesn't want to be, she needs a mate to protect her from the others. Can't you scent how strong her blood is? Deathwish will tear her to pieces the first chance he gets. Are you really going to allow that psycho a chance to be king?"

Dr. Sharpe narrowed his eyes on Vincent, a jump of a vein in his temple finally betraying some kind of readable emotion. He didn't like Vincent—he didn't like him at all.

"The Elders have already made their decision, Feral. If Eros truly desires to take the throne, he'll take care to treat the princess with respect, as it is she who will be doing the choosing." His death-cold gaze shifted to me. "Provided she does so in the allotted time frame."

A chill shot through me.

Vincent looked to his brother, his expression desperate. Sterling couldn't see him, but Vincent's tone perfectly mirrored his plea. "Sterling..."

The silver-haired vampire just gave a small shake of his head, his frown tugging at the corners of his eyes. He didn't need to say anything for the rest of us to understand.

There would be no changing the council's mind.

"I want to go home. You can't keep me here." I swallowed thickly, pushing back angry tears. I wouldn't cry in front of Dr. Sharpe. I wouldn't cry in front of any of them. But it was hard not to break down. The long night was catching up to me, and a moment later, I realized I no longer had a home to go to. Not a friend in the world, except for maybe Corry. But if he was forced to compete with his brothers, that brief friendship was pretty much all over.

"This is your home now, Ms. Baxter," Sharpe's unfeeling voice rang out, sealing my fate. "You will spend the next four months getting to know the ways of our kind and our coven. The princes will be personally responsible for teaching you how to feed, how to protect yourself, and how to navigate the human world discreetly. You are not to leave the grounds until you have gained control of your bloodlust."

I could barely hear what the doctor was saying anymore. I felt like I was a world away as his words came at me through an echo, bouncing off walls and making my head rattle.

Vincent hadn't freed me at all. He'd rescued me from my room in Quincy just to bring me to another prison. That's what this was. Just another prison.

I'd been so stupid to believe Corry when he'd bought me the phone, assuring me I wasn't a prisoner any longer. He was a fucking liar.

The word "queen" had thrown me off. Queen's got to make their own decisions—they were the ones in charge.

The head bitch. But I wasn't queen yet. I'd have to choose one of my father's progeny before I would be queen. Then what? He'd make all the decisions for me?

Fuck that.

Fuck this place.

Fuck everything.

I had to get out of here.

I had to battle every fiber in my body that screamed at me to run. If I ran now, I wouldn't get out of the mansion before someone caught me. Hell, I probably wouldn't even get out the door of this room. My gaze flickered to the moon that now dipped behind the horizon. Dawn was coming, and if I had one advantage over these jerks, It was that I could walk in daylight. I'd make my breakout then. Because there was no way I was playing this fucked-up version of *The Bachelorette*.

Sure, maybe I'd be into it if I had

to stick around. But if there was one thing more important to me than having the fun and adventure I'd dreamed of, it was freedom.

And no one was going to take that from me ever again.

I stepped out of the steaming shower of my new suite, pulled a fluffy white towel from the rack, and wrapped it around my frame. If I wasn't so freaked out by the fact that this room was basically just another prison cell, I might have been more taken with how fancy it was. The bedroom, bathroom suite was at least three times the size of the one I'd grown up in back in Quincy, so at least there was that. And no pink walls, thank fuck for that.

The bedroom felt old with its creaky wooden flooring that groaned with every step. The wallpaper was black, with a pretty floral pattern etched in silver. The bed was giant, with four carved posts and a velvety black canopy draped overhead. The furniture was old, just as old as the home it seemed, but the bathroom was brand new. Complete with marble floors and stainless steel fixtures.

The water pressure was also better here, and nobody was screaming at me from downstairs to be careful not to run the water bill up.

Stepping out of the steamy bathroom, I approached the window beside the bed. The first time I noticed the window, my attention went immediately to the huge steel shutters mounted on either side. For a second, I had an unpleasant flashback, but I quickly regained composure when I realized there was no lock on the shutters. The shutters weren't meant to keep me in. They were meant to keep out the sunlight. This is a vampire coven, after all. All the rooms were probably outfitted with the same exact device.

I moved to the door and turned the handle.

Damn it.

After the meeting with the Elders, Sterling had shown me to my room. He was so eerily quiet, and not a word was spoken between us as I'd followed him up to the mansion's third floor. Even though he was blind, he seemed to have everything memorized because he didn't stumble once, nor did he stretch out his hands or use anything to find his way.

I'd ached to ask him the boatload of questions weighing on me, but I couldn't bring myself to say anything. There was this kind of awkward tension between us I couldn't explain.

Once I was inside the room, he told me he'd come for me at sundown. Then, with regret etched into the shadows of his face, he closed the door with a deafening click of the lock from the outside.

I thought an hour-long shower might do the trick to distract me, but I had only stewed in my anger.

How was I supposed to escape the coven when I couldn't even get out of the room? I was on the third floor, too high to jump out the window. Besides, the house was built on the cliffside, and right below my window were ragged rocks and the ocean. Even if I did manage to jump and miss getting skewered on the rocks, I couldn't swim.

I'd drown.

Wrapping the towel tighter around my body, I stuck my head out the window, watching the spew of white, foamy water every time a wave came crashing against the rocks.

Yeah, we'd have to call that Plan B.

I moved to the armoire and opened it to find an array of clothes inside.

They'd been expecting me alright. While Sharpe could have probably guessed my size from his many visits, he hadn't exactly pegged my style. Not like he would care even if he had. Everything hanging was vintage, frilly, and black. Okay, so the color was right, but most of the garments were traditionally gothic dresses that smelled musty and maybe even a little moth-eaten.

Not exactly my vibe.

Unwrapping the towel from my body, I gave my red hair a quick rub down before pulling on my Ramones hoodie and flung myself into bed. It wasn't my intention to fall asleep. I had to hatch an escape plan. But no sooner than my head hit the pillow, I was out.

Dreams filled with red eyes, sharp fangs and stolen kisses teased my mind when an obnoxious beep jolted me awake. Blinking back the fog of a restless sleep, I reached for the cellphone Corry had bought me on the nightstand.

Corry: Hey, Red. Thought I'd check on u. U ok?

I cursed when I saw the time. 8:35 PM. I had slept through the day. Everyone would be up now. Not that it mattered much. It's not like I would have been able to make a getaway unless someone came to unlock the door.

As I re-read Corry's text, an idea occurred to me. For a second, I wrestled with the implications of it. I didn't really want to manipulate the one who'd been the nicest to me so far. But Corry was still a vampire. If I didn't go through with this plan, I'd be forced to stay here, and that wasn't in the cards for me.

"Sorry, Corry..." I mumbled to myself as I typed out my angle.

Ruby: Fine. So when u gonna take me on that bike ride you promised me?

My pulse began to climb, faster and faster with each second I waited for the youngblood's response. A part of me worried he'd see right through my plan. I was so out of my element and if I panicked, he'd see right through my bullshit. There there was the added fact that wasn't supposed to leave the ground without Vincent's supervision, and I wasn't allowed to leave at all.

But there was another part of me that knew he wanted to be the first to get in time with me, time alone so he could have a shot at being the one I "picked."

I just hoped he liked me enough to overlook the possibility that it was some trick.

Because it definitely was.

But his dick would convince him otherwise. I was almost sure of it.

I nearly jumped when the phone buzzed with a new text notification.

Corry: Tonight?

A wild grin shot across my face, and the bloom of hope fluttering in my chest was enough to drown out the guilty sensation knotting my stomach.

Ruby: It's a date.

Chapter Eighteen

BASTARDS, LIES, AND GREEN EYES

I almost jumped out of my skin when a knock on my door sounded. I knew it was Corry, ready to set me free on the pretense that we were going on a date. Casting one last look at my reflection in the mirror mounted to the vanity, I sighed.

I looked great. I'd styled my freshly colored red hair into French braided pigtails, and I'd managed to find a PVC-style club dress amongst all the frilly old-fashioned clothes. The person who'd owned it before me had been thinner, so the material stretched tight over my curves, making my boobs pop just a bit too much out of the dress. I'd taken a piece of velvet ribbon from one of the velvet frocks hanging and tied it around my neck like a choker, tying it in a bow in the back. It wasn't the most ideal outfit for making a getaway, but I wanted Corry thoroughly distracted. This would do the trick.

I thought doing myself up for a date would make me feel better because it was something I'd yet to experience. But my appearance in the mirror only made my gut twist into knots.

Maybe because I was using Corry to win my freedom.

Which was a reasonable thing to do when I was literally locked up in a house full of dangerous vampires, saddled with the task of choosing a mate to rule the vampire legions by my side.

Yeah, no thanks.

No one was going to force me to do shit. That chapter of my life was over. And if I had to use the most naive guy here as a way to win my freedom, I would.

"Ruby," Corry's voice whispered from the other side of the door.

"Come in," I whispered back, looking around for a pair of shoes. There was nothing to match my dress that fit my size seven feet, so I opted for what I'd come in; my bright red converse high tops. They didn't exactly go with my outfit, but they'd be more functional for my getaway. And they matched my hair.

The clink of a key unlatching the door rattled in my ear, and a second later, the door pushed open, Corry peering at me from the other side. His blue eyes widened to saucers the second his gaze landed on me. "Shit, Red. You look..." His throat twitched with a swallow. *"Good."*

"Thanks. Do I have to worry about you tonight? You're not allowed to bite me. Not tonight anyway," I said with a flirtatious smirk.

A corner of Corry's mouth lifted into a wolfish grin. "I already fed. But I'll have room for seconds when you change your mind."

Hearing he'd already fed, my mind flashed to the argument the youngblood had had with his brother the night before. Corry wasn't allowed off coven grounds because he had killed innocents.

Another jab of guilt struck me in the gut.

I was leading a wolf to the sheep. But I couldn't let myself be responsible for crimes Corry *might* commit. I had to focus on saving my own skin.

I eyed him warily. "Don't tell me it was another prostitute."

"That was an accident," he muttered, his expression hardening. "I never mean to hurt anyone. These days I'm only allowed to feed on the coven's livestock until I can be trusted to gain control over my instincts. You can't understand the full force of the lust, Ruby."

At the mention of blood and lust, my throat burned like it had been set on fire. I knew perfectly well what it was like to thirst for something for two decades and not even know what it was my body craved. Locked away in my room, my mother shoved piles of food at me in pathetic attempts to curb my appetites. It had never been enough. The pills Dr. Sharpe had prescribed had helped, but it had never taken away the edge. None of it had been enough.

"I know what it's like, Corry," I rasped on a grated whisper.

"At least you're half-human. You don't *need* blood. That's a blessing."

Blessing. Anger coursed through my veins, turning my blood to lava. That word infuriated me, and something inside me snapped. I didn't like being kidnapped or being told what my future was going to be like by some elderly dead fucks who didn't know shit about me. I was tired of being lied to, tired of being a prisoner.

Nothing about my life was a blessing.

I wanted to go home. But I didn't have a home to go to anymore.

I didn't have anyone.

All I had was myself.

Before I realized what I was doing, my hands slammed into Corry's chest, and he went flying back onto the bed. Something predatorial was in the driver's seat now, something that had me scrambling onto the bed after him, straddling him with my hands around his throat. I felt my entire body pulse with rage, strength coursing through my limbs just like it had in my room when Vincent had attacked me.

Corry's eyes widened as he looked up at me, his chest heaving with frantic breaths. But I felt no pulse against my palm where I gripped his jugular.

"You don't fucking know me," I seethed, low and deadly so as not to alert anyone else lurking in the hall.

I expected the youngblood to fight back, to get angry. If this was Vincent, I'd probably already have my throat ripped out. But this wasn't the vicious Vincent Feral. This was his younger, kinder brother, who looked up at me with soft, blue eyes, his mouth tugged up into a smile that warmed me all over.

He reached up to tuck a rogue coil of red hair behind my ear, his chest rumbling beneath me with a chuckle. "But I want to know you, Ruby-Red, soon to be Queen of the Dead. There isn't anything I want more than to just know you. And that's saying a lot because I have a hot virgin vampire princess straddling my junk."

With his other hand, he dug into his pants pocket and extracted two familiar-looking pills, offering them up to me. "Here, take these. They'll make you a little less hangry."

I swallowed the pills down without argument. Their effect, along with his tender words and affectionate gesture, immediately calmed me. Suddenly I felt very weak. Uncoiling my hands from his throat, I collapsed against his chest. "I'm sorry I..."

"Shh, it's alright, Red. You've had a pretty weird day." His arms banded around me to pull me close to his muscular chest. It was the first time I can remember anyone ever holding me like this.

It felt good to be in his embrace. I felt safe. I wondered if I could trust it. Was he being affectionate with me just because he hoped I would pick him as my mate? Was this just part of the game?

No matter his motives, I didn't care. It was intoxicating being this close to him.

"You smell so good."

His chest rumbled beneath me with a chuckle. "Yeah, I bet I do. You're probably starving. Sterling and Vincent should be staked for sending you to bed without anything to eat. I'd let you bite me if we had the time."

I sat up on my heels, looking down at the male I straddled on the bed. The ravenous hunger inside me was building by the second, and I was afraid I'd explode like a volcano. The mere mention of biting the vampire caused an odd sensation inside my mouth as if my fangs might punch out of my gums at any moment. I wouldn't even know how to bite him, and that was if it even worked the same for half-bloods.

But damn it, did I want to bite him. I wanted to bite him *bad.*

The texted conversation we shared in the car came rushing back. I wanted to feed, but not if it meant tying myself down to Corry.

"If I were to bite you, would that mean I'd be choosing you as my mate?"

His chest rumbled beneath me with a chuckle. "No. Vampires drinking from other vampires is serious business, but not so serious if it's just a bite and nothing more." He propped himself up on his elbows, his smile slipping into a suggestive smirk. "If you were to bite me, the entire coven would be able to scent my blood inside you. It sticks in your veins longer than human blood. The claiming bite is when you fuck someone *while* you feed from them. There's nothing like marking your mate by pumping them full of your blood *and* cum. Though, picking someone to pop that cherry of yours and letting one of us claim you can be two different things entirely."

My cheeks burned with a blush. "Are you saying you guys would actually be okay with me sleeping with all of you?"

He shrugged one shoulder. "All I'm saying is the game isn't over until you pick a king. You're free to do what and who you please until then. But you'll want to be careful, Red. This will get pretty dicey, say if you end up hate fucking Vin, then you end up picking me as king. Or if you let Deathwish touch you at all, Vin and Sterling will probably go into conniptions."

I scrambled off the bed, my mind in a daze. "But I don't even know Deathwish. I don't know any of you."

Corry waved his hand dismissively. "He's a psychotic bastard. I guess all of us are on a different level. Just be careful. This can end badly in a lot of ways. We're not super competitive, but jealousy is inevitable when you've got everything to win."

This was insanity. It was already a dangerous game. Vincent had warned me about this in the Walgreen's bathroom. There would be fights for the throne, my blood, my freaking virginity.

I had to get out of here. But first I needed something to eat.

"I need to eat something, Corry... The pills aren't enough. I need food. I don't have to feed on livestock, do I?" I suppressed a shudder at the idea.

"Nah, that's just my punishment for the accident that Vin decided to tell you all about in the car. Besides, you probably aren't going to be able to bite anything until you figure out how to drop your fangs. Usually, that happens under pressure or extreme hunger, so it may not happen for a while yet. In the meantime, I'd thought I'd take you out for some fast food burgers."

Burgers didn't sound half as good as blood, but I still perked at the idea. For years I'd watched fast food commercials on TV, and sometimes Mom would bring me some on the way home from work to push under the door. But I'd never been through a drive-thru, as God intended.

Sensing my eagerness, Corry clasped my hand and led me out of the room.

"Will you get in trouble?" I asked in a hushed voice as we hurried down the corridor toward the stairs, passing door after door.

"Absolutely. Probably means more dinners spent out in the barn. But hey..." He glanced back over his shoulder at me, winking. "I'm sure there's some way you can thank me for busting you out of jail."

A nervous flutter of butterflies tickled my stomach, then turned to angry hornets in the next breath when the door just before us ripped open, and out ran a woman, crying. Human by the pound of her heart and the sweet honey scent of her blood that laced the air.

"Fucking *bastard*," she sobbed.

Everything inside my body seemed to still for a second when I registered several punctures in her neck and chest, fresh and glistening red. She smelled so damn good; it was intoxicating. My mouth began to water as I watched her fling herself into another room.

For several thunderous heartbeats, I watched the door she disappeared behind, my chest tight with a myriad of emotions. I didn't like the little nagging voice in the back of my head telling me to follow the girl, her scent still lingering in the air like tracks leading to prey.

Corry jerked on my arm, tugging me along. "We have to go."

I stumbled after him, the urgency in his voice spurring my feet forward. But his hand was ripped out of mine when a second person came stomping out the room from where the girl had fled. I slammed into the newcomer, his brick-wall-like build knocking all the air from my lungs.

I took a tremulous breath as I tentatively lifted my gaze up a sinewy chest, over a cotton t-shirt peppered with bloodstains and raven tattoos that twitched over the taut tendons in his neck, to rest on pale eyes the color of olives.

Vincent Feral, prince of the dead, had green eyes. They narrowed to deadly slits as they slowly slid down the length of my neck like it was a foldout in a *Playboy* magazine.

I watched, completely transfixed as his eyes slithered lower, taking in my exposed cleavage.

Like blood being dropped in a pond, the murky green depths of his irises stained crimson.

His lips curled in disgust, everything about his expression saying "whore" when he took in the rest of my outfit. But those red eyes were a dead giveaway of how he really felt about my chosen ensemble.

"Where are you taking her?" Vincent demanded, veering his baleful glare in Corry's direction.

"Out to get burgers," he answered coolly, even though every muscle in his body was balled with tension. "Sterling said we could if we went through the drive-thru."

The older vampire's blood-crusted mouth twisted into a heart-stopping sneer as a guttural growl slithered out. "Don't fucking lie to me, Youngblood!"

"It was my idea."

Vincent's attention snapped back on me, his gaze deadly and full of hatred. He grabbed my arm and yanked me against him, arching down to press his lips to my ear.

"I know what you're doing," he growled, his voice too low for his brother to hear. I shivered in his grip, hating the way my body heated against him. "Consider this your last chance to save yourself from me. From all of us. If you come back, you're playing the game, Princess. And I promise you, I'll win."

My throat burned with a rebuttal, but Corry was within earshot, and I didn't want to risk spoiling the plan.

If only I was stronger. If I didn't have to worry so much about my life expectancy in a place like this, maybe I would stick around just to knock down this prick a few notches. Maybe I'd let Corry take my virginity, mate me, and I'd pick him to be king just to see the look on Vincent's stupidly gorgeous face.

Shoving me back into Corry's embrace, Vincent turned on his heel and stomped down the hall. He paused outside a door not far from my own, rapping on it once with a slam of his entire forearm. A moment later, the door opened, revealing the dark-haired woman he'd called Lexi. His arm looped around her waist and pulled her up to his lips in a crushing kiss, consuming her muffled cry of surprise.

By the way she responded, she was used to this kind of caveman behavior. Her eyes were closed, but Vincent's remained open and fixed to me.

I didn't like the dark, confusing emotions twisting around in my belly as Vincent pushed her into the room and slammed the door shut behind them, leaving a ringing sound in my skull.

Corry and I stood in the hallway for a few moments, completely speechless. The atmosphere still crackled with the lethal energy Vincent Feral had left behind.

"Holy shit," Corry muttered after several more moments. "I can't believe he let us go."

I watched the spot where Vincent had disappeared into what I surmised to be Lexi's room.

"Holy shit, I can't believe he's such an asshole."

I hated him.

I hated the way his words stuck inside me like sunbaked tar, repeating over and over again on a loop.

I'll win. I'll win. I'll win.

His eyes had been red, and right after he'd fed. He wanted me. It pissed him off that he wanted me, maybe as much as it pissed me off that I wanted him.

Which made me wonder why he was giving me one last chance to get out of here?

Maybe because he had a less clear shot of the throne now that he had to compete with his brothers. Because there was no way in frozen hell, I would pick him to be my mate or king.

Sure, he'd be a hot fuck. Hate sex had always intrigued me in the darker novels my mom brought home for me on occasion. But sex with Vincent Feral was completely out of the question when I didn't trust him not to bite me.

Some dark part of me still ached to stay and let Feral do whatever he wanted with me. But my fucked up attraction for the monster didn't quite override my desire to stay out of a body bag.

The fact that this dark thought sent a flutter of warmth to my core was all the more reason to get the hell out of here.

Vincent Feral and his brothers didn't scare me.

It was my own fucked-up fantasies about them that frightened me most.

CHAPTER NINETEEN

PRETZELS, ZOMBIES, AND A KISS

I paid close attention to the way Corry handled the motorcycle he'd called a "Ninja." Everything from the way he sat on it to the way he turned it on, changed gears and worked the turn signals and headlights seemed pretty easy.

I was almost excited to steal it.

As we zipped down the streets of a larger town called Barnstable, I relished the way the air stung my skin. I craved every jump of my heart as Corry zig-zagged around other vehicles and blew through traffic lights, going speeds that would be at home in *The Fast and the Furious* franchise. If I were any other girl, I'd be pissed and scared out of my mind. But this was exhilarating, and Corry seemed to be on an entirely alternate plane of awareness judging by how he expertly maneuvered his way through the streets. He may not have had Vincent's brute strength or ability to mesmerize people, but Corry's talent seemed to be his lightning-fast reflexes.

After about an hour of driving, Corry pulled the bike into a parking lot of a large concrete building with a flashing neon sign that read, "Roller City." Beside the sign sat a huge model roller skate, its wheels lined with twinkling lights. Muffled 80s glam metal music poured into the parking lot, and I couldn't help but shake my head with a laugh. He'd taken me to a roller rink.

Cutting the engine, Corry pulled his helmet off and twisted around to help me with mine. "So, what do you think?"

My arms dropped from where they'd been wrapped around his waist for the last hour, and I smoothed down my hair, laughing. "I think you're crazy."

He raked his fingers through his mashed brunette locks, teasing them back up into the spiked style he seemed to prefer. "You've had so many other experiences taken from you that I thought it might be nice to take you out for a normal first date. Well, as close to normal as you can get on a date with a dead guy."

I found myself smiling. My heart pounded hard, not from the intense drive but from something else. Something I desperately wanted to ignore.

"It's nice, Corry. Thank you. You're the only one who has cared enough to try and give me normal experiences."

He pulled himself off the bike and held out his hand. "Well, I figured we owed you a little bit of normalcy. Come on, Red, I'll buy you a pretzel."

It was easy being with Corry. He made me feel...human. Maybe it was the fact that he was close to my age—twenty-one, I found out while standing in line to get our skates. Or maybe it was the way he treated me like an actual person and not a monster. When we got our skates, he sat me down on a bench and knelt on the colorful carpet in front of me to help lace me into the clunky shoes, chatting with me about music, bikes and other normal things. I watched with quiet fascination as he pulled on the bright orange laces, his youthful features lighting up with a display of glow sticks for sale behind a counter selling skates and protective gear.

"You really were turned only six months ago," I found myself saying in a hushed voice, recalling the argument where his brother had chastised him for his age.

Corry looked up, his expression growing stony. "Yup, that's me. The stupid, reckless youngblood."

"I didn't mean it as an insult. I like how human you seem. It's nice. I hope you stay like this."

His brows crinkled. "What do you mean?"

I swallowed, choosing my next words carefully. "It's only that Vincent seems to have lost much of his humanity. I'm guessing he's really old. It would make sense for a vampire who—"

"You've got it wrong," Corry cut me off, his tone flat. He got up and sat on the bench next to me, yanking on his own skates. "Vincent is thirty-two years old. He was turned when he was twenty-two. He's only been a vampire for a decade now. He's an asshole because that's his personality. He likes to think it's because of what Master did to him, but Sterling had to put up with that sick bastard for a thousand years, and he's one of the kindest people you'll ever meet."

"What did my father do to Vincent?"

"It's not really my story to tell, Red, and I only know bits and pieces anyway."

I sat for a moment, staring at all the skaters on the rink, going around and around in loops just like my thoughts. Maybe Corry was being a bit harsh on his assessment of Vincent's "personality." I didn't have the nitty-gritty details of what my father had done to the eldest of his sons, but torture had a way of changing people regardless of the method. Maybe Sterling was just the exception. Everything about the silver-haired prince was an anomaly.

I clung to Corry as he slowly rolled me onto the rink.

"Stop laughing at me," I chastised him through a grin. "I've never done this before."

"Maybe we should have opted for the helmet and knee pads, babe. Maybe a couple of pillows and some duct tape too. I can't believe I'm saying this, but I hope you've got underwear on under that dress because you're gonna be flashing the whole rink if you don't gain your balance."

I shot him a withering glare, using my free hand to pull down the hem of my skirt. "If I knew you were taking me here, I wouldn't have worn a dress."

"Here, let go of me, and I'll show you how it's done."

Reluctantly, I released him and clung to the edge of the rink's balustrade as I watched him skate circles around everyone else, weaving between skaters and darting around with the same precision he had on his motorcycle. I didn't miss the way other girls watched him, either. Hell, practically everyone in the place had their eyes glued to Corry. When he came around again, he grasped my hand

and pulled me along with him, cackling as I struggled to gain my balance.

"Corry, you jerk!"

"Trust your feet, Red. You're only stumbling because you're second-guessing yourself. Don't think, just focus on me and move."

Simple advice, almost too simple. But I took a deep breath and watched as the show-off skated backward, grinning at me as he pulled me along after him.

His eyes were so beautiful, the way their blue depths lit up with his smile. And that damn dimple. I found myself staring at it, almost transfixed when his words of praise pulled me out of my daze.

"That's it, see?"

"What?" I looked down at my feet to see them moving in rhythm with his.

"Sometimes, you just have to trust your body to take care of you even if you're in an unfamiliar situation. It's why vampires move so fast and why they are so damn hard to kill. Your instincts will know what to do even if you don't, so long as you don't get in your head and let fear take over."

I skidded to a halt, my feet somehow knowing to use the little bumper on the edge of the skates.

"What is it?" Corry asked, stopping to look at me with a confused expression as I gaped at him.

The youngblood might not be able to show me how to mesmerize humans or feed like a vampire since he could hardly keep a lid on his own self-control, but he was still showing me how to be a vampire and fit into his world, in his own special way.

"You're pretty awesome, you know that?"

His eyes brightened. "Awesome enough for a kiss?"

"I know what you're doing, Corry."

"Oh yeah, and what's that?"

"Trying to butter me up, so you can be king."

The smile stayed plastered to his lips, but some of the light drained from his eyes. "What if I just like you? How about that? Newsflash, Princess. Before you got here, I didn't give two fucks about being king. But now that being king means having you as a mate..." He shoved his hands in his pockets, shrugging. "Maybe now I care."

"Corry—"

"Look, I'm sorry. We don't need to talk about this right now. Am I still awesome enough for that kiss?"

"How about we start with that pretzel you promised me? I'm so hungry that if you were to kiss me right now, you probably wouldn't escape with your lips."

"Oh, threats of mutilation? Good thing Deathwish isn't here. He'd have too much fun with you."

I followed Corry off the roller rink to the concession stands, frowning. "This Deathwish guy must be pretty messed up, from what I'm hearing."

"Ha. *That's* the understatement of the century. He's a sadistic psychopath. There was a reason Vin threw a fit when the Elders decided to let all four princes have a shot at courting you or whatever. It will be best for everyone if you make a decision before he gets back from his trip."

A mixture of disgust and intrigue swirled in my gut at the mention of my father's most depraved progeny. Almost enough to put off my appetite until Corry shoved a fat, steaming pretzel into my one hand and a cup of cheese dip into the other.

The delicious scents of hot bread, salt, and cheap cheese were enough to cause a hungry growl to rattle up from my chest.

"Hey now," Corry said with a nervous chuckle while steering me away from the crowded concession stand. "Keep the predator noises on the down-low there, Killer. You'll freak out the humans."

I blinked several times, taken aback. It was the same sort of sound Vincent had made in my room and in the pharmacy restroom, the one that had sent a rush of heat through me.

"I've never made that sound before..."

"It's pretty common for our kind. Whether you're hunting, or fucking, or irritated. Though this is the first time I've seen anyone make it over a soft pretzel."

I pulled off a chunk of pretzel, but before I could eat it, Corry grabbed my wrist and pulled it toward him, snagging the piece for himself. My protests turned to weak whimpers as he sucked my fingers clean of salt, his gaze fiercely holding mine. I shivered from the way his tongue stroked over my skin, soft and reverent, and I was almost sad when he broke away, brushing off the brief moment we'd shared with a chuckle.

I ate the rest of my snack, watching him as we strolled through the rink, past the lockers to the arcade portion where dozens of blinking, tittering video game cabinets sat.

"I'm surprised by your restraint tonight, Youngblood."

"How do you mean?" he asked, flattening out a five-dollar bill to feed the coin machine.

"I mean," I dropped my voice, leaning against the coin machine, "when you made me mad back at the house..."

He looked up with a wicked glint in his eye. "You mean when you threw me onto the bed and straddled me?"

"Um, yeah."

"That was hot. But I'm not going to bite or fuck you without your explicit permission, Red. Even if I was that evil of a shithead, Sterling and Vincent would kill me if I tried anything you weren't down for. The goal is to earn your affection here. Vin might be blowing it big time, and I can't vouch for Deathwish because he's a sadist with a fetish for the word 'no.' But I want you to feel safe around me."

I *did* feel safe around Corry. And that was the problem. I didn't want to feel anything when it came to Corry. What I needed was to get on with my plan.

"You wanna shoot some zombies?"

"Huh?" I muttered, pulling myself from the plan running through my mind.

The vampire jabbed a thumb at a machine with two plastic guns attached to rubber cords. Zombies ambled across the screen with a fluorescent sign mounted on top of the cabinet reading 'House of the Dead.'

"It's a classic."

Curiosity won out, and the details of my plan fizzled away as I stepped up to the game. Corry pressed two quarters into my palm, and I gave a sure nod when asked if I knew what to do. I'd seen enough Chuck E. Cheese commercials to get the gist. I pushed the coins into the slot, and the machine came alive.

"Here, I'll show you how it works."

Corry came up behind me, his warmth pressing into my back. Books had always made vampires out to be ice cold, but Corry had a pleasant heat to him that enveloped me like a blanket. His arms encircled me, his hands guiding mine to the gun.

The game started, and we were doing terribly, mostly because neither of us seemed to be paying any attention to the mission. We were both distracted by how close we were to one another.

Corry's hard chest pressed against me, trapping me against the arcade game. He was leaner than Vincent, sharper, and even through his denim jacket, I could feel his rock-hard muscles. He didn't have an ounce of fat on him.

Every human instinct ingrained in me screamed in the back of my head to run, to get as far away from the youngblood as I possibly could. Under his bleached-tipped hair and his bright blue eyes and playful smirk, he was still a predator. A predator who hadn't yet gained complete control over his need for blood.

But I ignored what my survival instincts were telling me. Not because I was adrenaline starved from my years spent in suburban captivity, but for some stupid reason, I felt safe with Corry.

He made me feel normal.

"Why are you doing all this?" I whispered, my voice strained with a sudden wave of emotion.

He grinned, his arms still wrapped around me, the gun still pointed toward the screen. "Why am I showing you how to survive in case of a zombie uprising?"

"No. You're showing me all these human things, stuff I never got to do or have. Then you were teaching me all that reflex stuff. You're letting me experience both worlds I've been suddenly thrown into, and you're doing it in a way that makes me feel..."

"Cared for?"

I gulped back a lump, my head bobbing with a slight nod. "Yeah, something like that."

He pushed closer to me from behind until there was no space left between us. I could feel every inch of him, from the swell of his pectorals, the ripple of his toned abdomen, all the way down to his semi-erect shaft pushing against the valley of my ass cheeks.

I should have wanted him to stop. His cock was throwing a major wrench into my whole escape plan. Of course, seducing him had been my plan the entire time, at least up until the point where I could steal his keys without him noticing. But all these emotions weren't meant to get tangled in the details.

His brow rested against mine, his blue eyes searching my gray ones.

"Do you want me to stop?" he asked me on a breath so soft it took my own away.

I bit my lip and shook my head, my cheeks heating under his hot-blue gaze. "No."

CHAPTER TWENTY

JUST LIKE THE REST OF THEM

Corry went in for the kiss, but I pulled back and he froze, seeing my look. "How do I know you're not just doing this to get the throne?"

"Ruby, I already told you. I didn't give a shit about being king until you came along. I only want the throne now because it means I get you. Hell, even if Vin ends up king, it's not like he'd own you."

My eyes practically popped out of my head with that. "You mean...*share* me? There is no way he'd go for that."

"As queen, you get to do whatever the fuck you want, babe. Plus, he throws around his body like it's God's gift to women, so why should you be expected to be monogamous if he's not going to give you the same courtesy?"

Molten ire simmered low in my belly like lava, hearing about Vincent's sex life. What made me angrier yet was that I cared. Why should I give a fuck if he threw around his dick like free grocery store samples on half-off deli sausage? It wasn't my business. Still, there was something that really pissed me off with the way that Lexi chick had looked over his shoulder at me with that smug smirk while they were mauling each other in the hallway. Like she was rubbing it in my face.

"I would *never* pick Vincent to be king," I said with an incredulous scoff. Little did Corry know, I wasn't going to pick anyone to be king. I wasn't going to play this stupid game when I had my life to think about. This was all too stupidly dangerous, even for me.

But deep down, I *wanted* to play the game. I wanted to mess with Vincent's heart, make him think he had a real shot at being king, then rip out his heart and fucking eat it by sleeping with Corry or something even more fucked up. Something petty, something borderline evil.

Because he deserved it.

He deserved it for ripping me so brutally out of my sad little reality without so much as a kind word or a gentle pat on the head telling me it was going to all be okay. Yeah, so he freed me. But it wasn't out of the goodness of his heart. The Elders had forced him to. The prick would have just left me there to rot in suburban hell if it had been up to him. He would have preferred to keep me there so I wouldn't interfere with his plans on inheriting that stupid throne.

"If you don't pick Vin, that pretty much leaves me, babe."

"What about Sterling? And what about Deathwish?"

Corry let out a cold laugh devoid of all humor. "You're not going to like Eros. *No one* likes Eros. There is a reason the Elders keep him away from the coven a huge amount of the time. He's the grunt, doing all the dirty work no one else wants to do. And that's saying something. I mean, we're vampires. We're not afraid of blood and gore. But Eros takes it to the next level. When the king died, and no successor was immediately crowned, the other covens started to get ideas about crowning one of their own as king. That's what Eros is off doing. Making examples out of those stupid enough to think they can knock the Cape Cod Coven off the top."

My guts twisted. "And Sterling?"

"Sterling is…" Corry sucked in a sharp breath and then exhaled slowly, seemingly searching for the right words. "Complicated. He's been through some shit with your dad. Some pretty fucked up shit. He's loyal to the coven and wants what's best for us. And for whatever reason, that computes to him not being king. He also prefers his solitude. In the six months I've been with the coven, he's never had a mate, not even one of the human donors that work for the coven."

"Corry, know that I don't want to be queen. I don't want to play this stupid game. No one gave me a choice, and I don't want to think about this shit right now."

He finally let go of the gun, and it clattered onto the arcade cabinet. Folding his arms all the way around me, he drew me in tight, chest to chest. "Then don't think about it. You've got four months to decide. If you take anything away from this, it's that all I want out of this whole thing is you. I don't care about anything else."

Hell, I almost believed him. There was something so genuine about his words, the tender cadence of his voice. The way he held me like he never wanted to let go.

Even if it was all just an act, I wanted desperately to believe it. I wanted to believe it so much I didn't pull away when he arched down and pressed his lips against mine in a reverent kiss.

Corry kissed like it was an art. He poured his soul into the connection, his lips soft and attentive. It was the complete opposite of the kiss Vincent had stolen in the pharmacy bathroom. Though calling that a kiss was a stretch. It had been an assault to my senses, a show of dominance.

It was a warning.

But Corry's mouth was pure decadence, like a sweet dessert that I'd never had. I couldn't peg the exact flavor, although it reminded me of the wedding cakes I'd see on baking shows, specifically, the beautiful icing flowers crafted so perfectly they looked like actual flowers. My mouth had watered every time I laid eyes on those flowers, desperate for a taste of the forbidden dessert that never in my lifetime would I get to taste.

Corry's kiss was nothing but sweet.

Until I gathered my courage and pushed my tongue into his mouth. I knew I was pressing my luck by making out with a bloody thirsty, baby vampire. But hey, I deserved a redo at this whole kissing thing.

As soon as my tongue passed his lips, I regretted it. His fang came down over the tip of my tongue, puncturing it.

I whimpered, and a growl just like the one I'd made over my pretzel rattled out, low and gravely. He sucked on the tip of my tongue, coaxing out a few drops of my blood. The most erotic, masculine moan rolled off his tongue and onto mine, hot and heavy. His nostrils flared.

Gone was the taste of sweet frosting, and in its place was the coppery tang of my own blood.

"*Fuuuuck*," he groaned.

His fingers turned from gentle and soft on my back to possessive and greedy. They dug into my shoulder blades, causing me to wince. He thrust his pelvis into mine, grinding his now fully erect cock against my groin.

"Corry, not here..." I muttered a feeble protest, my eyes darting around to see if anyone was watching. This time of night, the joint was packed with people our age, raunchy PDA all over the arcade, the food court, and by the scent my acute nose picked up, there was even a couple banging one out under the bleachers on the other end of the rink.

But if things kept escalating between Corry and me the way they were, people were going to start noticing at any moment.

His hand slid up my thigh underneath my dress to grip my butt cheek.

"Come with me into the restroom then. You deserve a better first time, but Christ—" His voice fractured on another ravenous growl that sunk straight through me, curling up between my thighs. If his hand dared to make the venture from my ass to my pussy, he'd find me soaking wet already. "I want you so bad it hurts, Ruby-Red."

My first time.

His words sent a rush of heat through my veins. He wanted to take me into the ladies' room and fuck me. My breath went short, my lungs emptying of all air like slashed tires.

For one intense heartbeat, I actually considered the offer. Losing my virginity in the restroom of the local roller rink seemed kind of pedestrian, a bit dirty, and cheap. And that was precisely its appeal.

Aside from my choice of partner, it would be wonderfully ordinary. *Human*.

If I lost my virginity to someone like Vincent Feral, I imagined sacrificial altars, chanting, and a knife involved.

With Corry, it would just be safe. It would be like what I'd seen on teen sitcoms on TV. He would once again be giving me another experience my mother stole from me. And that mixed with the appeal of sating this deep, clawing hunger to mate him was enough to make me agree to the whole thing.

"Do you trust yourself not to feed from me?"

He searched my gaze as if he'd find the answer rooted somewhere inside me. By some miracle, his irises were still blue, but the whites of his eyes were bloodshot all to hell.

"No," he admitted after several tense seconds, "I don't."

I didn't trust him either. He'd already pricked me as soon as I entered his body. What bloody, fucked up bullshit would he pull when he entered mine?

Corry's fingers dug tighter into the flesh of my ass and slipped beneath the seam of my panties.

I jerked in his arms as his index finger stroked over my labia, his movement slow, agonizing, calculated. He buried his face into my neck and inhaled deeply. Tiny, blaring alarms were sounding in my head. A vampire's fangs were mere millimeters from my jugular. My heart pounded so hard I knew Corry could feel my pulse hammering away against his lips. I could feel him salivating against me.

"Your virgin's blood is so damn sinful I'd sell my cock to Satan for just another drop," he gritted in my ear, his other hand fisting in my hair.

I nipped teasingly at his lower lip, earning me a husky growl. "If you sold your cock to Satan, how would you be able to taste my virgin pussy, Youngblood?"

Another heady groan erupted. His finger slipped past my folds, sinking in no deeper than his first knuckle. I ached for more, so *so* much more.

"Then I'll sell my soul—shit no—I don't have that anymore. I'll sell Vincent's cock to Satan. How about that?"

"Now that's a plan I can go along with," I rasped, my breath hitching as his fingertip pulled out of my slit, dragging back over my ass cheek. Using my own wetness, he traced something on my flesh.

"Corry," I whispered the word as I felt him spell his own name out on my rear.

He flashed me a panty-melting grin, his tongue flicking out to clean any traces of my blood from his lips. "Hearing my name in your mouth is almost as good as tasting your blood in mine."

My heart ricocheted off my ribcage like it was trying to jump out of my chest. Two nights ago, I believed this much heart-pounding excitement would mean almost certain death. I wanted a night like this so bad, I'd been willing to trade my life for it. For what? Roller skating, a pretzel, a video game, a lusty kiss right in front of everyone. And I would have jumped at the chance if only those bars hadn't been in my way.

At twenty-three years old, I'd never had anything close to a sexual experience, with the exception of what just went down with Corry's fingers in my panties five seconds ago.

I contemplated taking up his invitation to the restroom and opened my mouth to respond, but another woman's voice filled the space instead.

"Corry? Corry Cross?"

Corry jerked out of my arms, and his eyes darted around frantically, searching for the source of the voice who'd called his name. "Shit. Shit. Fucking *shit.*"

CHAPTER TWENTY-ONE

QUESTIONS AND ANSWERS

"What is it?" I asked, dazed.

"Look, for the next few minutes, my name isn't Corry, alright?"

There was no time to ask questions because just as I turned in the direction where Corry was looking, I saw a girl approach with a guy I assumed to be her boyfriend at her side. She had shoulder-length brown hair and eyes as blue as Corry's. She was beautiful and young. In her early twenties, if I had to guess.

"C–Corry?" she asked again, her voice tremulous and her pretty features pinched with some sort of emotion that made my stomach flip. When she spoke his name, she sounded so unsure. It was like she'd never seen his face before and was going off a description.

"Uh, sorry, lady. That's not my name." He turned back to the game, feigning interest.

Her mouth slanted into a dubious frown, her scrutinizing gaze slowly roving over Corry. He threw me a quick glance that screamed, "help."

"Derrick." I tugged on his bicep, a slight whine to my voice to sell the act. "I'm done playing this stupid zombie game. Come back onto the rink with me, please?"

The girl's brows wrinkled with confusion. "I'm sorry, you just look like someone I know."

I felt sorry for the girl. She recognized Corry, but for some reason, he was brushing her off as a stranger. And she didn't seem sure enough to call him on his bluff.

The guy with her spoke for the first time, chastising her with a "What kind of dumb bitch mistakes a stranger for her own brother?" Gripping her wrist tight enough for her to wince, he jerked her arm and led her away.

I watched them go, my jaw hanging open in astonishment.

The youngblood let out a low hiss, his molten-glower hot on the boyfriend's back. "I hate that prick. If he doesn't start treating her better, I'm going to—"

"What in the actual fuck? That was your *sister?*"

Corry's expression hardened. He plunked down on a nearby bench and began ripping off his skates. "Yeah. Her name is Corra. She's my twin."

I paused, waiting for his face to crack. Anything that would hint at the joke he was playing on me. But there was nothing about Corry's expression that was even remotely funny. His gaze remained fixed on the laces as his hands began to shake with the fury he was holding back. The laces snapped in his grip on the second skate when he jerked a little too hard on the knot. "Fuck."

Taking the seat next to him, I put my hand on his knee, and the simple contact stilled him immediately. "Tell me what's going on. How does your sister not recognize her own twin's face?"

"I wanted this to be a normal, human date for you. I don't want to bring down the mood with my shit."

"It's alright," I said with a weak smile. "I'm quickly learning normal isn't really my speed."

"I didn't have the easiest time with my transition. Thomas Knight turned me pretty abruptly, just like the others." Corry heaved a sigh, his fingers sweeping through his hair. "I didn't take it too well. First thing I did was run off to see my family. Only not before accidentally killing someone on the way over, out of a blood lust-driven panic. Imagine your son, who's been missing for three days, just show up at your door covered in blood, reeking of death and babbling on about a secret underworld filled with vampires and covens. If you'd only seen the look on their faces."

His face was as white as a sheet—even paler than usual —as he stared blankly into space. It was like he was reliving that night, his bloodshot eyes glazed with painful memories. "There was so much screaming. Master and Sterling came in and mesmerized everyone. Wiped all memories away from that awful night and replaced it with a story about how I contacted them after three days, telling them I was going on an impromptu bike trip across Europe with no return date. They also muddled the memory of my face in their heads, just in case shit like this happens."

"What about photographs?"

"We cleaned out the house of any pictures and had to get the coven's security guy to take down everything on the internet. It was a whole mess and partially the reason why

I'm still saddled with the equivalent of vampire training wheels."

"You mean Vincent?"

"Yeah. Why he decided to let me off my leash tonight of all nights, I can't fathom."

I sat back in my seat, stunned. This moment of vulnerability from Corry gave me a whole new perspective on the youngest vampire prince. "That's so horrible. I'm sorry that happened to you."

I could feel his muscles unwinding beneath my palm. "I'm getting over it. The others had way worse transitions than me."

"That doesn't make your experience any less painful."

He shrugged, hauling himself to his feet with his skates in hand. "I'll get over it. Time heals all wounds or whatever bullshit thing people say to make you feel better. And if I've got anything, it's time." As fast as a snap, his demeanor changed from somber to his usual cock-sure self. "Now come on, I promised you burgers."

With his face awash with the light from glow sticks and blinking video games, a pair of skates dangling from his hand, Corry looked so human. Like an average twenty-one-year-old.

It felt natural being with him.

It felt safe.

And yet, I knew I couldn't trust that feeling making my stomach warm and tingly like a schoolgirl with her first crush.

Because nothing about Corry was natural.

Nothing about him was safe. All this, the skating, the pretzel, the video games, the flirting... It was all an illusion of normalcy that could be enjoyed. But not trusted.

Corry may walk and talk like a harmless guy I could fall for, but by the tiniest residual smear of my blood on his lips and the way his gaze occasionally wandered to my neck, I knew he was a monster.

Just like the rest of them.

It didn't matter what he was after, the throne, my virginity, my blood... Whatever it was, he wanted to take a piece of me. And if I didn't get on with my plan and get out of here fast, I might just let him.

Corry made good on his promise to stuff me full of hamburgers. He took me to a locally owned burger joint called "Clown Car Burgers." The rusty fluorescent sign was shaped like a clown car with ten clowns popping out of it holding burgers. It was surreal, watching a vampire order the "clown pack" and excitedly receive a cardboard container shaped like a clown car, supposedly packed with a dozen burgers.

Sitting out on the curb outside, I watched with fascination as Corry devoured what had to be his fifth burger. "I thought vampires couldn't eat regular food."

"We can," he said, his mouth pursing into a grin over his food. His lips looked so enticing, even when coated in grease. Damn, I was hungry.

"It just doesn't give our bodies any nutrients. Basically, it's just for the taste. Most in the coven don't bother, but I guess it's pretty common for youngbloods to eat. Habit and all."

I gave a thoughtful nod. "What else about vampires isn't true? You can see yourselves in mirrors as long as it's not an antique kind backed with silver, right? And obviously, the thing about vampires having to be invited into a house isn't true. Otherwise, Vincent wouldn't have busted into my mom's house the way he did."

"Well, the whole thing with sunlight is a pretty harsh reality." He let out a low whistle. "Let me tell you, if you don't respect curfews now, wait till you get a load of the next poor bastard who misses bedtime. Not pretty. The thing with crucifixes is a bunch of bullshit. You can look at one, lick one, fuck one. It's just a piece of wood." He paused, cringing. "Unless it's made out of silver. Silver is deadly in most contexts. It's also pretty common for vamps to have allergies to garlic for whatever reason, but it's not like it's lethal or anything. Sharpe gave me a medical explanation once, but honestly, I wasn't really paying attention."

"So Sharpe *is* an actual doctor?"

"Yeah, back in the day," he snorted. "When dentists were considered 'doctors' for pulling out people's teeth, armed with nothing but a pair of pliers and a tin of morphine."

My stomach writhed at the visual, but I took another bite of the burger, enjoying its flavor way too damn much to be put off. "Bloody hell, this is good," I moaned as the hot meat exploded with flavor in my mouth.

A low, rattling purr slipped out of Corry, just like the one I'd made over the pretzel. But I wasn't sure if it was because of his meal, or my reaction to mine.

For several moments we just sat in silence, eating. It was a cool and clear night. It had to be about midnight right about now, and the Clown Car parking lot was completely empty, save for us. Any minute now, I would continue with the plan. But right at this second, I was enjoying myself too much to leave just yet.

I watched the moon with a newfound appreciation. It looked so much better without the bars on my window blocking my view. Everything was so new, so interesting. My gaze wandered to the telephone pole just a few feet away, littered with a smattering of wanted posters, event advertisements, and "lost cat" notices.

My mouth went bone dry and my body went hot then cold again when my attention settled on a poster with faces that I recognized. "Corry, what is *that?*"

CHAPTER TWENTY-TWO
THE MAN ON THE FLYER

The flyer featured two half-naked men built like tanks. "The Feral King vs. The Deathwish," the poster read. It was advertising a fight set for one week from now.

Corry followed my line of sight to the poster. "Oh, shit. I forgot all about that fight. Guess Eros will be home sooner than everyone would probably like. He'd never miss a chance to beat up on Vin."

I don't think I'd envisioned Deathwish in my mind at all, but if I had, this was not the image I would have put together for the infamous "sadist" everyone had been whispering about.

My chest tightened as I took in the details of the man opposing Vincent.

The man nicknamed 'Deathwish' was brutally gorgeous. He had several piercings, including snake bites, eyebrow piercings, and gauged ears. Even his nipples were pierced. He had long blond hair tied up in a bun on his head with a dark blond beard to match. It was hard to tell from the angle of the picture, but it looked like he had a tattoo of the grim reaper on his chest, the scythe so huge its blade stretched up the side of his throat.

He was fair-haired and light-skinned. But there was a nebulous darkness in his gaze that caused my skin to erupt with goosebumps.

Vincent was a stark contrast, with his short hair as black as death and his raven tattoos that stretched from his wide jaw all the way down the side of his bare torso to slip into the waistband of his shorts.

I remembered in the car last night, Corry had mentioned something about Vincent being an MMA fighter. But this didn't look like anything official. This looked like some underground shit.

I couldn't peel my eyes away from the blond-haired man, who looked like a terrifying Viking of old.

The hatred between the two vampires was palpable, judging by the way their fists were raised and the gleam of murder in their eyes.

"I didn't think Deathwish was a fighter too."

"Oh yeah. They were both at the top of their game in the MMA long before they were turned. They'd always had this brutal rivalry thing going on. And Master got such a huge kick out of it he turned them both right around the same time. Now they're forever at each other's throats. Their hatred for one another pulls in a ton of dough. You should see the fights. Vicious as fuck. Humans go crazy betting on those two. Vin likes to think he's the strongest, but Eros gives him a run for his money once in a blood moon."

"But doesn't anyone notice that they look different now? They're both as pale as death and Vincent's got his bulgy black arm veins going on. And don't people get weirded out by all the black blood?"

"If they were still in the MMA, sure. But these fights are different. They are underground, literally. The place is dark, filled with all sorts of creeps who just want to see bloodshed. they thrive off the gritty theatrics of it, and they don't ask questions. They don't grapple for the logical. Besides, even if they did suspect anything, they wouldn't dare spread rumors. People in that world disappear all the time for asking too many questions."

I couldn't tear my gaze away from the two vampires on the flyer, throwing punches meant to maim, their muscles flexing beneath sweat-slick skin. They looked deadly, and as much as I hated to admit it, hot as fuck.

"You don't want to get caught between those two, Red," Corry said, reading my pinched expression. "And you don't have to. Sterling doesn't want the throne or a mate, so expect him to sit out this whole suitor thing, but those two will fight for you, and it won't be pretty."

It was obvious what Corry was getting at. I was pretty sure this whole night was just one big "Corry for King" campaign.

I had the youngblood wrapped around my finger. Which was exactly where I wanted him.

Feigning a shiver, I wrapped my arms around myself. "Shit, it's cold."

On the next breath, Corry was shrugging off his jacket and draping it over my shoulders. I could feel the bulk of his motorcycle keys weighing down his pocket.

Bingo.

Just one last thing to do. And that would be it, that would be the last I saw of Corry. Of any of them.

That would be the end of my short-lived life as a vampire princess.

I stared at my half-eaten burger, trying my best to ignore the hallow cavern in my chest.

There was still so much I wanted to learn, but there was no time. Unanswered questions about my father swam to the surface of my mind. This was basically my only chance at getting some answers to the questions that had been hanging over my head.

"Can you tell me a little bit about my dad, Corry?"

The youngblood's expression stretched with surprise. "Er, I'm not really the person to ask, Red. I only knew him for six months."

I fully intended leaving the cape—hell—probably Massachusetts altogether. I had no intention of coming back, so this was my only shot to fill in some blanks.

"Tell me what you can. I get that he was a horrible monster. But for someone as old as him, there had to be more depth than that. *Some* shred of good in him."

Corry sent me an indecipherable look and shifted uncomfortably on the curb, balancing his elbows on his knees. "I dunno, Red. I didn't know him like the others did. I know bits and pieces of what he did to Sterling and Vincent, and..." his voice quivered and died, seemingly unable to say the next words. "Horrible things. *Unspeakable* things. His favorite hobby was turning the strongest men unfortunate enough to cross his path and making them his playthings. He delighted in breaking them down until they were nothing more than dust. He kept alive only the ones strong enough to survive him."

My blood ran cold, and I inhaled on the question, "There were others he turned?"

"Countless others. Sterling, Vincent, Eros, and I are the only ones he bothered to keep alive."

"All men?"

Corry gave me a nod.

I pulled his jacket tighter around me as an actual chill shuddered through me. To think the vampire king, my father, stole the lives of countless men over the course of his stupid long life, turning them into monsters, and killing the ones who didn't measure up.

Maybe Vincent Feral had been a soft, kind man before he was made to suffer through whatever it was the vampire king had done to him.

Regardless of what kind of person he'd been before, Vincent had had a life. A promising career in the MMA, and all of that was robbed from him. I wondered if my father had tipped over Vincent's world as swiftly as he had tipped over mine.

Then there was Sterling, who I barely knew. But something told me the silver-haired prince had been broken so many times that he eventually became unbreakable, unshakable, like a proud and picturesque statue, untouched by time while the world around him shifted and changed.

My gaze went back to the pierced, blond-haired man on the poster who looked every bit as vicious as his dark-haired brother. Deathwish seemed to be the most like my father, a typical monster who got off on the suffering of others.

And Corry was a perfect counterbalance to all of them. I wondered what he'd experienced under the cruel hand of Thomas Knight.

As if reading my mind, Corry took my hand in his, pulling my gaze back into focus as he said, "He was a terrible bastard, Red. But I think there was a shred of good in him. I won't tell you lies and say he was kind to me. But he didn't do the things to me that he did to the others."

My breath hitched. "What did he do to the others?"

His jaw hardened. "Those aren't my stories to tell. What I can tell you is that the circumstances under which he turned me were a complete accident. You might even call it an act of mercy."

"Mercy?" So far, what I knew of the vampire king, mercy had no business being in any sentence where he was included.

Corry's body went completely still, like stone. "The night I died, I'd been speeding down Route Six. I did it all the time. My family lives in Boston, and every Friday night, I'd get on my bike and get out of the city. I'd go as fast as my bike would handle, and I'd go all night. The Cape's the perfect place for it, especially up north where the roads are completely empty, and it feels like you're all alone."

Corry's gaze locked with mine, his face expressionless, stony. "But that night, I wasn't alone. The vampire king liked to take joy rides that time of night too, and his car collided with my bike going one-fifty."

"That's when you died in the car crash," I nodded, remembering what he'd told me from before. Though, it was only an offhanded mention. I was eager to hear the rest of the story.

"I should have," he said, bobbing his head as if a part of his brain was still trying to process it. "Should have died instantly. Instead, I died in the arms of the guy who hit me. And it was just my lucky night, I guess, because it happened to be the vampire king on the one day in his life he felt merciful."

"Do you ever wonder why he did it?"

"Pretty much every damn day, Red. The guy had been through countless wars, plagues, genocides, some of which he was the cause. Human life meant fuck-all to him. He'd killed so many people, all of them as inconsequential as squashing a fly. But he decided to save me, some kid he didn't even know."

"He probably felt guilty."

Corry scoffed, the sound grating and filled with frustration. "Thomas Knight didn't know the meaning of the word."

Letting out a sound that was half animalist growl, half sigh, Corry scoured his hands over his face, his fingertips buried in his hair. "I know how you feel, you know?" he muttered, not looking at me anymore.

My brow furrowed. "How could you?"

"I don't feel like I belong in this world, this dark existence filled with death and suffering. My family bought the lie about me going overseas to bike through Europe because that was my plan. I was about to start my last year at college, and I was majoring in engineering. My twin was in the same school, same year. Biology major. We were going to take the trip together to celebrate our graduation." His voice dropped, pinched into a pained whisper. "She had to be so crushed when she found out I dropped out of school without warning and went on the trip without her."

"But you didn't!"

His head shot up from his hands, his eyes full of darkness. They were terrifying with the neon flicker of the clown car sign reflected in them. "She was made to think that I abandoned her. For the last six months, I've been pretty miserable. Wondering why this happened. But maybe your dad..." He shook his head, unable to voice his train of thought.

"Maybe he what?" I prodded, sliding my hand over Corry's back. His expression softened at the contact.

"He knew he was going to die. He knew he was going to name you his heir. I don't think he turned me out of pity. I think he turned me because I was your only shot of having someone kind of normal. Someone who hasn't forgotten what it's like to be human. I'm not hardened and jaded like Eros. And Vincent? Hell, *no one's* like him. I don't even think he was ever human. And I'm not some ancient vessel of knowledge like Sterling. I'm just...me."

Holding my breath, I gaped at the vampire as his words slowly sank in.

What did he mean by Vincent not ever being human? What could he have been before?

My attention wandered back to the flyer. There was no question by the stacks of muscles that Deathwish was a deadly predator and a formidable opponent for Vincent. But other than his pale skin, he could pass as human. The Feral King, on the other hand, his skin so white, the fans who followed his MMA career had probably thought he'd painted himself as part of the act. Playing up the stage.

They probably thought the bulging, ink-black veins were makeup too. It wasn't a stretch to imagine him as more monster than man even before he'd been turned. Which begged the question, what exactly was he?

My mind slipped to the other thing Corry had said. Did my father choose to turn Corry simply for my benefit? Because he thought his friendship would be a relief amongst the other inhuman, deadly princes vying for me?

Maybe.

By keeping himself out of my life, maybe that was another act of mercy. Another sign that he... *cared.*

That was enough for me. That was the little tiny flicker of light that I needed to exist in the otherwise noxious ball of hatred that swelled in my chest whenever I thought about my father.

There was just one more question I needed an answer to. "How did my father die?"

Corry's whole body went rigid and by the way his face contorted, I knew I wasn't supposed to know the answer.

When he didn't reply, I pulled the dirty card. Because there was no way I was leaving here not knowing what happened to my dad. Even if he had been the world's biggest prick, I had to know.

"Corry, tell me how my father died or there is no way you're getting into my pants tonight."

"That's not fair," he groaned. "Also that's kinda fucked, Red."

"Yeah well if you want me to be kinda fucked tonight you better spill the beans, Youngblood."

CHAPTER TWENTY-THREE
THE MONSTER INSIDE

F or the briefest moment, a flicker of conflict crossed the youngblood's face. A second later, he recovered and nonchalantly shoved a fry in his mouth. "As much as I want to seat myself between those pretty thighs, this isn't how I want it to happen. I can't be spilling coven secrets all for the sake of getting my dick wet."

I glared daggers at him. "Aren't I in the coven now? Shouldn't I be let in on all these secrets if I'm going to be the queen of the freaking *vampires?*"

"You're not queen yet, Red."

"Oh come on!"

"You should ask Sterling."

"I'm not asking Sterling. I'm asking you."

The skin around his eyes tightened with a grimace. "The guys don't want me talking about it. We're trying to keep it under wraps, so the other covens don't use it as ammunition against us."

"It's not like I have the other covens on speed dial," I snorted. "Even if I did, how would they use that info against you?"

"What happened... It's not how anyone thought the vampire king would go out. Makes us look weak."

I was burning with curiosity, but I decided not to push it any further. It didn't matter anyway.

"Well, at least that's more information than I'd be able to pry from Feral. This has been a really nice date, Corry." I smiled at him. "Thank you. If my dad really did turn you just so I would feel more comfortable and at home, then it wasn't in vain."

And that was true. Without the youngblood, I wouldn't have any means of escape.

My heart twisted in my chest when Corry sent me the warmest smile, the dimple on his left cheek popping up.

Bloody hell. Why was this so hard? Why was I dragging this out? I had the keys. All that was left was one final step, and it would be so easy.

While Vincent's game was to taunt, mock, and play the part of the cruel monster that, for some stupid reason, made my lady parts melt in rebellion, Corry was going straight for my heart.

I couldn't delay any longer.

"Hey." I forced myself to perk up, snatching the empty paper cup that had held my Diet Coke. It had done nothing to sate the scratchy ache always lingering at the back of my throat. "Would you get me another refill?"

The youngblood perked right up as he took the cup, the fist around my heart squeezing tighter as our fingers brushed. "Sure, Red. Anything for you."

By the cadence of his voice and the warmth in his blue gaze, I knew now that Corry wasn't selling an act. This wasn't some play for the throne.

He genuinely liked me. If he actually believed my dad had turned him just for my sake, it had to be a relief that we actually clicked. That he hadn't lost his twin, his family, his future for nothing.

That thought made my heart freeze over with ice as I watched him stride into the restaurant.

Scrabbling up from the curb, I dug out the keys to the motorcycle, slapped myself onto the seat, and kicked up the stand. I stuck the keys into the ignition, and the engine roared to life. I didn't bother to look back over my shoulder as I tore out of the parking lot.

I wouldn't be able to stand the look of betrayal on Corry's face should he have heard the rev of his bike.

I refused to feel guilty for putting myself first.

For the average girl forced to her own bedroom for two decades on the pretense of a deadly heart condition, driving a motorcycle at night at speeds fast enough to outrun a vampire should be terrifying. But I've never been average or normal. I've lusted for the kind of danger where I was the one in the driver's seat, controlling the speed. If I wanted to die, that would be my prerogative. The point was, for the first time in my life, I was in control. And it felt fucking good. That is until it started to rain. It felt good at first, just another normal thing any living creature was given the courtesy of experiencing except for me.

My grip tightened around the handles as I zipped along Route Six toward Boston. Then, as if in tune with the turmoil of emotions inside me, the rain turned bitterly cold and started to pound on me without mercy.

I was sure Corry was trailing me. I couldn't see him behind me, there was no sign of anyone tracking me, but his rage was almost palpable as the freezing drops of rain stung my skin like needles.

I just need to keep going for a few more hours. He'll have to turn back well before dawn.

But my hope bottomed out with the rest of my stomach when the gaslight blinked on the dash.

The wind tore away whatever curses and prayers fell from my lips. I wasn't a religious woman, but I sent out a quick jumbled prayer to whoever would listen for Corry not to catch up with me. He lacked the chilling brutality of some of his brothers, but he was still an impulsive youngblood who'd probably retaliate for getting played.

I pulled into a gas station off the side of the road in the middle of bum-fuck nowhere. There were no lights from any nearby buildings, no trace of civilization, save for the blinding white lights illuminating the covered area where the gas pumps sat. The mini-mart was closed, the inside completely dark. My skin erupted with goosebumps, and my breaths fell into short, trepid sucks of air as I fumbled inside Corry's pockets.

Fuck.

His wallet must have been in his jean pockets, not his jacket. I didn't have any money to gas up the bike, and there was no one around to bum some cash from. I jumped when my pocket vibrated. Pulling out the cheap cell Corry had bought me at the pharmacy, I forced myself to read his text.

Corry: "It's cute how u think u can run from me, backstabber."

All my blood drained from my cheeks as I read the text a second, then a third time. The single sentence was accompanied by a knife and blood drop emoji. A threat? Or just an extra emphasis on the backstabber bit?

Panic began to set in, sinking into my bones and making me cold all over. What was I going to do? Run? No, that would be stupid. I couldn't outrun a full-blooded vampire.

I started to run through the very short list of options I had when the deep voice of a man called out, causing me to jump.

Whirling around, I found myself staring at two men who'd appeared out of the blue, both of them leaning on either side of the gas pump. They were both moderately handsome, but there was something about the way they looked at me that set me on edge. Wherever they came from, it hadn't been from a car by the way their hair was plastered to their foreheads. But there was no time to ask who they were and why they were sneaking up on me. There was a literal monster tracking me.

"You scared the hell out of me," I gasped, trying to frantically stuff down my fraying nerves. "But I am kind of relieved to see someone here. I just ran out of gas, and if you guys could maybe spare a few bucks so I can get out of here—"

They exchanged a look over the gas pump that froze the words in my mouth. It was a look that chilled me to the core, one that didn't need any words to know what they were thinking. They weren't going to help me, but they were certainly going to try to help themselves to something I wasn't selling.

I threw back my head to let out a scream, but they moved so fast, they were a blur. One was already behind me, pinning my arms behind my back with a single hand, and the other slapped down over my mouth.

The second guy arched his spine, so he was at my eye level, leering at me with a seedy grin. "Did you hear that, Mal? She's trying to make a getaway. What's the matter? Trouble in paradise already, Princess?"

Every muscle in my body went rigid as the last word slithered over my skin, mingling the man's breath on my cheek.

These men weren't random thugs. At least, not human ones. They were vampires. Now that they were closer, I realized they had no heartbeat. Pale skin. *Red eyes.*

"The king's rabid princelings not good enough for Her Royal Highness?" the one named Mal hissed behind me. I thrashed against him when his hand came sliding up the back of my thigh, lingering just below the swell of my ass. "Maybe she's scared," he snickered, the sound of him licking his lips in my ear spurring me to fight harder against him. "Maybe the halfling bitch needs a little lesson in vampire cock before she picks a king to rule us."

"You know what?" the one in front of me snarled. "I don't think I like the fact that the Elders expect this halfling bitch to select our next monarch. Maybe we should do the picking for her."

"Yeah," Mal said with a slimy purr-like growl. "You think if I seal the mating bond with her, I'll get to be king?"

My blood froze in my veins. *They know about the Elders' decision. How could they know? Who told them? They couldn't be from the Cape Cod Coven.* None of them would be stupid enough to incite the princes' wrath by putting their hands on me like this. Right?

Or maybe this was planned. Maybe Vincent had let me go because he saw it as an opportunity to get rid of me for good and clear his way to the throne.

No. If Vincent wanted to destroy me, he wouldn't send two grunts to do his dirty work. He would do it himself. If the last twenty-four hours had taught me anything about Vincent Feral, it was that if he was going to make me suffer, he would want it to be by his own hand.

The monster in front of me stepped closer, his fingers curling into the lowcut neckline of my dress. With one swift yank, he tore the dress all the way down to my navel. I screamed against the palm clamped over my mouth. The one holding me pressed his nose to my neck, my blood crystallizing when I felt the needle-sharp tips of his fangs pressing to my flesh. "Fucking hell," he moaned, his teeth nicking the delicate skin of my throat with the movement. "You smell that, Al? *Virgin's blood.* Maybe that's why she's been locked away, keeping her pure."

A single drop of ruby red slid down my neck to pool in the hollow of my throat.

Al's pupils dilated, creating a thin ring of red around a disk of black. His lips peeled back to reveal his dropped fangs. "Maybe that's why the old fuck offed himself. Keeping a piece like this all locked away, untouched. What a waste."

Offed himself. My father killed himself? No, that couldn't be. They had that wrong. Ancient, narcissistic vampire kings did not commit suicide.

My spinning thoughts stalled out when Al's hand slid around from my ass over my hip, down to the crevice between my thighs. All my insides shriveled, seeing the way his lips spread into a maleficent grin. "Knowing how old-fashioned your sire was, I'm surprised there's no chastity belt."

Mal cackled, then he made the mistake of letting his hand slip from my mouth to caress my breast.

I didn't think about my next move. Just as Corry had instructed, I let my instincts take the driver's seat. Twisting my head around, there was a pressure in my gums I never felt before. At first, there was a skull-spitting ache and then relief. Before I could process what was happening, a male's screech of pain rang out, and blood blurred my vision.

Black blood.

The thick, inky liquid gushed from the gaping hole of flayed flesh. Something had torn out his throat.

It's like my train of thought had left the station without me. What was happening? I was barely keeping up with my actions, processing them after they'd already happened. I'd ripped out the throat of the vampire called Mal. He released me, stumbling back from me with his hand slapped over his throat, thick gobs of oil-like blood seeping from his fingers.

"You—you bitch!" he stammered through a spittle-laced snarl.

He was livid. Surprised by my strength.

Join the club, buddy.

While any human would already be face down on the concrete in a pool of their own blood with a wound like that, the vampire acted as though it were a mere paper cut.

What the fuck.

Before I could decide what to do next, those deep-seated, monstrous instincts were already pushing me into action. I leaped at the vampire, tackling him to the ground. He was surprisingly easy to pin down, like I weighed a thousand more pounds than I actually did.

He hissed at me, his gaze full of murder. He screamed something, but I wasn't listening. The world around us stalled out as my attention honed in on the gruesome tattering of his throat. Wounds like that weren't going to kill an immortal.

My hands clamped down over his ears, and with all the strength I had, I ripped his head clean off in a spray of gore. I let the head fall to the concrete with a sickening *thunk*. His blood on my lips tasted like euphoria. Like the thing I'd hungered for all these years without actually knowing what it was my body craved.

I was lost in the flavor of it, sucking my fingers clean and licking my lips as his body twitched beneath me, his life draining away.

I was lost to the monster inside me.

Chapter Twenty-Four

DIRTY DEAL WITH THE YOUNGBLOOD

It wasn't until the fog slowly melted away that I regained some awareness, the ringing in my ears dying away to be replaced with the sounds of a fight behind me. Twisting around on the headless body I was still perched on, my heart lurched when I saw Corry lunging at the remaining vampire. I had to have been out of it for longer than I thought because they were both covered in scratch marks. Corry must have snuck up on him because Al was worse for wear, with his face covered in claw marks, his clothes hanging in shreds. He was having a hard time keeping up with his opponent, who was moving too fast for him. Even I couldn't track Corry's movements. All I could make out was Al's body shuddering with every blow. He must have understood that he was losing the fight because a moment later, he took off sprinting into the dark.

The youngblood raced after him, leaving me completely alone with Mal.

I glanced over at the head, its eyes still open and staring at me with shock. My hands were shaking as those eyes watched me fumble inside his jacket pockets for a wallet. There was no time to panic, no time to process the fact that I'd just ripped off a man's head with my own bare hands.

A cry of relief dropped from my lips like a prayer as my fingers closed in around a wallet. It was fat with cash.

Ripping out the wad of bills, I scrambled to the gas pump and shoved money into the machine. Between my trembling fingers, my utter lack of knowledge on how to pump gas, and my gaze flicking up to scan the darkness for any more blood-thirsty vampires, I was getting nowhere.

Bloody fucking hell.

By some miracle, I managed to keep myself steady long enough to screw off the cap to the tank. Turning toward the pump, I took the nozzle and moved to insert it into the tank when strong fingers slapped down on my wrist, stopping me.

My chest squeezed as my gaze slowly slid up my captor's arm to rest on the bloodied features of a *very* angry youngblood.

"Stole my bike, broke my heart, and you got blood all over my favorite jacket. Plus, I had to chase off some punk ready to take what belongs to me and my brothers. That's not cool, Red. Not cool at all."

I was quickly coming to realize the strength I possessed. Who knows, maybe I was stronger than Corry. But I didn't want to fight him. I didn't want this to end the same way it did for Mal.

"Let me go, Cor," I advised, my voice fraying. "I'm not afraid to shoot," I added, pointing the gas nozzle at him. But my attempt at easing the tension with a joke was futile.

Moving lighting quick, Corry slapped the gas nozzle out of my hand with a guttural growl.

"Let me go! I don't want to hurt you."

"Hurt me?" he choked out in a dry laugh. His fingers gripped my wrist tighter, and I bite back a wince of pain. "You've already done that. You used me. All that shit you said about being comfortable with me, about my life getting fucking stolen from me not being in vain—"

"It *was* true!"

"Liar!" he roared, his bloodied face contorting in anguish. "You're a fucking liar, Ruby."

The hurt in his tone pierced my heart like a knife. "I'm sorry. I didn't mean to hurt you. But you were my only way out of that place. Understand that what you call home was just another fucking prison for me. I'm done being locked up! I'm done being told what to do. My life needs to start, Corry."

"It *has* started. We freed you. You can't compare the coven to your mom's house."

"For the last two decades I thought my heart was a ticking time bomb. That any moment if I did anything too exciting, it could give out." My voice jumped up an octave, growing shrill and desperate. "There is nothing wrong with my heart now. It's beating, and I want to keep it that way. If I stay, my life is on a timer just like it was back in Quincy. I know you want me to participate in this insane courtship the Elders brewed up, but I'm still half-human, Corry. I don't belong in your world while I still have a beating heart."

Corry's brow furrowed, steeping most of his physiognomy in shadow. He kept my hand fixed to the

Ninja's gas tank, the motorcycle the only thing standing between the vampire whose heart I had broken and me.

"You don't belong in the human world either, Ruby-Red. Trust me, you don't."

I tried to swallow down my heart which felt as if it had lodged in my throat. "Shouldn't that be my decision to make?"

"Not when the fate of my world hangs in the balance."

"You–you can't make me stay."

"I can, actually," he replied in an icy whisper that froze all remaining warmth between us.

I'd meant it when I told him I didn't want to hurt him. Okay, so maybe that ship had kind of set sail, but I didn't want to physically fight him. I had no idea if I actually had a shot of winning, and if I did, was it worth the cost? Using Corry's emotions to win my freedom seemed like a few steps less drastic than ripping his head off. And if I actually harmed him, his brothers would come after me looking for revenge.

I shivered at the prospect. No, there had to be another way.

"Come on, Corry. Let me go. Please," I said with a little whine in my voice, hoping to stir the vampire's compassion. I gave a hard jerk to my hand, but his grip remained steady. It only pulled him closer under the lights, the fluorescents chasing away the shadows masking his face.

My heart pulsed, seeing the way his irises were now red, his pupils fixed to my chest like a starving man eyeing a hunk of meat.

My dress now had a plunging neckline all the way down to my belly button, courtesy of the vampire Corry had chased off. My breasts were still contained in a black bra, its lacy material crusted over with a mix of red and black blood. The cut the vampire had given me when he'd been seconds away from a full-on bite was worse than I thought. My neck and chest were streaked with dark red, and it had even seeped into the padding of Corry's jacket, the metallic tang of my blood mingling with his dark, spicy scent ingrained in the coat's lining.

He didn't look like he was ready to force himself on me like the other two vampires had attempted.

Despite some of his mischievous quirks, Corry Cross was a gentleman. Vincent seemed to distrust his youngest brother around me, but it seemed the youngblood had more restraint than everyone let on.

I knew if I offered, he wouldn't be able to resist. And now, there was no one else to stop him. No moral quandaries that I didn't know what I was getting myself into.

I forced my muscles to relax in his grip, and I softened my voice as I said his name, smooth and sweet in my mouth like candy. "Corry. Let me go. Let me go, and as a goodbye, I'll..."

His eyes narrowed, his head canting to the side. "You'll *what?*"

Before, the youngblood struck me as the least dangerous of all the vampire princes. But right now, with my arm pinned to the gas tank of his motorcycle, his predatorial gaze brewing with a heady mix of hunger and hurt, I was recalibrating my assessment.

"You can bite me," I pushed out on a fractured breath.

His lips quirked into a sardonic smirk. "Not good enough, babe."

"Wha–what?" I balked with a series of aghast blinks. "How is that not enough?"

"Don't get me wrong. I want to taste you. I want it so bad the fucking sight of your blood makes me hard."

He wasn't exaggerating. The testament to that was straining against the dark denim of his jeans.

"But you used me. Played me like a fucking fiddle, and now you owe me."

Lifting my hand off the gas tank, he pulled on my arm so that my body was forced to lean over the bike. His lips pressed against the skin behind my ear, the knuckles of his free hand gently grazing my jugular. When my breath hitched, and my heartbeat lurched into a gallop, the fringe of his lashes fluttered, and his nostrils flared.

"Now it's my turn to play with you."

I was no longer battling against his touch. Despite the prickly details of our tense stand-off, his touch felt just as safe and inviting as it had in the roller rink.

I didn't trust it for a second. And of course, that just made messed-up me want to risk it all the more. Because I knew what he was suggesting as payment for my freedom.

"I won't be your mate, Corry. You can't have me in that way," I said, my breath coming out in pants as his tongue slowly skated down over the length of my throat, cleaning off any traces of the other vampire.

"The difference between a bite and a claiming mark is that my cock has to be buried inside you, along with my fangs, Red. My brothers and I made an agreement right after the council's meeting that the only one who gets to do that to you is the one you pick as king. You're free to spread your blood and cunt around however you wish, but we've all agreed to no double-dipping until you make a decision."

My blood heated, the warmth sinking straight to the place between my thighs. They made rules, contingencies to this little fucked up game of *The Bachelorette*. And I wasn't even there to throw in my two cents. I'm just the prize, the piece of meat to fuck and feast on and sit pretty on the throne beside them.

Fuck that. If I had the strength and the power, I'd bring every last one of them to their knees and take the throne for myself while leaving all four of the fucked-up princes in the dust.

But that wasn't on the table, not when I was still very much a mortal.

"I want to have fun with you, Red. But I won't be taking your V-card, not tonight."

"When you're done, I can have your bike?"

"You can have my bike."

Stealing a breath, I closed my eyes and nodded. "Alright."

CHAPTER TWENTY-FIVE

BITTER GOODBYES AND BLOODY BARGAINS

"Straddle the bike, Red," Corry commanded, pointing at the motorcycle between us. He let go of my arm and waited for me to obey.

My heart took off like a jet engine in my chest, my pulse roaring in my ear. "W–wait. You don't mean for us to do it here?"

I didn't care if we weren't having full-blown sex. We were at a gas station, standing under a bunch of fluorescent lights. If anyone happened to drive by, we would be lit up like a freaking national monument.

"It's one in the morning, and we're off the main road. Hardly anyone comes this way in daylight, let alone at night."

Swallowing the lump in my throat, I sat down on the bike's seat. My short dress—or what remained of it—rode up my thighs as they parted to straddle the vehicle.

Corry's crimson eyes blazed with something carnal as they slid over the length of my body, making my skin burn despite the fact that I was still soaking wet from the rain.

He finally released my arm and strode around the bike, drinking in the way I looked with my sopping red hair plastered to my blood-streaked skin and my ripped dress, which failed to cover most of my body.

"Fuck me, Ruby Renada Baxter. You look good enough to eat."

I struck him with an icy glare, trying to hide how damn hot he was making me with just a single look. "That's what those other vampires thought."

The youngblood's expression hardened as it slipped to the body that still lay on the concrete. "Part of me is glad Allister got away. He'll crawl back to his coven and let them know the Cape Cod Coven isn't to be fucked with. We'll ship Malachite's head back to them just in case they don't believe his brother's story."

"Malachite and Allister?"

"Two of the Boston Coven's messenger boys. Their coven is one of the few not a part of the council. They've been trying to take over for fucking years. They never liked your father as king. Makes sense that they would attack his daughter, especially since you're only a half-blood."

"But doesn't it seem kind of random that they just happened across me?"

"There was nothing random about it. They were looking for you. Which can only mean there's a snitch on the council, someone who is slipping information to them."

"That would explain how they knew about the way my father died."

Corry's brows shot up. "Shit! What did they say?"

"It doesn't matter now," I snapped. "Fucking bite me, and let's get this over with so I can get the hell out of this nightmare."

"Stop that. You don't get to do that."

My eyes narrowed. "Do what?"

"You don't get to act like you don't want me because we both know you do. I can scent your arousal. It's so strong we're lucky for the rain. Otherwise, it might attract other vamps in the area."

I hated how right he was. I wanted him so bad it fucking hurt. Everything in my body was twisted into tight, aching knots, begging me for release. The pool of need swirling low in my belly was almost enough to pull my mind from the latest worry. *Almost.*

Whether it was because there was a traitor among the Elders or another reason, the Boston Coven knew about me. They'd sent their goons after me. I wondered if they'd leave me alone after I decided to abandon the crown. Something told me it wouldn't be that easy.

Then there was my father. According to Malachite and Allister, he'd taken his own life.

Why? What would compel an unfeeling monster like him to take his own life?

All my thoughts of Thomas Knight and the Boston Coven disintegrated when Corry pulled out his cell phone.

"What are you doing?" my voice splintered with panic.

His thumbs paused mid-text. "Just texting Sharpe back. He asked us brothers if anyone had remembered to give you your pills to sate your vampiric abilities."

Corry glanced back at the headless Malachite and chuckled. "Lucky for us, I don't think the pills are really doing a good job."

"I thought they were just to quench my bloodthirst."

"They are." He shoved the cell back into his pocket and sat down on the bike, with his back facing the handlebars and his face just inches from mine. The curve of the leather seat cradled us together, so we were practically in each other's laps. We were so close I was sure he could feel the heat of my blazing cheeks on his cool ones.

Reaching up, this thumb stroked along my bottom lip. Then it slipped into my mouth to feel the fangs that had miraculously appeared in the panic to protect myself.

"They're also supposed to prevent you from dropping your fangs. A fat lot of good that did. But I'm pretty damn happy the pills failed to work. Looks like you took my advice and just trusted your instincts to protect yourself."

Now that I was coming down from the adrenaline rush that had swept over my whole body, I began to tremble against Corry. His arms wrapped around me, pulling me flush against him. "Hey, it's okay. You're fine, Red." He stroked my hair with calm, soothing motions and his voice dropped to a quiet hum as he comforted me. "You're more than fine, actually. You're damn near perfect."

Despite how fucked up this whole night was, how shook up my nerves were, I managed a laugh.

He pulled back with a perplexed look on his face. "What's so funny?"

"I'm not perfect. I'm filthy. I'm covered in another vampire's blood and half-naked."

"Hey, in our world, we just call that foreplay, babe." Corry's eyes lit up with a cock-sure smirk. "So you figured out how to drop your fangs. The baby vampire is taking her first steps. Tell me, how do you feel now that you've had your first taste of blood?"

I thought about it for a second before answering. "Pissed off and horny."

"Those are common side effects to having vampire blood. If it makes you feel better, you can unwind some of that tension on me."

"What do you mean?"

He tilted his head to expose his neck to me, his smug and sexy smirk still plastered on his face. "Bite me, Red. You know you want to. You've been drooling over me all night."

My mind blanched for a second as I stared at the pale flesh wrapping his throat. There was no pulse, but the urge to bite him was still strong, almost like my primal instincts could detect the flow of blood there.

I chewed my lip, unable to look away. "I thought you were supposed to be biting me... That was the deal for the bike."

"That is the deal. But this isn't going to be any fun for me if you're not enjoying yourself, Red. So go on. Don't you want to wash the taste of that rapey asshole out of your mouth?"

Mal's blood had been disgusting. It tasted like how I imagined the flavor of freshly paved asphalt after a heavy rain. Corry, on the other hand, had a spicy, masculine scent that made my mouth water.

In spite of the fact that whatever was about to go down between us was a result of the seedy trade we'd made for his bike in exchange for him to do whatever he wanted to me, I still felt safe with Corry. It felt like he cared.

And I was going to feel bad for leaving him after all this, especially after he told me that he thought my father had turned him for me.

As much as I liked Corry, it didn't change any of the facts. I had to get out of here.

So this would be a bitter goodbye. Might as well make it as sweet as we could before it was over.

So I bit him. My fangs sunk into his skin like a hot knife through butter. The gush of liquid—cooler than blood probably should have been—gushed into my mouth. I let out a moan against his flesh, and he let out a noise that had the hybrid of a chuckle and a husky growl.

"Gentle, Red." One hand cupped my head, holding my mouth to his neck and his other grasped my thigh, fingers biting into my flesh.

The last thing I wanted to be was to be gentle. His blood was like a drug, one that drove my senses into a mad frenzy. I sucked on him, unable to get enough of the delicious liquid into my mouth. Despite how cool the black blood was, it made my entire body hot and feverish.

I needed more, *more.*

I began to writhe against him, grinding up against the erection contained in his jeans.

"Red, ease up, babe..." Corry groaned in half pleasure, half pain.

I did not ease up, though. I didn't know how. I didn't want to. I could hear his words, but it was like my brain was holding all messages until I'd gotten what I needed.

"*Ruby!*" Corry's hand against my head turned mean. He snatched a fist onto a thick lock of my hair and yanked my head away from him, jerking me off his neck. I snarled at him, blood streaming down my mouth and dripping onto my breasts.

Both our chests were heaving. He looked pissed but even more turned on if that was even a thing. Thomas Knight's progeny were teaching me that yes, being horny and filled with rage were very normal things around the vampire royalty.

Corry's lips parted, revealing dazzling fangs that dripped with his own saliva. "My turn."

His fingers clamped down tight on my arm, and he wrenched me off the bike. He pressed my back against the gas pump, grabbed hold of one of my legs, and propped it up on the bike with the other planted on the ground.

Then he fell to his knees and ripped the rest of my dress down the middle. My cry of shock was replaced with a swollen whimper as the youngblood trailed his tongue and teeth from my knee up to my inner thigh.

By the stroke of his tongue and the predatorial glint in his eye, I had a feeling Corry Cross was going to do much more to my body than bite me.

Chapter Twenty-Six

FANGS IN THE THIGH, KNIFE IN THE BACK

I twitched against Corry's mouth, my heart thundering hard in my chest when his tongue paused at the base of my leg, mere inches from my core.

He looked up at me, and my panties damn near melted seeing him on his knees, his red eyes framed by his brunette hair that had come undone from the gel in the rain. Inky blood soaked the color of his shirt, but the puncture wounds where I'd bitten him had already healed. He held eye contact as his tongue dragged over the flesh of my inner thigh. His lips curved up in a devious grin when my breathing turned sharp.

"There is a major artery here. I've always wanted to try feeding from here."

"Is it going to leave a scar?" I asked on a shaky whisper.

He frowned. "Only mating marks leave scars. But fuck, I wish I could mark you. Any time you'd take a lover, they'd see that I was here first."

Without any further warning, he sunk his fangs into my thigh, and I slapped a hand over my mouth to cover my scream.

This should have felt wrong. Here I was, leaning against a gas pump, standing in nothing but a bra and panties, with a guy's jacket on, the shredded off remains of my dress at my feet and a vampire buried between my legs. Not to mention the headless prick who still lay beyond the ring of light we stood under, the mess I'd created shrouded by the night and the downpour of rain.

But it didn't feel wrong. It felt...*good*. I hated just how good, in fact. It's just like how I killed Malachite without really thinking. Like my instincts were in the driver's seat, not me. Now with Corry, my instincts were still the ones in charge, making my core grow hot and wet with need.

Sensing my hunger, Corry's hands gripped my thighs so hard I knew he'd leave bruises. As his lips suckled at my flesh, he grazed his knuckles over my sex, which was still wrapped in lace. My knees began to wobble, and I leaned against the gas pump for support as he pushed the crotch of the panties to the side and slid a finger through my arousal.

"*Christ,*" I muttered, dazed and drunk from the sensation.

Corry unlatched from my thigh and glanced up at me, his jaw ticked, his lips dripping. "He's not here. Try again." Then he sunk a finger inside me, so slowly it was torture.

"Fuck, *Corry!*" I panted, clenching around him as he pushed inside all the way up to his knuckle.

"That's better," he crooned through a bloodied grin as he stroked me from the inside like it was a carnal praise.

The pleasure of his body inside mine was mind-blowing. How could a single finger bring me to the edge of complete bliss?

The walls of my sex clamped down onto the invading digit, shuddering for more. Almost like he could read my damn mind, he pushed a second finger into me. My core was dripping, making it easy for him to slip in and out as he pushed me higher and higher toward something incredible. I'd touched myself before, but it was never like this, not anywhere in the same universe.

"More," I groaned.

A heated grin jerked the corners of his mouth. "I could give you so much more." He withdrew his fingers and licked my arousal clean from them.

I didn't need to be good at puzzles to sort out what he meant. One of his hands was still hooked into my panties, keeping them pulled to the side, but his other dropped to grip his erection from the outside of his jeans.

He'd said he wouldn't take my virginity, and I knew if I turned him down, he'd drop the idea. But damn, I wanted him to take me. After tonight, I'd never see him again. I wanted it to be him.

"You won't be marking me as your mate or whatever?"

"Only if I bite you again while I'm inside you, Red."

"How do I know you won't?"

His gaze softened, and some of the blue even returned to his eyes. Even before he reassured me, I knew he wouldn't. Not if I didn't want him to. "I don't think it would be so bad for you to carry my mark. It could ward off other males, weak ones anyway. But I made a promise, not only to you but to my brothers. Only the king gets to claim you. And since you plan on running off, well, it won't be my right either way."

I gave a thick swallow and nodded. "Alright."

He canted his head, his stupidly sexy smile, complete with his dimple, stretched wide. "Alright, as in...?"

My eyelids fluttered shut, heavy and delirious, with the swell of lust taking over me. "As in, I want you to fuck me, Youngblood."

I shivered in euphoria as his lips planted a kiss to where he'd bitten me, and he pushed my panties back into place. "Music to my ears, babe."

He pushed to his feet and pulled me in for a soul-consuming kiss that demanded my attention. Then he guided me back to the bike and bent me over it. I peered over my shoulder to watch him as he examined me for a second. He pushed my stance wide with his feet, his hands caressing the backs of my thighs then curving over my ass.

My belly tingled, the muscles in my thighs clenched, and my spine arched. A thick growl rattled from my chest, and Corry returned it with one of his own.

"*Fuuuck*, if you could only see you right now, Ruby. You look so goddamn gorgeous bent over my bike, ready to take me. And your scent is so goddamn good. Like your body is begging me to take you."

I wiggled my hips, grinding into him. His cock throbbed against me, and an animalistic growl grew deeper, guttural. My skin prickled as he arched over me, pressing me into the leather seat of the Ninja, making my heart pound hard against the bike.

"Ready?" he gritted into my ear, his fingers slipping back into my panties.

I opened my mouth to give him my answer, but bright headlights from the road brought everything to a screeching halt.

My mind blanked out like it didn't know what to do. Run? Stay here and let the car drive past and hope they didn't notice? It's not like anyone would notice the headless corpse unless they turned into the gas station.

My heart damn near dropped to my ankles when that's exactly what they did. The car pulled into the parking lot, the lights blinding me. I straightened, pulling the jacket tight over my body in an attempt to cover myself.

Oh, God. Corry couldn't mesmerize people. We were going to go to jail for murder. Or he would just be compelled to kill them for what they were about to witness. Corry swore under his breath. "Shit, I didn't think he'd get here this fast."

I blinked, trying to understand what was going on here. The car came to a halt, and the door opened, the figure of a man stepping out.

I couldn't see him through the downpour of rain combined with the bright headlights shining right in our eyes, but the voice that called out to us turned the freezing fear in my veins to molten rage.

"Get in the fucking car, Princess."

Chapter Twenty-Seven

GOOD LITTLE MONSTER

"You fucking bastard!" I lunged at Corry, tears of rage stinging my eyes like acid. But Vincent was already between us, his dark hair plastered down from the rain and his white shirt clinging to his heaving chest.

"Knock it off," he ordered, his booming snarl oozing with authority. His dark glare flickered between us and settled on me through the rain. "Your instincts have been awakened tonight, Princess. They're out of whack. If I let you near Corry right now he might just end up like that poor bastard," he nodded toward Mal's headless body.

"Fucking good!" I seethed, fists balling at my sides. "He lied to me. We had a deal and he stabbed me in the back!"

Corry stood behind his brother with his hands in his pockets, unflinching. "That's right. Your body for my bike. You held up your end and I plan on holding up mine. You can have it. Just don't expect to be allowed to leave coven grounds with it anytime soon."

I stared at Corry over the larger vampire's shoulder in disbelief. "Unbelievable. You used me."

The youngblood's chest heaved with a sigh, his expression stony. He didn't look like he was getting any pleasure from the play he'd made. But what pissed me off the most was that he refused to look me in the eye. "Doesn't feel so good on the receiving end of it, does it?"

A cruel fist squeezed my heart, the pain of it making the tears flow steadily. "I'm sorry I ruined your damn pride, Corry. But this is my freedom on the line."

He finally met my gaze. The pain I saw in his blue eyes made my stomach heave with guilt. "You're right. This is about your life. And I saved it. I can't believe you still wanted to leave after those two thugs from the Boston Coven tried to rape and murder you. Wake the fuck up, Ruby. Did you think they'd just forget about who and what you are after you left us? There is a traitor in our midst. Now you're going to need to stay closer to us than ever."

I hated to admit it, but he was right. Corry had only played my own damn card against me, and he'd done it to stop me from running off and getting captured by more of the Boston Coven later down the line. Who was to say Allister wouldn't have turned right around and finished what he and Malachite had started? I almost felt dumb not considering how the other vampire covens were going to take the news of a half-human ruling them. Especially the vampires that weren't in alliance with the Cape Cod Coven. It was doubtful that they'd just forget about me even if I did run away. But I wouldn't apologize for fighting for my freedom.

I wasn't sure if it was the adrenaline leaving my body, lack of sleep, blood loss, or a combination of everything, but my vision began to blur and my head started to spin. My knees buckled, and the concrete—stained black with Mal's blood—rushed to meet me. But instead of hard ground, strong arms caught me.

My head lolled back and Vincent came into focus as he peered down at me with something almost akin to worry banked in his eyes. He scooped me up in his arms, carried me over to his car, and ripped open the back door to lay me across the backseat. Even though I could barely focus, I could feel his eyes scrape over my nearly-naked body. All I wore were panties, a bra, and Corry's jacket.

"What the fuck," Vincent hissed under his breath. I twitched as I felt his fingertips ghost over where Corry had bitten me on the inside of my thigh. "You tapped into her femoral artery." His voice shook with anger, which was a stark contrast to the way his fingers grazed over the puncture marks. It was the most gentle he'd ever touched me.

"So what?" Corry's voice muttered behind him.

"You could have killed her!"

"She drank me and that other vampire, I thought that would have been enough to replace what I was taking."

"There was no way you could have known how much she took. You shouldn't have bit her at all. You don't have enough control. I shouldn't have let you leave with her in the first place."

"So why did you?"

"So she'd have a chance of escaping us."

"Yeah well look what's happened. There's a rat in the Elders, bro. Someone who's slipping the Boston Coven intel. They knew that master offed himself."

Vincent let out a rattling growl that made my skin erupt with goosebumps. "That explains how they knew about our little princess here. No surprise they aren't fans of a half-blood taking over the throne. What were the Elders fucking thinking."

"We can't let her go now, Vin. They'll kill her the first chance they get."

"Or worse," Vincent's voice turned lethal. "They keep her alive and use her as a way to get support from the other covens to elect a king from their own coven."

My heart fell when I felt Vincent step away, his warmth leaving me as he instructed his brother to help get the Boston Coven member into the trunk. Angling my head, I could barely make out the princes picking up the headless Malachite and a second later the Rolls-Royce shook from the weight of the body being thrown in.

I listened as Vincent gave instructions to his brother, his words now completely cloaked by the rain. A second later the car jostled again with the trunk slamming shut and several moments later the rev of Corry's motorcycle started and he coasted away. Feeling Vincent's imposing presence press in around me, I peeled my eyes open to see him looming over me. Despite my brain fog, I could make out Vincent's eyes as they analyzed me. I probably looked like complete shit, soaking, covered in crusted blood, half-naked. But there was no disgust in his olive-colored gaze. Only concern.

"You've lost a lot of blood, Princess." The softness of his tone caught me by surprise.

"What do you care?" I spat, my tongue thick like cotton.

His eyes narrowed but the cadence of his voice remained silk-soft. "I'm here, aren't I?" That was probably the closest he could come to saying 'I care.'

His fingers brushed over my hip and I jerked under his touch. It was like he was made of fire, and my body was pure ice. My teeth began to chatter. "W-why am I s-so cold?"

"The Youngblood took more of your blood than he should of. Everything else you've been through tonight probably isn't helping. Your body is spent. You need blood and you need it now."

He disappeared from my vision for a moment and on the next breath, the car purred to life and the heaters from the car turned on.

When he returned, I felt his arms wrap around me and lift me out of the car. "Wrap your arms around me," he urged. I did as he asked, banding my arms around his neck. Cradling me close to his chest, he got in the back seat and held me on his lap, closing the door after us. My breath began to rush out in sharp, unease exhales as I watched him arrange my legs so that I was straddling him with chest pressed to his.

"W-what are you doing?" I asked as his hands came up to peel off Corry's jacket.

"You're still shivering. This thing is soaked. You'll warm up faster without all this wet clothing." He paused, waiting for my permission to remove it. I gave him a shaky nod, wondering if he could feel the rapid hammer of my heart slamming against my rib cage as he slid the garment from my body, leaving me in just a bra and panties. Tossing the jacket to the floor of the car, he moved to remove his own soaking-wet t-shirt and my breath caught in my throat when I took in the glory that was his bare chest. I'd seen him in only pants before, on the poster. But it didn't do the real thing justice.

At a closer look, even I could tell the raven tattoos that littered his throat and torso were more than just pretty ink. There was something dark about them, almost like they had an aura of their own. I reached out, grazing my fingertips over the largest tattoo that covered the majority of his right pectoral. His muscles unwound beneath my touch and I felt him relax against me. I hadn't realized just how damn freezing I was until his warmth wrapped around me like a blanket and I eased into him, my delirious fog helping me push away all other opinions of him for the time being.

"Why are you so hot? You're like a damn heater. I thought vampires were supposed to be cold. You're dead."

"I'm more alive than you think, princess." The vampire's hands gently touched my back, tracing the curves of my shoulder blades. "Now, you know how to drop your fangs?"

I gave a weak nod.

"Good." He angled his head to the side, exposing the most delicious, mouth-watering stretch of his throat to me. His neck was the most masculine, erotic thing I had ever seen. But maybe that was just my monstrous hunger talking.

He was all sharp edges, hard muscles, and white ivory flesh wrapped up in dark ink of the ravens that stretched from his neckline up to his stubble-covered jawline. Tendons twitched and his Adam's apple bobbed as he watched my reaction to him offering himself up to me.

"Y-you can't be serious."

"Oh yeah, because I'm such a fucking joker," he muttered on a grated chuckle. "Be a good little monster and feed on me. You need blood and mine is much stronger than Corry's. It's special."

I blinked at him, my gaze affixed to his throat. "Special how?"

"Try it and you will find out for yourself, princess."

CHAPTER TWENTY-EIGHT
APHRODISIAC

There was nothing I wanted more than to sink my fangs into Vincent. My fangs ached and an embarrassing, animalistic growl slithered up my throat. But all shame erupted into lust when the vampire's own hunger hardened beneath me, his breathing growing sharp and fragmented.

My body must have been craving what he offered because my senses were hyper-aware of his presence. From the way he felt beneath me to how fucking good he smelled. His scent was the ocean air just before a storm, salty and charged with electricity. And underneath that, there was a hint of something lush and sinful.

His hands skimmed up my back, reverent and kind. They felt like someone else's hands.

Maybe Vincent Feral had been possessed or something. Maybe I was just delusional from all the blood loss. Because this was not the asshole I'd come to know over the last two days. Whatever it was, I was completely transfixed by this new side of the vampire prince.

He threaded his fingers through my hair, playing with the strands gently. I closed my eyes and leaned into his touch. "Wow, you're really eager for me to bite you. Your blood filled with poison or something?"

He planted a series of gentle kisses over my collar bone, his lips curling into a grin against my skin. "If I wanted to kill you, do you really think that's how I'd do it?"

It was almost disturbing how reassuring that was.

"You're right. Poison isn't your style. You'd probably just strangle me while you drained me dry of every drop of blood I have."

His cock twitched beneath me and I squeezed my eyes shut as a shaky exhale left my body. "You're fucking demented. You know that?"

His brows arched. "You know I wouldn't intentionally hurt you?"

My voice came out in a hoarse whisper. "Do I know that?"

He sat back, his hand hovering over my skin but not quite touching me as he caressed the curve of my throat. My pulse burst into a gallop when his fingers gently clamped down on my throat like a collar.

"Don't play that game with me." His voice dropped, low and dangerous.

It swept over me, making my belly pool with need. "W-what game?"

His lips peeled back into a cocky grin. "Pretending you don't ache for the way I touch you."

"And how do you touch me?"

"Like you're not something easily broken."

I sat back on the vampire's lap, taking a long look at him without any of his shields erected. This gentle, attentive side he was allowing me to see was something so out of character for him, I was left questioning the true depths of my delirium. Because right now, all I wanted to do was please him.

"Show me your fangs," he crooned.

"Are you mesmerizing me?" I whispered as I sat back to bare my fangs for him.

His chest rumbled with a dark chuckle. "That trick only works on full-blooded humans. You're obeying me because your body is eager to please me. And why wouldn't it?" His voice was as soft as silk and as dark as a witch's curse all at once. He reached to brush the pad of his thumb over my fang and pulled back so I could examine it, a thick drop of inky blood streaking down his skin. "I have what it needs."

The sultry invitation combined with the intoxicating scent of him was too much to ignore. I latched onto him, drinking like I'd been stranded in the desert for two weeks. And that's exactly how his blood hit my tongue. It was the most refreshing thing I'd ever had the pleasure of tasting.

His head leaned against the chair, his jaw going rigid in an erotic expression that made me suck harder on his digit.

Vincent Feral was the perfect blend of brutality and beauty. Exotically masculine. His muscles clenching tight, tendons going taut in his neck, nostrils flaring as I took what he offered.

Holy. Shit.

Corry's blood had been sweet like candy but Vincent's was rich and decadent.

It was almost obscene how good he tasted. I wasn't an expert, hell, I barely knew what I was doing when it came to pretty much anything. But I knew by the first drop of Vincent's blood in my mouth that Corry's inkling had been right.

Vincent Feral wasn't like the others.

He tasted dark, forbidden.

His rich flavor was almost otherworldly.

It was like he'd never been human to begin with.

I'd never done drugs, apart from whatever was in those suppressant pills Dr. Sharpe gave me. But Vincent's blood was like how narcotics were always portrayed in books and movies, completely and utterly addicting.

A swell of renewed energy filled my whole body, the pain and lightheadedness evaporating in an instant. I almost felt like a different person, like I could run forever, like I could fight a million men and win.

Then there was a new sensation.

My skin flushed, pebbled of perspiration peppering my brow as a flood of heat settled low in my belly, inspiring a new kind of ache.

The fucker had given me a damn aphrodisiac.

Corry had mentioned the slightly differing effects of drinking vampire blood over human blood. One sated blood lust and the other inspired carnal lust.

They had warned me that vampires drinking from other vampires was an intimate affair, usually reserved for mated couples.

With the way Vincent's eyes shone bright with hunger through the dark of the car, there was no doubt he wanted me to take more than his blood.

I bit down hard on his palm, enjoying the way he hissed through clenched teeth as he watched me take more of him into my mouth.

"Your lips look so goddamn good painted in my blood."

I rocked in his lap, rubbing my pelvis into his and I chuckled into his palm when his head dropped back on his shoulders and bit his lip to hold back a guttural grunt.

"Fucking hell," he muttered, his hands slipping down to grip my thighs over the bruises Corry had left. "I want you so damn bad, Ruby. I want you so damn bad it fucking scares me."

His words sunk straight through my core, turning my insides molten.

Hearing my first name in his mouth was more erotic than any dirty line he could have come up with, and I was sure a virile male like him could fill a whole book with panty-dropping filth.

Seconds ago I'd been so damn cold but with the combination of the heaters, Vincent's blood coursing through my veins, and his bare chest pressed against me, sweat dribbled down my back.

The windows were beginning to fog and all I wanted to do was fuck this vampire. Maybe then I could kick the stupid crush my vagina had for Vincent fucking Feral.

Watching him react to me like this was probably going to become a very annoying addiction of mine. I didn't want to like him. He was a grade-A prick. He didn't care about me, not really. This nice-guy act was probably just a play for the throne, it had to be. It was just like he said earlier. He was giving me one last chance at escape and if it failed, we were playing the game.

And he was playing to win.

Earlier impressions had led me to believe that his method of winning the crown was to bully me into submission. But that wasn't his plan at all.

The bastard was straight up seducing me.

CHAPTER TWENTY-NINE
HIS BIDDING

"I know what you're doing." My voice was fraught with something that scared me to my damn core. It was tiny, tremulous, and bore a shred of hope. Vincent was showing me a side of himself I'd yet to see, a side that showed me there were more layers beneath the douche bag act.

But for all I knew, it was just an act to get me to lower my defenses.

"Taking care of my girl," he replied, his cadence sinfully soft as he watched me through lust-filled eyes.

I ran my tongue along the crease of his palm, earning another whine as I bit down on him again. "I'm not your girl, Feral."

His lips tugged into a sultry grin that oozed sex and arrogance. "Maybe not yet."

Canting his head, his attention centered on my mouth and my lips softened under the heat of his smoldering gaze. It was as if he was completely taken with my mouth, like he was moved by the sight of his blood dribbling down my chin. I watched, completely transfixed as he sucked his bottom lip between his teeth and bit down. An inky bead leaked from the fresh wound and then he whispered his next words so low, I barely heard them. "Your turn."

My eyes widened. He was referring to when he'd stolen that kiss from me in the pharmacy restroom, all for a taste of my blood. Before I could convince myself that this was a bad idea, I brought my lips down over his in a bruising kiss that left us both gasping for air. The first thing I tasted on his skin was something faintly feminine, like clementine oranges. Then it dawned on me, it was that other woman I was tasting.

Lexi.

The thought of him kissing her in front of me, and pushing into her room while he knew I was watching made my whole body throb with anger. So I bit down on his lips —hard—and devoured his pain-laced moan.

"Fuck, *Ruby.*" There it was again. My name, spoken like it was the most sinful thing he'd ever dared utter. I couldn't take it anymore. As much as this vampire rubbed me the wrong way, I wanted him to the point of pain. And his blood inside me only added fuel to the fire. I was bursting with hunger, to the point where it would tear me to shreds if I didn't sate this monstrous lust inside me.

"Touch me," I demanded.

He smirked. "You're going to have to ask me nicer than that."

"Touch me, please?"

He shook his head, his whole body rumbling with his mean laughter, which only made me rock harder against him, desperate for more friction. "You can do better than that, princess. Beg me."

Swallowing down the last fragments of my pride, I cast my eyes down and did as he asked. "Please, touch me. I want to be touched so bad it fucking hurts. Please, Vincent. *Please.*"

He purred his approval in the form of a grating chuckle that slid right through my body down to the place where I wanted him most. His hands came up to cup my breasts over my bra and he gave my nipples a pinch through the thin padding.

A soft cry tumbled from me and he came forward to consume the sound, his mouth crushing against mine in a savage kiss that touched every damn nerve in my body.

His hands slipped around my waist, and curved around my ass cheeks, slipping inside the black lace of my panties. His fingertips dug deep into my skin, squeezing out a pained mewl that leaked from my mouth into his. He pressed me down deeper into his groin, moving my hips so that my sex stroked his shaft straining through his pants.

"You feel that? I don't just hunger for your blood, Ruby Renada. I want it all. Your blood, your tears, your cum. And this is my oath to you. Before the vampire crown hits your head I will own every goddamn drop of you. You fucking understand me?"

I don't know what compelled me to nod. It had to be the way he spoke in that gravely baritone, how it commanded my body like it was a voice-activated toy that had been specifically manufactured for him.

"Good girl," he purred.

God damn my soul. This beautiful monster was working me into knots. I couldn't stand it any longer. I needed him inside me.

Unable to reign back my desire a second longer, I scooted back on Vincent's lap and went straight for his belt.

He caught my wrist, and his lips stretched into a mean grin that made my heart wither. "Did I say you could have that?"

"*What?*" I gasped, squirming against him. "I did what you asked. Didn't I beg hard enough? You want me to get on my damn knees?"

His eyes gleamed. "That's a pretty thought. But no. All I want is for you to say that you're mine. Say you choose me as your mate and king and I swear on the grave of my master that I will fuck you so hard you'll never forget the sensation of me, marking you as mine from the inside out."

I ripped my wrist out of his hold with a sneer of disgust. I *knew* it. This was just a move for the throne. "I'm not playing that game with you, Feral. I'm not so desperate for your cock that I'm willing to saddle myself with you for all eternity to get it."

He moved so fast, his hand was off my ass and in my hair before the words had barely left my mouth. He wrenched my head back and I choked out a miserable whimper as he craned my head so that my throat was exposed to him.

Leaning into me, he brought his face so close that I could feel his breath tickle my flesh, red eyes leering at me with an intense mix of lust and contempt.

"You ever think that maybe this is beyond us? Of course not. Because you're just a sheltered little brat. Who gives a shit if you hate me? This isn't about who you like best. It's about who will make a good king."

"I would pick Corry a million times before you, asshole."

He snorted. "You owe Corry an apology for acting like you did after he saved your hide. But you aren't so stupid to think he'd make a fit ruler. Just like you, he's too young and naive."

"Sterling then."

"Sterling doesn't want to be king. And before you go making me more pissed, don't even dare suggest Eros. You wouldn't survive one night in his bed, let alone an eternity by his side as his mate."

"So that's your angle? You're the least shitty option?"

"My angle is that I am brutal, I am ruthless, I was forged by your father, out of cruelty and malice and I stand before you as an unbreakable force, a formidable king."

"Shouldn't a king be soft, merciful?"

"Not one that sits on the throne of vampires." He released my hair and his touch suddenly turned gentle as his knuckles grazed over my hip. "Those things will be reserved for my mate when I take her into our bed."

He was playing mind games with me. He had to be, this side of himself he was showing me had to be fake. Just a ploy to get the throne. Not that I blamed him. Claiming the throne was important to him. But from the little I gathered of my father, would he really be that different of a ruler? He wanted it so damn bad, he was willing to do anything it took. Seducing me and break my heart being the least of it.

Hell, for all I knew, he'd wanted the throne so bad he'd murdered my father and staged it to look like a suicide.

That would explain why he'd been outraged when the Elders had decided to honor my father's long-time wishes of making me queen. Now I was his only way to the throne, it was in his best interest to keep me safe. Especially now that there was a risk of that enemy coven capturing me and using me to show that the Cape Cod Coven is weak and not meant to be in charge. He wanted me to be his figurehead. The pretty little queen sat alongside him. Alongside Vincent Feral, I'd been a queen only in the sense that I'd carry a title. All I'd really be was his plaything. And even though that idea held much appeal with my hormones, it would be insane to actually give into those dark, fucked up desires.

"I want to go home."

"Home?" His brows arched. "Does that mean you're not going to try to run away again?"

"No. It would be stupid if I did. I get that now."

The thing was, I felt it was also stupid to stay. Hell, for all I knew the vampires in the Cape Cod Coven were even more dangerous than the vampires outside it. The only thing I had going for me was that I would eventually be the head bitch of the whole place if I played my cards right. The difficult part would be surviving these princes for four months. The beginnings of a plan were starting to sprout in my mind and we rode back the whole way home in silence as I picked at the details.

CHAPTER THIRTY
A STUPID IDEA

Vincent pulled his Rolls-Royce into the hanger filled with the coven's eclectic collection of cars, and my throat constricted when my attention landed on Corry's Ninja—which was now mine I guess.

For all the good it'd do me now.

Vincent cut the engine and watched me with an indiscernible expression as I glared at the motorcycle with crossed arms. "You know, that's his favorite bike. He doesn't let anyone else touch it."

"So?"

"So, out of the three he has, he wanted to take you out on the one he's most proud of. The one no one else gets to touch."

I didn't bother with asking what his point was. He wanted me to apologize to Corry, and admittedly I owed him one. Unlike prince douche-bag here, the youngblood genuinely liked me. Even though he'd used my desperation to escape as a means to mess around with me, he lied and double-crossed me to prevent me from leaving. Not out of selfishness, but because he wanted to keep me safe.

"Yeah, so I was a bit selfish and short-sighted. I'll apologize to Corry."

"Good," the vampire grunted, unfastening his seatbelt to jab a finger out the window. "Because he's right there."

I got out of the car to see Corry leaning against the hanger door with his hands shoved in his pockets. I couldn't make out the details of his expression, with his back turned toward the moon he was wrapped in shadows.

"Finally," he gritted. He tilted his head back, his nose in the air as his chest swelled with an inhale. "Surprised she's still got her V-card by how damn long you took, bro."

"I was too busy fixing your mess, dickhead," Vincent ground out on an irritated growl as he stepped out of the car. "You nearly drained her dry. And with your blood in her body, you could have turned her."

"I made her feed from me first on purpose. It would have been the other way around for the change, right?"

"The fact that you don't know for sure means you shouldn't have fed from one another in the first place."

Grabbing Corry's jacket from the car, I shrugged it on with a shudder, hating how it was cold and crusted with blood. But it was better than standing in my skivvies. "Hey, I got a great idea. First, can we stop talking about smelling my virginity, please? I don't care if you've got drug-dog noses. It's creepy, not to mention that it's none of your business."

"Whatever," Corry muttered. He pulled his hand out of his pocket, tossed me the keys to the Ninja, and turned to leave. "Sterling is waiting for us in the council chamber, bro. I told him about the mole in the Elders."

"I'll be right there."

Corry slipped out of the hanger, leaving a heaviness in the air that made it difficult to breathe. I wanted to apologize but he clearly needed more time to cool off.

Glancing down at the keys in my hand, I frowned.

"I don't get it. Why did he give me these if I'm still on lockdown?"

"Because the Knight heirs make good on their promises, Princess. And you're not on lockdown now that you know how dangerous it is off coven property. If you want to leave and be the Boston Coven's new whore, that's your prerogative."

Vincent locked the car and strode toward the exit but I grabbed his arm, stopping him. He swung his gaze on me, his green eyes glittering with irritation. "What?"

"Uh, are we just going to leave Malachite in the trunk?"

"Deathwish will take care of it when he gets back."

"And when is that going to be exactly?"

His expression turned sour and he ripped his arm away from me, furious at the mention of Eros. "Why do you care?"

"Well if he's a suitor shouldn't I meet him?"

Vincent said nothing, violence and hatred hanging over his head like a storm cloud.

"Ha, wow. Jealousy is almost cute on you, Feral."

When I was met with another scathing glare I shrugged. "Fine, don't tell me. At least I know I'll see him next week at your match."

He folded his thick arms over his chest, a vein ticking in his jaw. "You're not going to that."

"Psh. Like hell I'm not. You'd have to chain me to my bed to keep me from missing that."

The corners of his mouth twisted into a wolfish sneer. "Don't fucking tempt me, princess."

Leaning against the side of the car, I folded my arms over my chest and slid him a smoldering smirk.

"So why do you hate him so much? Corry said you guys used to fight back when you were both alive?"

"Why don't you go ask Corry, since he's such a damn loudmouth."

"What if what I really want to know, you're keeping from him as well? In fact, I think you're keeping it from all your brothers."

I was venturing into dangerous territory here seeing as I was getting at my dad's suicide. Which had to be a cover-up. Because evil, power-grabbing, torture-happy vampire kings didn't take their own lives.

Vincent's brows twisted with anger and his knuckles flexed as he spun to face me. "What are you talking about? I don't keep anything from my brothers."

"So what you're telling me is that they know Thomas Knight's suicide was staged?"

For several intense seconds, a barbed silence settled between us. Feral looked like he was about to go bat-shit on me. Yup, I was definitely crazy for poking the bear. But hey, getting a rise out of him was so far my best way at getting some answers.

"I don't know what the fuck you're insinuating, but your father killed himself by drinking liquid silver. That's knowledge that only his progeny and the Elders were supposed to be privy to. Now that it's gotten out to the Boston Coven, we know there is a traitor in our midst."

"But that's not really how he died, is it?"

There was, so far, no hard evidence pointing to the fact that my dad's suicide had been staged. All I had was my gut instincts and the fact that no one loathed my father more than Vincent Feral, who also happened to have the world's biggest hard-on for the throne.

To me, it was a no-brainer.

The vampire strode toward me with terrifying purpose in his steps, easily eating up the distance between us. He was still shirtless, muscles shifting beneath raven-tattooed skin, a lethal miasma of fury oozing off of him like a damn gas leak. He slapped his hands down on the car, caging me between his arms as he loomed over me.

"You want to tell me what you're getting at?"

I swallowed. "I think you know what I'm getting at."

"I warn you—"

"What are you gonna do? Kill me, like you killed him?"

To my shock, the vampire's expression remained completely stony. If I had guessed right, there was nothing etched in the grooves of his face, not a twitch or a flicker in his eyes that would betray the fact.

He reached to brush a knuckle over my cheek, the gentle gesture turned menacing by the poison lacing his tone. "Sweet little princess, you think I killed your daddy? I fucking wish. Progeny can't kill their masters. It's impossible. There was no one stronger than him that could have forced him to drink that silver. It would have had to have been his own will."

I jutted my chin out, glaring. "Even so. My father wasn't the type to kill himself."

"You don't know shit about your father."

"I know that you're more like him than you care to admit. And I know you would rather be ripped off the throne by a pack of wolves than surrender it by drinking silver. You think I'm so damn naive. That may be true, but I'm not a total dunce. You have to know, I don't care. Who gives a shit if you murdered him? He was an evil asshole. You probably did a lot of people a lot of favors." I reached out to touch his chest, hoping to ease the tension between us but he shoved me away with a snarl.

"Keep your fucking hands off me. You have no idea the world of shit that's going to come down on you if you keep digging into my past. If you insist on playing Nancy Drew, help us figure out who the mole is."

He stormed away and turned to look over his shoulder at the hanger door. "The sun will be up soon. Go upstairs, clean yourself up, and go to sleep."

"No way! I'm going to your meeting. I deserve to be there."

His gaze raked down my body, hot and leering at me like I was something to eat. "Dressed like that? Are you coming as one of the Knight heirs or as a snack?"

"Let's get one thing straight asshole, I can be naked, wearing a potato sack, or a damn inflatable t-rex costume. I deserve to be at your little 'bro' meeting. I'm going to be your queen, aren't I? If you want me to be your mate on top of that you'll start thinking long and hard about what you tell me what I can and can't do. Now I'm going up to take a shower and find a change of clothes. Don't start the meeting without me."

I moved to march past him but he caught my arm and jerked me toward him. "Or what? What are you gonna fucking do?"

I held my head high, meeting his dagger-sharp glare with one of my own. "Oh, who knows?" I leaned against him as if I was flirting, and ran a teasing finger down his chest.

"There are so many ways I can piss you off. Maybe I'll form a 'We Hate Vincent Feral' club with Eros. We'll bond over how much we both hate your guts. Or maybe I'll just tell all your brothers that I think you're lying to them about their master's death. I don't think they'll blame you but they deserve to know."

His gaze turned dark as death, a thin ring of red bordering his blown up irises. He looked absolutely terrifying but I refused to flinch. "You're playing with fire, little girl."

"I'm not afraid of a few burns."

"The way you're heading, you'll be going down in flames."

I patted his chest, flashing him a coy grin. "Then you're going down with me, big guy."

With that I shoved past him and made my way toward the mansion, feeling his smoldering glare hot on my back.

Okay, so even I had to admit I had just done something incredibly stupid. My new obsession with riling up the most tightly wound of the Knight princes was *probably* going to get me killed.

But the plan that I'd hatched in the car was the first step in protecting me not only against Vincent but against the Boston Coven to boot.

In fact, I felt pretty damn confident taking on this whole queen thing if the plan worked.

All I had to do was convince Sterling that it was a good idea.

And that was going to be the hard part.

CHAPTER THIRTY-ONE
GIRL TALK

The eyes that watched me as I strode through the halls of the Knight Mansion were cold and mean.

Knowing that these vampires could probably scent Corry's and Vincent's blood inside me should have been unnerving. Instead, I felt powerful. Almost like it validated my decision to stop running, and accept my role as the half-blood princess.

Though, if Sterling agreed to my plan, I wouldn't be a half-blood for much longer.

Despite my lack of clothing, I held my head high as I ascended the grand staircase to my bedroom on the second floor.

Word had probably gotten out about their dead king's bastard daughter. Judging by their faces, I'm not sure what pissed them off more, the Elders' decision to slap me on the throne, or the fact that they were all probably told that they couldn't eat me.

When I got to the second floor, I was met with a frigid stare so chilling, there was no way there was a soul behind those eyes.

Lexi.

The beautiful vampiress with midnight black hair was leaning against her door, watching me with all the warmth of an avalanche intent on smothering me.

I forgot that her room was right next to mine. Joy. "Um, hi. You're Lexi, right?"

She sniffed, her unfriendly, pointed face etched with disgust as she took in my ensemble. "He ripped you out of your clothes? The barbarian." Her words chastised Vincent but the way she spoke, it was like it was somehow my fault.

"Um, no. We had a run-in with an enemy coven." I didn't bother specifying which one. I wasn't sure how much the princes would want her to know.

The skin around her eyes tightened as she glared at me, like an adult trying to glean a child's lie. "Right. Well, either way, you've had an eventful night."

"Um, yup." I stood there for a second, the atmosphere so awkward I began to inch away. "Anyway, I'm going to go get cleaned up—"

"So are you going to marry him?"

I froze in my tracks, gaping at her with naked astonishment. "What? Vincent?"

"Of course. That youngblood isn't even the same caliber as Prince Feral."

The way she said 'youngblood' you think it was some kind of dirty word. I frowned. "Um, I'm confused. Are you actually wanting me to marry Vincent? Aren't you two a thing?"

Lexi's lip curled at me like I was the most ignorant and insignificant person to ever grace her presence.

"This isn't about us. It's about who will make a fit king."

Barf. This Lexi chick had been spending too much time with Feral, that much was obvious. It was weird that she was angry that I was entertaining all my options before settling on Vincent, and even odder yet that she seemed okay with her boyfriend marrying another woman.

It made me uneasy. Like Lexi was tied up with Feral's plans on being king somehow. And that shit was unsettling as fuck.

I excused myself with a pointed 'goodnight' and hurried away to the sanctuary of my bedroom with Lexi's scrutiny stripping me down to the bone as I scuttled off.

After a satisfying but quick shower, I was standing in front of my armoire contemplating my limited options of outfits to wear to the meeting when someone knocked on my door.

Wrapped up in a towel, I cracked the door and cautiously peered out.

It was a woman I recognized immediately as the human that had fled from Vincent's room in a fit of tears earlier in the evening. I hadn't gotten a good look at her then, but I knew her right away from the scent of her blood.

Thanks to Corry's and Vincent's blood inside me, she didn't smell nearly as delicious as she had.

She was cute, with curly red hair pulled onto the top of her head in a loose bun and a smattering of freckles covering her fair cheeks and nose.

"Princess Ruby?" Her voice came out timid and unsure.

"Um, yeah?"

Her eyes widened. "So it's true. The king did have a human daughter."

I leaned against the door frame and folded my arms over my chest. "Half-human turns out. What's your name?"

"Mckenzie, but you can call me Kenzie if you want." She held up her hands, which were full of paper shopping bags. "Prince Sterling asked me to run to Boston and get you some things."

I opened the door and invited her inside but she stood where she was, her gaze flickering between me and the room. "Is it...safe? I'm not allowed to be alone with youngbloods."

My brows scrunched together in thought. "I'm not sure if I am a youngblood. I've been half-vampire all my life. But you don't have to worry about me, I just fed."

A look of relief washed over her face and she stepped inside, setting the bags down on my bed. My jaw fell open when I took in the massive haul of clothes. The only thing I knew about designer brands was what I saw from TV commercials. But even I recognized some of the labels. Dior, Chanel, Dolce & Gabbana.

For a girl who lived in sweats and sports bras, it might as well have been Christmas.

I started sifting through a couple of the bags, pulling out gorgeous tops, leggings, jeans, jewelry, lingerie. The crazy thing was, everything was exactly my style, or at least it was the style I'd always fantasized I'd have when I dreamed about life beyond my bedroom. Lots of short skirts, ripped denim, leather jackets. It was all black or red. My super religious mom never bought me stuff like this. For her, goth and punk fashion styles were for heathens and minions of the devil. Guess she was right.

"This is all for me?"

Kenzie nodded as she set to hanging up my new wardrobe in the armoire. "All yours! But not nearly enough for a princess. I'll make a second run soon. You can walk in the day, right? We'll go together! After all, we'll need to get you shoes since I had no idea what size you were. I thought I was gonna be able to tell how well I did guessing your style once I saw you but..." She took in my blood-crusted outfit-or what remained of it-but without any of the judgment that had been in Lexi's gaze.

I pulled out a leather jacket from one of the bags and had to stop myself from drooling. It was an Alexander McQueen biker jacket. It had a ruffled hem that fanned out at the waist, high in front and low in the back. It was perfectly feminine, and kick-ass at the same time.

Her face lit up when she saw how I looked at it. "You like that?" She held up my Ramones hoodie that I had left behind. "I saw this and I thought it would look cute paired with the jacket. I love this band too!"

Excluding Lexi, my mother, the cashier at the pharmacy, and a few randos at the roller-rink, this was the first girl I'd come face to face with that I actually wanted to be friends with. Having a girlfriend was yet another thing I'd never gotten to experience. Watching TV as I was growing up was hard. As I watched female friendships blossom over seasons, I was left with a painfully hollow loneliness. I'd been led to believe that the only connections I'd ever have were with the characters in my books and shows, and the pathetic relationship with my mother through my bedroom door. Nothing more.

It wasn't until Kenzie's hand was on my back, consoling me that I realized I was crying. "Hey, it's okay to cry. You probably haven't gotten a chance to do that yet. Not in front of..." Her voice was tight with anger. "Not in front of them. But you can cry in front of me if you want."

She guided me to sit on the bed, taking a seat next to me. I let her wrap her arms around me, consoling me with quiet shushes.

"I'm sorry for crying, I'm just..."

"Overwhelmed," she finished for me with an understanding bob of her head. "I can't even imagine what you've been through the last couple of nights. I don't know a lot about you but I do know you were kept in Quincy, and you weren't told anything about this life or who you were. It can't be easy, having your whole human life ripped away from you like that."

"My human life sucked, Kenzie. I'm glad I'm here... I think? Glad, but scared. I don't know what the fuck I'm doing."

Kenzie's hand dropped from my back and moved to her lap where she wrung her fingers nervously. "Can I tell you something?"

I nodded.

"When me and the other blood donors- the humans that work for the coven- heard about the Elders deciding you'd be crowned queen in four months, we were so happy."

"You were?"

"Heck yes. Having a queen on the throne who knows what it's like to be human is going to change the way vampires treat our kind."

My belly tightened with unease. The problem was, I didn't know what it was like to be human, not really. I wondered if her and the others who worked for the house would be so hopeful if they knew about my plan with Sterling.

I laid back on my bed, staring up at the swaths of the velvet canopy draped over the posts, and wrinkled my nose. "It's funny how every little girl dreams of being a princess and having a knight rescue them from their tower or whatever. But Vincent Feral ruined that fantasy for me." And ignited a few other, darker fantasies. But Kenzie didn't need to know about those.

At the mention of the prince, Kenzie's expression darkened. "You don't like him either?"

I snorted. "He's a total tool and a bully."

Kenzie shifted closer to me on the bed, the paper bags crunching under her knees as she studied me. "You're definitely not like the other female vampires here. All the women here go crazy for him. Heck, even some of the blood donors have tried to sleep with him during his feeding sessions."

"Ugh." I rolled my eyes. "Of course he'd sleep with his food."

"No, he always turns them down as far as I know. I think he only likes vampires."

Well, that's great, just another reason for him to hate me.

"How many other donors are there?"

"Three others."

"And you guys are here because...?"

Kenzie laughed. "We're not slaves if that's what you're asking. Some vampire dens have thralls but all covens under the Elders are required to have their humans on salary. Don't get me wrong, there is a crap ton of contracts we have to sign and the job can be pretty gritty, but we get compensated for it."

"And you're okay with them biting you?"

"Actually, most of them don't feed directly from the source. The coven paid for me to get my Phlebotomy license and I draw from the other donors and we put it in bags for them. Only a few of them feed on us directly."

My gaze dropped to the healing puncture wound where Vincent had bitten her earlier and her cheeks flushed when she noticed me staring.

"Did he hurt you?" I asked in a hoarse whisper.

She shook her head but I knew by the way she started to shake that she was lying. "I shouldn't be telling you this..." She rubbed the back of her skull with her hand, her eyes glued to the space of the bed between us. "But I heard about the Elders allowing you to pick the next king among the princes."

I sat up, suddenly intrigued by where this conversation was going. "Word gets around fast."

"Secrets are hard to keep here, so be careful who you trust."

I frowned at her. "What you're saying is, don't trust Prince Feral."

"I'm saying don't trust any of them." Her fingertips gently brushed over the place he bit her and her cheeks flamed. "Especially him."

"I'm figuring out pretty quickly all he cares about is the throne." Vincent had made it pretty clear from the beginning that all he cared about was becoming king. But there were little glimpses through the cracks of his douchebag act that suggested that maybe he did care about me. Maybe that was just another layer to the act he was trying to sell me.

"One thing I can't work out is that Lexi chick."

Kenzie's expression hardened as she rolled her eyes. "Oh, God. Her. She's a snake. Just because she's screwing one of the princes she walks around here like she's the freaking queen of the place."

"Which doesn't make any sense why she was pissed about me hanging out with Corry. She started talking up Vincent and how he'd make a good king. Like she wants me to take him as a mate."

"Well, once the king died everyone thought Vincent was going to get the throne. So Lexi was under the impression she was going to be queen. Now that you're in the way, she wants you to pick Vincent. Once he's crowned, who's to say he isn't going to toss you aside and take her as his queen?"

"Would the Elders allow him to do that?"

She shrugged. "He'd be king. The last one was capable of all sorts of evil shit. You think he'd be any different?"

Kenzie's words settled in my stomach like sediment at the bottom of a lake. I didn't want to believe that Vincent would so easily toss me aside for his vampire girlfriend, but why wouldn't he?

He never wanted me to begin with.

My fists clenched at my sides and I stood up and began to rifle through the clothes for an outfit. "That bastard. He thinks I'm a helpless idiot who can be easily manipulated. Two can play his fucking game."

"Wait, you're heading out again? The sun will be up in less than two hours."

"There is a meeting between the brothers downstairs. I'm going."

Something wicked flashed in her eyes and her lips quirked into a mischievous smile. "I have an idea. If you really want to get under Prince Feral's skin."

"What is it?"

She chewed her lip. "I'm not sure if you're going to like the idea... but it involves going down to the basement."

My brows pulled together in confusion. "What's in the basement?"

Her cheeks drained of all color, leaving her paperwhite. And her tone dropped to barely more than a whisper, as if she was afraid the vampires beyond my room would hear. "Deathwish's room."

Chapter Thirty-Two
A Death Wish

I t didn't surprise me one bit that Eros lived in the basement.

After everything I heard about the coven's most feared prince, whether the stories were overblown or not, it was just common sense to stay away from everything to do with him. But with a thrashing pulse, I ignored my human instincts blaring in the back of my brain, and agreed to Kenzie's plan. After all the horror stories revolving around Eros, curiosity would eat me alive if I didn't go.

And this was all to piss off Vincent, which was as good of a reason as any. I didn't want to believe that the only reason he'd shown that other side of himself to me tonight was all to gain my trust. Just so he could toss me aside and place Lexi on the throne after he was crowned king.

It had felt all too real. From the way he snapped when Corry had taken too much of my blood, to how he healed me. Not to mention how he touched me like I was his. And he held me like he'd fight the whole damn world to keep it that way.

I didn't trust his words, those were easy to warp. But could a touch lie?

Maybe Kenzie's plan was petty. It was just going to rile up the brutal prince. Not to mention what Eros would do when he found out I stole from him.

Sweat beaded on my brow and my breath came out in shaky patterns as I followed Kenzie down the creaky, narrow staircase leading down to the mansion's basement. The stairs were lit by a single naked light bulb that hung just over the door that stood before the last step, its brown paint peeling away and cobwebs dangling from the wooden ceiling beams. "This feels like a bad idea, Kenzie."

"Don't you want to see Feral flip out when he gets a load of you in Deathwish's hoodie?"

"Not if it's going to get us murdered! Isn't he going to scent us in his room?"

"He's not due back for another four or five days. The scent should fade by then."

"Are you sure this isn't some hazing thing you and the blood donors are in on? How do I know I'm not going to be beaten with socks filled with soap bars the second I walk in."

Her freckled nose crinkled as she fought back a laugh. "Maybe if this were TV but as a general rule, the humans in the household don't 'beat' the vampires. We generally like the whole living thing. I just want to help you get back at Feral. The face he's gonna make when he sees you in Deathwish's hoodie. It's one that they sold at his merch table at matches right after he broke Feral's winning streak. The image on the front is him smashing in his nose."

I blinked at the old door, imagining the horrors that could possibly lie beyond it. For all I knew, the place was booby-trapped.

"I'm not sure if the sweatshirt is worth it."

"Wearing that hoodie to the meeting will make Feral jealous. Hell, maybe if you can drive him and Deathwish to kill each other that would only leave Corry and Sterling to worry about."

"I can't decide if you're an evil genius or if you're insane and need to be fired."

Kenzie gave me a grim smile. "In my line of work, we don't get fired. We get put down. With you as queen, you have the power to change the way vampires view humans. I want to help you become queen, and we have to make sure we keep pricks like Deathwish and Feral off the throne. Because they won't be changing shit for us."

The redhead made a good point. Vincent needed to understand that I wasn't afraid of him or his wrath. More than that, I couldn't snuff my blazing curiosity pushing me to see what lie inside the room that knew Eros so intimately.

"Alright, ready?"

"Oh, I'm not going in with you."

"What?! But this was your idea!"

"Yeah but you're going to be queen. If we get caught you can't be eaten as punishment!"

I gave an indignant snort and reached for the doorknob. "Tell that to the princes. Go back upstairs then, I don't want you to get caught down here."

"Are you sure?" Kenzie asked, but I could already see the relief passing over her face so I nodded.

"Yeah. Don't worry, I'll be right up. I'll just grab the hoodie real quick and get out. Won't be more than a minute."

Wishing me luck, Kenzie made her way back upstairs. When she was out of sight, I turned toward the door and steeled my nerves before reaching for the handle.

The first thing that met me was complete and utter darkness. I used my cellphone to light up my immediate vicinity, the white light from the LCD screen illuminating the brick walls. Finding an ancient-looking light switch, I flipped it. There was an audible click as the light bulbs mounted in industrial steel sconces flicked on, washing the room in warm, yellow lighting.

For a second, I stood completely frozen. I'm not sure what I'd expected, but it wasn't this. Eros' room looked like a medieval dungeon that had been decorated by a modern twenties or thirties something guy. The floors were cobblestones, the walls were exposed brick, and thick wooden support beams ran down the length of the ceiling. This house had to have been built around the 17th century but somehow the basement looked even older. It smelt musty, with centuries worth of memories ingrained in the porous brick. And by some dark, mysterious stains on the walls, not all good memories.

Huge metal racks were pushed to the perimeter of the walls, displaying dozens of crude weapons. By the rusty metal, they had to be ancient. Stepping closer, my stomach twisted when I realized they weren't weapons at all.

They were torture devices.

Thankfully, it looked like they hadn't been used since their hay day.

So Eros collected medieval torture devices. That was...
kind of cool. In a really creepy sort of way.

Foisting my attention to the rest of the room, I began
inhaling every detail. MMA posters littered the walls, some
of them his own posters and some depicting other fighters.

What surprised me the most was that the entire
basement was relatively tidy. It was obvious this place had
been used for storage long before Eros had ever taken over
due to all the dusty crates and barrels pushed off to the
corners of the room, but everything had its place. The item
that drew the most attention was his bed. It was a wooden
four-poster behemoth that was oddly eloquent compared to
the rest of his furniture, such as the barrel he was using as
a side table and an old Coca-Cola crate that appeared to
hold an assortment of trophies.

I wondered how he'd managed to get the bed down here.
Or if he even used it. The black bed coverings were
smoothed down nicely, and the pillows plumped.
Everything about this place was a mix of hard and soft,
beautiful and crude. A testament to Eros, maybe.

My attention settled on what I'd come here for. A
dresser at the foot of his bed. I slowly stepped up to it,
taking a moment to examine all the little knick-knacks
covering the top. A pack of cigarettes, a pair of handcuffs, a
bowie knife wrapped in a bloody sock—vampire blood by
the color. A lighter with gothic script reading DW stamped
on the front. Hand wraps. A mouthguard.

The collection of items illustrated Eros as strange, but
evil wasn't exactly popping into my head when I took in
his room and all its contents. Dangerous, definitely crazy,
but not exactly evil.

Holding my breath, my hands hovered over the dresser's brass handles that had long since had the finish worn off from decades of use. Was I really about to rifle through his clothes? This was definitely an invasion of privacy. Was Kenzie right about my scent fading before he got home? Some dark, twisted part of me wanted him to know what I'd taken from him.

To see what he would do.

Maybe I did have a death wish after all. And what a match made in Hell we could be.

I was beginning to learn things about myself in the company of these vampire princes. Fucked up things. Like the phantom sensation of Vincent's hand wrapped around my throat that first night we'd met. How his expression had been carved up with hatred, but his eyes had been banked with lust. Even thinking about it sent a rush of tingling heat to my sex.

Would Eros be just as heavy-handed? Or would his brand of torture be more skilled and practiced? My dark fantasies began to unfurl in my head, but all the images of me splayed out on my back in the bed before me slipped away as I opened the drawer and a plume of masculine scent washed over me, heady and potent.

"Holy fuck," I whispered to myself as I pulled out a black t-shirt and buried my nose in the fabric, inhaling Eros's scent. It was metallic, like blood and steel, with the vaguest notes of cloves and cigarette smoke.

The fragrance was gloriously male, one that belonged to a monster. More unsettling than that, was the way it swept over me like a palpable touch, making my mouth water and my knees wobble.

Putting the shirt back, I only had to dig a little deeper to find the hoodie. It was black, with gothic lettering reading 'Deathwish Dethrones the Feral King!' and sure enough, there was a black and white picture of him in the ring, landing a huge fist in Vincent's nose.

A devious smile curved my lips, thinking how Eros might react once he found out I'd broken his brother's nose the night we'd met.

I quickly tugged the hoodie on, breathing in the prince's spicy aroma. It was huge on me, covering my denim shorts and red crop top I'd chosen from Kenzie's haul like a damn tent. But it was cozy, and more than that, it felt like armor for some reason. Closing the drawer, my curious gaze swept over the bed one last time before making my way for the door.

I'd already been here too long and if the guys had bothered waiting for me to start their little meeting, I doubted they'd wait much longer.

Reaching for the door handle, my hand froze in mid-air when I heard footsteps echoing down the basement stairs.

My heart launched into my throat as I listened closely.

The steps were too heavy to be Kenzie's.

Then the scent hit me.

Metal. Cigarette smoke. Cloves.

Deathwish was home, early. And he was about to find me in his room, wearing his clothes.

Chapter Thirty-Three

TIME TO PLAY

There was someone, or something, accompanying Deathwish as he descended the basement stairs. With every groan of a step, there was a thud of something dragging behind, knocking against the wood with a sickening thud.

Panic struck me like a lightning bolt and for a second all I could do was stand there and hyperventilate.

As the footsteps got louder my instincts took over and before I knew it, I had flung myself to the far end of the room where all the crates and barrels sat.

When my attention fell on a door, hope soared high in my chest, thinking I had found an exit and pushed higher yet when I discovered it was unlocked.

Throwing myself inside, I pressed my ear to the door to listen.

"You're a heavy fucker for how skinny you are, Al," Eros grunted. There was the slide of something weighty dragging across the floor, followed by the click of the door shutting.

My heart rate vaulted, hearing Eros' gravelly voice speak a name that would probably give me nightmares for a while.

The door I was hiding behind was old-fashioned, with a keyhole made to fit a large skeleton key. It was just big enough to peer through and make out the scene on the other side.

The blood in my veins turned red-hot then froze into ice as I registered the man on the floor.

Sure enough, it was Allister of the Boston Coven, the goon at the gas station who tried to rape me.

After I'd ripped Malachite's head off, Corry had chased his coven mate off. I thought he had escaped, but it turns out he hadn't made it far at all.

The sight of him on the ground, bloody and battered was a satisfying one. He was bound and gagged, a trail of blood smeared on the stone floor where he'd been dragged in.

Standing over him was the man from the poster in front of Clown Car Burgers. He was even more imposing in person. He was tall, stacks of muscles wrapped up in skin that was tanner than his brothers. His long, coarse blonde hair was wrapped in a bun on top of his head. In the picture, he had a long beard braided like a Viking's but he had since shaved and had started growing out again in an appealing, rugged scruff.

The scythe of his reaper tattoo could be seen poking out of his shirt and grazed his jawline. He wore a black t-shirt like the one I'd found earlier that hugged his brawny torso like a dream and camo pants flecked with dark stains that were either mud or blood, I couldn't tell from this distance.

Eros stared down at his captive for a few moments, his features wrapped in shadows.

Striding to the dresser, Eros reached for the carton of cigarettes and the lighter that sat on top. "You know, you're pretty damn unlucky I got a text from my little brother when I did. Otherwise, you might have gotten away. You want to know what he told me?"

Al grunted a muffled 'phuck you' through the gag and Eros let out a guttural chuckle, scratching his chin. "I'm going to take that as a yes. His text told me that our little halfling princess has finally been sprung. We've all been waiting a long time to meet her. Now that the Elders have declared her heir to her father's throne, she's more important than ever."

He pulled out a cigarette and put it to his lips. He went to light it but paused.

My heart squeezed as he tilted his nose in the air, his huge chest expanding with a great inhale. "Fuck me, this whole place smells like virgin cunt now. So sweet, like candy. You scent that, Al?"

He lit his cigarette and took a deep drag. His snake bites and brow piercings gleamed in the light of the cherry-red embers and for a second his eyes lit up. They were a warm brown, topped with brushy blonde brows and underscored by dark eye circles like he hadn't slept in a while.

Eros placed his combat boot over his captive's head, and slowly pressed down, a pathetic whimper bleeding past Al's gag. He pinched his cigarette between his fingers and leaned down, smoke swirling around him like a demon fresh out of Hell.

"You know that scent, don't you? You've smelt it before, tonight, when you put your hands on her."

He knew.

Corry must have texted Eros the same time he'd texted Vincent to come get me at the gas station. It explained why Corry was so at ease when he'd lost Allister's trail.

He had gotten another brother to do the hunting for him.

And apparently, Corry had filled him in on details I would have preferred to keep private. But something told me the youngblood had told Eros exactly what Allister and Malachite had planned for me at that gas station on purpose.

Deathwish was freaking scary when he was pissed off. And that wouldn't bode well for Allister.

The prince appeared cool and collected but I could feel the rage and fury rolling off him, even from here.

All because they had touched me.

He hadn't even met me yet.

It hadn't been more than a few hours.

And Eros was already carrying out revenge in my name.

"Feef a phucking haf bud!" Allister snarled through his gag, a scream replacing his words as Eros' boot pressed down harder on his skull.

"Doesn't matter if she's a half-blood. She isn't yours to touch."

He took a slow drag from his cigarette and blew the smoke onto his victim. "Do you know why they call me Deathwish?"

My stomach roiled with disgust when the sound of cracking bone filled the basement, somehow still audible over Allister's screams. Thick beads of black blood began to leak from the vampire's eyes, nostrils, and ears, pooling around his head in an inky puddle.

"Because anyone who fucks with this coven, fucks with me. And the only people who dare fuck with me have a death wish."

Eros lifted his boot from Allister's skull and brought it down hard. I had to turn away with a wince, slapping my hand over my mouth to muffle the sound.

The screams ceased and everything fell so still I could hear the sizzle of Eros taking another drag of his cigarette.

With my attention pulled away from the grisly scene, my eyes had adjusted to the dark of the room that had provided me sanctuary.

I had to bite my lip to hold back the gasp rising in my throat.

Eros was tidy. The reason that the rest of his room was relatively normal was that he kept his messes in here.

It wasn't a closet or an extra storage room that I had stumbled into. I had flung myself right into Deathwish's torture chamber.

It was damp, with no windows or other means of escape. Chains with huge, sinister hooks dangled from the ceilings, and shackles were bolted to the walls with bloodstains marking the stone beneath, the stains leading to the drain at the center of the floor.

Pushed against the wall was an ebony coffin, the first I'd seen since coming here.

Next to the coffin was a workbench filled with all sorts of tools. These tools were different from the ones in the next room. These were much newer, made of silver and dark wood. By the bottle of alcohol and jar of cotton balls on the bench, they were cleaned meticulously. Over the workbench was a display of even crueler devices. Stakes, knives, hooks, pliers, whips. There was even a gun sitting next to a tray of what I surmised to be silver bullets.

My hand shook as I reached for one of the stakes. I didn't know what compelled me, but it was in my hand before I realized what I was doing. It was heavy, with a deadly sharp tip and was all silver, with a rounded end that was decorated in dozens of tiny little red jewels—garnets by their dark red tint—and arranged in the letters 'DW.'

Jesus.

I put the stake back into its mount and examined my fingers. They were completely unmarred. Vincent had been right. Being a half-blood meant I was immune to silver. The box of latex gloves on Eros' bench confirmed that he was not.

My breathing stilted and my heart lunged to my throat when yet another ominous feature of the room snagged my attention.

It was a fucking furnace installed into the brick.

My skin prickled when my gaze fell to a set of iron rods propped in one of those little brass holders meant to hold implements for sweeping up ash and poking fire logs. I inched forward and picked up one of the rods. My entire body went cold when I examined the end. There was a stamp, made of silver with Deathwish's initials.

It was a brand.

Holy *fuck*.

Eros liked to initial everything, including his victims. Another brand had the monogram 'CCC' and another that read 'Traitor to the Crown.'

The basement and its collection of wicked instruments should have horrified me. In a way it did, but what scared me more was the fact that I was more captivated than anything.

There was more to the sadist than Vincent and Corry were letting on. Deathwish was the coven's protector. Sure, resorting to torturing the coven's enemies was extreme. But in the world of vampire politics, there probably weren't a lot of other options.

Part of me felt cheated that he had ended Allister's life so quickly.

Just as I was beginning to imagine what I would have done to my assailant if I were in Deathwish's boots, a gargled scream ripped me from my fucked up fantasies.

I peered through the keyhole and I couldn't believe my damn eyes. Allister was still alive, his skull knitting back together as Eros glared down at him with thinly veiled boredom.

"Hurry up and heal so I can break you again."

I knew vampires could regenerate quickly, but I didn't know it was to this extent. His skull had been crushed, yet he had come back to life in under a minute.

Eros grabbed his victim's ankle and dragged him over to the room where I was hiding.

Fuck, fuck, fuck.

Any second he'd find me, and his torture room wasn't the ideal place for him to discover I'd broken into his room and stole from him.

I frantically searched for a place to hide. When my gaze landed on the coffin, I scrambled inside and cracked the lid just enough so I could still see the room.

The inside of the coffin was lined in soft silk that had the prince's dark and spicy scent ingrained in the fabric.

Somehow his coffin and his hoodie made me feel safe. It felt like a different version of him as I watched the dark angel of vengeance burst through the door with Allister slung over his shoulder.

Dumping the vampire unceremoniously on the ground, he stepped up to the bench, coming dangerously close to my hiding place. My heartbeat spiked, pounding so loud I was afraid he would hear.

He pulled his cigarette from his lips and snuffed it out on the table. As the smoke evaporated and its scent faded, he paused, his brown eyes slitting and his nostrils flaring.

With the way my heart was slamming frantically against my rib cage, maybe I would die from a heart attack before he could kill me himself. But whatever demented god had sanction over this fucked up place must have been on my side, because Allister had chewed through his gag. When he spoke his voice came out loud and clear.

"Go ahead and kill me, you deranged fuck. There is a traitor in your den, leaking out all your secrets. We know what happened to your master, the coward king who took his own life! And how your precious Council of Elders plan on putting his half-blood bastard on the throne. You think our coven is the only one that turned against the Elders? Just wait, there is a whole fleet of us waiting to come down and obliterate you. And we won't stop there. We'll rip apart any coven that remains loyal to you. The Elders will be destroyed and all that will remain is the one true king and those loyal to him."

Eros coolly grabbed a set of latex gloves and pulled them on, then took a set of shackles from the workbench and spun around, cocking his head at the victim at his feet. "The one true king? And who might that be?"

"Dagon Knight."

A pregnant silence filled the air. I'd never heard the name but even so, it sent shivers down my spine. Whoever this Dagon Knight was, he carried my father's name.

"That's impossible," Eros growled. "He died centuries ago."

"He's alive. He's coming for all of you. You just wait and see what he has in store for your little half-blood cunt. If you'll be alive to see it."

Eros was on top of the other vampire so fast, I hadn't even seen him move. He crouched down, ripped the rope from his wrists, and clamped the shackles on him so his arms were over his head. With impressive strength, he hauled the vampire up with one hand and slung the chain holding his wrists together onto the hook dangling from the ceiling.

"You're wrong," Eros growled between clenched teeth. He peeled off his shirt and moved to the furnace to light it. When the flames sprung to life, the room lit up in an eerie orange, chasing the shadows to the far corners of the room.

Bathed in firelight, I could now see Deathwish clearly.

He was devastatingly gorgeous, even flecked with Allister's blood and covered in a thin sheen of sweat that made his tattooed skin glisten.

Picking up one of the iron rods, Eros stuck it in the furnace and turned the dial mounted on the wall to adjust the heat. "You know why you're wrong, Al?"

The vampire gave only a snarl in response, thrashing against his shackles, making the chain rattle.

Eros pulled out the iron and strode back to his prisoner, examining the red-hot tip of the brand with a diabolic grin. "You're wrong because even if Dagon is alive, I'll be king long before he gets here."

With that, he slammed the brand between Allister's eyes. Blood-curdling screams filled the air and the stench of singed flesh stung my nose.

I should have been horrified at the display before me. Instead, nothing but raw satisfaction filled me as I watched the man who'd tried to rape me writhe in agony.

Eros continued with the torture, switching between making wounds that would almost immediately heal, and cutting off bits that he'd toss in the fire that couldn't regenerate. Each slice, each stab, each burn was made with extreme precision and calculation, all to drag out his victim's pain.

The male before me was no man. He was the fucking grim reaper.

And watching him dole out my due in flesh and blood was more than inspiring. I was falling face first into one fucked up love affair with this depraved creature, and we hadn't even met.

"Just kill me already," Allister spat at his captor. "I'll never tell you who your traitor is. They may bow to your half-blood princess but only under the solace that Dagon Knight is coming for her and the throne, long before she's crowned."

I couldn't see Eros' expression, with his muscular back facing me. Even so, I could feel the lethal energy rolling off him, charging the room with something dark and wicked. My hair rose on the back of my neck and my breathing turned erratic when he next spoke.

"Maybe I can't get you to spill all you know. But maybe someone else can. Someone who hates you even more than I do."

Allister looked up, his beaten and swollen face shifting with a mixture of fear and confusion. "What? Who?"

Eros turned to face the coffin, only his blazing eyes of brown distinguishable through the shadows that swathed his features.

"You can come out now, Ruby. It's time to play."

CHAPTER THIRTY-FOUR
A CHOICE IN BLOOD

M
y heart stilled when the beautiful monster of a man called out my name.

You can come out now, Ruby. It's time to play.

His words permeated through my mind, filling me with a jarring coalescence of terror and curiosity. He knew I was here, spying on him at work. He had known the whole time, but not a twitch of a muscle or a bat of his eye had betrayed that fact. It was freaky how collected he was at all times. He never seemed to betray any emotions he didn't want others to see. He was the epitome of control.

A little voice in the back of my head screamed at me to run. I wasn't supposed to be here. I'd only dared step into Deathwish's world to grab his hoodie, a power move against Feral. Now I found myself completely frozen in place. My human instincts were telling me to flee, and my vampire instincts were pushing me forward.

Before I could will myself to move, Eros strode forward and lifted the coffin's lid.

I should have been freaked out of my mind but instead, I could only peer up at the dark angel of death with nothing but complete fascination glittering in my eyes. Maybe he could even tell how aroused I was, not by the torture of course, but by the fact that this male was handing me my revenge on a silver plate.

With the fire roaring in the furnace at his back, I couldn't penetrate the shadows that masked his features. But I could hear the rasp of his heavy breathing, and I felt the weight of his gaze pinning me down.

"Look at you," he rasped. "So small, like a little doll."

He knelt down so we were at eye level and when he reached out for me, his eyes glinted through the dark as he probably could hear the wild thrum of my heart. His fingers—still wearing the black latex gloves—took a lock of my cherry-red hair and felt the silky strands between his thumb and forefinger. Then he dropped the piece of hair and held his hand out for me.

"As much as I love the sight of you cowering in my bed, little doll, it's time to come out."

Without hesitation, I took his hand. The second his thick fingers curled around mine, a chill rushed over my flesh and I felt myself being lifted from the coffin. He set me on my feet and stepped back as if to inspect me.

Now I could see his features better, wrapped up in shadow and firelight. When his line of sight landed on the hoodie I was still wearing, his piercing gleamed as his expression contorted with surprise.

"Why?" The single gravelly word was all he needed to say for me to understand. He wanted to know why I'd broken into his room, to steal his sweatshirt of all things.

I lifted my chin, my eyes sparkling with unapologetic defiance. It was a little embarrassing, having him catch me wearing his clothes, hiding in his coffin, and witnessing his grisly work. But I wasn't about to apologize.

"To piss off Feral."

Something dark and wicked passed over his face. His chocolate orbs banked with a delicious fire that sent flames lapping at my core. "Fuck me, you're perfect."

He reached out with a gloved finger to trace his name on the hoodie. Since the garment was so huge on me, it sat just below my belly. I swallowed hard, my cheeks blazing with heat and sweat began to bead on my brow.

Damn, it was hot in here.

The furnace fire made this entire room a sweltering oven, and Eros' touch wasn't making things any cooler.

"Careful princess," the voice from the other end of the room spat. "This one might get attached to seeing you wear his name."

I was so wrapped up in Eros' deliciously dark aura that I'd almost forgotten we had an audience. I glared daggers at Allister, who was strung up by his wrists and dangling from a huge chain bolted to the ceiling. Now that I was closer, I could see the fresh brand stamped on the vampire's forehead.

Deathwish.

From his collection of brands, Eros had chosen to mar Allister's flesh with his own name.

The dark prince stepped up to his prisoner and punched him in the gut so hard, my own bones rattled from the force of the blow. The chain rattled and the vampire's head lolled back on his shoulders, black blood spewing from his mouth as he wheezed and coughed.

"Don't fucking speak to her unless she asks you a question, Boston Coven trash," Eros snarled, his command laced with a warning that sat heavy in the air; a brutal promise for what was to come.

Composing himself, Eros twisted to face me. A fresh splatter of Al coated his tattooed torso, the grim reaper's blade coated with dark blood as if it had drawn it itself.

His skin was slick with sweat and gleamed in the glow of the firelight. He was so perversely beautiful, it hurt to look at him. But something I was learning about myself was that I was a bit of a masochist because I couldn't look away.

His lips twisted in a grin, his snake bites twitching with the movement. Then he dug into the pocket of his camo pants and extracted his phone, glancing at the screen before placing it on his workbench. "The sun is going to come up in about five minutes, doll. That means you have a choice."

"A... choice?" My palms began to sweat with nerves.

"The basement door is on an automatic timer. When the sun rises, it locks. It won't open again until sundown. You can leave now, and come back at night. But there won't be anything left of our friend Al here. He's not surviving the day."

My heart began to pick up pace again, as I was beginning to see where this was going.

Eros stepped closer to me, his scent of metal and cloves wrapped around me tight like a vice. Heat radiated from his body and when his thumb came up to stroke the edge of my jaw it was all I could do to keep myself from melting.

"Or you can stay. Take out your retribution, Ruby. He deserves to feel your wrath. Make him scream and beg for forgiveness for daring to lay his unworthy hands on the princess."

My gaze went to the torturer's bench and my mind went wild with all the ways I could make Allister pay for trying to rape me. I knew I wouldn't get the same enjoyment for dealing out pain on the same level as Eros, but fuck, did I want to make this asshole hurt. I'd killed his coven mate so quickly, it left a pit of regret in my stomach. They both deserved to suffer for touching me like they did. If my vampire abilities hadn't come to my own rescue with Corry swiftly following suit, they would have raped and fed on me. Then they probably would have brought me to this Dagon Knight person.

Who knows what he had planned for me.

Making Allister suffer, with the added bonus of potentially getting him to spill what he knew about our mole, was worth spending the day locked in with Eros.

I reached to grab a dagger from the bench, my fingers closing in on the leather hilt but Eros grabbed my wrist and held it in front of us, with the knife glinting between us.

"Wait. Think harder about your decision."

"I want to stay," I gulped. His fingers cinched tighter around my wrist, squeezing a small moan-laced wince from me.

His brows twitched with thinly-veiled surprise and his lips curved into a devilish smirk. He jerked me against him, my body flush against his hard, muscular mass. His mouth grazed the shell of my ear, making me shiver against him as he whispered, "Maybe you can survive my world. You have the scent of a virgin but your pussy weeps with an even stronger scent. It's practically begging for me. No woman has ever been in here, seen the real me, and then looked at me with desire."

"I want to stay," I repeated on a shaky exhale. "I have seen the real you and I'm not afraid."

No, I wasn't afraid. I was *enthralled*.

I felt Eros' chest rumble against mine with a guttural purr that seemed to call to something deep inside me. "Understand that if you stay with me, I'm not going to want to sleep, little doll. I'm going to want to show you every bit of my world."

"But I've seen your world," I blinked, pulling back to meet his hunger-banked gaze. I had already seen him literally torture a person. What more was there to see?

"You've seen the worst of it. I want to show you the best of it," he said on a purr-like growl. With the knife still held between us, he guided my hand so the blade was pressed against my cheek. My breath caught in my throat as I felt the cold metal cut into my flesh. "Stay, and I'll make you bleed. I'll make you cry, and writhe, all while you beg me for more."

He dragged the blade down my cheek, a shallow cut slicing across my skin. The scent of my blood tinged the air and Eros' pupils dilated. He leaned forward, his lips pressing a kiss to where he'd cut me. His tongue, hot and wet, slid over my flesh, and he let out the most deliciously erotic growl when my flavor hit his taste buds.

Then I felt it. The wound was lacing up on its own.

He pulled back, held the dagger up, and licked the blade clean of my ruby-red blood, uncaring that he drew some of his own in the process.

His eyes fluttered closed and his chest rose with a great inhale like he was trying to center himself. "*Bleeding fucking hell*, you taste so damn good."

"Run little girl," Allister taunted from across the room. "He's gonna carve your pussy up! He'll drain you dry! Leave the torture to the real fucking vampires."

He was trying to scare me off. But his words had the opposite effect. In any case, I'd already made up my mind.

I stepped up to Eros, licked the combination of our blood from his stunned lips, and took the blade from his hand.

As I approached Allister, I looked at him dangling on the chain, bleeding and broken. Not broken enough yet. Not until the fucker was ash in my palm.

"I'm staying."

No sooner than the words were out of my mouth, there was a loud click from the other room.

The door had locked.

There was no turning back now.

CHAPTER THIRTY-FIVE
MERCY

Allister's skull-splitting scream shook me down to my damn core as I slammed the dagger into his eye socket. Blood gushed in a torrent of ink-like ooze, splattering on the floor like he was a sacrifice and me, his dark god.

I left the knife sticking out of his head so the wound wouldn't heal and stepped back to admire my handiwork.

The vampire looked absolutely miserable. The sight of his broken body would have made me feel sick to my stomach if it wasn't for the fact that this soulless bastard had it coming.

"Are you going to tell me who's been slipping your coven intel? It has to be one of the Elders, they were the only ones who knew about my courting arrangement with the princes. It couldn't have gotten to anyone else by the time it reached you."

Al spit a gob of bloody saliva in my face, his eyes flashing with hatred that burned just as hot as the furnace flames behind him. "Fuck you, half-blood bitch. You killed Mal!"

Eros was sitting on top of his coffin with his arms folded over his chest, watching me work. When Allister spit on me, he started forward but I put a hand up stopping him. "I got this."

He settled back into his lounged position, watching me with a hooded expression as I stepped up to the workbench and pursued the collection of torture tools. I didn't know what most of them were, but when my gaze settled on an arrangement of vintage dental tools, I grinned like a madwoman.

When I picked up the pliers, I noticed Eros' expression shift with the faintest shades of approval.

Feeling confidence radiate throughout my body, I went back to Al and held up the sinister-looking tool. "This is how it's going to go, shit head. Tell me who told you about the courting arrangement, and about my father's suicide while you're at it. And maybe I won't pluck out your fangs."

"Fuck you bitch! Boston Coven doesn't squeal, unlike the pigs in your den."

I went to grab Allister's head but he began to thrash around, hissing and snapping. I looked back at Eros and without a word, he read my expression and gave me a jerk of a nod. He strode behind the vampire and clapped his head between his palms, his huge hands acting like a vice. For a second, it was hard to focus on anything but the way Eros' huge biceps flexed, muscles shifting beneath sweat-soaked skin as they worked to hold our prisoner still.

"Be good for the lady, Al. This is the closest you'll ever come to a woman again, so behave and maybe I'll let you die with my beautiful girl here being the last thing you'll ever see. Should be an honor, really. Seeing as most of my enemies die with both their eyes plucked out.

"You two are fucking psychopaths! Go fuck each other!" He roared.

"That's the plan," Eros gritted through hooded eyes, his attention glued firmly to me. "But first we've got some housekeeping to do. You do the honors, doll."

I nodded and gripped Allister's jaw, peering inside his mouth. "His fangs aren't dropped."

"Good luck getting them out, stupid bitch. You think I want to fuck you now? I'd rather eat my own cock."

"Don't give her any ideas." Eros chuckled behind him.

I did have an idea, and thankfully it didn't have anything to do with touching Allister's dick. Maybe he wasn't turned on, but that wasn't the only reason a vampire dropped its fangs. Gripping the dagger's hilt that still stuck out of his eye socket, I gave it a jerk and ripped it out of him. He screamed and thrashed but Eros held him still and they both watched with slack jaws as I took the knife and cut my own arm.

Hissing from the pain, I gritted my teeth and held it up to Al's nose. His irises turned as red as the blood seeping from my flesh, and his pupils blew up. As soon as his fangs had dropped I let the dagger clatter to the ground and took the pliers to his mouth. I thought it would be hard to pry out the tooth but with the adrenaline coursing through my veins and my supernatural strength, it ripped out of his gums as easily as fraying toilet paper.

His screams sung a different tune now. He was in complete and utter agony. I went for the other fang but he let out a pathetic whimper that gave me pause.

"W-wait, please. I don't know who your mole is. But my coven leader, Erik Thorn has been in direct contact with them. Thorn is the one you should be torturing."

"That day will come, Al," Eros growled. "But right now you're the worm on my hook, not Thorn. You got anything else to tell us? Anything that's actually useful?"

"Dagon Knight is coming."

"You already said that," he snapped.

"There are rumors that he is trying to awaken the old king."

A chill settled over me. The old king... as in my father? I didn't like the sound of that, I didn't like it at all.

"That's impossible, vampires can't cast magic like that. He'd have to have witches' blood running through his veins."

"All I'm telling you is what I've heard."

"Let's pretend for a second that he's capable of magic like that. Why would he want to resurrect the old king?"

The smile that Allister flashed me while addressing Deathwish at his back was one that sent chills skittering down my spine. "Dunno. Something to do with clearing his way to the throne. You better be careful. He might just take your little half-blood cunt here and claim her as his own mate and queen."

For the first time since I'd stepped into this room, I felt like I might actually be sick. Yet surprisingly it had nothing to do with all the torture. God, I hoped it was only a rumor. But something settled in my belly, a sharp foreboding that suggested that it was all too real. And that whoever this Dagon Knight was, he was coming for me.

I had so many questions. But right now, my vision shrunk to pinpoints and all I could focus on was the fact that the man who'd assaulted me tonight was still breathing. Going to the workbench, I picked up one of the wooden stakes, and moving faster than I ever had before, I was slamming it into Allister's chest cavity before his shrill scream could leave him. His mouth was affixed into a silent cry and his face was etched with the deepest pain a creature could ever know.

Right before my eyes, his body began to shrivel in on itself, as if his corpse had been mummified hundreds of years ago. For a second, Eros and I stared at each other with a new kind of weight heavy in the air. Blowing out a steady exhale, he began to break apart Allister's brittle body and toss it into the fire.

I watched the planes of his bare back as he burned the final traces of the enemy, a bitter taste in my mouth. It was almost like I could taste Al's ashes. I didn't feel regret.

I only felt scared.

"How come Mal didn't turn to jerky when I killed him?" I asked in a whisper, trying to distract myself from the troubling information we had extracted.

Eros' shoulders tightened but he didn't turn to face me. "There are two ways to kill a vampire. Rip off his head, or stake him. When you stake him, they turn to 'jerky.'" He chuckled as he repeated my phrasing, and finally turned to look at me with a grin on his face. It slipped when he saw my expression.

"You're shaking."

"I just killed a man."

Deathwish's expression darkened. "That wasn't a man. He was a monster and he would have done worse to you if you'd let him."

"But doesn't it bother you what he said? About this Dagon Knight coming to—" I couldn't even repeat the words. Thankfully, Eros spoke before I forced myself to say them.

"No," he said firmly on a deadly growl. He prowled over to me and paused with his face inches from my own. Standing directly in front of me, his stature was formidable. My mouth went dry as my gaze drifted over his piercings, down his blood-spattered, tattooed chest. I ached to reach out and touch him.

But I couldn't. I was frozen under his intense stare as he reached to touch my lips with a gloved finger, as if he was just as entranced with me as I was with him.

"I don't think it's true," he said after a moment, his gravelly voice stirring the tension. "I don't know much about Dagon but I do know he was one of your dad's progeny, turned around the sixteenth century. He was one of many who didn't survive him. He's nothing but a ghost story. Don't let it scare you."

"I am scared," I admitted.

"Are you scared of me?"

"No, not you."

"Then nothing should frighten you, baby doll. Nothing."

I couldn't hold back for another damn second. I wrapped my arms around him and buried my face into his chest, inhaling his smokey, spicy scent like it was a drug.

He stilled, almost like he was shocked by the display of affection. Whether Dagon Knight was a rumor or not, other covens were coming for me. I already knew the princes' solution. They'd want me to pick a mate and king to protect me. Hell, I'd even heard it right from Eros' lips.

Even if Dagon was more than a ghost story, he wasn't worried because he was going to be king before he could get here.

The cocky bastard.

At least he was honest and didn't resort to mind games like Feral. There was nothing wrong with wanting to be my mate if he genuinely liked me. I doubt he had another bitch he was planning on slapping on the throne beside him the second we mated.

Vincent Feral's hate boner for me was hot as fuck, but it wasn't anything to build a relationship on. Corry had some stuff to work out. And Sterling... So far he didn't seem interested in me in the slightest.

I hoped Sterling would agree to turn me into a full-blooded vampire. Now more than ever, I knew that was the best way to protect myself from the other covens and the princes. Maybe that would help me survive long enough to sort out all the baggage with these princes and help me figure out who I could actually trust enough to make my mate and king.

Right now, all I wanted was someone who was fucking honest with me.

Vincent and Corry had failed in that area.

"Why do you want to be king?"

"Do you know why I live in the basement?"

I shook my head.

"Because they made me live down here. Like a beast to be ashamed of. They treat me like a monster, a necessary element of the coven but one to be kept to the shadows beneath everyone else. If I'm king, I get to be on top."

That wasn't such a crazy notion. Hell, I related. For all my life, I had been locked away like a damn animal. It made me feel close to Deathwish.

For the first time since meeting the princes, I felt like I was on one of their levels.

I tilted my face toward his, my lips softening under his fire-filled gaze. "I want you to make love to me, Eros."

His blood-flecked face contorted with a sneer. "I don't make love, I fuck, *hard*. I'm not going to be gentle with you. You want gentle, go beg Sterling for a fuck."

"I don't want Sterling right now. I want you. I want you, all of you. The fucked up parts and all."

Another eternity passed as he looked at me, a thousand thoughts brewing behind his dark eyes. Calculating. Plotting. It was like he was mapping out my entire domination in his head before saying a single word.

"At any point, if I'm doing something that you want me to stop, say 'mercy.' Got that?"

My lips split with a nervous laugh. "You're giving me a safe word?"

He grabbed my jaw and forced my gaze in front of his, my smile dissolving in an instant. "It's not fucking funny. I might be fucked but I'm not going to do anything to you that you don't like. My brothers may like to paint me as a monster but I don't fuck around with that shit. Do you understand?"

I nodded in his grip as best I could. "I understand."

CHAPTER THIRTY-SIX

BLOOD, LACE, AND A TOUCH OF DISGRACE

I stood before Deathwish with my heart beating so hard, I could feel it in my throat.

But it's just like I'd told him. I wasn't afraid. I stood there in his sweatshirt, my skin heating as his appraising gaze slithered over me from head to toe. He circled me, like a predator stalking its prey.

"Answer a question for me, doll. You're a virgin. But you've got the blood of my brothers coursing through your veins. Vampires typically only do that when they're fucking."

My eyes fluttered shut, and even still I could feel him watching me with an intensity so hot it charged the air with electricity, coiling tight with the bitter scent of Al's ashes.

"I let Corry touch me in exchange for my escape. But that didn't happen. Vincent showed up before it went very far. He took too much blood from me so I drank from Vincent to recover."

I opened my eyes to see Eros standing in front of me once again, his expression pinched with an indiscernible emotion. "Did *he* try to fuck you?"

Eros' tone was so cool, it sent a rush of goosebumps over my flesh. He was just as collected as always but I didn't miss the flash of fury in his eyes. His fists were clenched at his sides, and his anger was practically radiating from his taut shoulders.

"Why do you two hate each other so much?" I found myself dodging his question, mostly because I didn't know how to answer.

"That's not something I care to discuss right now. I don't want him touching what ought to belong to me."

My heart fluttered in my chest. "I don't belong to any of you. Not yet. I don't want you thinking this whole thing that's about to happen between us means I'm picking you as my mate, Eros. I want to get to know you all first before I make a decision. You have to be okay with me spending time with the others."

The vampire's jaw tightened, a tendon ticking as his teeth ground together. But he didn't protest. "Fine. I know you're a virgin but tell me what hard limits you think you might have."

Hard limits. Jesus. Was this going to be a mistake? Girls were supposed to have their first time be vanilla, that was the norm. But nothing about my relationship with Deathwish, or any of the princes for that matter, was going to be normal. And I had accepted that fact the moment I agreed to stay in the basement during daylight hours.

"You can't claim me, so no biting while you're inside me. And you can't turn me." While I wanted to venture into the dark world of Deathwish's bed, I did not want him to be my master. At least, not *that* kind of master.

His brows shot up in surprise and he let out a grating chuckle. "That's it? Those are your hard limits? Don't feed while I fuck you and don't turn you? Damn. You're fucking perfect."

Before I could respond, his lips came down over mine in a bruising, ravenous kiss.

Holy fuck. He tasted like he smelt, like blood and spices and sin. He kissed like a demon intent on claiming my soul with a simple swipe of his lips. It was so good I moaned against him, and his tongue took the opportunity to slip inside my mouth, filling the hollow of it with the silent promise that soon he'd fill more of me.

I felt his fangs extend but he didn't bite me, not yet.

His arms banded around my waist and he lifted me, carrying me over to his workbench. He set me down and stepped back, his wolfish gaze drinking in the sight of me nestled among his cruel collection of tools. Both our chests heaved in unison from the wake of the smothering kiss and for a second we just stared at each other with wild eyes as if bracing for what was to come.

"Take that off," he demanded, pointing at the hoodie.

I peeled it off, revealing my red crop top and the tiny black skirt beneath it.

His pupils dilated when he took in my body clothed in the skimpy clothing. "Good girl," he rasped, his tone guttural and dripping with need. "Now spread your legs for me like a good little fuck doll."

When I parted my thighs so he could catch a glimpse of my lacy black panties beneath, a guttural moan slithered from his throat. "Feral's going to kill me after I've had my fill of you."

"Why?"

"Because when I'm done, there will be nothing left for him. Place your hands against the rack."

I should have been rethinking my decision to agree to this kind of torment, especially for my first time. But that dark, messed up part of my brain wouldn't let me bail now. I was too intrigued, too eager to feel myself come apart under Deathwish's skilled hands. Placing my wrists against the steel rack that held his tools, Eros clamped iron shackles down on my wrists, spreading my arms wide on either side of my head.

"You're shaking," he surveyed as he peeled his black latex gloves that were still covered in Al's blood in exchange for clean ones. "Having second thoughts?"

I shook my head. "No."

"That's my brave little doll," he chuckled as he grabbed another knife from the rack beside my head and began slicing off my clothes. I shook beneath the knife as the blade nicked my skin, red blood seeping into the fabric as it fell away. He arched over me, and his tongue followed the blade of his weapon as it ran toward my navel, lapping up the trail of blood before the wound healed.

He pulled off the shredded top, revealing my bare breasts to his heated gaze. He arched down, as if to take one of my nipples in his mouth when the hoodie—that had been tossed onto his coffin—vibrated. His brows scrunched with irritation as if annoyed he'd been interrupted. Setting the knife down, he pulled my phone out of his hoodie pocket and read the text I'd received.

My stomach cartwheeled when his mouth peeled back into a manic grin.

"Who is it?" But I already knew. It had to be Corry, wondering why I hadn't shown up to the meeting.

His crazed expression was washed in the bright light of the phone's screen as he began to tap away at the phone.

Oh *no.*

This was bad. Real bad.

Deathwish didn't seem to have the best relationship with his brothers, and my phone in his hands had to be an excellent weapon of warfare, especially considering the kind of position I was currently in.

Then my heart damn near gave out when he raised the phone, and the device clicked with a bright flash.

He had taken a picture.

I never considered myself a girl that would be comfortable sending nudes.

But with my arms stretched out and bound on his torture bench, a still-healing cut sliced between the valley of my bare tits, this was next-level deprecation.

"Eros, don't! Corry is already pissed off at me, don't send that to him."

The vampire's grin stretched wider. "It's not Corry I'm speaking to. You said you wanted to piss off Feral. This is way better than wearing my hoodie."

Oh.

Fucking.

God.

Everything in me went cold, then hot again as the phone made the beeping sound it made when a text had been sent.

I couldn't even imagine the kind of reaction Feral was going to have when he laid eyes on that text. I did want to piss him off, but this was going to make him come down like a bomb on the whole basement. His wrath was going to be explosive, and fuck me, why did that make me so damn wet? Eros must have scented how hot his power move had made me because his eyes went blood red and his lips peeled to reveal his dropped fangs. His hand went back under my skirt, caressing my thigh as it slowly made its ascent up to my soaking seam.

Then his phone rang. It lit up, vibrating on the workbench where he'd left it. The display lit up with the name 'The Feral Fuckin Asshole.'

He reached for the phone with one hand and with his other, he slipped a finger into my panties. Just as he picked up the phone and held it to his ear, he slowly sunk a finger inside me, earning him a swollen moan.

"Hey, Feral. Guess what I'm doing right now."

CHAPTER THIRTY-SEVEN

A DANGEROUS GAME

W hen I had decided to come back to the mansion with Vincent and consider this whole vampire princess thing as a serious possibility, I had spent a lot of the car ride trying to imagine what my life in the coven would be like. Not for one damn second could I have imagined getting mixed up with these princes would have involved being strapped to a torturer's bench in the basement, getting finger fucked by a dangerous sadist with the body of a Nordic god, right after we'd killed a man together.

Nope, this was not how I'd thought this evening was going to go. But here I was, cuffed to a rack of torture tools with my legs spread and my tits completely bare. Eros stood between my legs, still wearing latex gloves like he was conducting some kind of science experiment with his finger slowly stroking my insides. His other hand pressed his cell to his ear, his face wearing a cool expression as Feral issued death threats on the other end.

It amazed me, the way Eros' eyes held mine, the reflecting of the furnace fire dancing in his darkly sensual gaze. How he kept calm in spite of Feral in his ear, threatening him with obscene and creative threats, all of which only made Eros' lips curve with smug amusement.

"Let her go, Deathwish. End your fucked up game now, and maybe I won't come down there and make your intestines into my new hand wraps."

"As fun as it would be to see you try, you're going to have to wait. It's sun up. The door is locked. You're not getting in and she's not getting out."

"The second it opens, I swear—"

Just then, Eros curled the tip of his finger inside me, hitting a sensitive spot that made my knees weak and my lower belly twist. I tried to bite back my moan but it only made a miserable little whine dribble past my lips.

The line on the other end went dead quiet for a few intense seconds, the only sound that filled the space being the embarrassing noises coming from beneath my skirt.

"Let me talk to her," Feral said, his choked growl making my heart squeeze. Maybe it was just my scrambled brain, which was currently getting blown by Eros' fingers, but Feral actually sounded worried.

"She's kind of busy right now."

"I want to know she's okay."

Eros' eyes narrowed into slits, his brow piercings gleaming in the orange firelight as a mischievous thought flashed over his face.

He set the phone down, jabbed the speaker button, and withdrew his finger from me. "She's here. Talk. Make it fast because I tend to get tired of your voice pretty damn quick."

"Ruby," Vincent gritted, my name on his tongue laced with emotions that made my chest squeeze. "Are you hurt?"

"No," I panted on a shattered breath. "I'm fine."

"Why the fuck did you go down there? I can't come and get you until sunset."

"No one's asking you to save me, I'm not some princess in distress," I said, trying to keep the worry out of my tone as Eros plucked a set of crude sheers from beside my head. He pushed the hem of my skirt up around my hips and my heart spiked as I felt the cold bite of steel against my opening as he slid the crotch of my panties between the sheers and sliced them off.

He pulled the shredded lace off me with a swift yank. "Open wide, doll," he muttered through a wicked grin that lit up with the flames dancing in his eyes.

"Wait, wha—" As I began to question him, he stuffed the black lace in my mouth, soaking up my gasp with the fabric. Before I could spit it out, a roll of black duct tape was in his hand and he pulled off a piece with a loud rip and slapped it over my mouth.

A muffled cry left my mouth when he picked up the silver stake I'd noticed from earlier.

"Ruby!" Vincent shouted on the other end. "I swear I'll kill you if you hurt one fucking hair on her head."

Ignoring him, Eros slid the pointed end of the stake from my inner knee up my thigh, making a shallow cut, his tongue trailing behind the blade to lap up the blood. His hot, soft tongue was a stark contrast against the cold bite of silver on my flesh.

My muscles unwound some when he spun the stake around so the hilt faced me, the garnets spelling out his initials glinting wickedly in the light. When he pressed it against my entrance, I quivered against the cold metal.

"Moan for it baby, tell me how much you want it inside you. But if you want to invoke my mercy, blink twice and our game will end."

That's when he decided to hang up on Feral with the brandish of an impish smirk. He probably wanted to leave him hanging, stewing in the possibilities of all that could have happened during the day while I was chained up in Deathwish's fucked up torture room.

Deep down I knew Eros wouldn't hurt me, not really anyway. But Vincent definitely wasn't of that same opinion. The second the sun set, he was going to storm down here and it wasn't going to be pretty. Part of me felt bad for making Vincent worry. Because he *was* worried. The way he shouted my name couldn't have been an act. No one was that good at feigning concern.

Once the sun went down and that door unlocked, I feared that Eros and Vincent might kill each other. Like for real.

Until then, I had several hours to revel in Deathwish's deviant ways.

There was still time to turn back. I knew if I wanted to stop, he would. But I had already come so far. Between Corry bending me over his bike, and straddling Vincent in the back of his car, they had worked me up into a frustrated tangle of need. And Deathwish carried a promise in his eyes that he was going to deliver on, helping me coax out the little ball of delicious heat that was beginning to build low in my belly like a dirty, sinful promise.

So I didn't blink. Instead, I moaned a loud and shameful noise that bled through my panties and duct tape.

"That's a good fuck doll," he crooned through a grated purr. With one hand, he slowly began to sink the hilt of the stake into me while his other gripped my shoulder, his thumb pressed into the hollow of my throat in a possessive yet gentle hold. I moaned, low and lusty into the wad of lace in my mouth as he pushed the stake deeper yet.

My chest heaved as my breathing quickened, thighs shaking as my body took in the invasion. He brought his forehead to rest against mine, his scent of cloves and smoke wrapping around me like another set of bindings.

His breath feathered over my skin like a delicate touch, an enticing contrast paired with the way his gloved fist worked to fill me with a dangerous weapon.

"You take it so well, baby doll," he said with a heated kiss to my brow. "I can't wait to see how you cry and writhe for me when I'm feeding you my cock."

My spine arched off the tool rack as he began to ease the stake in and out at an excruciatingly delicious pace. My own body was so wet with need, it coated the silver in my arousal that soaked my entrance and left the interior of my thighs glistening.

"You're so damn beautiful spread open for me like this. I can scent that you're close to climax. Do you want to come for me, doll?"

I gave a delirious nod, my forehead knocking against his, the delicious warmth swelling and coming to a torturous head. My whole body convulsed with a blissful shudder and stars dotted my vision. Without warning, he ripped the duct tape and the panties from my mouth and I let out a yelp-laced moan that he swiftly consumed in a brutal kiss that had me melting against him.

Orgasms weren't something new to me, not when one of the few things to keep me entertained in my bedroom prison had been my extensive collection of spicy romance books.

But the oh-so-decadent pain brought on by Deathwish's skilled hand introduced a whole new level of pleasure.

Coming down from the peak of ecstasy, I sagged in my shackles, my eyelids struggling to stay open.

"You're exhausted. You should get some rest."

"Wait, that's it? I thought we were going to..." My cheeks flared with heat as my mind was filled with images of his body pushing into mine. I wanted to see his cock, to feel it as it stretched me, hot and throbbing.

My skin flushed as I watched him discard his gloves and stride to a utility sink in the far corner of the room. He came back a moment later with a basin of hot water and set it down on the bench next to me.

"We will, doll. But I want you awake when I fuck you. You can barely keep your eyes open." He was right, I needed to sleep. His muscular form, bathed in firelight, began to blur. The last thing I saw before I closed my eyes was him wringing out a cloth. I twitched slightly as I felt his bare skin brush mine, followed by the warm cloth as he ran it gently between my legs, over my navel, and between my breasts.

He was cleaning me.

I probably desperately needed it, considering I was coated in crusted blood, sweat, and my own arousal. But somehow it felt like the intimate gesture meant more than that. His touch oozed with devotion. Like I was his treasured plaything, a doll he would protect and care for even when he'd push me nearly to the point of breaking.

The sound of unlatching shackles ribboned around my ears and I felt myself being lifted and carried to the next room. I sighed against the heat of his bare chest, inhaling his masculine scent. He set me down into the cool satin sheets of his bed, and the mattress dipped under his weight as he joined me, tugging me into the sanctuary of his brawny frame.

"I'm going to make you mine, Princess of Vampires. All mine."

The last thing I felt was a kiss to my head before sleep's embrace pulled me down into the darkness.

My dreams were filled with flashes of eyes. The ocean blue eyes of Corry, glaring at me through the rain as I was dragged away from my one shot at freedom. The olive green eyes of Vincent started soft and twisted with hunger-filled hatred as they turned red. The white, eerie eyes of Sterling as they watched me with an unknown emotion. And finally, the chocolate gaze of Deathwish as they swirled with a heat hotter than his sinister furnace.

"Wake up, doll," Eros' voice called to me, pulling me from the realm of sleep. Opening my eyes, I looked to see Eros spooning me, his arm wrapped around my bare torso, holding me flush against him.

While I'd slept, he had pulled his blonde hair from the bun on his head and now it fell in loose waves around his shoulders. I never thought long hair on a man was masculine before now. But paired with his piercings, and his beard, and his tattoos, he reminded me of a Viking warrior.

"You're so damn beautiful it's scary," I said without thinking, still waiting for my haze of sleep to clear.

He chuckled, the rough sound sinking straight through my core and curling up into the place I still ached for him. As if sensing my renewed need, he pressed his hips forward so that I could feel the swell of his own hunger against my ass.

"What time is it?" I whispered, my breath hitching in my chest.

Eros drew me into his arms, leaving no space at all between us. "We have time before the door unlocks," he muttered in a tone that suggested he knew exactly where my train of thought had wandered. A shiver ran down my spine, as my gaze fell to the basement door. As soon as the sun went down, Vincent Feral was going to come through it like a wrecking ball.

It was selfish and immature of me to want them to fight here, out of the ring where rules and onlookers would keep them from killing each other. But part of me did want Feral to fight for me. To see that possessive conviction burning in his eyes, the sort he couldn't fake.

As much as it pained me to admit, I wanted to desperately believe that he truly wanted me. And right now, there was so much evidence proving my worst fears. That all he wanted was to use me for the throne, and toss me aside when he was done with me.

It was a dangerous game, coaxing out that shred of genuine care for me like this. It was selfish. And it wasn't fair to either of them. But damn it, I wanted to see it again. I was addicted to that little spark I'd seen in the car. That little flash of excitement where we had, for one crazy moment, pretended like there was a possibility of us being more than bitter rivals.

Eros' mouth to my ear, kissing and nipping at the shell was enough to make all thoughts of Vincent fizzle away.

"I've barely slept at all. Having you in my bed is driving me fucking mad."

I angled my head to look back over my shoulder at him, wincing softly as his fingers dug into the naked flesh of my hips. "Why?"

I already knew the answer, but I wanted to hear him say it. I loved watching his reactions to me through the cracks of the calm and collected mask he always wore.

"Because I can't stop thinking of your body as it took my torture so damn nicely. You look so fucking hot, writhing and moaning under my touch when everyone else flinches and screams."

"I flinched and screamed for you too, Eros." Pushing against his erection, I swayed my hips to stroke his cock with the somewhat clumsy sway of my ass. But my lack of skill in this area didn't seem to be a concern of his. If anything, it was making him even more crazed, wanting to be the first to venture between my legs.

In a blink, he was on top of me with my back pinned down into the mattress.

He loomed over me with a look in his eye that made my nerves ball with tense excitement. He had shed his pants, leaving him in nothing but black boxers which did little to contain his swelling cock. "Do you want me to take your virginity, Ruby?" Eros asked on a growl, his hips pressing his hunger down between the apex of my thighs, the only barrier being the thin fabric of his boxers.

I bit back a gasp, feeling the rock hard heft of him against the most sensitive part of me. I nodded frantically, unashamed of my eagerness. So far, my virginity had been nothing but a giant ass headache. Something for the guys to fight and drool over when it shouldn't have fucking mattered at all.

My V-card was nothing but a pain and I was ready to hand it over. Because finally, everyone would stop talking about smelling it.

"You're not sore?" Eros asked, surprised by my enthusiasm.

"A little," I admitted, butterflies swarming in my belly. His presence over me was a dark cloud, like a dangerous rainstorm that could drown me if I wasn't careful. But for some reason, I was only attracted to his dark energy.

This was a man who could be my ally, maybe even my king. But I got a sense he could so easily turn into my enemy. And seeing this beautiful monster at work, I'd rather be smack dab in Boston Coven territory than on Eros' shit list.

Despite all that, I still wanted to play his twisted games.

I lifted the hem of the skirt I still wore and flashed him an inviting smirk as I spread my legs wide for him.

It was almost like I had a death wish or something.

CHAPTER THIRTY-EIGHT

ONCE BITTEN

E ros' dark eyes pinned me down to his bed, his face surprisingly expressionless as he watched me practically beg for him to take me.

"What's the matter?" I asked, blinking up at him. Just a second ago, he'd seemed so eager to fuck me. Now I could almost see the conflict etched into his cool scowl.

"You have to know that venturing into my bed is on a whole different level than fooling around with Corry Cross."

"Yeah, I got that from all the knives and duct tape."

"It's not just that. You fuck me, the whole coven is going to know. And not everyone is going to take kindly to the prospect that you might choose me as your king."

"I don't care what they think."

He inspected me through narrowed eyes, almost like he was trying to assess my sincerity. To prove just how serious I was about taking this step with him, I wrapped my arms around his neck and delivered a fierce kiss to his lips. His shoulder muscles flexed beneath my hands as he leaned into the connection.

It was a kiss unlike the others he had given me. They had been hard, demanding, and bruising. This one. This kiss was so damn good, I could feel it pierce my soul and stretch all the way down to my needy center. His mouth took as much as it gave, demanding I be present in this moment. His hands went to my hair, holding me close as he licked a trail of kisses over my jawline, down my throat, and over my collar bone. It was there that he nipped at me, his teeth sliding over my skin and making me shudder beneath him.

I felt his breath fracture, and his arms trembled as they held me. I could see his blood-red eyes, affixed to my bare throat. With the way his tendons went taut in his neck, I knew he was holding himself back from biting me. But for whatever stupid fucking reason, I trusted him.

Maybe it was because I was so desperate to have someone on my side.

I swallowed hard, I closed my eyes as I savored the way he felt against my skin. His scent was so damn intoxicating it made my head swim and my legs weak. "Is it going to hurt?"

His shoulders tensed and even though my eyes were closed I could feel his gaze on me. "When you're with me there's bound to be a little pain. But you like a little pain, don't you doll?"

I felt my whole body burn with a blush. "I... I think I do."

Gleaning my embarrassment he sat back on his heels. My eyes flicked open to see him kneeling between my spread legs. He looked so goddamn good framed between my thighs. Like he belonged there.

My mouth went dry as I found him staring at me with an expression on his face that lit something inside me on fire. "Liking pain is nothing to be ashamed of. Others might try to shame you for what you're into but down here with me, you don't have to pretend."

His fingers brushed against my hips and my skin went hot at his touch as he eased my skirt—the last remaining article of clothing I wore—down my legs. Tossing it aside, he grabbed my knees and splayed them wide open, exposing my bare sex to him. He arched down and slid his tongue through my wet heat. His eyes flashed through his screen of golden hair as he watched my reaction to his carnal kiss.

Bloody hell.

His lips and tongue against my center were warm, wet, and oh so damn good.

When the point of his tongue found my clit, my hips bucked and I ground myself onto his mouth, arching into him. "Fuck!" I gasped, flopping back and twisting my fists into his sheets, stunned by how good it felt. I felt his lips spread against me into a grin as he continued savaging my cunt with stroke after stroke of his surprisingly strong tongue.

My head spun when he abandoned my clit and ducked down further, angling his head deeper between my legs. When his tongue pushed past my folds and filled me, my hands flew to his head.

I held onto his hair for dear life, my whole body shaking as he made the most deliciously masculine sound against my center, like a ravenous animal. I bucked against him, silently begging for more. He glanced up, and what I saw made me gasp. His eyes were wild and crazed. Like I was the tastiest thing he'd ever put to his mouth.

"Fuck, you're so damn tight," he ground out as he lifted his face from my pussy. His lips, his chin, and his snake bites glistened with my juices and it was all I could do to keep myself from coming by the erotic sight of him. "If my little masochistic likes pain so much, it's a good thing you didn't let my brothers touch you yet. If you had, this would hurt a whole lot less. And you don't want that, do you doll? You like feeling pain. Because you weren't ever allowed to feel it back at your old home, were you?"

My eyes widened and for a second I was paralyzed beneath him, stunned by his perception. It was like he peered into my soul and so casually strewn in such a personal fact that I was barely coming to realize myself. And he had just thrown it down like it was just another article of our clothing forgotten at the foot of the bed.

"You're right," I said on a slow and shaky exhale. "I like pain and torment. That's probably why I came back here to the coven. I think I can handle the pain of courting four fucked up vampire princes. But I wonder, how are you going to handle it when I let your brothers touch me?"

His scowl carved a deep V into his brow. "It's going to piss me off."

"I need to pick a king and I don't want to deal with any drama between you and Feral. You can't be possessive."

"Well *I am*," he snarled. "I don't have a problem with Sterling and Corry. Just know that if you come down here smelling like Feral, I will wash away the scent of his blood and cum by covering you in my own. Understand?"

I couldn't stop thinking about his bare abdomen when he'd stepped out of the shower, the perfect cluster of muscles dusted with wet droplets that I'd give damn near anything to wipe clean with my tongue.

The ravaged crucifix tattoo.

His jawline, so sharp it could cut glass.

That damn mark that wasn't mine.

Freaking everything about this male drove me crazy.

I threw myself at him again, this time moving so fast the air whistled past my ears and stung my skin. But his reflexes were unparalleled. He maneuvered away from me, around the towers of books, as if he wasn't blind at all. I grabbed one of the thick books off a stack and whipped it at him. He snatched it out of the air like Mr. Miyagi grabbing the fly with chopsticks in *The Karate Kid.*

Sterling frowned at me as he carefully stowed it on a nearby bookshelf. "That's no way to treat my darlings."

Ugh. Of *course,* he loved books. At this rate, this male was going to make my ovaries explode.

I continued stalking him for what felt like forever. Each time I came close to him, he evaded me, as if he could see my every move with his own two eyes.

I wasn't keeping track of time, but the moon began to dip in the night sky, making the piles of books cast long shadows that stretched across the room.

My limbs began to grow heavy with fatigue, my chest heaving with my splintered breathing, while Sterling hadn't broken a sweat. The human side of me wanted to call it a night and snuggle into the vampire prince's comfy white bed, but the monster in me wouldn't give up. My vampire instincts wanted to claim the male for myself and wouldn't be satisfied until I was in that bed, with Sterling buried between my thighs and my fangs buried into the flesh of his throat.

I could practically picture it, his pale skin pebbled with perspiration as he slowly fucked into me, the sensual slide of his Adam's apple as he swallowed, his eyes clamped to mine like he could see all the darkest fantasies and desires buried deep inside me.

Suddenly, the air was filled with a new scent, something heady and sweet.

And it was coming from *me.*

The scent was nothing like I'd ever smelled before, a new aroma that my body was putting off, almost like it was meant specifically for my chosen mate.

Sterling's nostrils flared, and the muscles in his body tightened. Sweat beaded on his brow, and he let out a heated, masculine groan.

Whatever my body was putting off, it was affecting him, and for the first time since meeting Sterling, I could see him making a visible effort to restrain himself.

"What's happening?" I asked in a growled whisper.

We began to circle the room, almost moving in unison, slow and steady like an ancient dance that had the steps ingrained in the fabric of my being.

He watched me with intensity, as if he was using every sense available to him. His head tilted as he listened, his nostrils flared, and his tongue frequently ran over his lips to taste the air we shared.

"Fascinating," he murmured. "I've heard of this happening, but I've never seen it myself since female half-bloods are so rare."

"What's happening?" I asked again as we continued to circle the perimeter of the room, weaving between books.

"Your functioning ovum and your vampiric instincts are co-mingling to create a pheromone to entice your chosen mate."

"Meaning?"

He licked his lips again, tasting the air for the dozenth time. Then his eyes closed shut for just a moment, and a shaky exhale left his body. I could see he was doing everything he could to stay in control and keep all evidence of his reaction to me off his face.

Aside from his heaving chest and the beads of perspiration soaking into the collar of his sweater, he was doing a good job. With everything north of his waist, that was. His hunger pressed against his sweats, the girth of him pretty damn huge for how lithe he was. A lick of heat tickled my core as I registered the size of it. A girl could seriously hurt herself on that thing.

In spite of his raging erection, he remained cool and collected, his lips pressed into a troubled frown. "Meaning, your womb is fertile, Miss Baxter. And your body is trying to tempt me into claiming you by putting off a powerful pheromone. Similar to a beast in heat."

A beast in heat. Like an animal, or a monster. In this moment, I felt like one. A fierce huntress with my prey lined up in my sights.

I purred again, crouching low as I prepared to pounce. This time, I dragged the call to my chosen mate out, a low and sultry song meant only for Sterling. "Well," I hummed. "Is it working?"

Chapter Forty-Four
STERLING

Sterling held my gaze with an emotion burning behind his spectral eyes that made me weak in the knees. He didn't answer my question, but he didn't have to. Whatever pheromone my body was putting off to entice this male, it was working. I could tell by the way the prince's composure began to slip.

And something told me Sterling never lost control.

A dark curiosity filled me, making me burn with a dangerous desire to push him over the edge, where together, we would both topple over into a world I'd never experienced. A world that brimmed with sinful promises, where only we existed.

It was like there was something written in the fabric of my very being designating me as Sterling's mate. As if his name was stamped into my soul, and all he had to do was sign on the line to claim what was his.

But something held the vampire back, even though I could see his body reacting to my call. Every muscle in his lithe frame was coiled tight, his fists clenched into balls at his sides. His chest rose and fell in heavy succession, and his eyes... Before, they had been serene and calm like the rest of the tower, but now they were filled with something wild that called to the monster inside me.

Not to mention that cock, hard as a rock, pressing against his sweats like it was about to bust through at any second.

I moved with speed I didn't even know I was capable of. This time, I could see him beginning to dodge me. His body shifted to the left, and I recalibrated my path, slamming into him just as he swerved to avoid me. I moved to bite him, but his hand snapped out, catching my jaw, my fangs gnashing nothing but air.

I whined, pushing out another sultry purr that came from a place inside me I hadn't even known existed, a depraved stream of desires that had awoken from an ancient sleep the second Sterling came into my orbit.

I wanted to press my body into his, but he held me at arm's length, keeping a frustrating amount of distance between us.

"Sterling," I whispered on a seductive purr, as soft as a prayer but as sinful as a whore's confession. "Claim me."

Holy fuck.

The expression his face made at my invitation was almost enough to make me come right then and there. A vein twitched in his jaw, his brows knitted together, and his eyes banked with a heat that could keep a girl warm all night long.

His skin on mine was like fire and ice. I was melting beneath him into a pool of wet need. He couldn't see me, but damn, it felt like he could by the way his steel-cold eyes sliced into me, stripping back all my layers to expose my deepest parts.

My body ached for him, making me purr and growl and thrash in his arms, curving my hips to press into his. With how he held me, I could barely touch him. It was a mean way to tease me, so close yet so far. My gaze flicked down to see his generous hunger, oh-so-faintly kissing my thigh.

There was a tiny wet spot in the fabric where his pre-cum had bled through, and fuck me, seeing his dick thirst for me was one of the most erotic things I'd ever seen.

Then there was the matter of his scent. His aroma was still reminiscent of salty ocean air, cashmere, and paper, but now there was another quality to it. It was like his body was already releasing some kind of delicious fragrance to entice me, perfectly male and perfectly mine. He smelled so damn good, it hurt.

That's what he was doing. He was hurting me by inciting this ache between my thighs and torturing me by refusing to sate it.

It was so frustrating I felt like I could shatter apart in his grip.

Whatever was happening between us went way beyond physical attraction and basic chemistry. There was something profoundly terrifying about the way our bodies were being pulled toward one another. It was something neither of us could control or see. But by God, we could feel it.

So why the fuck was he holding back?

We should've both been naked by now, our sweaty limbs tangled together, consummating our mating bond.

"Sterling, touch me." This time I wasn't asking. I was demanding.

His nostrils flared again. He licked his lips, and I watched, enraptured as his tongue seemed to slide over his flesh in slow-motion. My mouth went dry, and another feminine growl bled from me.

Normally I wasn't this demanding, this desperate. With the other guys, I'd been coyer and more dignified. Well, sort of. But with Sterling, all my inhibitions seemed to fall away with the rest of my humanity.

His fingers quivered where they held my jaw. "Miss Baxter..."

My brows arched, and I let out a gravelly chuckle. "Given the circumstances, you can call me Ruby."

His features pinched in frustration, his brow carved with a disapproving scowl. "That would be inappropriate."

I blinked. Nothing about this situation was *appropriate.* I had come up here to ask him to turn me into a vampire, but my vagina had other plans, and now, here I was, my body literally begging for him to mate me.

"Sterling, I don't know shit about the whole vampire instincts thing or how it works. But whatever is happening between us, it has to mean that you're supposed to be my mate. My king."

I reached to touch his stomach, feeling the tight cluster of his abdominal muscles beneath the fabric of his sweater. I watched his reaction to me carefully, enjoying the way his breath hitched as my fingers hooked the elastic of his sweats. His arm went slack, allowing me to step closer.

As I slipped my hand inside his pants, his teeth clenched, and he let out a hiss when I made contact with the velvety skin of his erection. I moved to pull him out, but his other hand caught my wrist, stopping me.

"What are you doing?" I snapped, my voice practically shaking with a volatile mixture of frustration and anticipation.

He squeezed his eyes shut, releasing a shaky exhale. "No. We can't do this."

No?

He had grasped my wrist, but it felt like he had fisted my heart and gave it a vicious squeeze instead.

Was he really *rejecting* me?

"Sterling," I said, trying to gather what little control over this situation I still had. "I pick you as my king. A lot of shit is confusing me. I'm trying to figure out not only how to be a vampire but how to be me. Literally, everything is new to me, and I'm so confused. I'm not sure about anything. But the second I came in here, I was sure about you. You're supposed to be mine. You're supposed to be my king. It's you. I choose *you*."

By the look on his face, one would think I had just told him his dog died, rather than telling him he got the very thing the other guys were fighting for.

"Miss Baxter... Over my lifetime, I've had my fill of kings. I have no desire to sit on your father's throne."

"Even if I'm sitting beside you?"

He looked so pained, like it physically hurt him to say the words. "Even then."

Something dark and ugly stirred my insides as if he'd stuck my heart in a blender and set it to puree. "But, that's not fair!" My hand squeezed his cock harder, and he let out a deep growl, laced with both pleasure and pain.

"That's not just unfair to me. That's unfair to your people! You would be the best king of all of them!"

He sucked in a breath. "Pick one of my brothers."

"W–we don't need to decide now. We have four months before any decisions have to be cemented." Four months for me to convince him. And I'd start with that convincing right now. I gave his shaft a firm stroke, and he winced like he was using every shred of his will to resist me.

I didn't like how he made me feel like an evil seductress rather than his true mate.

"My answer won't be any different in four months."

Desperation began to seep into my soul, replacing the flames of lust inside me with molten ire. Turns out, my monster didn't handle rejection well. "*Please.*"

"I won't take the throne. I won't do it."

I ground my teeth. "You've got balls, rejecting me when your cock is so hard for me it could cut a bitch right now. I know you want me—the evidence is sitting in my palm!"

I gave him another squeeze for emphasis. I began to stroke his shaft in a slow, torturous motion. I'd never done anything like this before, but if my movements were clumsy, Sterling didn't seem to mind. His head fell back against the wall, and his eyes fluttered shut.

As I worked his cock, my attention clamped down on his throat. His neck was one of my favorite features, long and wrapped in perfect, marble-smooth skin. The contours of his throat were so freaking erotic, each little muscle that twitched accentuated by his pale skin and bathed in a sheen of sweat and moonlight.

But that damn mating mark stood out, taunting me.

"Will you not claim me because you're already mated?"

His eyelids flicked open to reveal surprise-filled eyes. Then his expression darkened with something that made my stomach twist. "It is..." His breath came out labored and disjointed. "But not for the reason you think."

What the hell was that supposed to mean? Did he have a mate or not?

My hand stilled, but I didn't take it off his cock. "Who is she?"

"No one," he answered me on a whisper so quiet it was almost swept away by the gust of breeze that rushed in through the window. "Not anymore."

"She's dead?"

He gave a nod.

A heavy sensation settled in my chest. I extracted my hand from his sweats, feeling dirty, desperate, and confused.

"Did you love her?"

He gave a slow shake of his head. "No."

"Then what's the problem?"

A vein pounded in my temple when he said nothing in response. Goddamn this infuriating male with a body so freaking gorgeous it wasn't fair. It wasn't fair how much I lusted for him. It wasn't fair how hot he made me burn and that he refused to quench this fire.

And it wasn't fair that he wouldn't tell me why.

"Am I not good enough for you or something?"

Again, he said nothing. The silence that pulsed between us flayed me like a bullwhip. It was a form of torture that didn't feel good, nothing like being strapped to Eros' workbench.

Sterling's refusal to claim me was a pain that didn't feel so good.

The distance between us, the silence, it felt all *wrong*.

Even more frustrating, I knew Sterling wanted me. He wasn't saying it, but he didn't have to. His body told me everything his words refused to.

"You were the one to tell me to give in to my instincts. That's what I'm doing. So why can't you give into yours?"

My question was met only with more silence.

My blood began to boil with anger, filling me with a rage so pure, the little purchase I had managed to gain over my control began to slip again.

And once more, my instincts had shoved their way into the driver's seat.

Without thinking, I sank to my knees in front of him, grasped the waist of his pants, and pulled them down over his hips. I paused for a split second to see if he would stop me. He didn't though, In fact, he let out a rattling growl of encouragement and pushed his hips forward.

So I guess it was cool for me to suck him off, but claiming me as his mate and queen was off the table.

His delicious length sprung out into the open, and for a beat, all I could do was stare at it, completely enthralled. I wanted to shove myself on it, to make him moan and writhe while he was seated inside me. But the heady scent rolling off his cock fell into the background noise as my senses honed in on the dark veins in his hips and thighs.

I arched forward as if to take his length into my mouth, but instead, I sunk my fangs into his thigh, taking out my rage induced by his rejection in the form of my blood lust.

The cavernous growl that tore from his throat rattled my bones, shaking me to my core. Taking a handful of my hair, he wrenched me to my feet, pinning me down with a baleful glare that made me squirm.

With his free hand, he wrenched his sweats back up, blood and pre-cum staining the fabric like some perverted abstract painting.

Eros had offhandedly mentioned in his room that if I wanted a gentle lover, I should seek out Sterling. But I had a feeling I was seeing a side of this vampire prince that no one else got to see. Just as he was seeing a side of me no one had yet seen, including myself.

"Get out of my room," he muttered through a voice so steady and calm, it made the little hairs on my neck stand up. "Go find one of my brothers to claim you because I won't do it."

"I'm not leaving until you either claim me or give me a damn good reason why you won't."

There weren't words to describe the wave of frustration that ravaged my body. I wanted Sterling to the point of pain, and I knew he felt the same. So why was he rejecting me? Whoever his mate had been, they were no longer in the picture. There was an inexplicable force pushing us together, and yet, for reasons he wouldn't say, he was going out of his way to resist it, and he was hurting me in the process.

Blind with rage, I twisted in his arms and bit him again, this time over the mark on his throat. I knew my bite wouldn't permanently cover it, not unless he was buried balls deep inside me. But damn it, I wanted it on his flesh forever. More than that, I wanted him to want it as badly as I did.

And the fact that he didn't left a bitter taste in my mouth that his salty-sweet blood failed to wash away.

"Ruby! Stop this!" He wrenched me away, holding me at bay in his arms. His black blood trickled down his ivory flesh, soaking into the collar of his sweater. Even covered in sweat and blood, he was beautiful.

"I need you. Please. I don't know what reason you're resisting this—whatever *this* is—but please don't." I should have felt pathetic begging for him, but the only sensation left in me was the excruciating pain in my chest, where my heart had broken into a thousand pieces. "You're supposed to be mine. Can't you feel it too?"

"Of course I do!" His lip peeled to reveal sharp fangs that glinted in the moonlight. I resisted the urge to step back as his face twisted with the fury he could no longer bridle. "Listen to me. I want you so bad I can feel it in my balls. But I'll never be yours. I won't be anyone's ever again. Do you want to know why? Because your father ruined me! I don't want anything to do with him! I don't want his throne! And I don't want you!"

Sterling still held me, with one hand in my hair and one on my wrist. But I couldn't feel him. I had gone completely numb.

I hated my dad.

I'd never met him, and I hated him with every fiber of my being. He had taken so much away from me, a chance at a normal life, a normal family. And now that I found something I actually wanted, that felt right, my father had gone and ruined that too.

I swallowed thickly, trying to hold back the thick tears that stung at my eyes. "I don't look like him, you know. If you're wondering."

Sterling's expression softened some, the anger fizzling away to leave only hurt etched into the corners of his eyes.

A long beat of silence swelled between us. When he finally spoke, his question came out in a tentative whisper, free of all the hurt and anger that had been present in his voice before. "Can I look at you?"

I wasn't really sure what he was asking, but I found myself nodding.

Releasing my hair and my wrist, he brought his hands to my face. His fingertips went to my chin first before trailing up to trace my lips. He took his time feeling them out, exploring their shape. Then he felt out my nose, the apples of my cheeks, my brow, even my ears.

He was mapping out my face with his hands, and when he finished, he gave me a doleful smile that deepened the ache in my heart.

"I may not see in the traditional sense, but my senses have developed so much over the centuries, I can make out things that humans and even other vampires cannot."

"Like what?"

"Sometimes, I can see heat patterns. I can detect the vibrations in the air. I can even see the kind of energy gathered around a person."

"Like...auras?"

He nodded. "Yes."

"And what does mine look like?"

His hands dropped from my face, and he took a step back, placing distance between us once more. All traces of the smile he'd worn were now gone. "Like your father's."

My heart froze, and suddenly I felt so damn cold. I wrapped my arms around myself, my gaze falling to the floor. "I'm not like him."

"I know."

"Then why are you letting him get between us? He shouldn't have anything to do with us."

I watched Sterling as he moved to his bed and sat on the edge of the mattress, resting his head in his hands with his elbows propped on his knees. "Miss Baxter... Understand that ours is going to be a complicated relationship. I already knew that even before discovering the way our bodies seem to respond to one another."

I moved to sit beside him, keeping about a foot between us. When he felt the bed creak with my weight, he looked up from his hands, and the expression he sent me caused all air to empty from my lungs. It was that same hollowed look the painter had captured in the painting I'd seen in the library.

"You are the daughter of the man who haunts my every nightmare. When I see your aura—*his* aura—I want to hurt you. But when I scent you, and I touch you, I want to do the opposite. I want to hold you and feed from you, and I want—" His voice dropped an octave, and when he spoke next, his words came out in a rasp, like he was confessing some dark fantasy. "I want things from you I've never wanted from anyone before."

"Like what?"

"Like..." He looked right through me, eyes warm with something that sent a rush of fire through me. It was a wild heat that burned so hot I thought I might turn to ash. And if the flames didn't eat me up, I was sure the terrifying darkness swirling in Sterling's blind gaze would. "Like someone to call my own. Someone to warm my bed. Someone who knows the things that have been done to me yet still looks at me with desire rather than pity."

"I can give those things to you." I reached for his hand, lacing my fingers through his. For a second, I thought he might pull away, but he didn't. He stared down at where I held him as if he was imagining my hand and how it might look nestled in his.

"But to do that, Sterling, you have to tell me what my father did to you."

CHAPTER FORTY-FIVE

REBORN WITH A SILVER SPOON

Sterling let out a heavy sigh that felt like it carried the whole weight of the world. His hand tightened around mine, giving it a squeeze. He then unfurled his fingers from mine, patted my knee, and got up from the bed. I watched as he crossed over to one of the windows and leaned against the wall, staring out at the ocean with an unreadable expression on his face. I could almost see his frustration not being able to see the view of the ocean that stretched beyond the window. Or the view behind him stretched out on his bed. His shoulders fell, and he ran a hand over his face. With where he stood, the moon created a halo effect around his head, bathing the tortured prince all in silver.

"You don't have to tell me," I amended. "I thought it might be a relief to get things off your shoulders."

"You're asking me to tell you things I haven't even told my brothers."

I frowned. "You act like you guys are close."

The vampire turned his head in my direction, his lips quirking into the faintest of smiles as his blank gaze bore right through me. "Vincent and Eros may butt heads, but they won't be at odds forever. We're den mates, the closest to family creatures like us have."

For a hot second, I considered telling him about Eros and Vincent's little bet over Friday's fight but quickly pushed the idea away. I wasn't sure I had the energy to weather both their tantrums when they eventually found out I'd ratted on them. Plus, I didn't want to change the topic and give Sterling an out.

I was venturing into tricky territory by asking the silver prince to fill me in on the torture my father had subjected him to. I felt bad pressing Sterling on such a sensitive and personal topic. But I was eager to thoroughly explore the man behind all the walls he had erected around himself for protection. And unlike Vincent, I felt as though Sterling was eager for me to see that side of him.

"Speaking of my brothers, it seems Eros has already placed his mark on you."

My skin flushed as I felt the fresh mating mark burn on my shoulder. Since stepping into Sterling's domain, I had almost forgotten about it. Of course, Sterling could scent it, but why he hadn't chosen to mention it until now was beyond me. Maybe he was deflecting, using it as a means to redirect the conversation. "It was an accident. Things got... heated."

I searched Sterling's features, half expecting to find traces of jealousy or anger. Instead, he gave me a nod, a pleased look briefly passing over his features. "I'm glad he's found someone in the coven who can stomach playing with him."

My eyes narrowed. "You're changing the subject."

"Miss Baxter, say I tell you everything about the grim and complicated relationship I had with your father. And let's say you still somehow want me after you uncover my skeletons. What good will it do? I will never take the throne. It would be a waste of time spending these four months with me."

I rose from the bed and walked over to him by the window. I don't know what compelled me to do it. Maybe it was the swirl of hormones that knotted my insides, filling me with a confusing tangle of emotions. Or maybe it was simply the fact that with Sterling, I felt like it was safe to let my guard down. Which wasn't a stage I had come to with the other guys. Not yet.

I took his hand and guided it to my cheek so that he could see me. He turned toward me, letting his fingers roam over my features, pausing with his fingertips over my mouth. My lips pursed into a smile against him.

"I just met you, but for some reason, I know that any time I spend with you won't be a waste. Even if you still won't take the throne with me at the end of this, our time together won't ever be a waste."

"How can you know that?" he asked in a stony whisper.

"Because I like you," I answered simply, shrugging a shoulder. "You smell good, you feel good. You feel *right*. That's enough for me... For now."

I emphasized the "'for now" part. It sucked big time that I seemed to have a deep, instinctual connection with the one prince who wasn't interested in the throne. He was right, though. It would be heartbreaking to become attached to him and, at the end of the four months, marry another prince. But I came into this whole thing knowing it would be complicated.

Then again, I still had four months to decide and four months for Sterling to come around.

Before he could pull away, I pushed onto my toes and brought my blazing lips to his cool ones.

He didn't pull away like I thought he might. Instead, his lips softened beneath mine, and he moaned against my mouth like it was more lecherous than anything else we could do.

Somehow the kiss connected us both in ways I couldn't even begin to fathom. It was as if our souls were trying to fuse through the simple connection. I felt that dark, confusing part of me trying to claw its way out again, driven mad by the combination of his scent mingled with his old mate's.

Something buried deep inside my being ached for more of him. My desire for him went well beyond sex. He was attractive, sure, but no more so than the others. Unlike Corry, Eros, and Vincent, Sterling was an ancient mystery, wrapped up in a package my lethal curiosity burned to unravel. It was like he was the most prized book in the library's vast collection, a thick and ancient tome written in a foreign language.

I couldn't even begin to fathom the stories he held tight inside him. If only I could crack his code and spill out all his dark secrets.

I broke the kiss but pushed myself against his hard frame. He seemed hesitant for a split second but wrapped his arms around my waist, holding me close against him.

I studied him with complete fascination. He was so measured and calculated that when he did move, I was hypnotized. His moonstone eyes seemed to soften when I was near him, sensually hooded and accented with thick, frost-colored lashes.

He was magnificent in every sense of the word, a beautiful man who had been turned in his prime—his early thirties by my estimation.

I had so many questions about the thousand-year-old man before me. What color had his eyes been before he had been turned? Or his hair, it couldn't have always been silver. Where was he from? What happened to his family?

"You don't need to give me the whole story on what exactly happened between you and my dad," I assured Sterling again. "If you want, you can. But only if it's baggage you're ready to unpack."

"I do want to tell you something," he said after a moment of contemplation. "Something I've never told anyone."

I perked in his arms. "What is it?"

"My name isn't really Sterling."

I blinked. "Really?"

He nodded, his eyes darkening as old memories seemed to surface in his mind.

"What's your real name?"

"I don't remember," he admitted on a pained sigh. "Sterling is a nickname that your father gave me."

He paused, a beat of silence pulsating between us, but it wasn't awkward this time. I understood it was hard for him to come out of his shell when he'd probably spent countless years being reclusive. With each breath he took, I could feel the muscles in his body unwind. I felt giddy, knowing he was about to share something with me that he hadn't trusted anyone else with. On the flip side of that, I couldn't seem to tramp down on my rioting nerves, knowing full well the story he was about to tell would be a sad one.

"I was a monk a thousand years ago in England. I was devoted to the Lord, living a simple life in a monastery. There was another monk, a mad fellow who disappeared for long bouts of time, doing missionary work. Or so he claimed. I discovered later he was a monster hunter. Well, he came back after some months away, in pieces."

"In pieces?" I swallowed.

"Indeed. Stuffed in a bloody potato sack tossed over Thomas Knight's shoulder. That was the first time I ever laid eyes on the former king."

"I remember so little from back then, but I will never forget how the hairs on the back of my neck stood up when I laid eyes on the dark-haired devil, wearing a manic grin painted in blood. That sight alone made a few of the monks piss themselves, and those who hadn't wetted themselves followed suit with those who had when he introduced himself as Satan."

My stomach cartwheeled, and my body went ice cold in Sterling's arms. For the past three days, the other princes had laid out clues as to just how horrible the old vampire king had been. But no one had provided exact details.

The depths of my father's cruelty had been left to my own imagination. I hadn't let myself dwell on it too much. But now, I had a feeling I was about to discover just how evil Thomas Knight had been. As much as I wanted to stay in the fantasy world where my dad had been a halfway decent guy, that ship had left the port.

At this rate, the only solace in my blossoming hatred for my dad was that maybe it could bring Sterling and me closer together.

"Go on," I urged on a waif-thin whisper, searching his haunted expression. "I'm listening."

Sterling gave me a solemn nod. "Well, suffice to say, the vampire king wasn't happy about the loss of his mate at the hands of the now-deceased monk. I still remember the look in Thomas Knight's eye. He was grinning, but it was a mask. Beneath his blood-crusted mania, I could see his anguish. He was completely crushed. For all I know, maybe he had been a good man before he lost his mate, a man capable of love. And when she was murdered, perhaps that was when he'd become a monster."

"What happened next?" I asked, feeling like a little kid, listening to a bedtime story, a fucked-up bedtime story where the villain was my own father.

"He ordered every monk to swear their fealty to the devil and said that if they did, he'd give each a great gift."

"Let me guess. Those who did he turned, and those who remained faithful, he killed."

Sterling gave me a morose smile. "If only. Every single monk fell to their knees, pledging their allegiance to him, the devil. Only one was fool enough to refuse to forsake the Lord. To this day, I regret it."

A fist of dread squeezed my heart, causing me to shudder. "What was the gift he gave to those who pledged themselves?"

"Death," Sterling murmured coolly, his gaze sliding past me to the moon outside that he couldn't see. "The great gift was that they got to meet their Lord. I watched as he slew my friends one by one. But he made it quick for them. I wasn't given such mercy. Maybe the devil would have changed his mind if I hadn't provoked him."

"What did you say?"

Against all odds, the prince let out a dry laugh, almost as if he found it funny. "The stupidest thing I could have. I told him that I wasn't afraid of him and that he could do his worst because, in the end, the last thing I would see would be the face of my Lord and Savior."

"That's when he blinded you."

Sterling chewed his lip, appearing steeped in thought. "Your father always had a sick sense of humor. He bit me, then forced me to drink his blood. I got so sick... I was lying on the floor of the monastery's chapel, too weak to move, surrounded by the bodies of the monks with the crucifix looming over me and my new master's arms wrapped around me like a cage. It was utter hell, but when I came to, I felt...fantastic. Like I'd never been sick. I could practically smell colors. And the things I could *see*. For those first waking moments, I thought I had died and gone to Heaven. But then I noticed your father, standing over me with a spoon in hand."

"A spoon?"

"Silver, from the monastery's storage."

My jaw fell open, and horror filled my lungs like concrete, making it hard to breathe. "He blinded you with a silver spoon?"

Sterling's arms dropped from my waist, leaving me even colder than before. He closed his eyes, and for a second, I wasn't sure what he was doing. Then I realized he was showing me his eyelids. The scars were so faint, I hadn't noticed them before. But now, I could make out the curved scars of where a spoon had been pushed into either eye.

"After he blinded me, he locked me in the cellar. Left me there for... I lost count. Years, probably. Maybe even decades. I drank the monastery's wine stores, and when that ran out, I lived off rats. The cellar was opened by humans years later who discovered me."

"Who were they?"

Sterling's brows knitted together, an expression so sad, I felt his agony deep in the marrow of my bones. "I didn't ask before I slew them all. I was so hungry, and I didn't understand what I was, what I had become. But I felt this *pull*—a youngblood's link to their master. I followed it, all the way across the country, to find the King of Vampires. I was delirious with terror and bloodlust. When I finally found him, there were so many things I wanted to say to him, and yet, the first thing out of my mouth was to ask him if he remembered my name. But he hardly recognized me. In fact, all he remembered about our encounter was the sterling spoon."

"That's how you got your name," I muttered, barely able to move or say anything more. I was horrified beyond belief. I felt horrible for Sterling.

The story on how he'd gotten his nickname had to be a drop in a bucket of fucked-up memories he had of my dad. The worst thing I was feeling, though, was *guilt*. Which didn't make any damn sense. *I* wasn't the one who'd shoved a silver spoon in the vampire's eyes. I hadn't tossed him in that cellar and left him to survive off rats like an animal.

But my father had.

How could I have spawned from such a monster?

Vincent had called me "little monster" on occasion, and now the nickname felt appropriate. I was the direct blood descendant of pure evil. A normal girl in my situation might be afraid of the four progeny princes that my father had tormented—afraid that maybe they'd take out their vengeance on me.

But nope.

More than anything, I was afraid of myself. Something was lurking just beneath the surface of my being. It was that monster who had taken off Mal's head without a second's hesitation, and it was the same thing that had fought to hunt and claim Sterling.

Sensing my rising panic, Sterling arched down and pressed a reverent kiss to my forehead. "It's alright, Ruby. He's not here anymore. He can't hurt either of us any longer."

Tears pricked my eyes. I wasn't sure if it was from the joy of hearing my first name in Sterling's mouth or from the unsettling revelation that maybe there was a part of Thomas Knight inside me, a part that could hurt us both.

"I don't understand," I sniffed against him, rubbing my tears away by angrily grinding my fists into my eyes. "How can you stand touching me after what he did to you? You said you can't claim me or the throne because you don't want anything to do with him. I get that now. But there is a part of you that *still* wants me."

A gentle smile tugged at Sterling's lips, and he placed another soft peck on my cheeks, kissing away my tears. "Yes, there is a part of me that wants you."

"But why?"

For the first time since meeting him, Sterling's expression showed everything. His mask had fallen away, his walls crumbling like the ancient ruins they were. His eyes begged for a connection, something real, something he could trust. "Because Thomas Knight owes me something good."

I pressed my hands against the prince's chest, feeling the sculpted muscle beneath his sweater. He grasped my wrists, holding my hands against him as if showing me he wasn't afraid to be close anymore.

A lump formed in my throat as my fingers grazed over the scars of the ruined crucifix tattoo. "I'm not an expert in medieval priests, but you couldn't have gotten this tattoo before you were turned. So after all the vampire king put you through, you still have your faith?"

A melancholy smile touched Sterling's lips. "My faith comes and goes depending on the century. If there is a God, I don't believe he cares for me much. The tattoo was more of an act of rebellion against your father."

Before I could respond, a huge raven landed on the windowsill, giving an obnoxious squawk. I jumped in surprise and moved away from Sterling, who looked thoroughly irritated by the interruption.

"Whoa, you are a *big* bird." I stuck out my hand to see if it would hop onto my finger, but Sterling waved it away with an impatient flick of his hand.

"You don't like birds?"

"I like birds just fine, but that one will be trouble if we let it inside tonight."

Confused, I decided not to ask him to elaborate. He latched the window shut and began pulling down the metal shutters that seemed to be affixed to every window in the mansion. "It will be sunrise before too long. While it seems you've come down from your youngblood tantrum, you're still putting off pheromones that will, to put it politely, excite all sorts of creatures, be it human, vampire, or otherwise."

A familiar heat bloomed between my thighs as I began to catch on to his meaning. "So, what do you suggest we do about it?" I purred a growl, releasing some of the feminine scent he was referring to.

The vampire's lips slid into a smooth smile that unleashed a flutter of butterflies in my stomach.

"I'm suggesting you stay with me for the remainder of tonight and into the day."

Chapter Forty-Six

GOLDEN GIFT FROM A SILVER PRINCE

Since Sterling had shuttered and locked all the windows to ensure protection from the oncoming sunrise, I was confused when he turned to leave the tower, pausing in the doorway, beckoning me to follow.

"Where are we going?" I asked with my gaze clamped to his broad back as he descended the stairs. "Isn't the sun going to be up soon?"

"It is. The tower isn't my only dwelling place. I like to have full run of the east end of the manor. I don't have much of a stomach for small spaces anymore, not after those dark years spent in the monastery's cellar. I like to move about, even during daylight."

"But where will we be sleeping? Not among the books?"

"Would that be so terrible?" He chuckled, twisting to face me from over his shoulder, his sinful lips stretching into a smile as if he could see me and the excitement on my face. Hell, if he could see auras, maybe he could feel the giddiness bursting out of me, like a swarm of fireflies were buzzing in my belly, lighting me up from the inside. I was alit with a mixture of curiosity and arousal that had yet to fade. In Sterling's presence, with the sleek body of marbled perfection and a pouting mouth made for sin, I doubted that sensation would ever go away while I was in his presence.

"I would love to sleep among the books. Or make a fort out of them." I let out a nervous laugh, afraid that he might think I was childish. Of course, in a lot of ways, I was, at least compared to him. This gorgeous creature possessed a wealth of knowledge that made me weak in the knees just thinking about it. Here I was, a sheltered twenty-three-year-old whose knowledge didn't stretch beyond a basic home school education, a meager book collection that was a joke compared to his, and lessons learned from cable TV. But if Sterling thought me pathetic, he didn't show it.

He turned to face me when we got to the bottom of the stairs and leaned against the doorway, crossing his arms over his chest. The corners of his mouth pulled into an amused grin, his brows cocking. "A fort? And what are we defending against, fair princess?"

"All these males who supposedly will be drawn by my womanly half-blood pheromones or whatever. That's why you asked me to stay with you through the day, isn't it? To protect me from them?"

"While I think it's true that both genders can get savage during breeding rituals, I think in this case we're protecting the males from you. If one of my brothers tried to offer themselves to you in your current state and you find them lacking, you may attack them."

I rolled my eyes. "If that's the case, bring Vincent in. A few of these heavy-ass books have his forehead written all over it."

Sterling's ghostly pale eyes pinned me down with something that made me shift uncomfortably.

"You like him," he mused with scary accurate perception. "Don't you?"

"*No*," I retorted, a little too quick on the draw.

Sterling's smile stretched into a knowing smirk that looked too good on his lips for me to be angry. "Your heart rate makes a liar out of you, Miss Baxter."

"Vincent Feral is an asshole. He's cruel, and he's a bully. Plus, he's with that Lexi chick. If I was stupid enough to pick him as king, he'd toss me aside and give her my throne."

"Alexandra?" Sterling's brows popped so high I thought they might come off. "No, the Elders would never allow that. Even if we did, why would Vincent choose that ice-cold harpy as our queen over you?"

A deep warmth bloomed in my chest to match the blush on my cheeks. Sterling's tone suggested that the notion of Lexi being queen over me was a ridiculous fear, easing my nerves about the whole thing in an instant.

Sheesh. I should have come to Sterling way sooner. When I met Lexi, her frigid-bitch glare instantly set loose a parasite of doubt in my stomach that had been eating me alive ever since. And Sterling had squashed it with just a few words.

"I thought that maybe because she was a full-blood..."

"You're still a vampire. And you're the blood heir of Thomas Knight."

I felt stupid saying my next words, but I was already addicted to Sterling's soothing words of comfort, his reassurance. "Doesn't Vincent only go for full-blooded women?"

Sterling's nose wrinkled. "He doesn't like to take human mates, but to say he doesn't care for half-bloods, well, that would be very hypocritical of him."

The enticing curve of Sterling's lips curled downward when he realized what he'd just admitted. It wasn't anything I hadn't figured out myself. Vincent was only half-vampire, like me. But from the obscenely delicious flavor of his blood and how his imposing energy wrapped around me like a chloroform-soaked cloth, he wasn't half-human.

"What is Feral?" Might as well come right out with one of the many questions weighing on me and try my luck. Sterling was way less aloof than the others so far. Well, except for Corry. But judging by our conversation at Clown Car Burgers, Corry didn't know what Feral was either.

"He'll tell you when he's ready," Sterling muttered, moving through the library. I trailed behind him, weaving with him as we worked our way through the maze of shelves, various furniture, and stacks of books.

"Vampires really love their secrets, don't they?" I tutted.

"What else do we have, if not our secrets?"

"I don't know. Being so powerful that humans still fear you but somehow still want to have sex with you? Plus, you can live forever."

Sterling whirled around so fast I almost slammed into him. I stumbled back, catching myself on a table. My throat constricted when I took in the severity of the scowl on his face.

"And to you, all these are good things?"

"I–I don't know. Being a full-blooded vampire has to be better than being half. Lately, I don't feel like a human or a vampire. I just feel like—" My voice began to tremor dangerously. I sagged against the table, hanging my head. Suddenly I felt so exhausted. I hadn't told Sterling about my plans on asking him to turn me into a full vampire. And at this point, I had decided not to tell him.

Because I had changed my mind.

When I laid eyes on his mating mark, something inside me had shifted. The idea of being a full-blood still held appeal, of course. Once I became queen, the other covens' loyalty would be easier to keep if I was a full-blooded vampire on the throne. But Vincent wanted a kid. He'd come right out and said it in a very unsubtle manner. The cleft between my thighs still throbbed at the memory. Eros and Corry had been a little more subtle about it, but they had more or less hinted at wanting kids too. And even though Sterling was more guarded when it came to his desires for me, he wanted it. I could feel it.

And damn it. I wanted it too.

I had to admit it to myself. No matter who I ended up picking as my mate and king, I wanted to give them an heir.

When I became queen, I would want to have a baby.

"Miss Baxter, look at me," Sterling whispered on a soft coo, pulling me from my thoughts. I don't know how he knew my gaze was currently rooted to my feet, but I obeyed and lifted my eyes to his, finding a tender smile on his face. "I think I know what's on your mind. I hope I can ease any feelings of inadequacy by telling you that you being a half-blood is a gift."

"It is?"

"Yes." My heart clenched as his voice shifted to a gentle whisper like a tender cadence meant only for a lover. "You can control your instincts better than a full-blood. You can still walk in the sun. You can touch silver. You can have a family, a child forged out of love, rather than a vampire progeny whose life you would have to steal."

Something in my chest stirred, making my heart heat with an intense fire that melted my insides. I leaned against Sterling and closed my eyes as I felt his arms draw me against him.

"But I would be stronger as a full-blood," I countered. "And what will the other covens think when the news of the half-blooded heir spreads? The Boston Coven has already started rebelling."

Sterling pressed his knuckle beneath my chin to lift my gaze to his. Even though he was blind, at that moment, I felt as though he could see me. "You would be stronger, but even as a half-blood, you are a force to reckoned with. I heard about what you did to that Boston Coven member when they tried to ambush you during your botched escape attempt the other night. Evil as he was, Thomas Knight's power was unmatched by any other vampire, at least on this continent. You must have inherited some of that power. And you will live plenty long. Hundreds of years, if not more. As for coven loyalty, that much is true. But having a male like Vincent as king, he would rule with an iron fist. Most would be too terrified to defy him. Eros too."

"What about Corry?"

"Corry is... fresh from the human world. He could be a great comfort to you. As vampire queen, your life won't be ordinary, but at least he could provide you with some semblance of something normal."

I frowned against Sterling's shoulder and wrapped my arms tighter around him. "I don't like that I have to choose. Why do I have to pick a king? Can't I rule on my own? This is the twenty-first century, after all. Queen Elizabeth doesn't need a king, so why do I?"

The vampire prince plucked me away from his chest and held me away from him, giving me a hard frown. "Do you think if Queen Elizabeth was only half-human she would be so beloved by her people? With a strong, full-blooded king by your side, there will be far less chance of rebellion from the other covens."

My glare eased, and I felt those butterflies resuming flight in my belly. "What if I pick you?"

His shoulders tensed, and his serious expression locked back into place. "We already talked about this. I haven't changed my mind. I won't take the throne."

I made a low-rattling growl of frustration, baring my fangs at Sterling. He didn't flinch, though. Instead, he shoved his hands in his pockets and showed me those beautiful pouty lips of his turned down into a scowl that made me ache with an unmet need.

"Are you going to attack me again?" he asked. "Before we even get to my den?"

My heart pulsed in my chest as a hot rush of heat simmered low in my stomach. Those monstrous, confusing tangles of hormones inside me seemed to react to the mention of his den. "We're going to your den?"

"Yes. Do you know what that is?"

I mulled over my answer for a second before giving it to him. "It's a separate room where you keep your coffin? Like your hidey-hole?"

"Yes." His brows twitched in surprise. "How did you know?"

"I kind of saw Eros'... I think. He had his main bedroom with a normal bed in it, then he had this back room that was tucked away, with his coffin and er...personal items." I wasn't really sure what to call Eros' cruel collection of instruments, but I doubted Sterling wasn't privy to them.

"Yes, sometimes we'll have little spots we burrow behind. Places we feel most comfortable being ourselves, away from the eyes of others."

"Of course, vampires would have formal bedrooms," I chuckled, feeling my smile return as my weird monster hormones settled back down. "So you're taking me to your den? Are you going to drag me back kicking and screaming and suck my blood? And then I'll be turned from the lowly pauper girl to your hot queen of the night?"

Sterling had blinked only a handful of times since I'd been with him tonight, and he chose that moment to give me a blink. "What?"

"Um, never mind. You haven't read enough dark vampire novels, and it shows."

"No, I suppose I haven't. But the library is filled to the brim with archaic dribble. It's time we order some new books for the coven's collection. We'll get whatever you want, and you're welcome to come here any time to read."

"You're promising a girl infinite books and a beautiful library to read in, any time I want?"

"Why not? You'll soon be queen. It will be your manor, your library. You can have whatever you want in it."

Everything except him.

"Wow, you're giving me a library? Way to get a girl all hot and bothered."

A wolfishly sensual smile stretched his lips, making me whine and squirm with a fresh wave of need. "Well, it was that, or your little fantasy from the vampire novels, where I'd drag you back kicking and screaming."

My jaw fell open, a lustful haze settling between my thighs as I watched him turn around and continue leading me through the library. He paused in front of what looked to be a dead-end and reached to pull on the head of a marble bust nestled between a copy of *The Divine Comedy* and *Paradise Lost*. If his naughty teasing hadn't gotten me properly turned on, the shelf that swung open with a groan to reveal a hidden passageway sure did.

Holy shit. This was every nerd girl's dream.

Sterling's "den" was a proper secret room in an ancient library, and I could only imagine what secrets lay beyond the darkness at the bottom of the stone steps.

The air wafting from the passageway smelled of dust, old wood, and beneath that, a mouth-watering scent that was all Sterling. It was all I could do to keep my instincts from going rogue again when the vampire prince held out a hand to me, brandishing a charming smile that had to have been the cause of many lost maidenhoods over the centuries.

"Are you coming, Ruby?"

Chapter Forty-Seven
LESSON IN BLOOD

S terling's den was much larger than I expected for a
secret room behind a bookcase. It was just as big as his
room at the top of the tower, if not larger. The walls were
stone-covered with thick swaths of velvet drapes and lined
with more bookcases. These shelves must have been filled
with his favorites because all the books here were in braille,
with worn-out spines from countless reading sessions.

I imagined the tomes in Sterling's hands, his long fingers
running over the bumps in the pages, stroking them,
building images in his head from what his fingertips felt
out.

Fuck me, what I'd give to be one of his books, for him to
read my body like braille.

My lusty daydreams were temporarily pushed to the back
of my mind when my attention landed on the center of the
room where a dark wooden coffin sat. It had elaborate
carvings cut into the panels, was topped with gold
hardware, and lacquered to make the whole thing shine.
The lid was propped against the side, exposing the coffin's

royal blue lining—probably silk—with embroidered flourishes done in silver thread.

Behind the coffin, there was a large fireplace with a sitting area, and to the right of that, a little kitchenette complete with a sink and a mini-fridge. It was a bit out of place among the medieval-style den, but the most surprising detail about the whole space was the grand piano pushed off to the far left corner of the room.

The sight of the instrument tugged at an old memory, and I couldn't keep myself from walking over to press a key. The note rang out, crisp and beautiful, echoing off the stone. I peeked back at Sterling to find him in the doorway, quietly listening to me as I took in the details of his sanctuary. "Do you play?"

He gave me a nod, a sensational smile flitting across his sharp features, making him look younger, if that were possible. "I do."

"But why do you keep it in here? Why not have it where other people can hear you play?"

His smile slipped some. "My music is something I prefer to keep to myself. But...I can play for you if you'd like."

By the luscious lilt in his tone and the mischievous smile on his face, I'd think he'd just offered to take his pants off rather than play piano for me. But my body was heating at his offer all the same because I knew just how intimate of a thing this probably was for him. "I'd love to hear."

Sterling's eyes glittered, and he looked so pleased, so happy.

Goddamn, things were so easy between us. How could he still be so resistant to claiming me when we were just so damn good together?

My body craved the darkness Vincent offered and the pain Eros promised. And I couldn't help but adore playful Corry. While I liked all of them equally for very different reasons, Sterling made my body sing for some weird, primal reason I wasn't sure I'd ever understand. His gentle, kind, and sage mannerisms had a way of driving me mad with lust, just as much as Vincent's possessive words, Eros' depraved tools, and Corry's greedy addiction to my blood.

I took a step toward the prince, and he tensed, as if he could glean my building arousal. "Before we do anything else, you need to feed."

My line of sight went to the mini-fridge at the corner of the room. I saw the biohazard sticker slapped onto the front, which told me this was where Sterling kept his blood. Knowing he wasn't offering himself as my meal, I started for the fridge, but in a blink, he was in front of me, blocking my path.

He extracted his cellphone from the pocket of his sweats and said, "Siri, call Miss O'Leary."

I blinked, wondering who Miss O'Leary was until Kenzie's voice answered. "You need me, Your Highness?"

"Yes. I need you to bring some pajamas for the princess down to the library den. Wear clothes you don't mind getting stained. We'll be taking a meal from you if you're feeling up for it."

I could practically hear Kenzie's shock from the rush of breath coming from her end. After a couple of seconds, she regained herself. "Um, My Prince, you never feed directly from the donors." Jeez, she almost sounded excited.

"This isn't for me. It's for the princess." Sterling ended the call and shoved the phone back into his pocket.

Kenzie's shock passed to me. "Wait. *What?* Aren't I basically a youngblood? Isn't it too early for me to be feeding directly from humans?"

Especially from one I liked.

Sterling's marble-smooth features completely lacked my concern. "With me as your chaperon, Miss O'Leary will be safe."

"Chaperon?" I snorted. "You act like I'm going to try to fuck or kill her."

He cast me a pointed look. "Considering your current condition, your carnal lust combined with your blood lust might make for a lethal combination. However, whether you prefer feeding from the source, from a bag, or you somehow learn to control your lust and stick to human food, you still need to know how to safely feed on humans." Sterling straightened, standing tall and imposing with that formal expression back on his face, letting me know this was going to be something I would need to take seriously. "I will teach you."

Kenzie took no time at all getting to the hidden room. I wondered how many other people knew about Sterling's den. At the thought of other females in here, my territorial instincts clawed at my insides once again. But this time, by some miracle, I managed to keep a lid on them.

To my embarrassment, Sterling's request to bring me pajamas had somehow translated to slutty nighty in Kenzie's mind. She gave a mischievous smirk when she presented me with an obscenely short black slip with a lacey see-through decoration on the front, one that would *definitely* show off my nipples...if Sterling could see them.

I took it from her, shooting her a look before slinging it onto the back of the couch. She gave me a teasing wink as if to say, *hey, you're about to suck my blood. The very least I get to do is pick out your outfit.*

"Miss O'Leary, please take a seat on the sofa."

Kenzie gave a dutiful nod and moved to obey the prince. She didn't seem nervous in the slightest, but maybe that would be different if Sterling wasn't here. He beckoned me to sit beside Kenzie, and I did. He remained behind us, his elbows propped on the wooden frame of the Victorian-style couch.

"Pay attention because this is important, Miss Baxter." He pointed a long index finger at Kenzie's throat. At this rate, Vincent's fang marks from the other day had completely healed. "Feel here."

I pressed my finger to where Sterling pointed, feeling a little silly. But that quickly fizzled when I felt the delicious hammer of Kenzie's beating heart thrumming against my fingertips.

"It's important to note the difference between arteries and veins. Arteries carry pulses, veins do not. Until you are a master of your blood lust, avoid feeding from arteries. Nonetheless, you should be familiar with them. The artery in the neck, famously known as a vampire's favorite place to feed, is the carotid artery. It may be tempting to feed from here, but don't."

"Where should I bite instead?"

"Here." His finger moved down to the joint in her arm. "It's called the antecubital fossa, the juncture of the inner elbow. It's far safer for a youngblood to bite here because it's a vein, not an artery like the carotid artery in the neck.

Biting the inner elbow will hurt less for the donor, so it's best to bite our own staff here. There are two types of blood in the human body, venous and arterial. Venous blood is deoxygenated, meaning all the oxygen it carries through the body has been distributed and is flowing back to the heart. This blood is darker and unfortunately doesn't taste as sweet as arterial blood."

"It's venous blood that flows through veins and arterial blood through arteries?"

"That is correct. Arterial blood is sweeter, but taking it can kill the donor far faster." Sterling's features darkened as if reminded of something unsavory. "Which is why Corry was very reckless feeding from your femoral artery the other night. It's the second deadliest artery to feed on. The first is the carotid artery in the throat. Only a master, perfectly in control of their bloodlust, should feed from these areas if they plan for the meal to survive."

A blush heated my cheeks. "You heard about that?"

Sterling's face remained perfectly void of all emotion, but something flickered behind his pale eyes, making me shiver. "I hear about most things in this coven."

I swung my attention to Kenzie, who looked positively giddy with being smack in the center of this weird as fuck conversation and not at all freaked out that I was about to bite her.

"Go on," Sterling gently urged. "Drop your fangs and feed. It will help sate your other appetites."

Well, boo to that. I wanted to sate my other "appetites" by locking myself away in this den with its naked master, only to emerge sexually sated, full of each other's blood, with our marks on each other's flesh. Was that too much for a ravenous vampire princess to ask?

I thought Sterling might have had ulterior motives inviting me to stay with him through the day, but maybe he really was just trying to keep an eye on me so that I didn't go ape-shit on the other guys like I had with him.

Sensing my disappointment, Kenzie mouthed "*sorry*" and held out her arm.

I didn't need to drop my fangs because they had been out from the second I had seen that mark on Sterling's throat. I hadn't been able to make them go back in. I wondered if it was like a persistent boner and wouldn't go away on its own without some encouragement. So with my nerves knotted in an uncomfortable jumble in my throat, I bit Kenzie where Sterling directed.

Human blood wasn't anything like vampire blood, and I was surprised at just how different it tasted. The guys' blood all had their own flavor, but each one was like a luxurious cocktail. At least, they tasted what I guessed a luxurious cocktail to taste like. The only alcohol I ever had to date was the cheap bottle of vodka Corry bought me at the pharmacy. *Gag.*

But Kenzie's blood was like a thick, rich soup. Instead of making me horny, filling me with adrenaline and need, I felt full, happy, sated.

"Damn, you taste good," I murmured against her arm.

"That's enough. You only need a little," Sterling said, but I was barely listening. His voice was just static now. The monster had taken over, and she was gorging herself on my friend's blood. No, *I* was gorging myself on my friend's blood.

And if I couldn't make myself stop... I would kill her.

Chapter Forty-Eight
Sate the Monster

"Ouch, Ruby, stop," Kenzie mewled, but her pleas were lost on me.

"*Ruby!*" Sterling's voice cut through my haze, and the next thing I knew, I felt myself being wrenched away from my meal.

I snarled at the male who dared interrupt me, spittle and flecks of blood flying in his direction. My two halves warred against one another. My vampire side was pissed that my meal had been cut short and even more pissed-off that my chosen mate wouldn't claim me in all the ways I know he ached to. I could practically feel his body aching for me, just as mine ached for him. Yet he was doing *fuck all* to sate this pain. Then there was my human half, who was horrified that I couldn't seem to get a hold on my control.

"Miss O'Leary, thank you for your services, but it's best if you leave now. I'm sure the princess will want to apologize when she's feeling more herself." Despite the fact that I had once again lost my grip on my humanity, Sterling's voice was cool and composed. He didn't look at all concerned, which just drove my ire hotter and hotter until I was fit to explode like a volcano.

Why couldn't he lose control with me? Why was he fighting this? We should've been fucking on the floor in a puddle of our own blood and sweat by now.

Why, why *the fuck* was he holding back? There had to be more to it than the fact that I reminded him of my dad. That had to be a cop-out because, damn it, I wasn't anything like Thomas Knight. I wasn't!

Was I?

I caught Kenzie's tearful gaze just as she scrambled through the room.

Oh, hell.

Maybe I really was a monster.

Hot tears welled in my eyes, my hatred for what I'd just done driving the rioting monster inside me to deeper bounds of unhinged insanity. I leaped at Sterling, slashing at him with my hands, my teeth bared. He easily dodged me and moved to the kitchenette so quick I barely could keep up with the blur of his body. He opened a drawer and pulled out an orange bottle filled with red pills. I bristled, knowing exactly what those pills were.

"It's alright, Ruby. You'll be feeling like your old self soon. You haven't yet come down from your body's urge to claim a mate," he told me coolly, extending an arm toward me with two of the pills nestled in his palm. "These won't make it go away, but they may take the edge off."

I snarled at him, slapping his arm away and sending the pills scattering. "Fuck you and fuck those pills! I hate them! And I hate you! You're cruel!"

Part of me felt like an immature kid throwing a tantrum after being denied a toy. But damn it, Sterling wasn't just something I couldn't have. I don't know how, I don't know why, but he was supposed to be mine. Something deep in the fabric of my being screamed at me to claim him. I felt like a junkie going through vicious withdrawals, even though I'd barely tasted him. Even with just a sampling, I was already addicted.

Finally, Sterling's mask fell away once again, showing his true emotions. His face twisted into a sneer as he bared his fangs. "*Cruel?* How *dare* you call me such a thing!"

"I had no problem until I met you! I hunger for you, but you refuse to ease the ache. You want to, but you won't, and that's why you're cruel. I get that I remind you of my father, but you have to know that I am not like him! You even said he owes you something good. So why won't you claim me as yours?"

Sterling donned that same hollow look he'd worn in that painting I'd found in the library. "It's not as simple as that. I can't claim you as my mate."

"Answer me this. Do you want to? Tell me I'm not the only one feeling this. Because you're making me feel like a desperate, pathetic *freak,* who's set my sights on a man who doesn't want me!" My voice jumped an octave, growing shrill and ragged with my frustration.

Sterling's fists balled, his knuckles cracked, and he bowed his head, silver strands falling to screen his face. "You *know* I want you."

"Then do something to sate this ache. Stop torturing me! *Please.*" At this point, the scathing ache between my thighs went beyond lust. I was breaking, fracturing from my desperation for him.

It. Fucking. Hurt.

Sterling jerked his head back up, and the expression on his face was like a blow straight to my chest. All the air left my lungs, and I was left wheezing. I staggered back against the piano, my legs unable to hold me up. On Sterling's perfect, marble-smooth physiognomy was a mean snarl that made my insides flutter, and the most delicious flames lap at my core

He was in front of me in a blink, slapping his palms on the piano, caging me between his arms.

"You think me not marking you is *torture?* No. If I wanted to torture you, I would drag you kicking and screaming down to Eros' den and order him to do his worst to you. I'd then stick around to listen to every scream, every splatter of your blood that hits the ground, every slap of his flesh against yours until he wore you to nothing. But wait..." Sterling grabbed a fistful of my shirt and tore it open, revealing my bare shoulder where Eros' mark sat. "You would get too much enjoyment out of that, wouldn't you?"

All I could feel was pain. Physically, mentally, everything hurt. "Whatever this is, we have to settle it, Sterling. It hurts too much."

The vampire leaned in so close, I could reach his lips and kiss him. But I didn't dare. I was frozen under his ghostly stare, which burned with shadows and something else... Something that wanted to eat me alive, and I was game to let it.

"Listen to me, and listen closely, Ruby. I've lived for one thousand excruciating years, and I can tell you this. You know very little of pain. But you crave it, don't you? There is a darkness that clings to you. In fact, I think I've figured out why your aura resembles your father's. Like him, you crave agony, pain, maybe even death. But unlike him, it's your own suffering you long for."

"That's not true," I said, the lie tasting bitter in my mouth.

By Sterling's stern glare, he knew it was a lie too. He pushed off from the piano and tugged his sweater over his head with one swift movement. I gaped at his perfectly toned muscles, wrapped in ivory flesh, glistening with a thin layer of sweat.

"W–what are you doing?"

"It's pain you want? Fine. I can give it to you. But unlike Eros, the brand of pain I offer won't come from our physical coupling, but in the bitter disappointment you'll feel when your chosen mate will never sit beside you on the throne. I will not place my mark on you, and I will *never* be your king. If you acknowledge these things, the least I can do is sate your ache."

"I... I understand."

"Good. Now run, I'll give you a head start."

"R–run?"

"Yes. It's the mating hunt, like how you tried to hunt me in the tower. A cute attempt, but I'll show you how to do it properly. *Now run.*"

CHAPTER FORTY-NINE

CRASHING THE PARTY

With my heart thrashing in my throat, I raced out of the den and into the library. With the countless rows of shelves, haphazard stacks of books, and random pieces of furniture strewn between, the place was a labyrinth. It would be most kids' hide-and-seek fantasy come to life, but for me, I knew Sterling could find me within moments.

No matter how many great hiding spots there were here, no one could hide from an ancient vampire with the nose of a bloodhound.

Every single nerve in my body was tingling in anticipation, going off like fireworks inside me as I scrambled past row after row of bookcases, searching for a place that would provide me with an advantage. Although, I wasn't exactly trying to hide from the prince. Not when my body was practically in a hot sweat, desperate for his claiming.

The thing was, I knew this wasn't going to be much of a hunt. I knew I was fast, but comparing my reflexes to

Sterling's was like comparing a cheetah jacked up on espresso to a comatose sloth. Even though I wanted him to catch me, a deep, primal instinct inside told me to make him work for my submission.

It was obnoxious how much my body needed him in this moment. Sure, I was growing fond of all the princes—Vincent notwithstanding—but I didn't want to need any of them. Of course, the evil, twisted instincts inside me weren't giving Sterling or me an option in this matter.

As weird as this whole thing was, it felt almost...normal. Cathartic even. Like I was finally indulging in a side of me that was just beginning to emerge.

I twisted to look over my shoulder. My heart slammed against my ribs when I saw Sterling emerge from the passageway, shadows wrapped around his athletic form like a cloak. God Almighty. He was so beautiful, a predator eternally at his prime. For a moment, I was so mesmerized by the male that all the moisture in my mouth sank straight to my hot, needy core. There was something so hypnotic with how the muscles in his neck and shoulders shifted as he prowled forward, a dark smirk sitting on his lips.

"I thought I told you to run."

Remaining rooted where I was, I couldn't help but bathe in the masculine energy rolling off him in droves. "You're going to find out very quickly that I'm not so good at following rules."

"Well, I'll just have to teach you a lesson, won't I?" As he spoke, he flung an arm out, his fingers barely brushing my hair as I lurched away from him. My back bumped into a bookcase, and without thinking, I turned and scrambled upward, using the shelves as footholds. My heart burst into a gallop when I looked down to see Sterling climbing after me.

My foot landed on the spine of a book, and my weight made it shift. I almost lost my balance but caught myself just in time. The book went hurtling right at Sterling's face. He snatched it out of the air, catching it just in time.

Holy shit. How had he seen it coming?

Setting it down carefully on the shelf, he veered his displeased scowl in my direction. "Miss Baxter, I like to think myself a gentleman when it comes to women. But for you, I may have to make an exception if you continue to abuse my books."

"I'm sorry!" I made it to the top of the bookcase, and just as I was crawling over the edge, he seized my ankle. Taking another anchor-sized book, I threw it down at him. He managed to catch it just in time, but only by letting go of me. Pulling myself up, I moved to the end of the bookcase and turned to see Sterling already crouching on the other end. "I should have known threats would only provoke our masochistic princess," he murmured.

With where he sat, I could barely make out his features. Most of the candles had burned out, leaving only the thin slivers of moonlight that sliced through the gaps in the window coverings.

For several intense seconds, we stared at one another in silence, crouched and ready to spring into action at any moment.

Electric energy crackled between us, making my skin prickle with bumps and my brow pebble with perspiration.

"What is this?" I panted.

"I already told you," he muttered. "You're in heat. It's something that happens to half-bloods."

"No, that's not it. What's happening between us? What's this feeling, this freakish chemistry?"

"Sometimes, our deepest instincts pick our mates for us. Yours has selected me. And it's a sad thing because I will not have you, not as my claimed mate."

"But you're hunting me."

"I am."

"What are you going to do when you capture me?"

His throat twitched with a swallow. "I'm going to fuck you, Miss Baxter."

"And are you doing it as a favor to me, to sate my ache? Or is it because your instincts have chosen me as well? You're fighting this. You're being so damn stubborn. You don't want Thomas Knight's daughter as your mate, so you're trying to brush off our connection, but I can see behind your mask, Sterling, because it's starting to crack. You're losing the battle."

He let out a low, rumbling growl then leaned forward so that a strip of moonlight fell over his face. A violent shiver came over me as I registered his sharp, silver-bathed features. He was as terrifying as he was beautiful with his needle-sharp fangs and those snow-white brows and lashes. And his *eyes...*

They had turned crimson, but his ghostly cataracts made them gleam like a blood-red moon that had been coated in mother-of-pearl.

Knowing he was about to pounce any second, I spun and made a leap for another shelf. Maybe it was due to the fact that my focus was clamped to the vampire hunting me that I'd miscalculated. I didn't jump high enough. My body slammed into the top of the bookshelf instead, sending it toppling over.

I was thrown into the air, unable to reach for anything to catch my fall because all that surrounded me was a rain of books. Hitting the ground would hurt enough. The falling books would leave some bruises, but the shelf would crush me.

Before I could do anything more than brace for the world of hurt that was about to come slamming down on top of me, I felt myself being snatched out of the air.

Sterling drew his arms around me, pulling me protectively against him so that when we slammed into the ground, it was his body that took the blow. Books hailed down around us, and he crouched on top of me, shielding me from the downpour of ancient leather and paper.

My skull rattled when the shelf smashed to the floor, missing us by inches. The ground quaked under the weight of the wood, sending splinters and pages flying every which way. Sterling held me tight in his arms, protecting me from the debris.

As everything settled, we remained there on the floor among the wreckage, our chests battering together as we tried to get a grip on our breathing.

I didn't dare move. Maybe it was because I was in shock, seeing as I'd come within an inch of being crushed to death. Although, I was almost certain it had more to do with a half-naked man on top of me, who'd just used his own gorgeous body as a shield to save my own.

I could feel no heartbeat in Sterling's chest, but there was still something magnificent about the feel of his chest rising and falling against mine.

"You're right," he said on a long breath in my ear, his tone fraught with an emotion that pulled tight on my heart. "I want you so badly, the pain of it is almost unbearable. And after all I've been through, I thought I was impervious to pain. But that's not true because if I was impervious to pain, I wouldn't be so fearful of getting hurt. I wouldn't be so terrified of allowing myself to get close to you."

With trembling fingers, I reached to touch him, running my hands over the sculpted planes of his chest. His skin, cool at first, heated at the contact. I traced the crucifix tattoo on his pectoral with my index finger, then pressed my lips to it, letting my mouth linger on the ravaged flesh that I was sure my father had tried to remove.

I looked up at him with a reverence I hoped he could sense. "For twenty-three years, I've been closed off from other people too. Not as long as you, but I know what it's like to be alone. The only difference between my prison and yours is that you erected your own walls. You can choose to knock them down."

Sterling's mask fell away. All the shadows melted from him, and in that moment, he never looked so damn intoxicating, with a tender smile on his lips meant only for me and red eyes that betrayed his lust. Not to mention the rock-hard accouterment jabbing me in the thigh.

He cradled my head between his hands like I was the most delicate thing he'd ever held. The kiss was slow, descending upon me with a sensual gravity that reminded me of all those movies I'd watched when I was a kid. The ones where I would wear the VHS down because I would rewind to the scene at the end where the prince would kiss the princess, watching it over and over again, wishing it was me being kissed.

I never wanted it to end. It was as sweet as it was sinful. It felt like a moment stolen in time, a secret sanctuary from all the hurt and pain and all the fucking lies. Something that was all our own, where our walls had come down, and we both saw each other fully, with no armor, no deception. It was just us.

Sterling was blind, but I knew he could see all of me. There was nothing more erotic, knowing he was peering inside my soul, only to see the lust burn all the brighter in his gaze.

Using all my strength, I flipped him over so that his back was pressed to the rug, with me straddling the valley of his lap. He probably let me, and fuck, I'm glad he did, seeing how he looked, pinned beneath me.

He wore a thunder-struck expression like he knew he was just as powerless to break whatever spell had been cast on us, and by the smoldering heat burning in his gaze, he didn't want to.

"What I would give to see you now..." His voice dripped with sex as he worked his lip between his teeth. His hands gripped my waist and slid beneath my top to fondle the globes of my breasts. I let out a soft moan, his hunger growing harder yet at the sound.

"You fit so perfectly in my palms," he groaned, his head leaning back against a book as if he too was deliriously drunk from the magic suspended between us. "Like you were made for me."

The moment was shattered when the library door opened with a howl of ancient hinges. I jerked my attention to the entrance to see Corry standing there, looking as though he would have been less shocked to find a three-ring circus set up in the coven library than his eldest brother plastered beneath me.

Then he ran his gaze over the mess of books and the broken shelving unit. "Fucking hell, what happened in here? The whole damn house just shook. It's a little late for furniture breaking sex, don't you think?"

I opened my mouth to speak, but Sterling beat me to it. "Don't come in here!" His muscles clenched beneath me, and he wrapped his arms tight around my waist, pulling me against him as if he was afraid I'd be ripped away.

But it was too late. Corry had moved inside, and the second he did, his pupils blew up, and his nostrils flared.

He tipped his nose to the air and inhaled deeply. "Holy shit..." His eyes snapped shut, and I knew exactly what was happening.

Because it had happened to me twice tonight. His youngblood instincts were taking over.

When his eyes flew open, a twisted smile stretched his face, and his blood-red eyes ran me through like a stake to the heart.

"Damn, Red. You smell *good*. Good enough to breed."

CHAPTER FIFTY
SKELETONS IN THE ATTIC

C orry's eyes sparked with a blazing hunger as ravenous and dangerous as a wildfire. It had only been a handful of seconds since he'd stepped inside the library, but by the look on his face, he was already lost to his instincts.

He was about to throw himself into the hunt, and seeing as I was as horny as a bitch in heat, I would normally be super down for that. But I was already with Sterling. And while the thought of being with both of them made my body burn in ways I never knew possible, I doubted a territorial youngblood was in the mood to share.

Before I could react, Sterling rolled me over, so he was crouched over me in a protective position. His shoulders clenched, and his tendons stretched in his neck as every muscle in his body tightened. He was like a predator, protecting his kill from another beast.

"I was afraid of this," he whispered beneath his breath so Corry couldn't hear. "I shouldn't have let you leave my den.

I should have thrown you down on the floor right there and buried myself in you until sundown."

A rush of heat swept between my thighs, and my breath hitched in my throat. I swallowed thickly, watching as Sterling turned his blind glare on his youngest brother.

"Our princess is in heat, Corry. She's off-limits tonight."

The youngblood's lips peeled back into a twisted sneer. "So you can keep her to yourself?"

"No. That's not the reason. She's in pain, and she needs her ache sated. I am the only one among us with enough control to not harm her while she's putting off these kinds of pheromones."

Corry's gaze flicked to me. It made me shiver, knowing that the youngblood wasn't feeling like himself at this moment. Right now, he was more monster than anything else.

"I won't hurt her," he said after a beat, his hot-glower swinging back to Sterling.

"Her wellbeing isn't the only thing that concerns me. You're both youngbloods. She's liable to hurt *you* as much as you are to hurt her." Sterling was trying his best to talk his brother down, but I knew it was useless. I'd been in Corry's shoes. He was lost to his instincts, and he wouldn't come out of the fog until he either bred me, fed, or Sterling managed to force some of those pills down his throat.

Corry let out a rattling snarl, challenging his brother.

Sterling's expression hardened, and his lips curved into a mocking sneer. "You think you can best me? I'm nearly one thousand years your elder, Youngblood."

Corry crouched low, his eyes flashing dangerously, ready to pounce at any moment. But Sterling remained on top of me, shielding me, holding me.

"You can't just keep her to yourself." Corry spat. "It really pisses me off the way Eros and Vincent have been acting. Now you. Until she selects a king, she doesn't belong to any one of us. She's *ours*. You old fucks haven't watched your Sesame Street episodes on sharing, and it shows."

A warm, fluttery sensation filled my chest as Corry's words sunk straight to my core. Since I'd come here, I'd heard plenty of "you're mine" and "you'll belong to me" flexes, especially from Vincent's gloriously filthy mouth. But this was the first any of them had ever said that I was *theirs*.

Sterling slowly got to his feet. His knuckles cracked, and he rolled his shoulders, looking as intimidating as he was sexy in nothing but his blood-stained sweats, wrapped in the shadows and silver strips streaming through the drapes. "You're right. She *is* ours. But currently, you're not yourself, Brother. I won't let you touch her, not like this."

Corry was not pleased by this. He bristled, flashing his deadly fangs in a lethal hiss. "Can't you scent her? She smells so goddamn good it's making my balls hurt. If you won't mark her tonight, then I will."

"No one will be marking anyone, not while you're both delirious with lust in the throes of the youngblood state."

The tension in the room was so thick you could cut it with a knife. Corry cracked his neck, looking confident as hell. Not to mention hot as hell. He was wearing denim jeans and a black t-shirt that hugged his torso so perfectly it almost wasn't real, too perfect to be reality. I wanted to go to him, to let him claim me in all the ways I knew he was thinking of.

I wanted to let them both sate this ache that was tearing me apart from the inside.

Before I could dive deeper into that impossible—and a little fucked—fantasy, Corry lunged at Sterling. The youngblood moved so fast he was a blur of black fabric and bleach-tipped hair that slammed right into Sterling.

The silver prince was prepared. He caught Corry by the throat, his slender fingers clamping around him like a collar, and threw him down onto the rug in a spray of paper and splinters.

"Ready to give up?" Sterling muttered, his voice so calm it was almost eerie as Corry sputtered against his brother's grip, trying to pry his fingers from his throat in vain.

"N–never. Let g–go."

"If I release you, you must agree to leave the library and feed. You can apologize for giving me blue balls later."

Corry thrashed and growled like an animal lost to its most basic urges. My heart squeezed seeing him like this. I couldn't help but wonder what would have happened if I had gone into my heat state with Corry at that gas station and not with Sterling in the sanctuary of his library.

Or with Eros on his workbench.

Or Vincent, in the backseat of his car.

Corry was right. I belonged to all of them.

How could I ever pick just one?

Something deep in my being stirred, making my stomach tighten and my head swirl. I hated seeing them fight over me. Vincent and Eros was one thing, but I couldn't handle watching Sterling and Corry duke it out.

Before I even fully realized what I was doing, my feet were carrying me out of the library. I ran hard, practically flying up the main staircase and down the hallway toward my room.

I came to a screeching halt when I rounded the corner to see two figures standing just a few feet from my door, making out against the wall.

If I had been feeling shitty before, seeing Vincent basically swallowing Lexi's face was enough to push me over the edge into a dark place where I saw red.

Maleficent urges took root in my mind like weeds, intent on overrunning everything else good inside me. I realized the monster inside was imagining ripping off both their heads so they could both fuck each other in Hell, far away from me. And damn it, I hated how much I liked the idea.

New levels of exhaustion sapped my energy. Between Sterling and Corry, I didn't have the energy to deal with Vincent on top of it.

I couldn't even scrape together the willpower to walk past them to get to my room. Even if Vincent couldn't pry his lips from his cold bitch for two seconds to throw something snide in my direction, I doubted I could even handle his scent right now. Not in my current state of arousal, brought on by this damn heat cycle I never asked for.

Turning around, I made my way down the hall in the opposite direction in search of a spare room I could crash in for the day. Most of the doors were locked, probably because dawn was coming.

I climbed up to the third floor and found a door at the end of the corridor that was unlocked. Inside was a narrow staircase leading to yet another floor.

Curiosity wound through me, pushing me upward. The stairs creaked dangerously beneath my feet, wispy tendrils of ancient cobwebs brushed my face, and the air, heavy with dust, tickled my nose.

Whatever room I'd just stumbled on, no one had been here in a while. When I came to the door at the top of the stairs and pushed it open, it felt like stepping into a crypt. But it wasn't a crypt at all. I had found the coven's attic. It was stuffed full of an endless assortment of items, but all of it was organized in a way that made it feel more like a museum than a storage space.

The singular circular window at the far end of the room was boarded up, making it hard to make out the collection of antiquities. Noticing an old-fashioned candle holder with a half-burned candle mounted in the pewter dish and a box of matches, I lit it, creating a dim orange glow to illuminate the attic.

What I saw took my breath away.

It was a lifetime—several lifetimes—of antiques that could only belong to an ancient vampire coven. Moving around the room with the candle holder in hand, I took my time examining each item with a mixture of horror and fascination.

There were shelves of books, all older than the country they sat in and all bound in leather. But something told me it wasn't animal hide.

There was a stack of centuries-old maps that weren't even close to accurate, slumped over a globe. I spotted elephant tusks, human skulls, and an old box that looked like a vampire hunter kit from the late nineteenth century.

Scanning further, I saw a collection of swords and guns from blunderbusses and crude maces all the way to mid-century revolvers and ornamental weapons from *The Lord of the Rings* movies.

There was a chess set with pieces that looked to be made from vampire fangs and next to that a display case of bones with a nameplate probably proclaiming what poor bastard was in the case. I stopped to read it, rubbing the layer of dust away but was disappointed to find it in Latin.

Moving on, I paused in front of two suits of armor. One of them was ebony with an old velvet doublet over it, its once rich colors long since faded. The other was silver, with no doublet. It was carved with elegant little flourishes, masculine but feminine at the same time.

I reached to touch the visor of the silver set's helm when my eye slipped past it to see an alcove.

The alcove was small, with nothing in it save for a black coffin and a painting mounted on the wall above it.

A sheet hung over the painting, hiding whatever was behind it.

A chill swept through me, cold and harsh like a winter wind. The hairs on the back of my neck straightened with the feeling someone was watching me. It was as if whoever was in the painting on the wall could see me through the sheet.

This wasn't just the coven's storage. I was pretty sure I had found someone's personal collection of possessions, along with their den. The question was, who?

Once again, my human survival instincts and my vampire instincts went to war. Part of me said to run because I had found someplace evil, while the other part was filled with a dark curiosity that held me in place.

I took a step forward and then another until I stood beside the coffin. It was beautiful, luxuriously ominous with its Gothic touches. The lid had dainty gold filigree embellishments etched into the surface. It was like ancient Mesopotamian melded with Victorian style. It was awesome, like a relic right out of *Indiana Jones,* had he stumbled upon a tomb containing a vampire.

I don't know what came over me. It was a strange urge—no—a *pull*. Something had taken hold of me, and the next thing I knew, I was pushing the lid off the coffin to reveal what lay inside.

In the first second, the little ball of anticipation that had begun to build in my stomach suddenly dissipated like ash in the wind when I was met with nothing but ruby red velvet lining. Then it hit me like a meteor to the gut.

The scent.

It was the same infuriating scent permanently seared into Sterling's skin.

The scent of his mate.

I had found the den of Sterling's mate.

Now that I was looking at it more closely, I noticed a black and white polaroid of Sterling tacked to the underside of the lid, centered right where the coffin's owner would fall asleep looking at him every night.

I felt nothing but numbness as I walked over to the painting and wrenched the sheet away to reveal the portrait beneath.

Thomas Knight's impenetrable eyes found me through the dark, confirming the underlying fears that had slowly leached from the back of my mind like a poison.

Sterling, the prince who made my heart sing and my womanhood ache, was mated to my father.

I thought I might be sick.

Rage, confusion, and a pain so sharp that I cried ravaged my body, my mind, and my soul. I dropped the candlestick as the world around me slipped away, the flame snuffing out, plunging me into darkness similar to the one that filled me.

Spinning around, I was ready to run away from this coven. Far away from the world of Thomas Knight and his fucked-up princes.

But pale, moonstone eyes hovering in the attic's doorway froze me where I stood. Even through the murky dark, I could make out the raw look of pain etching Sterling's ghostly features.

"I was wondering when you'd find this room."

Chapter Fifty-One
MAGIC

"Don't come near me. Stay back!" I hated how my voice quaked, laced with the pain of his betrayal.

I felt so stupid. I'd made a fool of myself, chasing after a man who'd been involved with my dad. It was a new level of fucked-up. My stomach heaved, and I spun around, glaring at the portrait of Thomas Knight. Looking at him was easier than looking at Sterling at that moment.

"Ruby..." The way Sterling uttered my name, with tender reverence, made my chest tight and my heart pulse.

I didn't trust it. I didn't want to trust it. I was sick of wearing my heart on my sleeve in front of these guys and getting it broken for the trouble.

"Keep my name out of your mouth. I don't even want to share the same air as you, you twisted fuck."

Silence swelled around us, and I half expected him to turn and leave me alone. He didn't, though, and I realized I would have been disappointed if he had.

"I know this discovery is an upsetting one."

"*Upsetting?*" My cadence lurched an octave. "It's more than upsetting! It's deplorable! I was making a freaking fool of myself trying to claim you, and you said nothing. Fucking *nothing!*" My fists clenched, shaking at my sides. I dropped my gaze to my feet, unable to look at my father's portrait for a second longer. Here I was, caught between them, and he wasn't even alive.

I hated him.

I wanted to hate both of them. But I couldn't bring myself to hate Sterling. Still, I hated myself for wanting him all the more now. How fucked-up was that?

Thomas Knight ruined everything. He wasn't even alive anymore, and he still managed to come between the princes and me, crushing any hopes of a normal healthy relationship by all the hurt and pain he'd left behind.

Swallowing thickly, I tried in vain to stomp out all the hurt in my voice. But this time, it shook even harder, betraying the tears that threatened to spill. "Don't you think it would have been nice to mention to the girl interested in you that you were lovers with her father?"

"*Lovers?*" the blind prince murmured on a tight whisper that was all gravel. "Is that what you think we were?"

"He has a freaking picture of you in his coffin. You have his mating mark, meaning you fucked him. What other conclusion am I supposed to arrive at?"

The blistering silence that spanned between us made me turn to look at the prince for the first time since he'd entered the attic. The expression on his face sent an invisible knife through my heart. He didn't have to say anything for me to instantly understand. It was written all over his haunted gaze.

Sterling hadn't been my father's mate by choice, which was not a stretch to believe, knowing what I did about the massive fucking monster that was Thomas Knight. He loved inflicting pain. Eros had even said the old king loved turning men just to make them break. But that picture tacked to my father's coffin lid shed light on a different side of the relationship between the master and his eldest progeny. Sterling's face was worn on the polaroid as if someone had reached to touch it countless times.

"I... I don't get it. He kept a photo of you in his coffin. That's something lovers do, not rapists."

The vampire's expression hardened, and for a brief moment, his line of sight shifted to the painting of his former master as if he could see him, feel him staring at us both.

"I fully believe my master was under the impression that he loved me. But the only love Thomas Knight was capable of was a malformed and twisted thing. His demented obsession with inflicting pain destroyed any shred of good intentions he ever had."

"That's why you were trying to keep me at a distance."

Sterling gave me a grim nod. "I didn't feel right claiming you as my mate before you knew about..." His blank gaze shifted to the display cabinet filled with bones, knowing exactly where it was without needing to see it at all. He blew out a sigh, raking his slender fingers through his silver tresses. "The skeletons in my closet."

"Why didn't you say anything before?"

His brows crinkled. "Do you think it's easy for me to talk about it?"

"Of course not. I'm sorry I—"

"Don't apologize. I'm in the wrong here. Admittedly, I liked being the object of your lust. I didn't tell you because I knew your view of me would change when you discovered my sordid past."

"You thought I wouldn't want you after I found out?"

"How could you? I've lain with your father."

"It would be different if it had been your choice but... But if you're saying it wasn't..."

"When he first turned me, I was no one to him. He did it to torture me. It was nothing more than to bring me pain and suffering, a punishment for standing up to him at the monastery. In addition, I think I was getting a lot of the wrath that this one failed to survive," he added, pointing to the display case of bones. I guess that solved the mystery of who was in the case. It was the vampire hunter who had killed my father's mate all those years ago. "But after I was freed from that cellar and sought him out, he had a different reaction to me. He had a mating urge, just like you. I refused him, of course, and for another few hundred years, he continued to make advances."

"But he didn't force you?"

"He was aggressive with his advances, but there was a line he didn't cross. Until we moved to London. There, I met a woman. She was our human blood thrall who lived with us. We fell in love, but for obvious reasons, we had to keep our relationship from our master."

Sterling was speaking about something that happened several lifetimes ago, but his eyes were wide, brimming with memories that made his face contort as if the hurt from all that time ago was still fresh. When he spoke next, his voice was choked with emotion. "Then she became pregnant."

A chill, colder than anything I ever felt before, filled me, making my insides freeze over. This was one of those stories I knew had a horrible ending, and still, I couldn't help but keep reading. And even though I just knew there was no chance for happiness at the end of the book, I rooted for the characters even more.

"What happened? Tell me she lived. At least the baby, tell me the baby lived."

Sterling leaned against the wall opposite me and slid down so that we were facing one another. Something moved down his cheek, and I had to strain my eyes through the dark to see it. A single tear, slipping down his cheek.

"I tried to have her leave without me, but she refused. I begged her. Had she listened to me, perhaps both of them would have survived. Since I was weaker then, I eventually gave up trying to convince her. Neither of us wanted to be apart. So we risked everything and escaped together one night while Master was out feeding."

"But...isn't there a link between a master and their progeny? It's why you were able to find him after you were released from the cellar."

Sterling held his head in his hands, his fingers splayed over his face in shame. "Yes. And I was a fool for letting my love and my desire for a family blind my judgment."

I crawled across the attic floor on my hands and knees until I was kneeling in front of him. I reached to touch his hand, and he looked up in surprise, his cheeks crusted in fresh tears. "He raped me in front of her, Ruby. And that wasn't the worst part. When he was finished with me, he murdered her. He murdered my mate and my unborn child right in front of me. Then he used the same silver dagger—while it dripped with their blood—on me to make sure another 'accident' couldn't happen again. As if I were some naughty mongrel in need of neutering."

My throat burned with a swallow. Sterling's moonstone eyes were bright with tears, and as I stared into them, my heart broke a thousand times, shattering into countless pieces and lodging in my throat, making each breath painful. Then, I started to cry with him.

The injustice done to Sterling was deplorable and filled me with a hatred so pure and hot, I thought it might eat me alive.

Maybe that's why I had ached to place my mark over the one my father had left. I wanted to take Sterling's pain away. I wanted to replace all that hurt and fill that hole in his heart with as much of me as he would take.

"Do not weep for me," he muttered. "I do not shed tears because I am still hurting from what happened. It was five hundred years ago, and the pain has dulled."

"Then why?"

"Because I want you to the point of madness, Ruby Renada. It's beyond reason, stretching deeper than lust for your body and your blood. I want to claim you as my own and reclaim what Thomas Knight stole from me. He owes me a mate, one that I have chosen."

"Then why not claim me, here and now? Take your penance in flesh. I want you too. It has to be written in the stars or some dumb shit like that because I'm aching for you to claim me as yours, Sterling. From the second I saw you, I wanted you so bad it scares me." I dropped my tone to a whisper and leaned my brow against his. My eyelids drifted shut when I felt his cool palms on my blazing cheeks. "It still scares me."

Sterling's lips planted a kiss on my nose, sweet and innocent, his mouth lingering on my skin as he spoke. "How could you still want me, knowing that I won't claim the throne simply because I can't bear to sit where he once did? And I can never give you children."

"Sterling, I came to you tonight because I was going to ask you to turn me. I was prepared to never have kids."

He leaned back, a look of horror stretching his marble-smooth features. "I would never turn you. Ever. Nor would I allow anyone else in this coven to do so. After I was turned, I swore to never inflict that sort of pain on anyone else. Especially not anyone I love."

My pulse launched into a full gallop. "You...love me?"

"We might have just met, but my intuition is a deep and complex thing. I trust it more than I trust anything. So yes, Ruby. I wanted you the moment you saw your father's mark and desired to cover it with your own. Then when I touched you..." He reached for my face, his fingertips kissing the apples of my cheeks. "And saw you for the first time... I loved you."

I melted into him, pulling myself into his lap. His arms folded around me, gathering me against him. It felt so good sitting there against him that tears of joy seared my eyes. His lips moved to my brow, then he began planting a trail of gentle kisses on my eyelids, the bridge of my nose, my cheeks, my chin. It was like he was feeling out my face to get a mental image, but this time he was using his lips instead of his fingers.

I wanted him to kiss me and hold me like this forever. While I craved Vincent's brutality, Eros' sweet torture, and Corry's normalcy, Sterling's devoted reverence was the icing on an already sinfully delicious cake.

When he pulled back to look at me, I could see the thought in his eyes as he pieced together the mental image of me from all he'd just mapped with his mouth, and when the most tender smile that was so beautiful formed, a little gasp slipped out of me.

His brows twitched upward in question. "What is it?"

I touched his still smiling lips. "There's magic on your lips, Silver Prince."

He blinked. "Magic?"

"It's the first smile you've given me that hasn't looked pained. Like you're actually happy."

The smile stretched wider, and he kissed my mouth, pouring something truly freaking amazing into the connection. Whatever it was, it stretched deep down inside my being, touching all of me. I shivered in his arms, relishing in the beguiling magnetism pulling us together.

Sterling broke the kiss, his breath fanning over me, salty and sweet. "I am happy, Ruby. Now lie down. I want to do something I have been aching to do since the second you came into my room."

My breath hitched, a thrill flitting through my body, making my every nerve tingle. "And what's that?"

"Take off your clothes, and I'll show you."

Chapter Fifty-Two
Sins in Blood

Take off your clothes, and I'll show you.

Holy fuck, those magic words really did just come out of his beautiful mouth.

The energy in the room shifted in an instant. One moment, it had been romantic and sweet, filled with gentle kisses that hadn't been demanding or filled with any kind of sexual tension. But as soon as Sterling's words had slipped past those painfully delicious lips, the atmosphere in the attic grew hot and heady with something that made my skin prickle and my breath come out in short pants.

A flutter of butterflies took flight in my belly, making my whole body tingle. Everything inside me screamed for me to throw myself at Sterling, to let him dominate and claim me. But that was just my perverted vampire instincts talking. I was a hot mess of need, and my vagina was begging to be filled because of all these hormones. They were telling me to make it rough and fast. Maybe that's how it would be between Vincent and me if the asshole ever got Lexi's head out of his ass. And sex with Eros had been just that. Hard, rough, and fast. He'd been perfectly in control the entire time, and I was just clay in his hands. Well, until the end when both of us got swept away in the endorphins.

But Sterling was a whole different kind of beast than his brothers, and with him, it had to be different.

I wanted it to be slow and erotic, and sensual. If we had to hole ourselves in this attic for days, that would be just fine with me. I was hoping he wanted to make this last as long as I did, to drag it out until we were both trembling, sweating, a tangled mess of need, and when we finally brought each other to that long-anticipated edge, we'd both go tumbling over together.

Pulling myself out of his lap, I got to my feet and danced out of his reach as his hand swiped for me. "Get back here. I gave you an order, Miss Baxter."

"Oh, an order is it?" I laughed, watching with unbridled excitement as he slowly got to his feet, stalking toward me with purposeful strides. Predatorial energy dominated the air around him, making my mouth dry and my knees weak. "If I'm going to be queen, shouldn't it be me giving the orders?"

He tried to resume his serious expression, but I could see the shadow of a teasing smile lurking at the corner of his mouth.

"You forget I am an Elder and the current executor of the estate. Even when you're queen, there will be rules you'll have to follow."

"*Pft.* I already told you, I'm no good at following rules."

He stopped where he was, pausing for a moment. His expression was perfectly controlled, not a twitch of a muscle or a flicker of his snow-white lashes, nothing that would betray what was running through his mind. But his eyes couldn't keep the same secrets as the rest of his face. They had returned to that same hue of shimmering, murky red, like an eclipse plated in mother of pearl. And the best little tip-off of what was going through his mind was the erection straining against the blood-stained material of his gray sweatpants.

"Oh, dear little half-blood. I promise you, you'll want to follow my rules. If you do, I'll reward you."

A searing heat filled my throat and quickly sunk to my chest, then my tummy, and finally settled into a pool between my thighs. My heart rate catapulted into the stratosphere, and I had to lean against the glass case of the vampire hunter's bones for stability.

"What kind of reward?"

Canting his head, Sterling's serious mask dropped away, and the playful grin that had been lingering at the corner of his mouth unleashed in full force as he gripped the waistband of his sweats and shoved it down.

My lower lip caught between my teeth when his glorious erection sprung into full view. It wasn't the first time I saw the silver prince's impressive cock tonight, but I could swear it was even harder now that he wasn't holding anything back.

This prince was the one who seemed the most innocent and chaste out of all of them. Maybe that was just because he had manners. But there was nothing innocent or chaste about the massive piece slung between his thighs.

It's not like I'd seen a whole lot of cocks in my day. Eros' masculine heft had been sizable, but good God. There was no way I wouldn't need an ice pack after seating myself on Sterling.

He was simply gorgeous, with powerful muscles wrapped in a lean body that looked to have been carved from marble by a master sculptor.

He regarded me with an arched brow. "You wanted this, right?"

Hell yes. "I do."

"Good. Come here."

Goddamn. His voice was sensually dark and full of wicked promise. The monster inside me wasn't fighting anymore. All she wanted was to obey this male so he'd finally give us what we both desperately needed.

I approached him slowly. The attic floorboards creaked with every step, falling in line with my heavy breathing. It didn't matter that he was blind. As I neared, it felt like he could see every inch of me, inside and out.

I paused in front of him, so close I knew he could hear my pounding pulse.

My eyes dropped to his cock, which was still bare and on bold display. It was so heavy, it could barely stay up on its own. I only managed to tear my eyes from it when he gave me another order.

"I'm going to touch you now," he said in a strained whisper like he was also using every bit of willpower to tease this out nice and slow.

"Fucking finally." It was meant to be a joke, but Sterling's eyes lit with challenge. If he planned to be gentle with removing my clothes, he'd changed his mind.

He grabbed the neck of my crop top where he'd already half ripped it in the library and finished the job with a swift yank. The sound of ripping fabric was drowned out by my gasp as I felt his left hand curl around the back of my neck to hold me to him, and his right gripped the front of my lacy bra and snapped it off my frame like it was made of tissue paper.

"Don't wear undergarments when you're around me, Miss Baxter. Not unless you wish for them to end up like this." He held up the shred of lace fabric before letting it drop to our feet along with my shirt.

Well, shit. With a promise like that, I was going to be running up the coven's credit card bills from all the shopping trips Kenzie would be making for me.

Like Sterling, I was now completely shirtless.

It should have felt weird, standing half-naked in my father's den with his oldest progeny, about to do all sorts of sinful, bloody things. But it didn't. I could be anywhere with Sterling, and it would feel right. Then again, even if we wanted to leave and find a different spot to fuck, it was too late. Dawn had arrived. It didn't matter that the attic's only window was boarded up to prevent even a sliver of sunlight from creeping in. I could feel it. It was a bone-deep instinctual dread that told me the outside wasn't safe even though I was a half-blood and could withstand the daylight.

But it didn't matter. This was where we ended up, and this was happening.

"Touch me, Sterling," I whispered, my voice shaking violently.

I wasn't asking. I was begging him. The whole night had been a dance with him, and now here he was, about to give me the thing I'd been burning for, and I could barely stand to wait a second longer. "Touch me like you did in the library, and I swear to God if Corry comes through that door and interrupts again, I'll kill him."

Sterling's eyes gleamed with mirth as his hands slid to palm the globes of my breasts.

His touch was an experience the others had yet to give me. While the other brothers' hands were rough and demanding, Sterling handled me like I was one of his books. He was seeing me with his fingertips, brushing, stroking, teasing. His skin was just a whisper against my own, but the delicate contact heightened each sensation and made every damn nerve in my body light up like I was a freaking Christmas tree.

He pinched my nipples, and when they hardened to peaks, he stooped to take one in his mouth. A swollen whimper tumbled from me, and he chuckled against me, taking one of the sensitive buds between his fangs.

I went completely still against him, as terrified as I was turned on. "Sterling."

"Hmm?" he hummed against me, the vibration turning me to putty in this carnal embrace as he traced the perimeter of my nipple with the tip of his tongue. "By the scent coming from between your thighs, I'm almost convinced you want me to bite you."

Sweat beaded on my brow. "I...think I do."

He titled his head, surprise flashing in his hazy orbs. "You like being bitten?"

I gave him a nod, my eyes wide as he straightened to his full height, then brought his lips to my brow to plant a chaste kiss there. At least it would have been chaste if it wasn't for the fact that he still held my breasts in his hands.

"If I were to bite you, it wouldn't be there."

"Where then?"

He began another slow descent of kisses to my eyelids, my nose, my jawline. This time, however, his lips took their time moving across my skin, languid and deliciously skillful. A mouth like his had a precision to it that could bring me to my knees with just a single kiss. A soft whisper, a tongue stroke across his lower lip in a sensual sweep meant to entice. Bloody hell. All the pleasure that mouth could bring me, especially between my legs.

I was acutely aware of the heavy rise and fall of my chest as his lips skimmed down to the hollow of my throat and made their way to my jugular.

Every muscle in my body wound tight as I felt teeth and tongue swipe over the fragile stretch of skin. For one intense beat, I thought he was going to bite me. But he pressed yet another kiss there instead.

"Right here, the carotid artery."

"But you said—"

"I said it was dangerous and that only a master vampire should feed from here. As an erogenous zone, it's also an extremely erotic place to feed and can bring the donor a heightened sense of pleasure, so long as the vampire feeding from her knows what he's doing."

Another kiss, this time with more teeth. Still, he didn't break the surface. I was sure now that he was trying to work me into knots so that he could take his sweet time unraveling them.

"Will you make me a promise, Ruby?"

I blinked at him, a little side swept by the sudden shift in his tone. "What kind of promise?"

His hand left my breast to curve around the base of my throat, his grip gentle but possessive in a way that was perfectly Sterling. "Don't let any of my brothers bite you here."

My lungs emptied of all my air as I used my last breath to ask, "Why?"

His lips curved into the most intoxicating smile, his own labored breaths feathering over my skin, sending a delicious shiver down my spine. "Because I like to think this part of you should belong only to me."

Then I felt them, his fangs penetrating the flesh of my throat. I opened my mouth to shout his name, but all I could get out was a strangled mewl of delight.

My body against Sterling's was like an instrument in the hands of a master musician. He played me like a damn fiddle, using me for my blood, and, *fuck me*, it felt so damn good I wasn't sure I would be able to stop him if he insisted on taking every drop.

The ancient vampire let out a silken growl as he clutched me to him. His grip turned bruising, but I relished the sheer agony of it.

His arms banded around my waist, and he dipped me back as he fed on me. It was like some twisted version of those classic kids' movies where the prince swept the princess off her feet to kiss her. When I was little, I always dreamed of someone doing that to me. But this version was *way* better.

Thomas Knight's painting was in my line of sight. From my angle, he was upside down, but I could still see him glaring at us, witnessing the bloody scene that probably would have had him tearing Sterling to pieces if he was still alive. Licking my grinning lips, I flipped off the portrait.

Sterling pulled me upright, my heart lodging in my throat when his blood-stained lips came into view. He took one hand off me and combed his fingers through his hair, leaving a crimson streak through his silver locks.

Jesus Christ.

He looked good enough to eat. As if he could read my thoughts, he flashed me a bloody grin.

"On your knees, Miss Baxter."

CHAPTER FIFTY-THREE

PRECIPICE

On your knees, Miss Baxter.

There it was again, another dark and decadent order that had me panting like an animal in heat.

This was exactly what I'd been aching for all night.

Him.

Every lean, luscious inch of him.

But now that we'd arrived at this point, the precipice of all the rising sexual tension, I froze. Here Sterling was, offering himself to me, and *this* was the fucking moment my human insecurities had to take over?

No matter how hard I tried, I couldn't seem to smother the little voice in the back of my head, screaming, "*What the hell am I doing?*"

I was a sheltered twenty-three-year-old. I had lost my virginity not even twenty-four hours ago, and Eros had been the one in the driver's seat. I had just laid back and enjoyed the ride. Sterling was *one thousand* flipping years old. I didn't even want to try and fathom how many girls had sucked him off. I didn't want to stand out as the one who did it wrong. And how the hell was I supposed to do this without accidentally dropping my fangs? I doubted Sterling would tell anyone about our time together like this but still, I didn't want to be known as the coven's dick biter.

As if sensing my rising self-doubt, Sterling tucked himself back into his sweats. I was sad to see that part of him slip out of view, but I had a feeling he was about to say something serious by the pinched expression on his face.

Hooking a finger under my chin, he guided my gaze to his. Ghostly eyes peered down at me, looking straight through me, and just like before, I felt like he could see all of me.

"You're frightened," he murmured. His fingers brushed over my chest, making my breath hitch beneath them, as if he commanded the very air in my lungs. "Are you afraid I'll hurt you?"

"No. That's not it at all. I am scared," I admitted on a shaky breath, "but not of you. I just... I have no idea what I'm doing. I don't want you to feel like you have to teach me how to do this sort of thing." I thought I'd be embarrassed admitting this to him. But the second the words left me, I felt a weight lift off my chest. And Sterling's gentle smile—which was a bit weird seeing while coated in my blood—made all my self-doubt fizzle away.

"Your human side may not know what you're doing, but your vampire instincts have chosen me as your mate. Let those same instincts guide you. If you trust in them, they will never fail you."

I gave a tentative nod. "Can I ask you a personal question?"

His chest rumbled with a chuckle. "I've told you my darkest secrets. At this point, I'm an open book."

Hearing those words out of his mouth was the most refreshing thing I'd heard from any of the princes. And I believed him. Transparency was one of Sterling's sexiest qualities. If I had to rank them, I'd put it smack between his endowment—which was currently pressed against my thigh—and the way he held me, gentle and possessive. In his arms, I felt like one of his books. He was clearly protective of them if his reaction to when I had lobbed one at his head in the library was any indication. And I loved how he used every opportunity he could to touch me, like I was filled with all sorts of stories he could glean with the simple kiss of his fingertips.

"How long has it been since you've been with a woman?"

The prince swallowed, his Adam's apple making a quick and delicious bob in his throat. "It's almost embarrassing saying it out loud. About a century ago is when I've last been with a woman like this."

"A *hundred* years?"

"I wish the saying 'that's not long for an immortal' was applicable in this context, but unfortunately, when it comes to sex, a hundred years is a long time for anyone. Especially with our kind's sexual drives."

"Why so long?"

His eyes drifted shut, and his hold on me tightened slightly. "After what happened with Elizabeth—my human mate—I was too frightened to get close to anyone else with your father watching, waiting for any excuse to punish me on the grounds of disloyalty." His eyelids flickered open, and he leaned down to kiss the place he'd bitten me, licking away any remaining blood. "But our kind craves vampire blood just as we do human blood. The longer we go without it, the more unruly our lust becomes. This was before Sharpe invented the sating pills. So your father inducted a half-succubus, half-vampire into the coven. Her blood sates us for longer."

"A half-succubus? Is she like...er..." I faltered. "Well, you know."

He straightened, his brows cocking. "She's not a prostitute if that's what you're asking. But seeing as a vampire's carnal lust can spike when feeding on another vampire, and given her nature, her services often lead to sexual intercourse. It was one such session that I decided to indulge in her advances. At that time, I hadn't been with another woman since..." His voice was strained, and he sighed. "Since before we left for the new world. I knew I wasn't risking your father's wrath, considering Alexandra has slept with half the coven."

My stomach flipped. "Wait. *Lexi?* She's the coven's blood whore?"

Suddenly it wasn't so hard calling the half-succubus names now that I knew who we were talking about.

Sterling smirked. "Indeed. But take care not to call her that to her face. It won't do to make an enemy of her."

I snorted. Too freaking late. The ship had definitely left the dock on that one.

It was weird, knowing that Lexi was half-succubus. She didn't look any different than the other coven's vampires, but it made sense considering how tight she had Vincent wound around her finger. Seduction was literally her job.

"I thought she was Vincent's girlfriend or something."

Sterling scoffed. "She doesn't give him anything she doesn't offer the rest of the coven. He's just her favorite, especially since she seems to be under the unfortunate impression that if she spreads her legs enough for him, he'll make her queen."

So Lexi had been with more than Vincent. She'd slept with Sterling, and maybe even Corry and Eros too.

I hated how my insides swirled with jealousy. It's not like they all belonged to me. It was only the twisted, greedy monster in me that seemed to think they should all be mine.

Sterling stroked my hair, pulling me from my thoughts. "The point of telling you this is so that you understand it's been a very long time since I've been with a woman. In my case with Alexandra, I didn't enjoy it. Nor did she. She called me cold and unfeeling."

My veins instantly heated in rage, my blood turning molten. *Oh, the next time I run into that bitch, I'll have a thing or two to say to her.* "Are you kidding me? She's the cold and unfeeling one."

"She wasn't entirely wrong. I was cold, detached. It didn't feel right with her." He brushed the pad of his thumb over my mouth, my lips softening against his touch. "But it's different when I'm with you. You make me feel again, Ruby. And it's been so very long since I've felt anything at all."

He drew his arms around me and pulled me up until my toes were barely touching the ground, and covered my lips with his.

His kiss was nothing short of nirvana.

There were no more walls between us. It was nothing but pure, raw, transparent Sterling. He poured all of himself into the connection, and even though I never wanted it to end, I broke the kiss, only to press a dozen more to his sharp jawline, his throat, his shoulder, his tattoo.

My movements turned hot and frantic, my tongue stroking down over the swell of his pectorals as I eased myself to my knees. I lapped up the little pebbles of perspiration beaded over the ripple of his abdominal muscles and paused when I got to the waist of his gray sweatpants.

I was now fully kneeling before him, using my torn shirt as padding for my knees. I enjoyed the way his muscles clenched beneath my tongue in anticipation as my fingers curled beneath his waistband and slowly slipped the sweats down around his hips.

His erection sprung out at full mast. I peered up at him, the sight of him bare and ready for me making my core drip with savage hunger.

Without any more hesitation, I cupped his balls. They were heavy in my palm, the skin smooth and cooler than I would have expected. He let out a hiss between clenched teeth, and his erection twitched a little at the contact.

Keeping him nestled in my one hand, I brought the other to grip his girth, my fingers failing to meet as they encircled his mass as best they could. I fondled his balls, enjoying the way his thighs quivered. Then my fingertips touched something, a deep scar sitting just behind his ball sack.

A chill settled over me, realizing what it was.

Just when I thought I understood the depths of Thomas Knight's maleficence, I was shown a deeper layer of his fucked-up nature. The eldest vampire prince was kind, caring, honest, and genuine, even after millennia of torment under his master's cruelty. I had originally thought that my dad had kept Sterling around because he'd been intent on squashing all those traits that might have been perceived as weakness by other vampires, especially Thomas Knight. But after seeing that photo in my father's coffin, I was pretty sure that he had loved Sterling. Not that dear old dad's brand of love was anything short of twisted and toxic. It made sense why he had murdered Sterling's mate and child and why he had tried to burn off the crucifix tattoo.

My father didn't want Sterling to be devoted to anyone but him.

I couldn't even fathom what the brutal vampire king would have done had he been alive to see his progeny and me together like this. I doubted he'd just sit back and let it happen. He was too jealous, too messed up.

So thank fuck the evil prick was dead.

My eyes flickered to the oil painting of my father, sadistic satisfaction filling me before I turned back to Sterling and pushed the head of his erection into my mouth.

CHAPTER FIFTY-FOUR

FILTHY MOUTHS AND FAVORITE SINS

A deep groan rumbled from Sterling as he thrust his hips forward, pushing more of himself into me. I thought it would be hard keeping my fangs sheathed, but it was easy keeping them reined back. Having him inside me, even in this way, almost felt natural, easy. Like this was how it was always supposed to be.

I began to suck the tip of him while my hands made steady-paced strokes up and down his shaft.

"Ruby." His hands flew back to my hair, fingers knotting in my red locks. "Bleeding Christ."

I smirked around his girth, and he shivered when I popped him out for just a second to look up at him. "A priest taking his Lord's name in vain?"

He tipped his head back, his face tilted toward the ceiling. His next words came out on labored pants, erotic, guttural, and wrapped in sandpaper. "One of the few benefits of never having to worry about being sent to Hell is that I can indulge in my second favorite sin as often as I want. *Goddamn*," he added on a sharp grunt as I swirled my tongue around the tip of his head, further accentuating his point.

"And what's your first favorite?"

"Drinking blood. Or it was." His hands clenched tighter in my hair. "I think I have a new favorite. *Christ*. Ruby! I'm not going to last much longer."

I sucked hard, taking way too much pleasure in his reaction. It was that spell, that confounding chemistry that sucked us both into a moment in time meant just for us. We were lost to the dark magic of it all, our inhibitions flung out the window and into the daylight where there was no hope of their return.

His hips moved back and forth as he used his hold on my head to fuck my mouth with reckless abandon. I painted him with long licks, sucking and stroking while matching his wild pace perfectly.

He shook and gasped, and by the way his cock throbbed, and his hands shook in my hair, I knew he was close to coming undone.

But this wasn't how I wanted it to end.

Nope. I was going to tease this out for as long as I possibly could. I wanted us both driven to the brink of madness before we went careening into bliss together.

"I'm so close," he gritted, his mouth hanging open, tendons going taut in his jaw. His breathing grew loud, and his thighs began to tremble violently. Pearls of pre-cum seeped out of him, peppering my tongue, but I didn't slow.

I pulled my hands away from the base of him, skimming them over the backs of his thighs to grab two handfuls of his ass. His toes curled against the attic floorboards, and just as I knew he was *oh-so-close*, I pulled him out of my mouth, dropped my fangs, and slammed them down onto the artery of his inner thigh.

His howl was a passionate cocktail of surprise, pleasure, and fury. I latched onto him, the same place Corry had fed on me at the gas station. The femoral artery. I hadn't forgotten what Sterling had told me during the feeding lesson in his den. It was the second most dangerous place to feed on, and only a master should attempt it. Too bad I had a little bit of a kink for inciting my mentor's ire.

"*Ruby!*"

Holy Mother of God. My name in his mouth was pure sex, the timber of his voice husky, betraying the depths of his own hunger. But it wasn't my blood he was craving at the moment. No. He lusted for my body to the point where I could feel it in the air, like a palpable touch that sank straight to my womanhood.

If I wasn't dripping before, I was now.

He ripped me from him with a strength that rattled me to the bone, his black blood splattering over my bare tits and gushing from his thigh.

Since he'd torn me off him like a band-aid, the bite was messy, but relief eased the tightness in my chest when I saw the wound begin to knit shut right before my eyes.

Wrenching me to my feet, the vampire's murky red eyes burned straight through me. For a second, I thought he was pissed and that I had ruined the moment. But his lips peeled into a devilish grin.

"You just love having me inside you, don't you?"

Cheeks blazing, I leaned against him, his member coming to rest against the apex of my thighs. "I crave your blood in my belly as much as I crave your cock in my cunt."

"That's quite a dirty mouth you've got there, Miss Baxter."

"If it's so filthy, maybe you should lick it clean."

The sly grin that crept across his heart-breaking features was so predatorial, I instinctually backed away. Stepping out of his sweatpants, he started for me. Somehow he was even more intimidatingly, completely naked. "Perhaps I'm far more interested in licking your other set of lips clean."

Heart racing, I launched into a full run to the other end of the attic, and just as I'd hoped, he charged after me. It was the hunt, a mating dance that seemed to be ingrained in me even though I knew fuck-all about vampire mating rituals. But it's like Sterling said, my instincts knew what to do.

I ran until I came to a table littered with old papers and managed to circle it one time before he caught me. His arms looped around my waist, ensnaring me. I wrapped my legs around his waist and clutched tight to him as he pressed my back down onto the table.

Looming over me, his hands began to run all over my body, my face, my breasts, my thighs. He was looking at me, mapping me out like he wanted to memorize this moment forever. Then he peeled my leggings off, unwrapping me like a long-anticipated Christmas present. My panties were the last thing to go, and just like the bra, he ripped them off with one jerk of his hand, leaving me completely naked.

I bit my lip to hold in a gasp as he grazed the very top of my inner thigh, so close that he brushed against the blonde curls of my pubic hair.

"Corry told me you colored your hair red."

My cheeks flamed as Sterling coiled a stripe of my hair around his index finger. For some reason, the innocent gesture felt more intimate than anything else we'd done yet. "Yeah. It's my favorite color."

"And this..." His palm hovered over my groin, then lowered to touch the thin patch of hair there. "This is blonde."

I gaped up at him in surprise. "How did you know?"

Twin stains of color kissed the prince's cheeks, and it took me a second to register that the ancient vampire was *blushing*. "Before you came here, I asked Dr. Sharpe to describe you. I wanted to know what you looked like. When he told me you were blonde, well, it filled me with a sort of joy that confounded me at first. I didn't understand why I cared what color of hair you had. But I cared very much. My master's hair was black. But before, back when I was human, mine was also blond. When Sharpe told me you had yellow hair and not black, I felt as though you belonged a little less to Thomas Knight and just a little bit more to me."

Before I could react, Sterling spread my thighs and dipped down to deliver the most sinful of kisses to my center.

And it was with that kiss that something dawned on me. Had it been Vincent telling me this story, I would fire off a quip that had quickly become an old favorite with him.

That I didn't belong to anyone.

Not anymore.

Yet, in Sterling's presence, it was easier to admit to myself that I wanted to belong to him.

And that monstrous part of me, the one that I was so scared I wouldn't learn how to control, wanted to belong to *all* of them.

Chapter Fifty-Five
An Offering

M y lungs squeezed, emptying of all air with a sharp gasp as Sterling's tongue split me asunder.

"Bloody hell!" I cried, my hands flying to grip the edge of the table I laid on. As he lavished my core, he splayed me open, with my most intimate parts exposed and at the vampire's mercy.

All thoughts that had been lurking at the periphery of my mind, becoming queen, Vincent and his mind games, Dagon Knight and the Boston Coven, it all just ceased to exist. In this moment, the only thing I could focus on was the searing caress of Sterling's lips, his tongue, his heated breath.

Eros had already done this for me, but to compare the oral skills of the coven's master of torture to the silver-tongued, millennia-old priest would be a crime against womankind.

Deathwish had gone to war on my body, laying siege on my entrance, hellbent on my surrender.

Sterling was making love to me with his mouth. There was no other way to describe it. Each lick, each nip, each flick of his tongue was done with devotion, a true master of the craft even though it had been years since he'd done it at all.

Sensual and perfectly paced, just like Sterling.

When his tongue began to slide into me, slipping past my soaking folds, in and out, picking up speed, I began to shake under the delicious assault. Sweat beaded my brow, and my thighs quivered around his head. I didn't know how much more I could take. My breath began to splinter with every gulp of breath I managed to take, and—*God*—he grinned against me, his lips pursing against my own.

"I've forgotten what it's like making my mate shake with pleasure. There's nothing quite like it."

His mate.

Those words... A stamp of ownership that I wished, how I wished they were true.

But the sad fact was, I wasn't his mate, not without his mark on my flesh. But it was still a nice fantasy.

"I think this was the part I missed the most," he murmured into my folds.

"W–what part?"

"Preparing your body so that it may accommodate my own."

Holy hot hell. How did he manage to be so filthy and eloquent at the same time? I didn't dare ask him out of fear that he'd stop doing whatever he was doing with his tongue. He swirled it around my clit in sensual circles and gave it an occasional flick.

"Don't mistake me, love. Seating my cock inside you will be nothing short of ecstasy. But nothing compares to feeling the pulse of your heart pound my tongue through the walls of your womanhood." To demonstrate, he plunged his tongue into me again, this time staying there for several beats. Spreading my legs wider, he skirted his fingers down the interior of my thigh, over the swell of my ass, then pressed his thumb to the ring of muscle—a place I was not ready to take a male, especially a male like Sterling.

But instead of pushing into that dark place, his hand fell away, and he released a deep masculine growl of satisfaction as my heartrate launched into lightspeed. "Yeah, just like that."

Oh *fuck*. The rumbling of his tongue sent a series of delicious convulsions thrashing through my body. And there it was, the final push I needed to send me over the edge, an explosion of pleasure going off in my lower belly like fireworks.

My limbs went hot, then cold. A sheen of sweat settled over every inch of my flesh, making me one thousand times more sensitive to his tickling breath over my labia. Stars filled my vision, and when they faded, Sterling came into view.

Bloody hell, he was a vision. An erotic, sweat-covered, masculine vision. The sight of him arched over the table, silvery strands plastered to his glistening brow, and his lips covered in my arousal was not one I would let myself forget anytime soon.

I flashed him a dazed smile. "Damn. You look good. You feel good. Just everything is so...*good*." I breathed a happy sigh, not even caring that my post-orgasm brain fog was seriously hindering any ability to articulate. But Sterling was all to blame for that one, and I was sure he was smug for it.

Chuckling, the vampire prince leaned over the table until our faces were lined up, draping his lithe frame over mine to plant a kiss on my lips. When he drew away, the most darkly divine smirk curved his mouth.

"What if I could make you feel even better?" he asked in a silk-soft whisper as he positioned himself so that his erection came to rest against my slit. "What would you say to that?"

"W–what would I s–ay?" I stuttered, words coming hard for me as he began to move his hips, his hot and throbbing shaft sliding between my soaking folds, touching in all the right places. "Oh, oh, fuck! *Sterling!*"

His mouth split with a seductive smile. "A perfect sentiment, Miss Baxter."

I shivered beneath him, reveling in the way our bare bodies slid together, flesh to flesh, our breath entwined, our chests heaving in unison. Lifting my hands from the edge of the table, I banded my arms around his shoulders, gripping the clusters of lean muscles that rippled beneath his skin as he moved against me. His mouth came to rest between the juncture of my neck and shoulder, making me gasp as his teeth grazed my skin.

"The second I enter you, are you going to bite me?" He grunted against me, his voice all husky and low with his own lust.

"You don't want to be my mate," I said in a quivering voice. "S–so I'll try not to. I'm still trying to get a lid on this whole control thing."

"What I said is that *I* won't mark *you*. That privilege rests with the male you choose as your mate." His eyes narrowed to nothing but slits. "Eros notwithstanding."

I gave Sterling a stunned blink as his words penetrated the haze still wrapping my brain. What was he trying to tell me exactly? Was he really saying it was okay to bite him?

No, that was insanity.

It's not like I knew all the nuisances with all this marking and claiming stuff, but it couldn't be normal for one vampire to carry another's mark but not the other way around.

Before I could dwell on all the complications of this whole weird game to find my mate and king, Sterling thrust his way inside me.

My spine arched, and I surged on a swollen gasp, but his body pushed me back down against the table, and he devoured my cry with an insatiable kiss, feasting on my lips like they were the tastiest thing he'd ever had.

"Christ Almighty," he purred into my mouth on a half-growl, half-groan. "You feel like paradise. Complete and utter perfection. Fuck!"

He unleashed another erotic groan of satisfaction, his brows pinching in euphoria, and slowly fed more of himself to me. "Do you feel me, Ruby? Do you feel this?"

I wasn't sure if he was talking about this terrifying magic binding us together or the way his massive cock spread my walls, making me stretch to accommodate him. Either way, I felt it alright. It was this tight, uneasy ball of tension hanging over our heads. It had been there since the moment we came into each other's orbit and demanded to be worked loose.

Squeezing my eyes shut, I savored the sensation of him inside me, filling me up until I thought I might break. It was painful, but only because of his size. He went slow, almost painfully so, easing himself inside me in a way that told me all he cared about was my comfort. He was so damn gentle, so careful with me, as if I was something precious he wanted to treasure forever.

Sterling felt so goddamn right sheathed inside me that I never wanted it to end. Hell, I could die getting fucked like this, and that would be A-okay with me. He called me paradise, but it went both ways. His body locked together with mine felt so perfect. It went beyond reason. It was maddening how freaking *good* it all was.

"Don't stop, Sterling. Please, whatever you do, don't stop."

The soul-stealing smile he gave me was enough to make all the pain from our size difference melt away, and just like that, there was nothing but blinding pleasure between us.

Just as it should be.

No more secrets, no more pain, no walls or armor to hide behind. There was nothing but the most amazing heat coiling where our bodies met as his hips flexed forward, surging into me with his mouth agape as if he was just as lost to this enthralling magic fusing us as I was.

My teeth clenched, and I lifted my hips off the table so he could get more purchase inside me. His hands slipped beneath me, cupping my ass as he held me to him, pumping into me, rolling his hips with strokes that already had me close to falling apart in his embrace.

His brow pressed against my own, and I stared into his ghostly eyes that seemed to sparkle with something that would have me moaning in pleasure even if he wasn't seated balls deep inside me, fucking like he had forgotten the bliss of a woman's body.

"Beautiful," he breathed. "Absolutely beautiful."

"But you can't see me."

His hands left my rear to smooth over my breasts, up my neck, over my face, and finally settle on either side of my head, holding me. "I see all the parts that matter. And you're fucking beautiful, Ruby Renada."

I don't know why I started to cry. Maybe it was from the searing bliss between my thighs as his cock continued to work me up to another climax. Or maybe it was the fact that for the first time since... Well, since ever, that I felt seen. Truly seen. And by the reclusive blind prince, no less. How was that for irony?

Sterling stilled for a moment, staring down at me with worry etched in the corners of his eyes. "You're crying. Am I hurting you?"

"No, I'm just...happy. I'm so happy it almost hurts."

"If you're happy, why does it hurt?"

"Because it has to end sometime, doesn't it? Eventually, we'll have to leave this attic, and I have to accept that you won't be king. I just have to pretend that I'm okay with that. And I'm not okay with it. I'm not okay at all."

Part of me felt pathetic for crying, especially right in the middle of what I had basically begged Sterling for. And now here I was, sobbing, with his dick still inside me. But if I felt at all stupid, he soothed it away with hushed *shhhh* sounds, his arms encircling my head, drawing me into him in a fierce embrace.

"I can never be king because I refuse to sit where he did, Ruby. And I won't mark you because that right should lie with the king. But understand, I want nothing more than for me to be yours. The only reason I wouldn't take your mark before is that I didn't think you'd want me once you discovered what your father did to me. But if you'll have me, I will always be here for you to guide you in your role as queen."

He pecked a sweet kiss to my jawline and held himself there, so close that his eyelashes tickled my cheek. He hadn't come yet, and I was still building up to my second climax. But talking about this, about us, it didn't ruin the moment. If anything, it brought us closer.

And I relished it.

He took a shaky breath, and the muscles in his body went tight. "And if you somehow still want me as your mate after knowing what you do, you can mark me."

Tilting his head, he exposed the section of his throat where Thomas Knight's mark marred his skin, offering his neck to me.

"Even if I don't feel right taking you as my own officially, you can have me. The least I can give you is that."

CHAPTER FIFTY-SIX
BLOODY UNION

For one moment that seemed to last forever, I stared at the bite scar on Sterling's throat.

He really was a beautiful man, and even though every inch of his body was gorgeous, his neck was among his best physical features, right up there with his cock, and his eyes. His throat was all sinewy muscle and dark veins, wrapped up in flawless ivory skin.

The only imperfection was his ruined crucifix tattoo and that damn mark, the physical proof of my father's abuse.

And here he was, asking me to place my own, right there, smack on top of it.

I felt like I was in a dream, that maybe I had blacked out and imagined this going almost exactly how I wanted it to. By offering himself to me like this, he was giving me more than his blood.

Since he was still buried inside me, biting him now would mean the wound would become a permanent fixture on his flesh.

My mating mark.

Not only would it be visible for everyone to see, but my scent would be woven with his, alerting everyone in the coven that he was mine.

Mine.

Forever.

For an immortal vampire, forever was a pretty damn long time.

It was amazing that Sterling was making such a commitment to me after having known me for only one night. The obvious reasoning for his decision was that my mark had to be better than carrying my father's. Maybe that was part of it. But deep down, I knew there was more to it than that.

This, *us*, as insane as it was, it felt right. Now, if only Sterling would claim me in return, everything would be perfect. Still, the fact that he wanted my mark was enough to make the monster that had been dormant inside me stir back to life.

My breath came out in short pants as I gazed up at him, my eyes wide with a mixture of fear and excitement. I didn't want to lose myself to my youngblood instincts, not when we were attached like this, not when he was offering me something I desperately wanted. I didn't want to give him any reason to change his mind.

My cheeks torched with heat that quickly sunk straight to where we were connected. Squirming beneath him, I wiggled my hips to encourage him to keep fucking me. Taking the cue, he picked up his pace again, pumping into me with harder thrusts. His grip on my hips went from gentle to bruising, and he bared his teeth with a guttural growl rumbling up from his chest.

One minute he had been the most gentle, attentive lover, and the next, his hands had turned rough and his movements battering. It was almost like he was trying to coax out that dark, savage part of me. And God—or whatever deity was brave enough to spy on this debauchery —help me because it was working.

I was losing it.

Gritting my teeth, I braced myself against the assault of his pelvis against mine. Sterling really could read me like a damn book because I was a sucker for pain like this, that intimate torture that pushed me higher and higher to that promise of yet another euphoric explosion.

Sterling didn't slow his pace at all, and there was no end in sight. He had the stamina of a freaking god. His lips came crashing down over mine in an earth-shattering kiss, making me take his tongue into my mouth as he fucked me.

The sear of his cock slamming home into my core, the clean and salty taste of him on my taste buds, the heat in his eyes, the slide of his throat against my jaw as he broke our kiss to nip my ear. The twitch of his veins buried beneath marble-smooth flesh, and *fuck*, the scent of him.

It was all too much.

"Losing control..." I managed to hiss through clenched teeth.

"Good. Let your darkest instincts out to play, love." When I opened my mouth to protest, he gripped my chin and forced my gaze to his, lights dancing in his ghostly gaze. "Don't worry, I can handle you and whatever else your youngblood manners throw at me."

Then, he bit his lip. Hard. The fang punctured his flawless flesh, and a thick bead of black oozed out and splattered on my upper lip.

That was my undoing.

I lost what little hold I had over the reins of my humanity just as I came violently, a brutal orgasm ravaging every nerve in my body. My skull split with a sharp pain that was dulled by the intense pleasure sweeping over me like a tidal wave as my fangs punched through my gums.

I screamed and moaned, feeling like a feral animal. If there was any sense or reason left in me to feel ashamed, Sterling never gave those emotions a chance to surface. He stroked my hair, beaming down at me with an undiluted adoration that I caught at the peak of my orgasm.

"There she is," he cooed on a honied purr. "My beautiful queen."

My heart, my vagina, my freaking soul, all of it turned to ash in the wake of the fire that this sullied priest had ignited inside me. It felt so good that for a second, I questioned if it was possible to die from too much pleasure. Maybe under the marble-hard, perfectly crafted body that was Sterling Knight.

Unable to hold back for another second, I sunk my teeth into his throat, right where my father had bitten him centuries ago.

For a beat, the vampire went board stiff against me, his muscles going completely rigid. Then his body jerked and twitched, and I could feel the movement deep within where we were still joined.

A pained whimper left him as my mark sizzled into his skin, but it only lasted for a few heartbeats until he was fucking me again, surging into me while keeping his throat steady so I could easily feast on his blood.

This was the moment. This was what the night had been building up to. As soon as my teeth pierced his skin, with him penetrating me in return, the tension shattered. And all that was left was pure fucking bliss, wrapped up so close in each other that I was positive there would always be a piece of him inside me, lodged deep within.

I couldn't get enough of his blood. It filled me and felt as necessary as oxygen, as intoxicating as a lethal narcotic.

Unable and uncaring to rein back my rabid instincts, I released a low growl, laced with a moan as the combination of his blood filled my mouth and the wash of his cum filled my womb in the wake of his release.

Feeling warm and full, I came undone with him, crying in the crux of complete rapture.

When I withdrew my fangs from him, he pulled himself up on his arms to stare down at me, as if he could see me perfectly, splayed out beneath him. Blood dripped from his throat, speckling my breasts, and he arched down to suck them clean.

"Fucking perfect," he said on a sated sigh that tickled my nipples.

Coming down from the adrenaline high, I peered up at him through my tangle of red hair, unable to look away from the mark I'd given him. Reaching up, my fingertips grazed the already sealing puncture holes to form a silver scar.

Brushing my hand over his jaw, a smear of his black blood streaked his skin. "You're perfect, now that my father's mark is gone. You belong only to me now, Sterling. And I'm never letting you go."

He titled his head to catch my fingers with his lips, kissing them. "Promise?"

"I promise."

With extraordinary strength, he grasped me by the waist and rolled us over so that his back was now pressed to the table with me straddling him. I grinned down at him, impressed that he was still hard as steel inside me.

"You want more?"

"More? I want everything." Then he slid me a smile that had me instantly wet all over again, igniting that flame deep in my lower belly where the head of him pressed. "Bite me, ride me, do whatever you want to me, love. I'm yours."

Had there ever been words as perfect as those?

Mine.

My mate.

Still seated on top of him, I lifted myself so that only the tip of him was inside me and slammed myself back down, taking way too much glee in the way his eyes popped and his jaw clenched.

Rolling my hips back and forth, I rode him, my pace frantic and wild, chasing that promise of yet another climax. Sterling gripped my breasts, smearing his inky blood all over me as I fucked him hard and fast. His hands fell away, pressing against my lower tummy as if he was feeling for the impression of his cock.

"Look at you," he groaned, peering straight through me with his messy, silver trusses screening his eyes. "A queen on her throne."

I smirked down at him, writhing on his body like it was made for me. "And what a perfect fit it is."

It was true. It wasn't just some dopamine-induced dirty talk. I meant every syllable, down to the marrow of my bones. And I knew he felt it too. With this coupling, I had lifted at least a little of the stain my father had left on Sterling.

And in Sterling's own words from earlier, it felt like he belonged a little less to Thomas Knight and just a little bit more to me.

As we both came almost simultaneously yet again, I couldn't resist biting him a second time over my mark.

"Take it easy, love." He tried to gently push me away, but I pressed forward, insistent on a second helping of his blood to match the second helping of his other fluid. "My blood is ancient and far more potent than the others. If you overindulge…"

As the wash of his blood filled my mouth, his voice faded away, his words echoing in the distance as if I was suddenly far away. My vision went black, and the darkness surrounded me. The last thing I felt was myself collapsing against his chest, his strong arms catching me. Even though he was now shouting my name in worry, the last memory my conscious brain could compose was how happy I was hearing my first name in his mouth.

And with that, I slipped into a deep sleep where I could pretend I belonged to him as much as he belonged to me.

Chapter Fifty-Seven
RUDE AWAKENING

The first thing I noticed when I came to was the white sheet covering my body, my *very naked* body.

The second thing was that I was tied down.

My eyes flew open to discover I was lying in a white, sterile room on a hospital-type gurney. There was a mixture of medical equipment, old and new, making it look like a modern-day doctor and an eighteenth-century surgeon shared the place.

Where the heck was I? How had I gotten here? And why the fuck was I tied down like some patient at a Victorian insane asylum?

Attempting to work the bindings loose to no avail, I considered dropping my fangs to try and chew through the nylon straps when muffled voices had me pausing.

Male voices bled from underneath the room's entrance, and by their sharp lilt, they were arguing. The hair on the back of my neck prickled when I picked out the baritone voice currently speaking as Vincent's.

"I still can't believe you let her mark you. The agreement was—"

"I'm well aware of the agreement's parameters," Sterling's cool voice countered, a steely bite to his tone. "We agreed that her chosen king should be the one to claim her. However, if she wishes to mark any of us, that is perfectly within her right to do so."

Vincent scoffed, his voice fraying with barely bridled rage. "Since when do you snake by on technicalities like that? I expect it from Deathwish but not from you."

"Do not lecture me, Brother."

"Stop acting like she belongs to you." It was now Corry who spoke. "Until she picks a king, she belongs to all of us, dickhead. Fuck it. I say even when she chooses a king, she should still be mated to all of us. Seeing her marked and claimed by all four of us? Hot as hell. Dibs on being baby daddy, though."

"Already got dibs on that, Youngblood." My heart squeezed, and the mark on my shoulder burned when Eros' voice wrapped around me like a caress.

All four of them were here, waiting outside the room for me.

"No way. I saw her first!"

"I fucked her first."

Corry sputtered for a second before he could form words. "O–only technically! I finger fucked and fed from her first!"

"I marked her first. Beat that."

"How about you two fucks shut up, or I beat you both?" Vincent snapped, his growl of warning making my breath catch in my throat. "This is the princess we're talking about, not riding shotgun. Your pathetic little 'dibs' is pointless anyway. The throne should have been mine from the beginning. I shouldn't have to compete against my own brothers."

"Get the fuck over it, Feral," Eros growled. "This is what the Elders decided. You want to be king, you've got to play nice with the princess. Maybe if you eased up on the whole douchey alpha thing, she might be able to stand you long enough to let you touch her."

"Says the psychopath who fucking tied her up and cut her during her first time."

"Yeah," Eros snickered. "And she was screaming for more the whole damn time."

There was the sound of thumping flesh, the crunch of bone, and the clatter of shit hitting the ground. A fight had clearly broken out between Vincent and Eros but was probably stopped right away because instant silence followed, and Sterling's voice rang out next.

"Save it for the match tomorrow. The whole reason I allow you two to keep doing them is so you can get this shit out of your system, away from the coven. It's especially important to not wrap the princess up in your bad blood."

Ha. Too flipping late for that. Apparently, Sterling still didn't know about the bet. Then again, why would he? I hadn't told him, and who knew if Corry was in on it. If he was, I doubt he'd nark. And holy shit, did he say tomorrow? The match was Friday, and if tomorrow was Friday, that meant I'd been out for two whole days.

"I say we go in there," Vincent announced after a few moments of silence. "I don't like leaving her alone with Sharpe. For all we know, he's the mole."

"Can't be the mole," Eros sneered. "Don't go accusing people just because you're too insecure to let other males around her."

"Shut the fuck up and think about it for a second. Doesn't anyone else notice that shit's not adding up with the doctor? We all know Master didn't want any of us to be king. He'd rather put a baboon on the throne than have one of us rule. So why have her go through this fucked-up courting bullshit with all of us?"

"Because you're right," Sterling agreed. "Thomas Knight would have put anyone on the throne so long as it wasn't any of us, especially his own flesh and blood. But the fact of the matter is, she's a half-blood. Ruby's not fit to rule on her own. She barely knows how to be human, let alone a vampire. She needs guidance. She needs a mate. That's the Elders' reasoning. Is that so odd, Brother?"

"But whose idea was it for her to pick a mate out of the vampire king's progeny?"

There was a moment's pause before Sterling said, "Dr. Sharpe."

"*Exactly.* Isn't that weird, seeing as he was supposedly some great friend of the king's? He seemed to support making Ruby as queen even though we all know Thomas Knight kept her locked up in that suburban hell to keep her away from us. He didn't want her mixed up in this world." Vincent's voice dropped to a whisper so low, I had to strain to hear. "Sure, she was his heir, but between us four, we know our master never planned on dying. To boot, Sharpe was all for having her choose one of us as king when we know her father would have hated both of those options. If Master were here today, he'd kill all of us for even so much as breathing in her direction. Especially Sterling."

"I don't think that's true," Corry spoke next. "Why would he have turned me if it wasn't to keep her company? To make her feel more human?"

"Maybe that's the case, but I can tell you, he sure as shit didn't turn you so you could stick it to his daughter, Cor. He was protective of her. He didn't want anyone to mate her, especially one of us. He was jealous and possessive, and he would have kept her there locked up forever if he'd had it his way."

Sterling cleared his throat, his voice pinched. "So what are you suggesting, Vincent?"

"We know there's a traitor in the Elders. How else would our cover-up for Master's murder have gotten out? Sterling only told the Elders about the whole 'suicide' thing. And now Sharpe is changing his tune on making one of us king?"

"That doesn't make any sense," Eros countered. "The Boston Coven member that Ruby and I tortured let it spill that Dagon Knight is supposedly, miraculously back from the dead and that all the opposing covens support him as king. So if Sharpe is loyal to Boston Coven, why would it be his idea to make one of us king?"

There was a tense silence that fell between the princes that allowed me to stop and gather my thoughts on everything I'd heard.

I already had my suspicions that Thomas Knight had been murdered and that it had been staged to look like a suicide, that the suicide was just the cover-up. And I still had a gut feeling that Vincent had somehow been the one to do the deed. The new thing I learned today was that all his brothers were in on it. Hell, maybe they even helped. They had at least covered it up to look like a suicide, and then the Elders had covered up the suicide—believing it was actually a suicide—to avoid making the coven look weak.

When I questioned Corry on our date, he lied to me to protect their secret.

Vincent had lied to me.

And Eros and Sterling had just chosen not to talk about it.

Meaning they didn't trust me with their secret.

It hurt, knowing I wasn't accepted as one of *them* yet. I mean, I'd barely been here even a week, so it wasn't a big shock. But that fact did nothing to ease the ache in my heart.

The big question still on my mind was, had they done it? If it was supposed to be an impossible feat for a vampire to kill its maker, how had any one of them managed to pull it off?

Then there was still the question of the mole. While I didn't like Sharpe one bit, I didn't agree with Vincent's suspicions. It couldn't be him. Whoever the nark was, they were loyal to the Boston Coven. And if I learned anything from the torture session in Eros' den, the Boston Coven felt this Dagon Knight should be the true king. So, it wouldn't make any sense for Sharpe to suggest I choose a king for myself among the princes if he was in the Dagon Knight for king club.

But Vincent did make a great point. Sharpe had supposedly been loyal to my father all those years, pretending to care about keeping me safe from the coven and the princes. But as soon as the king had died, the good doctor had changed his tune, throwing me into coven life, into this courting game that would probably spur Thomas Knight into a murderous rampage if he were alive.

My attention was foisted away from the guys' not-so-hushed argument when a small figure approached my bedside, heels clicking loudly against the flooring.

"You're awake," Lavinia observed in a placid tone as she strapped a blood pressure cuff around my upper arm.

The little girl took the stethoscope slung around her neck and put the plugs in her ears while pressing the cup to my antecubital fossa—something I recalled from Sterling's lesson—in the interior of my arm. She listened for several seconds that lasted for what felt like forever in the awkward silence shared with the ancient little girl that was Lavinia Sharpe.

"Um... So, what happened to me?"

Lavinia didn't bother looking up from her task. Her blonde brows pinched together as if annoyed by my question. "You had too much pure vampire blood."

"I didn't know it was dangerous to have too much, not for the person feeding."

She sniffed, not looking up from her task. "It's not dangerous to overindulge on a younger vampire's blood, but our Prince Knight is old. His blood is potent. As a mortal, you have to pace yourself."

She pulled the stethoscope from her ears and took off the cuff to write down my numbers on a clipboard that she seemed to produce out of nowhere. "Your blood pressure is ninety over sixty."

"Is that good?"

"Extremely. You're perfectly fine now." She tapped my arm where an IV—one I hadn't noticed until now—was taped.

"After the transfusion, that is."

I blinked rapidly. "Wait. Transfusion?" Swiveling my attention to where she gestured, I noticed the IV bag suspended beside my head, filled with bright red liquid. Human blood.

"Yes," Lavinia sighed like she'd grown tired of this conversation before it had even started. "You needed human blood to counterbalance all the vampire blood in your system. The O'Leary blood donor was kind enough to supply it."

Kenzie. My guts twisted with guilt, knowing I still owed her an apology for almost killing her during my first feeding lesson.

"Um... So, why am I naked, and why am I tied down? It's kind of freaking me out here."

"Dr. Sharpe had to examine you to make sure the blood didn't have any negative effect on your mortal body."

My skin crawled, knowing Sharpe had seen my naked body.

Lavinia continued. "We've seen mortals intake too much vampire blood while being turned, and before the change could happen, they've often gone mad. Similar to humans reacting to synthetic cathinone, the drug known as bath salts. Bruising is an early symptom, followed by tearing off their own flesh and eating it." She clicked her tongue, her blonde curls swaying around her tiny, heart-shaped face.

"Not pretty. But you aren't exhibiting any of those symptoms, so I suppose we can release you."

I gave a thick swallow. "That's good. So, will you untie me?"

Lavinia smirked before turning on her heel to march out of the room. "I'll leave that to your callers. They've been very obnoxious, waiting around here day and night for you to wake up. They've even had all their coffins hauled into my and Master's parlor, in the next room." She twisted in the doorway, sliding me a brittle smile that sent a shiver skittering down my spine.

"Oh, by the way. While he was at it, my master also inserted an IUD. Figured you would want it until you've selected a king. Especially since it was the only way to end your heat cycle. Well, with the exception of becoming pregnant."

I gaped at her, feeling pretty damn violated at this point. Sure, I wanted birth control. I'd been a little reckless with the whole protection thing. Eros hadn't finished inside me, and Sterling was sterile, but I had to be more careful in the future. Not to mention that those pheromones would have been bad news if I'd had to walk around like that, so horny and on the edge of snapping literally every minute of the day. Dark flames licked at my core, thinking about the way Vincent or Eros might have reacted to my heat state. If sweet, mellow Corry could get so dominant, how would those two have reacted?

Still, no one had *asked* me. Sharpe had just assumed.

Then again, that was him. The cold and unfeeling doctor who had lied to me all those years, feeding me pills, saying it was for a heart condition.

444   OUR SINS IN BLOOD

He'd always been a slimy bastard.

There was no concrete evidence that supported Vincent's theories on Sharpe being the traitor. Yet, something was definitely off about the coven's resident doctor, and I was thankful to the guys for staying close while I'd been unconscious.

But that didn't mean I was ready to have all of them be in the same room with me while I was tied to my bed with nothing but a sheet between us.

Before I could try to convince Lavinia to untie me and get me some clothes, she opened the door and summoned them inside.

Chapter Fifty-Eight
An Unexpected Moment

Lavinia moved away from the door, allowing the princes inside. When Sterling was the first to enter the room, she peered up at him with wide doe-like eyes. A furious blush broke out on her cheeks, the infatuation in her gaze completely unguarded.

Well, well. It looked like Lavinia and I had something in common. We both had a huge crush on the coven's eldest vampire prince.

Sometimes I forgot that Lavinia wasn't a normal child. She was permanently stunted, a three-hundred-year-old woman in the body of a prepubescent little girl.

It had to be horrible for her. It reminded me of a book I'd read once, *Interview with the Vampire*, where the little girl vampire had gone mad with frustration because her body would never bloom into that of a full woman's.

As bizarre as she was, I felt bad for Lavinia.

"Ms. Sharpe, how is our princess?" Sterling angled his head, so his moon-pale eyes bore through the child doctor, who, for the first time, looked like nothing but a shy kid as she peered up at the man who was at least twice her size.

"S–s–she's just fine, My Prince. In perfect health!"

Sterling gave her a nod along with a polite smile. "Thank you for taking care of her. Again, I'm sorry to put you and your master through all the trouble. We'll be more careful next time."

The little girl gave a tiny, bumbling curtsy and left the room, leaving Sterling and me alone for a beat.

He looked in my direction, a soft, radiant smile unfurling on his perfect lips. He wore that chaste grin so well, but its innocence was a lie. I knew what those lips were capable of. For a second, I couldn't breathe at the memory of them buried between my legs. My chest began to rise and fall in heavy succession, and my pulse thrashed in my ear as my attention slipped from his mouth down to the scar on his neck.

My mating mark.

The sight of it sent a rush of heat down my core, filling my lower belly with a kind of warmth that had me sweating on the outside and melting on the inside.

"Ruby?" My name in his mouth was still the sexiest thing I'd ever heard, like it was a piece of candy he wanted to suck on forever. My whole chest squeezed, and I squirmed in my bed, wanting nothing more than to throw myself in his arms.

"I'm here. I'm fine."

Just like that, the creases of worry etched into the marble planes of his face vanished, and his smile spread wider. "Thank God you're safe."

My brows arched in surprise. "I thought you didn't believe in God."

"What I said is that my faith comes and goes. I'm going through an uptick in faith, currently."

My heart fluttered as if a thousand butterflies were trapped in my ribcage. "Would I have anything to do with that?"

Approaching my bedside, he leaned down to plant a kiss on my brow, his cool lips heaven against my blazing skin. "You have everything to do with it."

Next, Corry strode in with his hands shoved in the pockets of his dark denim jeans. "Finally awake, Red? You've been out forever. That's some dicking Sterling must have given you to blackout for two days." The youngblood let out a low whistle, his gaze flicking around the room before it settled on me, the dimples on his cheeks appearing in the wake of his ear-to-ear grin. He ran a hand through his spiked hair, his gaze dipping to his toes. "Speaking of which, I'm sorry for the whole um... scene I made in the library."

"It's alright, Cor. It was kind of hot. I didn't know you could be so dominant."

The youngest prince perked right up, his face beaming with delight. "Yeah? Well, you haven't seen anything yet, babe. Speaking of which, that sexy scar you gave Sterling? When do I get mine?"

Before I could even think of an answer, Eros ambled in next. His snake bites twitched with an arrogant smirk as he came over to the other side of my bed, studying me with something wicked glittering in his chocolate eyes.

"There's our doll, finally awake to join the land of the not-so-living."

My shoulder burned like it had been set on fire, and as if he somehow knew, he peeled back the sheet exposing just enough of my bare flesh for the whole room to get a peek at his mark on my shoulder. Arching down, he pressed his lips to it in a surprisingly gentle kiss. The scruff of his unruly five-o clock shadow tickled me, and for some reason, the pain in my mark seemed to ebb away under the purse of his mouth.

Eros was quick to yank the sheet back up when Vincent entered, a storm of darkness brewing in his glare.

For a sliver of a second, he looked in my direction with something vaguely resembling concern, but it was gone so fast I wasn't sure if it had been there at all. "You're awake. About time."

"Missed you too, asshole. Can someone untie me and get me some clothes?"

Without them needing to coordinate, Sterling went for my wrist closest to him, Eros for the other wrist, and Vincent and Corry set to my ankles. It was embarrassing how hard my pulse skyrocketed, having all their hands on me.

Having all four princes in the same room at the same time was intense enough, let alone having them all touch me at once.

Especially when I was still buck naked.

And, of course, my traitorous body had a thing or two to say about the whole scenario by the way my nipples hardened, creating tiny peaks in the sheets.

But if anyone noticed, which they probably did by the way their smoldering eyes kept wandering over the outline of my bare body, they held their tongues.

"I'm sorry we had to resort to this, Miss Baxter. The Sharpes were concerned you might have ingested lethal volumes of my blood." As Sterling spoke, his voice dripped with guilt. Knowing him, he probably held himself responsible for not stopping me sooner.

He'd probably been beating himself up for it the last two days. I wish he hadn't. The night we'd spent together had been absolute perfection, and I'd do it all over again in a heartbeat.

Before I could assure him that everything was fine, Vincent's fingers dug into my ankle with a bruising force as he ripped away the straps. When he'd freed my leg, he didn't pull away like I thought he would. Instead, his hand lingered beneath the sheet, his digits digging into my flesh enough to make me wince. But instead of admonishing me, he pinned his hot glower on his eldest brother.

"I still can't believe you let her take so much blood."

Sterling's face remained pointed in my direction, but his impassive mask wavered for just a second, never completely falling away as it had when we'd fucked like bunnies in the attic. "I've already punished myself enough for what happened. I don't need your help in adding to my guilt."

At this point, I was now completely unstrapped from the gurney. But all the princes still stood right beside me, one at each corner of the bed, touching me.

Sterling held my left hand, clasping it tenderly in both of his.

Eros' index finger traced the mating mark on my shoulder over the sheet.

Corry was brushing his knuckles gently over my left ankle, and Vincent, in true Feral fashion, held me in a rough and possessive death grip.

Bloody hell.

Now that I'd decided to remain as a half-blood, I wasn't so sure I'd be able to survive these men. But fuck, nothing —and I mean nothing—was going to stop me from trying.

That meant that if I was going to earn their respect, I'd have to put on my big girl panties and go head-to-head with them.

I wouldn't take Feral's abuse unless I was flat on my back with his dick inside me. Then, maybe.

Donning a too-sweet grin, I shuffled myself up into a sitting position and ripped my leg away from Vincent while allowing the others to touch me. "You let me feed from you the other night in the back of your car, Feral. You didn't bitch when it was your blood I was taking."

When he said nothing, I narrowed my eyes and continued. "So let's say we fell into some alternate dimension where I might actually fuck you. You wouldn't want me to mark you?"

His lips peeled back in a vicious sneer. "Oh, so we're going to pretend like you didn't *beg* me for my cock that night, Princess? Too bad I have zero desire to join the little harem you're building for yourself. And if we were in some 'alternate dimension' where I would be interested in a girl who fucks my brothers more often than the other females in the coven change their panties, I would have stopped you from taking too much blood. I'd make you stay awake, eyes on me the whole time while you watch yourself taking my cock."

The mean grin that broke out on his chiseled features made my skin pebble with perspiration and the apex of my thighs heat with a different kind of moisture.

Damn him. Why did he have to have this kind of effect on me? Why did my vagina have such a soft spot for such a hardass?

I held tightly onto my hatred, pushing my lust for him way back into that dark part of me where it bubbled up from like some poisonous witch's brew. I didn't want to admit to Vincent's brothers just how much his bad-boy act got to me. And most importantly, I didn't want to admit it to myself.

"Fuck you, Feral." I averted my eyes, hating how much my cheeks flamed. I could feel his cocky grin, hot on my skin. He knew how deeply his worlds had dug into me, crawling inside me, touching me in all the places we both wanted him to dominate and claim.

If we weren't too stubborn to admit it.

"Fuck me, huh?" His tongue flicked out, tasting his bottom lip. It was as if he was imagining it in his mind, contemplating it. Then he shrugged and turned to leave the room. "Only when you realize that I'm the only male you'll ever need."

With that, he left without so much as a glance back.

The tension that settled between the three remaining princes and me turned smothering until Corry shattered the tension with another of his low whistles. "Damn, he's cranky. Ignore him, Red. He's all sulky and shit that it was Sterling you marked, and not him. Speaking of which,

Sterling got laid for the first time in like, what? A million years? We should be throwing him a party."

"Right?" Eros chuckled. "It's been so long since he's gotten laid, my own balls have turned blue in solidarity. We'll get him a 'congrats on your nut' cake."

The eldest prince's expression remained mostly impassive, with only a sliver of irritation bleeding through the cracks. "That won't be necessary."

I wanted to stay and experience the strange comradery between Sterling, Eros, and Corry. With Vincent gone, the tension had lifted, and there was a kind of ease shared between them that felt light and natural. I knew that when forced to pick, Corry sided with Vincent but seeing them together now, I could see that Eros and Corry did like each other. And, of course, it wouldn't be like Sterling to pick sides.

But as much as I wanted to keep a safe distance from The Feral King and his angsty, big-dick energy, I couldn't. His words had been like a knife to my belly, and I couldn't just let myself sit here and pretend he hadn't just slut-shamed me in front of his brothers.

Wrapping the sheet tightly around me, I slid off the gurney and swayed for a second while I collected my balance.

"Whoa, take it easy there, Red," the youngblood said, starting for me. But I left his protests behind, bolting from the room before any of them could stop me.

Wearing nothing but a sheet, I ran after Vincent with angry tears in my eyes, ready to give him a damn piece of my mind.

CHAPTER FIFTY-NINE

SHOWDOWN

A s I stormed down the hall after Vincent, I didn't care that I was practically naked. And I didn't care that there were vampires I'd never met, jumping out of my way with looks of bewilderment on their faces.

That dark part buried inside me—maybe not so deep down after all—didn't spare so much as a care to what any of them thought about me. If I was going to be the queen of the dead, it didn't matter if people liked me.

They needed to respect me.

And it started with Vincent Feral.

Winning any iota of respect from the coven's resident tool was like going into a wrestling match with a bear and expecting to come out without scratches. But I was going to do it anyway because, damn it, I deserved a hell of a lot more than he was giving me.

Over the last week, I'd had my sad little life turned on its head. I'd been kidnapped, ripped away from the only person who I thought loved me. I'd been manhandled and lied to and almost raped and killed. I deserved a little shred of happiness in this scary and dangerous world I'd been thrust into. Then there was Vincent, my dark knight, touching me like I was his whole universe on one breath and calling me a slut on the next.

"What the hell is your problem, Feral?" I screamed at him, watching his broad-shouldered frame halt at the end of the corridor as soon as his name left my mouth. It wasn't until I snarled his name again, doused in venom, that he glanced over his shoulder to look at me.

With his head turned away from the open window, the moonlight lit up his back while swaddling his face in shadows. All I could see were his red eyes burning through the darkness.

The little hairs on the back of my neck stood straight up, and a little voice in the back of my head told me to turn around and put as much distance as I could between this predator and me. No matter what I was about to say to him, this confrontation wouldn't be pretty. Too bad it was my pride in the driver's seat right now, looking to throw down a few words of vengeance.

From the moment I'd met him, I'd formed a fast addiction to poke the bear. Or whatever the hell he was.

Plus, the prick needed to be taken down a few notches. He had struck out to wound me, right in my heart. And that was a part of me he had no business touching, yet he'd infiltrated and infected it all the same.

I felt the weight of his glare heavy on my chest, making my heart pound wildly against my ribs in a mad rebellion.

"Problem?" he growled, his voice as deep as the darkest bowels of Hell. "I think I was pretty damn clear what my problem is."

Coming within several feet of him, we stood facing each other like an old west showdown, not daring to get an inch closer. I didn't trust him, and I especially didn't trust myself whenever I was within arm's reach of this cruel prince.

"You're a fucking hypocrite, you know that?" My voice shook, and my cheeks burned red hot when I heard my own hurt lacing each word. I didn't like Vincent knowing how much he got to me.

His eyes narrowed, and his nostrils flared. "How am I a hypocrite?"

"Are you *serious?* You just threw a tantrum, slut-shaming me in front of your brothers. That's rich, considering you're slipping your dick to the coven's blood whore every chance you get. The difference between us is that I'm *supposed* to be spending time with you guys so I can select a king. This was kind of forced on me, remember?"

"The Elders told you to pick a king. Since when do our skills in the bedroom have anything to do with ruling our people?"

Anger spread through my veins, making my blood run molten. I balled my fists, my voice shaking with violence. "I'm not just picking the next king. This is my future mate and husband we're talking about, asshole! The father of my future children. I need to be compatible with whoever I pick, and it's a lot of freaking pressure, okay? I didn't ask for you to break into my bedroom and throw me into this life. But here I am, doing my best. So fuck off and stop making my life a living hell."

"You know nothing of hell, princess. Not yet."

I threw back my head and let out a dry scoff that felt like sandpaper in my throat. "Living in this place with you, I'm starting to develop a pretty good idea. Even if this wasn't some important political decision, and I was just sleeping with your brothers for the heck of it, that's my prerogative. You're not my daddy, and you're not my fucking keeper."

The vampire's lips peeled into a sardonic sneer that was all fangs. "This isn't a game, princess. Your future isn't the only one at stake here. We have enemies. And if it's true that Dagon Knight is somehow alive and that he's coming for the throne, we need to act fast. The Elders said you have four months to pick, but *we* don't have four months. The throne is empty, and the Boston Coven and their supporters are getting restless. They are planning to seize the throne, and if Dagon Knight really is involved with their plans, we need to crown a king *now*."

I dropped my eyes to my bare feet and pulled the sheet tighter around my body. "I need more time."

I could practically hear Vincent's teeth grind as he spoke next. "The answer is obvious. Corry is too young. I *will* win the fight with Eros tomorrow, meaning I'll win the bet, and he'll have to leave the coven. And Sterling doesn't want it. That leaves me."

When he started toward me, I jerked my glare up to lock with his, warning him not to come any closer. Naturally, Vincent ignored the silent warning burning in my eyes and stalked forward, that arrogant smirk tugging at his perfectly audacious lips.

"There's just three teensy weensy problems, Feral. First, you're hiding shit from me." Taking several steps back to keep that precious distance between us, I stepped on a corner of the sheet I wore and stumbled. Falling flat on my ass, he was looming over me on the next heartbeat, looking down at me with a predatorial glint in his eye.

Instead of allowing him to intimidate me, I continued my rant. "I *know* you were involved with my father's death, and it's shitty that you won't give me the courtesy of the truth. Second, I don't care if Lexi is a blood whore for the whole coven. You're fucking her, and I don't like it!"

Crouching so that he was at my eye level, his gaze raked over my body that was still wrapped up tight in nothing but the thin piece of fabric. By the way his Adam's apple bobbed with a thick swallow, his raven tattoos twitching with the movement, I was sure he could see right through the paper-thin sheet.

"What's the third thing, Princess?" he asked, his voice raspy and guttural.

I mirrored his swallow, trying to look anywhere but in those infernal eyes. I'd drown in them if I wasn't careful. "The third is easy. I hate you. Simple as that."

His brawny chest rumbled with a dark chuckle. "But it's not that simple, is it? Not by the way you look at me. The way your body heats when I touch you." He extended his fingers toward me, acting as if he was going to touch my calf, which poked out from the sheet. Instead of touching me, he hovered just over my skin. He let out a gloating laugh when my skin broke out into goosebumps and flushed bright red, right beneath the shadow of his hand. "Then there is your scent. That floral, honey-sweet smell your cunt makes, begging for me to bury myself inside it."

He leaned into me, pressing so close I could feel his warmth bleed through the bedsheet. Brushing his hand down the length of my throat, he watched my flesh prick and heat at the kiss of his fingers. "If this is how you react to guys you hate..."

He moved to kiss me.

"Then I want you to *loathe me.*"

A heady mixture of panic and dark desire knotted my insides. Jerking my head back, I withheld my lips from his, and he snarled his disapproval, which only made the crux between my thighs burn all the hotter.

"I love Sterling," I blurted without thinking.

Vincent didn't pull away, but the look of pure shock was enough to make him freeze.

With a quick survey of the hall, I sent out a little thanks to whatever deity fucked enough to listen to vampire prayers for making sure there was no one currently around to witness this. Here I was, on my ass with Vincent crouched over me, nothing but a sheet holding together what fragments of my modesty I still clung to. Toss in my love confession, and I doubt I'd ever erect the kind of opinion I wanted these people to have of me.

The silence that stretched between us was agony. I expected Vincent to either make fun of my love confession for Sterling or restate what he'd already told me. That I wasn't capable of love. So when he didn't do either of those things, I was speechless.

"Fine. Keep loving him," Feral muttered, his voice taut with an indiscernible emotion. "Fuck knows Sterling deserves a little happiness. But the sad fact is, he won't ever be king."

That cruel fist of reality squeezed my heart, making tears of pain spring to my eyes.

I hated crying in front of Vincent, but I couldn't seem to make myself care enough to fend off the encroaching tears. This was the first moment I'd had to really process what happened between Sterling and me. I had found something deep and meaningful with the blind prince. The crazy, passionate, magnetic chemistry that had ignited between us in a single night had been bitter-sweet. And now that I was no longer in the sweet warmth of Sterling's company, all that was left was bitter tears.

"He'd be a good king," I sniffed.

Vincent cupped my cheek, the softness of his touch taking me by surprise. "He would."

"I can get him to change his mind."

While the vampire's caress remained tender, his gaze hardened. "No, you can't. There is nothing that can fill the gaping wound inside him, Ruby. Not even a love like yours."

The unexpected compliment, the gentle lilt in Vincent's voice, the calming stroke of his palm against my cheek... This was the version of Vincent Feral I had glimpsed in his car that night at the gas station. I was completely mesmerized by the sudden shift in his demeanor. It made me want to get closer, but I was too afraid I'd break the spell.

"Ruby, listen to me. Even if you were able to convince Sterling to take the throne, he can never give you children."

"I don't care about that." It was only partially true. I'd been prepared to ask Sterling to turn me into a full-blooded vampire, which would have made my reproductive organs useless. I'd made my peace with that, or at least I thought I had. When that primal side of me awakened upon seeing Sterling's mating mark, I realized I did care about having kids.

I cared a lot.

There was no doubt in my mind that one day, when I was ready, I'd be a mother. The sad fact that Sterling could never be the father sat in my stomach like cement.

Vincent studied me with furrowed brows. "You really want him to be your mate and king? Why him?"

"He's gentle, honest, and—oh yeah—he isn't fucking other girls!" The shrill in my tone settled, and I was back to crying. I felt so freaking vulnerable right now, basically naked, sobbing on the floor. I had put myself in the perfect position for Feral to completely crush me. But something had shifted in the dynamic between us, even if it was just for a moment. Both our walls had come down, and just like in the car, it felt right.

"I have no idea what I'm doing, Vincent. This whole queen thing was shoved at me, and I'm so terrified I am going to fuck it up. I don't know anything about being vampire queen. People already want me dead, and I haven't even been crowned yet.

"Don't get me wrong, I can hold my own," I went on. "The more time I spend here with you guys, the more I can feel some of my father's power, this raw, monstrous strength slowly bubbling to the surface. I need someone *strong* to show me how to control it."

The prince leveled me with a stormy expression, his bloody eyes brewing with a thousand thoughts. I would give damn near anything to know what exactly he was thinking. "It would be a waste to just control your power. You are a weapon, a dangerous one with unlimited potential. In the hands of someone like Dagon Knight, you could be the end of our people. You need a mate and king who can properly wield you."

Before I could ask Vincent to explain what in the world he was talking about, he grabbed me by the waist and hauled me over his shoulder.

"What the—*Ow!* Put me down!"

With me thrashing against him, he grabbed hold of me so that his hand gripped my upper thigh, keeping me firmly mounted over his shoulder. His shoulder blades dug into my cheek as he strode down the hallway, and it wasn't a bad view back here, where I could see his ass and reach out to smack it. But knowing Vincent, he'd only take it as encouragement.

"Where are you taking me?"

"Someplace I can show you just how much you and I belong together."

Chapter Sixty

What in the Hell is Vincent Feral?

With Vincent hauling me through the corridor over his shoulder like I was some war prize, barely clothed and thrashing against him, we turned a few heads.

But if anyone was concerned for me, no one said shit.

In their defense, you didn't get in Feral's way. Period. Well, unless you were me.

Moving into the main hall, my chest squeezed when I realized we were heading toward the staircase. Was he taking me to his room?

When he strode past the stairs and shoved through the double doors of the council chamber, my heart sunk a little. Was I actually disappointed that we weren't going upstairs? Realizing that I was a bit let down that he wasn't taking me to his bedroom made some seriously troubling emotions unfurl inside me, complicated emotions that I didn't feel capable of dealing with at the moment.

Inside the council chamber, Vincent finally set me on my feet, and I looked around to survey my surroundings.

I'd been here once before when I was brought to the Elders that first night. Now the place was empty. It was eerie, being in here with nothing but seven empty thrones and Feral, regarding me with a look in his eyes that told me it probably wasn't the best idea being alone in here with him.

Any other girl in my position might be a bit shaken up by the fact that she'd been hauled over the shoulder of a possessive, blood-thirsty vampire while in a state of undress and taken to some secluded part of the mansion for God knows what.

But fucked-up me was only excited by the notion. My pulse launched into a full gallop, and my breath came out in uneven bursts.

I could feel Vincent's gaze on me, stripping me down to my bones.

In an attempt to settle my nerves, I forced my attention to the large windows behind the thrones.

The red drapery was pulled back, the silvery sea serving as a breathtaking backdrop. The sight of the ocean still made my knees weak, having gone all those years with it being just outside of my bedroom window's view.

Moonlight poured into the chamber, painting long shadows across the floor. The shadow of my father's throne was the largest and stretched across the entire room, touching my toes where I stood by the entrance.

My gaze slithered up the shadow to rest on the throne, and I had to suppress a shiver. It was a creepy piece of furniture, made with black wood, with the backrest carved into a picture of a screaming woman. The woman had needle-sharp teeth, the wood stained with what had to be real blood. The velvet padding of the throne made up her dress, but the most gruesome feature of the whole thing was the real vampire teeth embedded into the wood to create a necklace for the woman.

The six other thrones of the Elders were way less elaborate, although I couldn't help but look at the one to the right of my father's, where I had seen Sterling for the first time. He'd been kind, the only source of relief during that meeting. I could even remember what he'd been wearing, a thick knit turtleneck sweater with a high collar that would have kept his mark hidden.

My attention jerked back to Feral as he strode to the other end of the room and sat on my father's throne.

Folding my arms over my chest, I flung him a baleful glare. "What are you doing?"

"Look at me, Ruby. What do you see?"

A gorgeous monster who has no right being so damn beautiful.

Of course, I didn't say that out loud. What I wanted to do was ignore his question and storm out of here. At least, that's what I wanted to want.

But I couldn't seem to pull my gaze away from the scene before me. Because holy fuck.

As always, Vincent Feral was as terrifying as he was beautiful. The moon sat in the sky just behind his head, creating a crown-like illusion. Shadows concealed his facial features, but his masculine frame was outlined in silver, which highlighted his raven tattoos and his black arm veins that stood out even more so against his silver-kissed skin.

The first time I'd seen my father's throne, I knew Feral would look right at home in it. But I didn't think he'd look *this* good.

Like it had been made for him.

"So what?" I snapped, hating how I couldn't keep my voice from cracking. "So you look good on the throne? How is this supposed to convince me that we belong together?"

He leaned forward and propped his elbows on his thighs. Fuck me, why did he have to look so damn good sitting where my father once had? And how Vincent looked shouldn't matter in the slightest. But there was no denying that he slipped into the evil piece of furniture with his casual and cocky demeanor, like a tailor-made piece of clothing.

He didn't just wear the throne well. As stupid as it was to suggest a chair of all things had any kind of sentience, it seemed to wear him right back.

"You said you want someone strong, Princess? *Look at me*. This throne is more than a fucking chair. Here sits the strongest vampire in the entire continent. This seat means enemies, powerful ones. It means allies who are just as dangerous if you say or do the wrong thing. It's a responsibility you can't even begin to fathom. You don't understand what it takes to sit here for many years on end. It's going to take a strong king to keep you alive, to keep you in power, and to keep you safe. That's what I can offer you. Stability and safety. Do you think Corry can give you that? He wouldn't last two days. Eros? He'd protect you from our enemies for a time, but what happens when he inevitably makes more enemies than he can stand to fight? Then there's me—"

"*You?*" I pushed out a cold laugh, interrupting him. "Let's speed up with the Vincent for king campaign, shall we? What can you do for me that an army of vampires can't? I'll be queen, right? Don't we have forces, other covens with warriors who will stand with us? Why do I need you?"

Shadows masked his features, but I could hear the smirk in his answer. "Because I have a secret hidden in my blood."

Completely lost, my brows crinkled in confusion. "What do you mean?"

"Come here, and maybe I'll tell you."

He lounged back and tilted his head just enough to the side, so moonlight washed over him, lighting up half his face. His dark brows arched as if daring me to obey him.

My feet began to move, carrying me to him before my brain had a chance to intervene. It's like my instincts wanted to obey him, eager to please the powerful male. The monster inside me gave me new reasons to hate her every day.

I moved slowly in his direction, taking my time to approach The Feral King on my father's throne. I should have felt ridiculous, or at least embarrassed, since all I wore was a sheet. But the spell between us hadn't shattered yet. He was looking at me like he had in the car that night.

Like I already belonged to him.

When I was directly in front of him, he patted his thigh. "Sit."

I wanted to defy him, mostly because I was quickly developing a mad love affair with getting under his skin. But if my time with Eros had taught me anything, I loved a dominant male who knew how to handle a woman. The question was, would Vincent continue to keep his walls down and handle me with that tenderness I also craved?

Too intrigued to turn back now, I bent at the waist and seated myself in his lap.

With a muscular body that could have been hewn from stone with a demeanor almost just as cold, snuggling up to him was like cuddling with a rock. But I was coming to learn that was just his armor. I was sure there was a soft interior because I'd seen glimpses of it. He was allowing me to see some of it now.

But I wanted more. Not only did I crave that oh-so-rare soft spot of Vincent's, but I loved how honest and vulnerable I knew he could be when he let that part of him out for me to see.

"Vincent, what kind of secret do you have in your blood? What the heck are you talking about?"

He reached for me, pulling me tighter against him. My skin heated under his touch, filling me with a fire that quickly sunk into my core. Grasping my wrist, his fingers stroked over my skin as if the smooth flesh there was something special to be savored. Maybe it was. We didn't have the sort of relationship where he could just touch me like this, as if we were already lovers with not so much as a drop of hatred between us.

It was a dangerous game of pretend.

Handling me with a sort of gentleness I didn't even know he was capable of, he turned my hand so that the inside of my wrist faced up and lifted it to his nose.

Inhaling deeply, his chest swelled with my scent-laced air, like he couldn't get enough inside him.

For one intense beat, I thought he was going to bite me, but he only pressed a kiss to the delicate skin. Then he slid the point of his nose up my arm and over my shoulder. I tensed when he paused, his mouth hovering over Eros' mark. Was he going to bite me now? The thought had to be going through his mind.

If I had ended up having that heart condition where I could die if my pulse became too elevated, and I had somehow managed to survive up until this point, this moment would have been my last. My kidnapping, my botched getaway, being pressed up against the gas pump with Corry buried between my thighs, Eros' workbench, claiming Sterling, none of it was as surprising as Vincent *kissing* Eros' mark.

Before I could think of anything to say—because for a second there I forgot every word of the English language— he moved his lips to the hollow of my throat. His mouth hovered there, his breath feathering over my skin. He moved his hands to grip the delicate juncture between my neck and shoulders. And then he just... *held me.*

There were no words that could describe my level of shock. Was this even Vincent? How could it be with the caress of gentle hands and the graze of lips that rained a trail of sultry kisses, oozing nothing but heart-bleeding devotion?

Fuck me. He was good.

If this was another one of his seduction tactics, working me into impossible knots only to demand I make him king before untangling them, it was working.

He flicked his gaze up to lock with mine while keeping his lips to my throat. "Bleeding hell. You used to smell like heaven. Now you smell like paradise and damnation."

I blinked, my cheeks burning up under his blood-red gaze. "Why?"

"Because I scent *my* blood running through your veins, coursing through your entire body. Along with mine, I scent all of us, filling you up. While Sterling's blood is the most potent, mine is the most powerful. Do you know why?"

All I could manage was a sloppy shake of my head. I was a trembling mess of nerves with my breath coming out in short little pants. Trying my best to keep my composure, it was a failing battle. Here I was, sitting on Thomas Knight's throne in the lap of his most lethal creation, naked and very, *very* turned on.

Vincent's mouth curved into a wolfish grin. "Because of what I am."

All the air in my lungs emptied, but by some miracle, I managed to find the air to voice a question that had been plaguing my mind from the moment I met him.

"Vincent Feral, what *are* you?"

Chapter Sixty-One
A Dangerous Deal

"What are you?" I asked again on a sharp inhale. I wanted to know what he was so bad that curiosity was practically eating me alive.

His grin spread all the wider as his tongue flicked out in an erotic slide over his lower lip. "I love watching you trying to solve a mystery. You don't like not having all the answers. You squirm, and your body burns. I can practically smell your blood boiling in frustration. It makes me so hard just thinking about the way your sweet blood heats the air."

Digging his fingers into my hips, he pushed me down deeper into his lap and ground his groin into my ass to demonstrate exactly what he was talking about. Then I cried out—more in surprise than pain—when his mouth flew to my chest, planting a kiss to the valley between my breasts just above the hem of the sheet.

"Then there is this delicious, frantic little pound of your heart." His voice dropped an octave, husky and banked with his hunger, as his breath fanned beneath the sheet, tickling my navel. "I can't stop imagining how hard it will beat when I finally sink myself inside you."

I wasn't sure if he was talking about sinking his fangs inside me, his cock, or—God help me—both, but my body heated at the obscene fantasy all the same.

With my current position—slung sideways in the throne with my feet dangling over one arm and my back pressed to the other—I rearranged myself so that I was straddling his lap, my chest pressed against his. This was the same position we'd been in that night at the gas station. Only then, I'd been wearing panties. Now, to get purchase I bunched the sheet around my hips and rested my bare sex in his lap. Which just made his erection strain all the harder in the confines of his jeans.

I had to focus. Vincent was trying to distract me, and it was working.

"Don't change the subject," I said through a thick gulp, failing to ignore the fact that his cock was lined up perfectly against my apex. I had to summon every damn fragment of willpower I had to keep my hips from moving. "Tell me what you are, damn it."

His sanguine orbs glittered with mischief. "A being not of this realm. There is magic in my blood. Consumed, it grants great strength and heightened senses. And it can even heal minor wounds. It's part of the reason why your father turned me."

Worrying my bottom lip, I crunched my brows. "You were turned only a decade ago, weren't you? But you're saying my father got his power from you?"

"He was powerful before then. The former king was almost three millennia-old when he died. Any vampire who survives that long is bound to be a strong mother fucker. But I elevated him to a whole new level."

I almost didn't want to ask, having heard the horrors of Sterling's past. But my curiosity wouldn't let me hold my tongue. "How?"

Vincent's expression tightened, a storm brewing in his eyes. "He fed from me almost every night, Ruby. I was his personal blood whore."

It took me a few uneven breaths to process what Feral was telling me. A blood whore? Vincent? It was hard to imagine him being the vampire king's personal feeding trough, but knowing my dad, it wasn't shocking. And I highly doubted it had been a consensual thing.

Leaning back in his lap, I skimmed the exposed parts of the prince, searching for any mating marks on his body. He didn't carry my father's scent like Sterling had, but drinking vampire blood had a way of getting people all hot and bothered, so...

"He only used me for my blood," he said, gleaning the unspoken question in my eyes. "If you're thinking what I think you're thinking, it was only Sterling that he lusted for that way."

"But if you're from another world, how did he find you? How did you come here? *Why* did you come here?" I had a million freaking questions flying around in my head. What was he saying? That he wasn't from Earth? Was he an alien? No, that's stupid.

"I came to the human world to find my father. He was a sort of diplomat for our people, a connection between the magical creatures of my home realm and the supernatural beings native to the human world. He never returned from his last trip. My search led me to Deathwish. At the time, Eros belonged to a guild of humans who specialized in killing supernatural creatures."

The blood in my body turned to ice. "I thought he was an MMA fighter."

"That was more or less his hobby. He made most of his living by killing all sorts of supernatural creatures. While the Helsing Guild specialized in hunting vampires, Eros didn't discriminate."

"Helsing? Like, *Van* Helsing?"

Vincent gave me a solemn nod while running his hands gently over my shoulders and down my arms. Normally the tender gesture might calm me, but it was hard staying calm after hearing that Eros, the guy I had lost my virginity to, used to *murder* our kind. And that he belonged to a whole group of these people who were just...out there.

"I didn't think Van Helsing was real."

"Once upon a time, you didn't think vampires were real either." Vincent's voice was all steel, his muscles coiled tight as he stiffened beneath me.

I knew this couldn't be easy for him. He seemed so vulnerable right now. Here he was, admitting that he'd been the vampire king's blood whore. Not to mention talking about his father. I doubted he spoke to anyone about this, and I wanted to reward him for being so transparent with me, to let him know that we could be open and honest and vulnerable with each other. That he could trust me not to strike when he exposed parts of himself he normally kept hidden beneath his armor.

I leaned into him and kissed his stunned lips. His mouth softened, and a little rush of air blew out of him that I quickly consumed with another, slow, languid kiss. I took my time kissing him, enjoying how his muscles seemed to unclench beneath my touch.

After a few moments, I pulled away, breathless. "Tell me more. Please."

I settled against his chest with my cheek resting on his shoulder, peeking up at him through my wild mane of red. For several moments, he just gawked at me. It was like he was just as stunned as I was that we were together like *this*.

It took him a second before he found his words.

"Once I discovered that Deathwish had killed my father, I vowed to make him suffer. I was just one male, though, so I couldn't take down his entire guild. He didn't have any family, so the first thing I decided to do was destroy was his precious fighting career. It was a long game, but I slowly worked my way up, winning match after match. Finally, I knocked him out of the championship title and won that stupid belt he idolized so much."

"But why would you go through all that trouble?"

"Because he murdered my father in cold blood, Ruby. I wanted to make him hurt, to make him suffer in every way I could possibly fathom."

Vincent paused, letting out a huff of breath. "I never understood why he had such a love for the stupid sport. Maybe because he's always loved every facet of violence. When I stole the championship title out from under him, he was emotionally crushed. Just like I'd planned."

"What did you do after that?"

A sickening smile spread across the feral prince's face. "I killed him."

Chills swept down my spine. Vincent had killed Eros as punishment for murdering his father. Not that I believed Eros had actually killed in cold blood. Or if he had, he must have had a damn good reason. If I'd learned anything about Deathwish, it was that he protected the things he cared about. He would only kill something if there was good reason. *Right?*

Vincent's father had to have been something dangerous, a creature with no business being in the human realm for Eros to intervene. I'd have to ask him about it later and get his side of the story.

"So, what happened next? That should have been the end of it, right?"

"It should have been. After over a year of planning, I'd executed my revenge exactly how I had imagined it. I mean, it would have been exactly how I'd imagined if he hadn't been an orphan raised in the foster care system. Then I could have murdered *his* father. Or if he didn't have one of those, a son. Or a wife."

I lurched into a sitting position, gaping at Vincent in horror. "You would *not* have killed his family."

Black brows arched, and a cruel smirk lifted his mouth. "Do you think I wouldn't?"

A lump lodged itself in the back of my throat. The honest answer was that I didn't know. My first thought was yes, Vincent Feral would have killed Eros' wife and children or his parents if he had any. Then again, maybe that's just what Thomas Knight would have done...

"I don't think you would kill innocents just to make yourself feel better, no," I eventually answered.

Vincent's eyes narrowed to crimson slits. "Well, that's beside the point. He didn't have a family, so with his fighting career destroyed and his monster hunting days over, I found my revenge, and that should have been the end of it. But as it turned out, we had a fan who had been watching our rivalry on television. It's common for fans of the sport to get wrapped up in the rivalries between fighters. But Thomas Knight always had a knack for taking things to the extreme. When he came to one of the live matches, he scented what I was immediately. He became obsessed with our rivalry, following our every move. Even the moment where I snuck into Eros' locker room after the match to kill him."

I gasped. "My father followed you?"

"Yes. At least he waited in the shadows while I got some semblance of revenge for my father's murder. But then, with Eros dead at my feet, the vampire king made his presence known. I tried to fight him. I lost. When I woke, Eros was alive, or at least he was a lot less dead than how I'd left him. We were taken back to the coven. I became the king's personal blood bag for the next decade, and Eros was just here to piss me off because that was the sort of thing your dad got off on."

My heart crystallized, and I suddenly felt very cold in Feral's arms.

"Are you sure Eros killed your father?"

The vampire's lips peeled back into a snarl. "He admitted it."

"But why would Eros kill your dad if he was no threat to anyone?"

"Because killing supernaturals was his job, Ruby. He thinks he was 'protecting' humankind."

"I'm sure he had good intentions."

Vincent's grip turned mean. I winced when his fingers dug into the flesh of my hips. I tried to pull away, but he held me on his lap, and as I struggled, he hardened beneath me once again. Sick fuck. Then again, who was I to talk? Here I was, with a pussy so wet I could feel the damp denim of his jeans hot against the bare flesh of my thigh.

"Look at me, Ruby! Look me in the damn eye and stop fighting me, damn it!" Surprising him and myself especially, I fell still in his grip.

"Good. Now listen to me. My father was a kind and gentle man. I'm nothing like him. And I loved him all the harder because of it. He wouldn't have hurt a damn hair on anyone's head. Eros killed him in cold blood. *That* is why I hate him."

For several moments that seemed to span beyond time and space, we just stared at one another. Even though I knew there was probably more to the story than Vincent realized or was willing to see, I understood him better now.

"So my father turned you not only because he had a sick fascination for your rivalry with Eros, but because of your blood? What's so special about it?"

"You tell me. How do you feel now that my blood is coursing through your veins?"

"Stronger."

"Exactly." He eased his hold over me and lounged back into the throne. "Make it a habit to feed on me, and you'll continue to grow stronger. And yours, in turn, will make me stronger."

"How? My blood isn't special."

"That's where you're wrong. Do you want to know why I feed from Lexi? Because of what I am, I need to feed more often than the others, human *and* vampire blood. Sharpe could give you a more scientific explanation, but the cliff notes version is that I have an extremely high metabolism. I need to feed every day. And I need to intake just as much vampire blood as I do human blood. I keep the blood donors busier than they'd like."

The memory of Kenzie fleeing from Vincent's room in a fit of tears surfaced to mind.

"And keeping Lexi makes it so that I have a constant supply of vampire blood."

A pang of jealousy flared in my belly. "But you don't need to *fuck* her."

Vincent gave me a look that screamed, *don't be stupid.* "You've ingested vampire blood. You know what it does to your libido. Once you're my queen, I'll feed only from you. With one bite, you will sate my need for vampire and human blood, and you feeding from me can grow your power. It's the perfect partnership."

I sat back on his lap, folding my arms over my chest. "Perfect. *Right.* How can it be perfect when there is still so much distrust between us?" In his defense, Vincent was currently being the most transparent he'd ever been with me. But he was still holding out.

His lips pursed with thought, and his eyes glinted with wicked intent. "What can I do to establish some trust?"

By the look on his face, I assumed he was about to offer sexual favors. As appealing as that sounded, I had him right where I wanted him. "Tell me how my father died. And for fuck's sake, tell me what you are."

"Let's make a deal. I'll sit here and answer every question you can throw at me. But you have to do something for me."

My body tensed in his lap. "I'm not making a decision to make you king right here and now, so don't even go there, Feral."

"I want you to pick me because you know that I will be the best king our world has ever seen and the best fuck you've ever had. So, let's make this a good trade for you. You don't like Lexi."

When I bristled at the third mention of her, he chuckled. "If you think she's more to me than just a decent lay and a source of blood, you're wrong. She thinks one day I'll make her queen. She couldn't be more mistaken."

"How do I know you're telling the truth?"

"To prove it to you, I'll dump her, and I swear to never touch her again."

I narrowed my eyes in suspicion. It seemed too good to be true. There had to be a catch.

"*But...*" And there it was. "You have to take her place as my blood whore. And if you agree, you feed me right here and now. And I warn you..." His hand cupped my ribcage, his knuckle brushing against the globe of my breast. "I'm ravenous."

His proposition had all the ice in my body melting, settling into a molten pool of need in my lower belly. I squirmed in his lap, hating just how much I wanted to accept.

Bloody hell.

My answer should have been *hell to the fucking no.* But things weren't that simple between Feral and me. While he wore his monstrous nature plainly on his sleeve, with his soft side hidden deep within, my monster was buried deep inside me, and damn it, his called to mine in a strange sort of language fabricated out of cold glares and heated words.

He called to the beast inside me. And Lord help me because she wanted to come out and play.

His eyes burned with a fire that threatened to consume me, waiting for an answer that could flip this violent hate affair on its fucking head. Crawling out of his lap, I stood and faced him, holding the edges of the sheet as if I was about to let it fall from my body.

"I'll accept, but I have one more condition."

He leaned forward, excitement dancing in his eyes. "Which is?"

"You finally tell me what you are. And you tell me how my father died. No lies, no half-truths. You tell me *everything* you know."

His greedy gaze roved up and down my body, then he shattered the pregnant silence. "I accept."

He extended his hand to me as if to shake on it but instead, he grabbed the sheet and ripped it from my body.

Embarrassment, rage, all the emotions that would make sense in this moment completely fizzled into the background, and all that filled me was a lust so raw and pure, I couldn't help but feel like a fucking goddess standing naked before The Feral King.

He raised his fist to his mouth, his fang scraping against his knuckle as if he was moved by the sight of my naked body. He slowly stood to his feet, never once taking his eyes off me. Stepping to the side, he pointed at the place he'd just been sitting.

"Now, get on your throne where you belong, and spread those pretty legs for me."

CHAPTER SIXTY-TWO
DARK PLEDGE

Get on your throne where you belong, and spread your legs.

His lewd command made my lungs slam against my ribs, and for a second, I couldn't breathe.

With the sheet torn away, I was naked. My father's cruel throne sat before me, empty and awaiting my bare ass. Then there was Feral, watching me like a ravenous predator ready to pounce on its prey.

He wanted to feed on me while I sat on my father's throne. I didn't really want to sit in it at all, to be where *he* once sat. But somehow, being in the buff with my father's blood whore ready to bury himself between my thighs seemed like a great way to stick it to dear ole dead dad.

So I sat and watched his reaction as I slowly spread my thighs for him. This wasn't the first time he'd seen me naked. When he'd burst in on Eros and me, all my clothes had already been ripped off and thrown to the floor. But this was the first time I was naked for him, the first time he was seeing *this* part of me.

The cold air of the council chamber tickled my bare sex, but the chill was chased away when Vincent fell to his knees before me, his hot breath spilling over my flesh.

I arched my brows, trying to pretend that the sight of him kneeling in front of me like this wasn't making me so wet that my arousal was soaking into the throne. "Is this the part where you swear fealty to me, Knight?"

His eyes blazed with a brutal reverence, and his next words were just as convincing. "I swear it."

Surprised by the severity of his vow, I closed my legs and sat up a little straighter. "What do you swear exactly?"

"To always protect you. To keep you safe. Why do you think I made that bet with Deathwish?"

"To thin out the competition for the throne."

Feral's brows contorted with thinly veiled fury. "I'm doing it to protect you from him. He already took my father away from me. I'm not going to let him take you away too."

My lips slanted with a frown. "Let's not talk about Eros right now. Before you feed, tell me what you are."

"No. First, I get what I want." His hands settled on my knees, and he slowly spread them apart. His eyes dipped down to my sex, then darted back up, a devilish grin on his face. "Then we'll get to you."

"Are you going to fuck me?" I found myself blurting.

His tongue flicked out to slide over his lower lip, a display probably meant to tease me. "Do you want me to?"

Oh, God. Fuck *yes*. But wait. No! Or at least no *should* have been my answer. If I let him fuck me, he'd probably mark me. Who was to say he wouldn't bite me right over Eros' mark? While I hadn't intended for Eros to claim me, the thought of his mark being erased from my body filled me with a hollow sensation.

There were a million things I couldn't trust Feral with, but if I could count on him for anything, it was to be possessive and overprotective.

"You don't need to answer," he chuckled, his breath washing over my core in an invisible caress, a promise of what was to come. "Your dripping cunt gives you away, Princess. Don't worry, I'll make you beg for me before I feed you. Whether it's my blood or my cock, I'll let you decide."

He licked a path from my knee to my inner thigh, and I couldn't suppress my violent shiver of delight. The hot appendage felt like fire against my cool skin. It was fucking freezing in here, but instead of being cold, I was hot all over. And where this was heading, I'd soon be wearing Vincent Feral to keep me warm.

His mouth continued its lazy ascent toward the very top of my thigh, where my leg met my core. I knew he was going for my femoral artery, but I was still a little disappointed when he didn't make the final move to cover the juncture between.

"You're going to drink from my arterial blood. Sterling says it's dangerous." A gasp tripped from me as Vincent's fangs scraped over the sensitive patch of flesh. His mouth was so close to my opening, I could feel his breath tease and tickle me. It was sublime torture.

He peeked up through his screen of raven locks. "Then you know just how fucking stupid it was allowing Corry to bite you here."

"Hypocrite," I sneered. I knew it was a bad idea taunting Feral while I was spread out for him like this, free for his taking. But the demented little pervert inside me couldn't help it.

"I'm not a youngblood. I have perfect reign over my darkest urges. If I didn't, I wouldn't have turned you down in my car the night you tried to run away. I would have mated you hard and marked you as mine. You weren't on birth control then, and I could scent how fertile you were even before Sterling triggered your heat cycle. What if I'd knocked you up that night, Princess? Would you have made me your mate and king?"

"Yes," I whispered without skipping a beat.

"I know you would have. And how about this for a secret? If I could go back, I wouldn't do things any differently. I plan to tease this out, to claim you piece by piece. Your blood, your tears, your cum, your womb, and finally, your heart. Until I own all of you. Every. Last. Part. Then to finish off one fucked-up love affair for the ages, I become the father of the first blood heir to the vampire throne and king of this whole damn, fucked-up world. So don't worry your pretty little head about my control. I may not have been a vampire for very long, but I'm old enough to be a master in patience. Look how I destroyed Eros. I can afford to play the long game with you, Princess. The question is, can everyone else?"

Before I could even begin to unpack the steamy load of secrets, oaths, and threats he'd just dumped on me, he chose that exact moment to bite me.

My hips bucked, and I spasmed in the throne when his fangs punched into my thigh. He didn't bother with being gentle, even less so than Corry had been when he'd bitten me in the same spot.

The pain might have been too much if it wasn't for Vincent's thumb, finding the sensitive bud of my clit. He applied pressure to it with such skillful precision, I was already moaning loudly, trembling, and rocking against him.

He purred his approval where he feasted on my thigh, his lips reverberating against me.

Then he spoke, his mouth breaking the seal around the bite site, blood dribbling down my flesh in thick gobs of red. "Mmm, you're going to be such a good little blood whore for me, aren't you? Already moaning and dripping for me. And I'm not just talking about your blood..." He took his thumb off my clit to sink the tip of his pointer finger into my wet heat. Unlatching from my thigh, he brought the finger to his blood-soaked lips and popped it inside his mouth, sucking my arousal clean from his digit.

For several ragged breaths, all I could do was gawk at him in lust-drunk reverie. Between my thighs, Vincent Feral was a freaking beast. And I wanted to take all of him, every filthy word, every bite, every delicious inch of cock, cum, and blood he was willing to give me.

The urge to feed hit me suddenly like an anvil crashing down over my head. I had to bite my own tongue to keep myself from latching onto him. I couldn't let myself forget that this was just an exchange, my blood for his secrets. Feeding on him right now would just trigger that feral side of me. But damn it all, I wanted to let my monster out to play. Letting that side of me run free was a dangerous move and would lead to a path I didn't want to tread down. If I did, I would probably end up claimed by Feral as his mate, and he'd be even more possessive of me.

But damn, it was a nice fantasy.

"If I ever let you claim me, where will you mark me?"

His bloody lips peeled back into a sinful smirk. There wasn't so much as a pause as he pointed to the spot. *He'd already thought about it.* "Right here..."

The most delectable heat licked at my center as I followed his gesture to the stretch of skin just an inch or so from my labia, right over my public bone.

"When I claim you as my mate, I am going to mark you here." Leaning, he pressed a kiss right there in silent pledge.

Sweat broke out over my body as he returned his finger to my folds and eased his way back inside, his jaw flexing as he watched me shake and shiver around him. "B–but h– how is that possible? I thought you had to be inside someone to make a mating mark. So unless you're some freaky shapeshifter with a rubber spine, I'm not sure how that's possible."

Vincent flashed me the most panty-melting smile that glistened and glittered with a mixture of my blood and arousal. "You haven't seen enough porn, Princess, and it shows."

"You mean like..." My cheeks flamed, which felt a little silly considering my current position. "Biting me there while you fuck my mouth?"

"You humans call it sixty-nine, and in my opinion, it's your kind's reigning achievement."

"Wow, you really don't think much of humankind, do you? But how can that work?"

"Mouth, ass, cunt, it doesn't matter. All I have to do is penetrate you with my dick and bite. You're lucky it doesn't work with fingers. Otherwise, you'd be covered with our mating marks, wouldn't you?"

He chased the first finger with a second, and I thought he was going to bite me again, but instead, he brought his mouth down over my opening and licked a bloody path from my occupied hole all the way up to the place he'd promised to mark me one day.

Gripping the underside of my knees, he positioned me so that my calves rested against his shoulders with my heels touching his back. He still wore his t-shirt. It was always a white one that struggled to cover his mass, his raven tattoos just visible beneath. I wanted to tell him to take it off, but I couldn't find the words. When I opened my mouth, the only thing that came out was an embarrassing little groan because just then, he got to his feet and placed his knees on the edge of the throne while pulling me forward so that I was almost flat on my back with my center completely spread and exposed to him.

He leered down at me, his bloody eyes glinting in the moonlight, his lips fixed into a wicked sneer. My heart seized when he bared his fangs, his blood-laced saliva dripping from his lips to pepper my navel.

"Since you've been such a good little blood whore for me, I'll let you have me now. But you only get a small taste. You only get both once I claim you as my true mate. So what will it be, my little monster? Shall I feed you blood... or cock?"

"Cock," I panted on a broken breath.

Looking pleased with my decision, he moved my legs so that they were slung, one over either arm of the throne. This freed his hands while keeping me spread open for him, watching me as he straightened to his full imposing height. He made a show of peeling off his shirt, perfectly shaped muscles rippling beneath pale flesh with the movement.

He was so goddamn delicious, both sets of my lips began to salivate. His raven tattoos looked so real, like they might try flying away any second. Then there was a light dusting of hair from his navel that slipped down into the waistband of his denim jeans. He was all starkness, white skin, with black hair, ink, and dark veins that wrapped around his formidable forearms.

Sinful, supernatural perfection.

His hand fell to the fly of his jeans, and he flicked them open, then lowered the zipper at an agonizing pace.

"Hurry the fuck up, Feral, or I'll find one of your brothers to finish the job."

My taunt hit him right where I wanted it to, like a dart to his big, ballooned ego. He snarled, one hand flying to grip my throat while his other shoved down his jeans and boxers, unleashing his cock.

Fuck.

Me.

It wasn't as long as Sterling's or as girthy as Eros', but it was still sizable and its real triumph was the way it was wrapped up in dark veins like the ones that ran through his arms.

Heart racing, I gave a thick swallow as his fingers tightened around my windpipe, restricting my air only slightly. His control was frightening. He squeezed just enough to make it pleasurable. "Watch your mouth, Princess. Or I'll fuck that too."

"At the same time?" I teased.

"While I do have a secondary form, unfortunately for you, it doesn't come with two dicks."

A secondary form, huh? That was interesting, but now wasn't the time to sort out the mystery of Feral's species. Besides, he'd be spilling the beans after we had our fun.

I looked up at him with hooded eyes and donned a wry smile. "Who needs you to grow a second dick when we can just ask one of your brothers to come in here so you two can double team me."

I thought Feral might be turned off by the suggestion, but his fingers twitched around my throat, and his cock jumped a little in excitement.

A nasty sneer twisted his chiseled features. "You're lucky I already instructed the Sharpes to implant the IUD, else I might be compelled to breed you right here and now with a mouth like that."

"Wait—*what?*" Instantly, whatever pleasure and excitement that had been coursing through my veins was replaced with lava-hot rage.

"We couldn't wait for you to wake up, Ruby. It was the only way to get your body to stop producing pheromones, and it was driving every male in the house up the wall. I didn't trust anyone not to touch you while you were being monitored for blood poisoning. It was to protect you."

His excuses fell into the background like TV static. I wasn't listening to him anymore.

He had no right to make that kind of call without asking me. I was so angry, it filled me until I couldn't feel anything but rage.

Something inside me *snapped*.

Chapter Sixty-Three
Midnight Snack

Slamming my foot right into Vincent's sternum, he stumbled back a few feet before regaining his balance. Surprised by my sudden show of strength, a look of shock flashed over his face before his dark glower locked back into place. He hurriedly stuffed himself back into his jeans, fangs bared at me. "What the hell is your problem?"

"My *problem?*" I seethed, my tone mocking and doused in venom. I lurched up from the throne, regaining a somewhat more dignified position. "*You* are my whole problem. I don't give two shits if I was giving every male in the coven—or the whole damn cape for that matter—a hard-on. That doesn't give you the right to make medical decisions for me."

The vampire's eyes narrowed into cold, red slivers. All the warmth between us, any shred of trust, *anything* good at all that we managed to build in the last hour was completely crushed by the weight of the same old shit.

Vincent's lip curled, regarding me like I was worth nothing more than any of the other blood whores stupid enough to fall willingly into his embrace. "Oh, *please.* You're acting like I had you sterilized. It's fucking birth control, Ruby. Don't tell me that you wanted to stay unprotected, stinking like a bitch in heat. What would have happened once you were knocked up? The new king would be selected not by merit but by the time spent between your thighs! That's no way to elect our people's ruler. This is exactly why the Elders shouldn't have placed this responsibility on the shoulders of a naïve half-blood *bitch.*"

His words cut deeper than they should have. I expected the brutal prince would turn up again sometime, that the tender moment shared between us couldn't last forever. I knew his walls, complete with the barbed wire, had to come back up eventually. Even though I'd been anticipating this, it hurt more than it had any right to.

Hot, angry tears pricked my eyes, and I did my damndest to hold them back. I would *not cry* in front of Vincent. He didn't deserve any more of my vulnerability. "Of course, I wanted birth control. I'm not ready for kids. But that doesn't mean that you get to make decisions for me, asshole!"

Feral's gaze hardened to stone and shifted toward the window, refusing to look at me. "I do when you're too unconscious to make them yourself."

"You know what I think the problem is? You're pissed I slept with Eros. It's not that you hate sharing me."

When Corry had flirted with me that first night, and when he'd fingered and fed from me on the second, Vincent had only been irritated by the fact that the youngblood wasn't more careful with me. And he almost seemed happy when I told him I was in love with Sterling. It's not that he couldn't share. He seemed mostly fine with me being involved with Sterling and Corry.

"You just don't want to share me with Eros. You had Sharpe insert the IUD because you don't want him knocking me up."

"Yeah, it must come as a real shocker that I don't want the man who murdered my father in cold blood impregnating *my* mate."

"How many bloody times do I have to tell you?" I marched in front of Vincent, putting myself between him and the window, so he was forced to look at me. I didn't care that I was still naked. In a weird way, it made me feel powerful, especially when Feral looked me dead in the eye, refusing to look anywhere else. If I wasn't mistaken, I could detect the hint of admiration banked in his burning red glare. As if he was proud that I wasn't cowering, that I didn't let the fact that I was naked deter me from holding my ground.

Or maybe it was just a trick of the light.

"I'm not yours, Feral. And at this rate, I never will be."

"It doesn't matter that you have the mating mark of that murderer disgracing your flesh..." He stepped forward, eating up the few feet of distance between us until he was just a kiss away. His fingers brushed the scar on my shoulder. His touch was still silk-soft, like that tender part of him I craved so much was still here even though his words were as cruel and bitter as ever. "You're already mine."

He brushed down to kiss my shoulder again, and this time, for the first time, I flinched away from him. "You're wrong. I'm never letting you touch me again, Feral. Not after this."

His face contorted into a vicious sneer, strips of shadows and moonlight accentuating his severely handsome features. It suited him.

Moonlight and shadows.

Black hair and ink, white skin.

Cruel monster and sensual lover.

Vincent Feral was two sides of one coin, and I never knew what side he'd land on.

I stumbled away from him, and he was there, charging after me with a vicious glint in his eyes that told me he'd bite me as soon as he was within reach of me. I had a feeling he wouldn't bother making it as sweet for me as he had when he'd fed on me in the throne.

"Stay back! Don't touch me!"

I tripped and fell. Scrambling back on my hands, my spine met the wall. I was trapped, cornered with nowhere to run. He was on me in the next pound of my heart, peering down at me with a savage grin stretching the mouth that was still crusted with my blood. Gone was the man who'd pleasured me with those very lips only minutes ago. Now he was just a snarling, ravenous animal, looking fit to breed or feast, I wasn't quite sure.

But I wasn't scared. I never felt that with Vincent, no matter how feral of a monster he was capable of being.

Gawking up at him in awe, I couldn't help but gasp. It wasn't made in fear, rather, complete rapture. Like I was staring up at a dark god who held my fate in his terrifying grip. I was completely and utterly transfixed by the dark energy and raw power rolling off him.

His raven black, sweat-drenched locks fell in pieces over his sanguine eyes, and for a moment, I wanted to give myself over to the male, to surrender to the dark magic lapping at my skin in places that made me shiver in wicked pleasure.

Whatever he was, it was something *powerful.*

"We had a deal," he growled in a voice that didn't even sound like his own. It was all gravel with a grating timber that had the marrow of my bones trembling. "Your blood for my secrets. Don't you want to know how your father died?"

I was so enraptured by this ruthless male that I thought maybe he'd mesmerized me. But that only worked on full-blooded humans. No, this was just my own body completely drunk on the potent and exotic allure of The Feral King.

I was at war with myself. My human side wanted me to run away and never touch this mess of a man ever again.

And the lusty female vampire side of me was absolutely riveted and wanted nothing more than to submit to him.

As if gleaning the conflict raging inside me, he stroked my neck with that gentle touch that had me purring beneath him. Arching down, he brought his lips to my ear and whispered, "Don't you want to know what creature it is you're about to mate?"

Goosebumps erupted all over my body, which made him laugh—a guttural, bone-scraping sound—and he trailed his lips down over my throat. When I felt his fangs brush the flesh there, I came to my senses.

He was going to bite me over the place Eros had already claimed. The place that would carry Deathwish's mark and his alone.

"Keep your secrets," I managed to say on a raspy hiss. "I don't want anything from you anymore."

Feral wore the terrifying expression of hunger and pain and rage.

It sent a bolt of electricity through me.

On top of me loomed a beast who was on the brink of losing his control.

I had to get out of here. *Now.*

I brought my knee up as hard as I could, right into his groin. He howled and lurched off me. I was on my feet in an instant, moving to snap the abandoned sheet off the floor. I jerked my eyes up to see Vincent had the same thought at the same time. We both went for it, but he was quicker. Plucking it from the floor, I almost crashed into him, and another predatorial growl burst from him. He hooked an arm out to snag me, but I was already on the other side of the room beside the door with my hand on the handle.

"You're going to need this." He held up the sheet as he slowly stalked forward. "Come be your king's good little whore, and I'll let you walk out of here with your dignity."

Conflict raged inside me, threatening to tear me in half. I didn't want to walk out of here completely naked. I'd still yet to meet most of the coven, and those precious first impressions would be all but fucked if they saw me bolting out of the throne room, naked and covered in blood and tears. Then again, how dignifying could it be slinking out of here wrapped in nothing but a sheet after I'd been ravaged by Feral?

Nope. It was going to be option A for me. I'd rather lose my dignity than have my pride completely fucked. "Keep it. You can sleep with it at night. It's the closest you'll ever get to having me in your bed."

I stormed out in a rage and was thankful to find the hallway empty.

It was no use trying to hold back the tears for a second longer. They streamed down my cheeks, creating little blazing paths that made my skin feel like it was on fire.

It took me a second to gather myself. What just happened in the throne room...? There would be no forgetting it. From here on, every time I looked the brutal male in the eyes, I'd think about myself naked and spread beneath that monster. The monster I lusted for so badly it made my cunt, my heart, my *damn soul* ache in ways that terrified me.

And how I'd almost gone through with it.

It had to be late at night. Everyone was probably in their rooms getting ready for dawn. I scanned the hall in both directions to make sure the coast was clear before taking off into a sprint toward the grand staircase. I made it to the top and rounded the corner, my heart soaring when my bedroom door came into view. Then all hopes of making it to the sanctuary of my room without being spotted crumbled when another door opened, and a familiar face appeared.

Lexi.

What in the hell did I ever do to the universe to deserve this kind of stinking luck? Was I some cosmic joke? Was God just toying with me, seeing how he could make my life more miserable? Because he was doing a bang-up job, I had to say.

The second I registered the dark-haired, ice-cold succubus, I fumbled for the nearest door just a few rooms down from mine and bolted inside. Sure, it was a bad idea to burst into random rooms totally in the nude, but whatever I stumbled into couldn't be worse than facing Lexi like this.

The room I'd fled into was dark, and it took a second for my eyes to adjust. I prepared myself for the worst. Creepy dungeon, a closet full of bones, anything was possible in this coven of bullshit.

What I was not expecting was a normal ass room. It was so normal, in fact, that for a second, it felt like I'd found a portal back to Quincy suburbia. The walls were painted blue and were covered in posters from *The Fast and the Furious* franchise and bikini-clad women. There was a desk in the corner with stacks of books, a laptop, random playboy magazines.

A king-sized bed sat in the center of the room. It was the first non-antique piece of furniture I'd seen in the whole place.

It looked like the room of a normal college-aged guy.

The single window was already shuddered and locked, which meant whoever this room belonged to, they were in for the night. My heart skipped a beat when I realized the bed was *occupied*.

The male in the bed sat up, his blue eyes instantly turning red when they fell to my naked body. "Red. What the hell? Why are you covered in blood? And you're *naked!*"

Oh, Bloody hell.

Why couldn't I have stumbled into a broom closet or something? Instead, I had found Corry Cross' room, who wasn't exactly renowned for his control over his youngblood impulses.

Before I could react, Corry was out of bed and stalking toward me with a lopsided grin on his face.

"Talk about a midnight snack."

CHAPTER SIXTY-FOUR

NIGHT WITH THE YOUNGBLOOD

"C —Corry!"

I squeezed my eyes shut as the hungry predator breathed down my neck.

Great. Just great.

Of all the rooms to fling myself into, it just had to be the one belonging to the coven's most impulsive vampire.

Had I escaped The Feral King, only to fall prey to the youngblood?

No matter how deep into his instincts Corry was buried, he'd never force himself on me. But he *would* bite me.

And I was too tired to fight him.

I needed rest but knew that even with the blood-thirsty vampire inside, Corry's room was the closest thing I'd get to sanctuary with Lexi prowling the hall.

Squeezing my eyes shut, I braced myself for the bite I was sure would come. When it didn't, I peeked at Corry and was stunned to find his ravenous red gaze had returned to calm, cerulean blue. Instead of hunger etched into the grooves of his pinched expression, there was only concern. Anger, even.

He reached to touch my cheeks, moving slowly, as if to wait for my consent. When I didn't pull away, he swept both his thumbs over my tear-swollen cheeks.

"Who made you cry? I'll kill them." The grit in this tone, fraught with an emotion that made my throat convulse, caught me by surprise.

I couldn't bring myself to answer. The words wouldn't come, and even if I found the right way to describe what had just gone down between Feral and me, I didn't want to talk about it.

Corry's line of sight made a slow descent down my body, but there was no lust in his gaze. With scrunched eyebrows and hooded eyes, I knew he was trying to piece the puzzle together himself.

"Last I saw you, you were running after Vin. You carry his scent on..." His attention dropped to my thighs, where Vincent had bitten me. The puncture marks had healed, leaving only streaks of blood crusted to my flesh. Damn, it looked like a massacre down there, like I had given birth to Rosemary's baby.

My nape prickled when I caught Corry's horrified expression. "Ruby, did he...?"

"*N–no!* Nothing like that. He only bit me. It was consensual."

The youngblood ran a hand through his hair as he blew out a sigh of relief. "The thought shouldn't have even crossed my mind. Vin wouldn't do something like that, but I know you two have been having explosive levels of—um...

well, disagreement. And he's changed a lot since you arrived."

"What do you mean?"

"Whatever he is—that side of him that isn't human or vampire—it's changing. It's growing restless now that you're here. Like it wants to eat you or something. But not it the same way vampires eat." As he spoke, he turned and went for his dresser, rooting around for something in the second drawer.

My eyes fluttered shut as I tried to gather all the fragments I had to this puzzle. Corry was right. Whatever Feral had been before he turned vampire couldn't have been a friend to humankind.

It did feel like he wanted to eat me, and he was using every ounce of willpower he had to keep that from happening. It was making him a hangry asshole because of it. That also explained why he was so aggressive toward me when he had every reason to be kind to me so he could win the throne.

Whatever Feral was, he not only lusted for my blood, he wanted something else, too. Something I couldn't afford to give him. With every glance, every bruising touch, every battering kiss, it was like he was trying to crawl inside me and devour my soul.

What in the bloody hell *was* he? Was he some kind of soul-eating demon? Maybe an incubus? He sure had the sexual energy of a sex demon.

Whatever he was, that dark part of me lusted for him, brutality and all.

And if it was my soul he wanted, I was afraid the monster inside me would eventually give it to him.

"Here, you can wear this," Corry said, turning away from the dresser to offer me a black t-shirt with the "Kawasaki Racing" logo stamped on the front. I tugged it on, the hem of the shirt falling about mid-thigh.

It smelled of denim and cologne and faintly of hair gel. Perfectly Corry.

"Thanks, Cor. I don't know what I would do without you."

The prince gave me a smile that made his eyes dance with something that had my chest filling with a fuzzy warmth. "Anything for you, Red."

Those were the same words he'd said to me outside the burger place, right before I'd stolen his bike. After what I did to him that night, I'm surprised he still meant them.

"How did you do it? When you were turned, I mean. How did you handle the sudden shift in your life?"

He let out a nervous chuckle, rubbing the back of his skull with the flat of his palm. "I didn't. The night of my turning, I went on a bloody rampage, killing a few humans between here and my parents' house. When I got there, I terrified them. I probably would have killed them, too, if it hadn't been for Sterling and Master bursting in to clean up my mess. My whole family had their minds mesmerized within an inch of their life to forget what they'd seen. That's not exactly what I'd called handling it."

"Well, I haven't exactly been great at handling this whole vampire thing either. I stole your bike and betrayed your trust."

Corry gave my arm a comforting rub. "Hey, I get it. It's not like our experiences are very comparable. It couldn't have been easy finding out you'd been lied to your whole life, locked in your room because you're a half-vampire, while not getting the benefits of either race. You never got to be human, to go to school and make friends and do dumb teenage shit. You never got to be a vampire and experience the companionship and support you get from a coven. You were alone, and the night we had together, you had a choice. Freedom or me and my brothers. I was angry that night not because you chose freedom, but because you didn't understand that escaping us meant almost certain death for you."

I pressed a smile, instantly feeling at ease with the youngest prince. Everyone always gave him shit, telling him he had no impulse control, and that was partially true. But Corry was good. Even if he was young and naïve, he made me feel normal. Understood.

With him, I never felt alone.

I knew the youngblood cared for me, and that fondness for me stretched deeper than his instincts ever could. When he'd seen me naked and covered in blood, any other youngblood would have probably bitten me. It had been the sight of my tears that had stopped him. His concern for my emotional wellbeing had triumphed over his bloodlust.

"I understand what you did for me that night, Corry. You didn't screw me over. You saved me, and I'm thankful. I won't try to escape the coven again. It's safest for me here. But if I was to escape again, this time I'd ask you to come with me."

"I believe you, Red. And trust me when I say I'd leave everything behind to go with you. I believe you belong here, as queen and ruler of the vampires. But down the line, if you change your mind, I'll come with you. Wherever you want to go. I'm there."

I felt the tears falling again, but this time they were tears of relief. Leaning into his lean, hard body, I relished the way he felt against me. He folded his arms around me, pulling me close to him.

Corry was shirtless, clothed in nothing but tight, black boxer briefs. He wasn't as tall as his brothers but just as built as Sterling, with sleek muscles that boasted his athletic prowess. He felt so damn good against me.

Pulling back in his arms just enough to meet his gaze, I searched his eyes through my haze of tears. "Why are you so damn sweet to me?"

"Because I like you," he said with that panty-melting smile of his. "And I'm not a total dumb-ass like Vin. If I want to be with you, I can't be tossing you around like some plaything. Not my style anyway. Besides, I saw what you did to Mal at the gas station. If that's what you do to guys who get a little too handsy, then I think I'll just wait patiently for you to come to me, babe."

Everything felt so right and easy with Corry. Just like that, all my worries about Vincent Feral were replaced with warm and tingling thoughts of Corry.

Leaning toward me, he brought his lips to the apples of my cheeks, kissing away the tears. When he went in for another cheek kiss, I titled my head to capture his lips with mine. He let out a tiny groan the second our mouths fused.

I pushed him toward the bed, and we fell together onto the mattress, our lips tangled and our mouths still exploring, searching, licking, nipping.

Corry rolled on top of me, holding me in his arms like he couldn't believe his luck that I was in his bed, and I might blow away in the wind if he didn't hold on tight enough.

While our kiss was deep and decadent, his lips on mine were unhurried, demanding nothing from me. They only poured his affection, planting tiny kisses around the perimeter of my mouth before delivering one last lingering peck to the center of my lips. Breaking our connection, he sat back on his heels at the foot of his bed to drink in the sight of me nestled among his pillows in only his t-shirt.

I propped myself up on my elbows to meet his gaze through the dark of his room, missing the heat of his closeness. "Come back."

"We don't have to do this tonight," he said as he adjusted himself in his boxers—a testament that he did, in fact, want to do this tonight. "Trust me, I want to. But you were just claimed by Eros, and you gave your mark to Sterling. Then there's all that messy shit with Vin. You have a shit ton on your plate right now."

"I do want to be with you. I like you a lot."

"I know," he said through a lopsided grin. "I like you too. But I already told you, I don't care too much about being king. All I want is you. I don't need the throne to have you. So when you're ready, I'm here."

My whole body went warm, tingly, and numb. I was so damn tired I could barely feel my limbs. I wanted to be with Corry, but he was right yet again. It didn't need to be now.

"Thanks, Cor. That means so much to me. Um... Can I sleep in here with you tonight? I don't want to be alone."

The youngblood's brows flew up so fast I thought they might fly off his face. "You're not afraid I'll bite you while you sleep?"

I shrugged. "You didn't bite me when I came in here naked covered in blood, so I don't think you'll bite me when I'm passed out snoring."

"Good point. Fuck yeah, you can stay. Hell, if I had my way, I'd have you sleep in my bed every night."

He held back the covers for me, and I crawled in. When he got off the bed and pulled them back over me without climbing in, I frowned. "Where are you going?"

"I thought I might sleep in my den. It's just my closet," he threw his thumb over his shoulder to gesture to the door behind him. "So I won't be far."

"Don't you want to sleep next to me?"

He blinked several times. "Really? You don't mind?"

I shook my head, my cheeks burning red. "I don't want to be alone tonight."

His eyes sparkled with excitement, but by the way he held himself, he looked a little nervous. His chest expanded with an inhale, and he lifted the covers to tuck himself in beside me. "I've never slept next to anyone before."

"Not even your sister when you were little kids?"

"Well yeah, my twin. But I meant I've never slept next to a woman before."

"Haven't you had lovers?"

"A few. I had a girlfriend in high school, but that was a sort of sneak through her window sort of situation. Then there's been a couple of women in the coven, but vampires rarely sleep next to each other unless they're a mated pair."

"If it makes you feel better, I haven't slept next to anyone either until the other night with Eros."

Had this been Vincent beside me, he would have shut down at the mention of Deathwish. But Corry's eyes lit up with curiosity through the dark. Positioning himself on his side, he propped himself up on an elbow to look at me. "What was that like? Mating him, I mean."

"It hurt a little. But it was pleasurable. It was a little weird being with someone with, um, his tastes for my first time. I don't regret it, though. It prepared me." It should have been awkward talking about my night of debauchery with the depraved prince, but it wasn't. I felt at ease with Corry, like I could tell him anything in the world, and he'd be happy to listen.

"For what?"

My cheeks flamed hotter. "Erm, for you four. You're a lot to handle. I figured if I could take on the brutal Deathwish, I could take on all of you."

A mischievous smirk streaked across Corry's face. "Like at once?"

A surge of heat blossomed low in my belly. "That is not what I meant." Holy Mother of God. I could barely imagine being with two of them at once, or three, let alone all four. I'd have to be a queen indeed to manage that.

Corry's eyes trailed to the place where Eros' mating mark sat beneath the t-shirt as if he could sense exactly where it was without having to see it. "So you don't mind carrying his mating mark? You know he'll be able to track you now, right? He'll always know where you are and vice versa."

"Really? I'd been experiencing this burning sensation on my shoulder, but I didn't know why."

"I'm not an expert on this sort of thing, but our coven has a mated couple who have been together for like a million years. I asked them about their marks once. Supposedly it will burn hot when he's near and turn freezing when he's far away."

Corry reached to fan his fingers over my shoulder. What was with these princes' fascination with Eros' mating mark? Even Vincent had kissed it. Instead of getting territorial over it, it was like they were paying homage to it. Respecting it.

There wasn't a shred of jealousy in the youngblood's gaze, just curiosity. After a moment, he let his hand drop to the sheets between us with a sigh.

"So, do you want to tell me what happened between you and Vin? We don't have to talk about it, but you can't blame me for being curious. You came in here looking like you just escaped from a sacrificial altar. All that was missing was the ceremonial dagger and the white dress."

"No dagger needed when we've all got fangs. And the dark god I was about to sacrifice myself to kept the white dress." Despite how fucked the whole situation was, I couldn't help but laugh. Corry's joke hadn't been terribly off the mark. "There isn't anything to talk about. Vincent is a possessive asshole who turns into a big baby when he doesn't get to control everything. He's also a secretive bastard who won't tell me the truth about my father's death."

I shot the young prince a sharp glance. Catching my hint, he heaved a sigh and shook his head. "It's not my secret to tell, Red. If you want to know, you're going to have to pull it out of Vin."

My lips slanted with a frown. "Then I'll never find out how my father died. It's not that I give a shit if Vincent murdered my father. I just want the truth. That's all."

"I know, Red. And you'll get it. When Vincent finally comes clean and tells you with his own words what happened, that will mean way more than me spilling his secrets for him."

"Yeah, I get it. I should get some sleep, Cor. It's late, and tomorrow night is the big fight."

Corry sat up, frowning down at me. "They will not want you to go to that."

My brows crinkled. "Who's they?"

"The Elders. Especially Sterling. The warehouse where they host these fights is on Boston Coven territory, and Sterling's apprehensive enough just letting Eros and Vincent go even though they're two of our den's strongest warriors. And I'm still not allowed off coven property. Even though these underground fights are mostly supernatural fighters and onlookers, there are still humans that attend. Me and my bloodlust don't really mix well with humans in rowdy, enclosed spaces."

"Take a shit load of Sharpe's lust suppressant pills and sneak out with me. Or don't," I sniffed with a casual shrug. "Either way. I'm going."

If Corry wanted to argue further, he held his tongue. "Alright, babe. Just close your eyes and get some sleep." He kissed my cheek, his lips lingering there as we both dozed off in each other's arms.

As the embrace of sleep closed in around me, I couldn't seem to shake the bet from my mind. If Vincent lost, he'd have to step back from his pursuit of the throne. And his pursuit of me.

Vincent leaving me the fuck alone should have been what I wanted. But it wasn't, and that fact made my stomach twist into painful knots. I'd come to crave the attention of my dark knight because I knew underneath that armor was a man who ignited a catastrophic fire inside me.

On the flip side of that, if Eros lost the match, he'd have to leave the coven. Even dwelling on the possibility of him leaving forever made my mark scorch hot with a pain that brought fresh tears to my eyes.

As a restless sleep claimed me, I tried to imagine my life without either of them by my side as king.

And I couldn't.

That's why I had to go to the fight tomorrow. Not to witness the fight.

But because I was hellbent on stopping it.

Chapter Sixty-Five
A PROMISE

I woke up to the mattress shifting. My eyes drifted open to see Corry sitting on the edge of the bed, fully dressed, with a small box in one hand and a glass filled with orangey-red liquid in the other.

"Wakey, wakey." He kissed my forehead, looking too damn awake for this early in the night. Groaning, I shoved my face into his pillow. "Five more minutes."

"C'mon. You've already slept in. You don't want to miss watching Eros and Vin clobber one another."

Like that, I was awake.

Clearly, neither Vincent nor Eros had let the youngest prince in on the bet. It made sense. Wailing on each other to get out some aggression was one thing, but staking one's place in the coven and the fate of the throne all on one fight was entirely another. I doubted Corry would rat them out to Sterling, but he might interfere. For a second, I considered telling Cor myself but quickly dismissed the idea. I could handle this on my own.

Stretching with a yawn, I sat up and took the glass he offered me. "What is this? It smells great." I eagerly gulped it down, the delicious nectar tasting as sweet as candy and as filling as a thanksgiving feast.

"I wasn't sure if you preferred human food or blood in the morning, so I mixed OJ with some O negative. Shouldn't have second-guessed myself, though. You strike me as an all-or-nothing kind of girl."

Watching me practically inhale the liquid, his brows wrinkled in concern. "Whoa. Take it easy there, Red. Drink it too fast, and it'll come up quicker than you got it down."

Downing the last drop, I slammed the empty glass on Corry's bedside table. "I'm in a hurry. I need to talk to Vincent and Eros before the fight."

Corry's mouth thinned with a frown. "Like I said, you kind of slept in, babe. They're already at The Warehouse. The fight starts in a few hours, so we have to get going, seeing as it's in Boston."

"*We?* So you've decided to sneak out with me?"

The vampire smirked. "Turns out sneaking won't be necessary at all tonight."

I blinked several times. "What? Why?"

He handed me the little box that I'd almost forgotten about. "Here. This is for you."

Confused and a little excited—because it looked like a jewelry box and I'd never been gifted a piece of jewelry in my life—I took the box and opened it. Nestled on a little velvet cushion was a silver tiara. It was dainty, with a pick on the end that could be tucked into a ponytail. The little crown was so discreet considering what it was, but fuck me, it was beautiful. Instead of a typical tiara, the silver had been shaped to look like vampire fangs, and tear-drop-shaped rubies dangled from the fang's tips to resemble blood droplets.

"Corry, this is incredible." On further inspection, I spotted the T&CO maker's mark stamped into the silver. "Wait. This is from Tiffany's? This had to be expensive."

He gave me a one-shouldered shrug. "The coven's rolling in it, Red. We don't need to eat, and we don't have a mortgage. We own the whole cape, so we get a shit ton from tenant rent, not to mention all the businesses Sterling has invested the coven's money in over the centuries. You can have a million more of these, and we'd still give mortal tycoons a run for their money."

"It's great. I love it. But what does this have to do with me going to tonight's fight?"

"I spoke with Sterling. He agreed to let us go on two conditions. The first is that I have to take a triple dose of blood sating pills and feed before I go. The second is that you have to wear the tiara. We had a tracking device put into it. Eros might be able to track you down now that you carry his mark, but the rest of us don't have that luxury." Corry's mouth pursed into an impish grin. "At least not yet. If we get separated, and you get into any trouble, we'll be able to find you."

"I didn't know Tiffany and Co made tiaras with trackers."

Corry let out an awkward laugh while running his hand through his gelled hair. "With the business the coven has given them over the years, they'd make us a diamond-encrusted nuclear bomb if we asked. It's also pure silver.

You can use it as a weapon on vamps and werewolves in a pinch."

"Werewolves?" I gulped. "There are werewolves around here?"

"Yeah, especially in Boston. That pack isn't much of a concern for us because of the treaty. But these days, you can never be too careful."

I gaped down at the tiara with a rapidly growing lump in my throat. A horrible foreboding sensation was taking root in my belly, and I just knew that tonight something bad was going to happen.

I doubted the little silver crown was going to help me much. But still, bad feelings aside, I had to go. If I didn't stop this fight, I'd be losing one of the princes tonight.

Logically, I knew I couldn't have both of them. At the end of the four months, I would have to pick one prince. I hated how much the thought of just having to choose hurt me. It wasn't fair.

I wanted all of them.

But if I was forced to pick at the end of this, I wanted it to be my decision. I refused to lose one of them due to some stupid dick-measuring move on their part.

Even if my chances at stopping this ridiculous bet were slim to none, I couldn't just sit by and do nothing.

"You take a shower and get dressed while I feed," Corry said as he hauled himself to his feet. "I'll meet you by the bikes in twenty."

I perked up at the mention of motorcycles. I hadn't had a chance to take the Ninja out for a spin since I'd stolen it from Corry and the thought of riding it to Boston sent a thrill through me. "We're going to take the bikes?"

He grinned, beaming at the excitement lighting up my eyes. "Hell yeah, babe. The Ninja is yours now. I'll take the Harley."

"I get to ride the Ninja by myself?"

"Why not? You've already done it."

"Yeah, trying to gain my freedom. Now that it isn't a life and death situation, shouldn't I get a license or something?"

"Only if you get pulled over." He shrugged. "If you do, it will be great practice to see if you're able to mesmerize people. Anyway, I plan on letting you drive in front of me. Need more material for the spank bank." He winked at me. "I can't wait to see that ass straddling my bike."

Parting on a quick kiss, I left Corry's room and went to mine for a quick shower. I opted to wear black leather platform boots with a chunky heel and thick straps that ran up to my knee paired with some high-waisted black jeans with torn knees. After some thought put into it, I opted to wear the "Deathwish Dethrones The Feral King" sweatshirt and tucked the front into my bra, so it created a crop-top-like effect.

For makeup, I went with a red lip and smokey eye, then pulled my red locks into a sleek ponytail mounted high on the top of my skull. The final touch was the fang tiara tucked into the base of the ponytail. Examining my reflection in my bathroom mirror, I couldn't help but grin. I'd never felt more like a vampire princess than I did at this moment.

Heading out into the hall, I froze with my hand still on the handle of my bedroom door. The upstairs hallway was totally packed. New and old faces crowded around the staircase, and all turned to face me. I felt my chest go tight as I realized pretty much every eyeball in the coven was centered on me. I blew out a sigh of relief when I picked out Kenzie's face from the crowd and moved toward her.

"What the heck is going on? What's everyone staring at?" I whispered to Kenzie. Apprehension twisted my insides all around, not only because everyone was looking at us but because I still hadn't had time to fully apologize to my friend for almost bleeding her dry the other night. I'd sent her a quick text thanking her for the blood donation, but a few words and a smiley emoji over text wasn't the apology she deserved.

If Kenzie carried any animosity for me, she didn't show it. She grinned, waggling her eyebrows as she took in my outfit. "Wow, the princess is looking hella good. And they're staring at you, duh."

I gave a hard blink. "Um, why?"

"Because word got out that you're going out tonight. Princess's first day out."

"So?" I wasn't accustomed to being the center of attention and found it hard having so many people gather around just to look at me.

"*So*, it's a big deal. That building where sups gather to fight will have a buttload of vampires from other covens there tonight. Now that word has gotten out about the new princess, eyes will be on you."

Great, so no pressure or anything.

All the niggling anxiety for the outing fell to the back of my mind when my line of sight slipped past the second-floor railing down to ground level, where a familiar face waited beside the manor's main entrance.

Sterling.

I gave Kenzie a quick hug and whispered "thank you" in her ear before hurrying toward the silver prince.

As I descended the stairs, I could feel all eyes glued to my back, but my full attention was on Sterling. He stood in the manor's foyer, a smile slowly stretching his lips as I came close.

My heart squeezed, and my breathing went uneven as my pulse took off. With his waxen eyes centered on me, my awareness of everyone else ebbed away.

The prince was as gorgeous as ever. With his silver hair swept back from his eyes, each strand fell perfectly into place.

He wore gray dress slacks and a burgundy sweater that made his pale skin and hair pop. The most notable detail was the neckline of the sweater. Crew cut, not a turtleneck. My breath hitched. His scar—my mating mark—was on bold display for the entire coven to see.

"Miss Baxter," he greeted coolly as I approached.

I stopped just before him even though everything in me ached to throw myself into his arms. Tamping down on the instinctual urge to be close to my chosen mate, I held back.

It's not like we were together, at least not in the traditional sense. He wasn't my boyfriend, and while he carried my mating mark, I didn't carry his, meaning we weren't "officially" a mated couple. So I wasn't sure how professional he wanted to keep things when we were in public.

When someone catcalled, I ripped my attention from Sterling to see the front door open, with two motorcycles sitting outside just beyond the door. Corry waiting beside them.

Sending him a scowl, I dragged my gaze back to Sterling. "Thank you for the tiara. It's beautiful. I feel so official now."

The elder vampire smiled, the wrinkles at the corners of his eyes making the ice over his chilly expression melt away. And there it was, that heart-breaking smile I'd seen for the first time when we'd mated in the attic. "I know you look radiant in it."

"She looks hot as fuck!" Corry shouted from outside in an attempt to be helpful to his blind brother. Cheeks burning to new levels of hellish inferno, I flung a withering glare at Corry. It was hard to be mad at him, though. The youngest prince was looking "hot as fuck" himself with how he lounged against his black Harley Davidson in a leather biker jacket.

Ignoring the youngblood, Sterling's marble-smooth physiognomy contorted with a frown. "Be careful tonight, love. We have no shortage of enemies in Boston. Don't draw attention to yourself. Watch the fight, then come straight home."

"Can't you come with?"

His frown shifted into a melancholy smile that I felt all the way down to my bones. "I never leave coven grounds unless I have to. Please don't give me a reason to tonight."

"I won't," I assured him.

Putting distance between us, I stepped toward the door to make my exit, but Sterling caught my wrist and pulled me against him.

Holding my head between his hands, my heart stalled out for one intense beat as he looked down at me with that devotion I imagined only a medieval-aged priest could pull off.

With every member of the coven watching, he kissed me.

His lips were gentle on mine, cool and perfect.

I never wanted it to end.

Drawing my arms around his neck, I stretched up on my tip-toes to deepen the kiss, and he dropped his hands from my face to loop his arms around my waist. He lifted me so I could get a better purchase on his mouth. With the way my body burned, I felt like I could catch fire, but I wasn't sure if it was from the heat of Sterling's kiss or the scorch of everyone's curiosity hot on our backs.

We finally—reluctantly—broke away from one another. He pressed one last kiss to my brow, and I relished the last moments of his bare skin on mine.

"Be safe," he murmured on a whisper so thin I barely heard it. He ran his fingertips over my face to glean my expression before pressing his lips to my ear. "And promise me something, Ruby."

"Anything."

"Keep pushing Vincent. You'll break through his barriers. Never yield to him. Keep fighting. If anyone can reach the man inside the beast, it's you."

"I will," I said with a shaky exhale. "I promise."

Chapter Sixty-Six
BATHROOM BREAK

I decided there were few things better than driving a motorcycle at top speeds down a deserted road, with the wind in my hair and the open sky above. Nothing beat the sting of the chilly night on my cheeks, the rev of the engine beneath me, and Corry right beside me, glancing at me every few minutes, blue eyes glittering in the bike's headlights.

It was freeing, completely exhilarating.

As we made our way toward Boston, the roads grew wider; the lights became brighter, and the sounds louder. It was almost overwhelming for someone like me, who'd never been to the big city before. If Corry wasn't here, centering me, it would probably be too much sensory overload. But every time the lights became too blinding or the sounds too grating, I flicked my gaze to his and relished in how he looked on his bike.

This was his bliss.

And seeing him revel in it was mine.

Once we got into the city, I let Corry take the lead and followed him through the streets to the waterfront, where all the skyscrapers and billboards and cars melted away. We slowed the bikes as we came onto a gravel road that led into an industrial area filled with heavy machinery and warehouses that dotted the docks.

Compared to the rest of the area, the place was eerily quiet and dark. The only lights were from the occasional lamp posts stretched along the dock and the few illuminating the gravel parking lot. For how quiet it was, there were a lot of cars.

"Are these people all here to see the fight?" I asked as I pulled my helmet off and slung it over the bike's handlebar.

Corry jammed the kickstand into place on his Harley and stood, sweeping his eyes over the filled lot. "Yup. The Warehouse fights are a hub for our kind to come and hang out over a beer and watch guys from different covens and packs and whatnot duke out some beef. But The Feral King and Deathwish matches always draw the largest crowds."

Corry threw his arm over my shoulder and steered me toward the dock. As we approached the building at the end, the line of people waiting to get inside came into view. My jaw dropped. The queue of people would rival the Disneyland ride lines during peak seasons.

It shouldn't have been surprising that the supernatural crowd was drawn to bloodshed, especially since these sorts of fights seemed to be legal within the community. They were a way to settle aggression without messing with peace treaties and alliances. But the fact that this many people were eager to see two of my guys rip each other to shreds didn't sit well with me.

"There's no way we can stand in this line. The fight will start before we get to the door!" The sudden panic in my voice made Corry's brows lift.

"Chill, babe. We're vampire royalty. We don't do lines."

I thought having the whole coven stare as Sterling and I kissed was nerve-wracking, but that was child's play compared to having every single person in line veer their glare on us as we cut to the front.

Sweat broke out on my back, and I tried to keep my heart rate calm, knowing a lot of these people would possess the ability to sense my nerves.

Corry's arm tightened around my shoulder, tucking me close against his side. "Hold your head high like the queen you are, Red," he whispered in my ear. "Imagine all these people—"

"In their underwear?" I finished for him. "I've heard that trick on TV, and I don't think it will work."

"No, pervert." He grinned at me, a teasing chuckle tickling the shell of my ear. "Imagine all of them on their knees, bowing before their queen. They'd be shaking in their boots right now if they knew what you were capable of."

Corry's words of encouragement were like steel support beams that had me standing a little taller as I emanated newfound confidence.

The bouncer at the door was a muscular man with a strong jawline, amber eyes, and a buzz cut. On the side of his skull was a silver scar reading 'SC.' It was a brand.

I was surprised by the ear-to-ear grin that broke out on the bouncer's face as we approached. "Well, send me to Heaven and call me a saint. It's the royal youngblood himself. I was hoping you'd sneak out tonight. Those den brothers of yours are going to be making Warehouse history tonight."

He held out a fist to Corry, who bumped it with his own.

"No need to sneak tonight, Zeke. I got my leash lengthened, all on the condition that our sweet princess here gets to hold it." Corry's hand dropped to my ass and gave it a squeeze. I should have been irritated by the possessive gesture, but something about the way the young prince was showing me off had me feeling like a queen. If it were Vincent next to me, I'd feel more like a tool.

Zeke's brows arched, and there was a cacophony of murmurs from the line behind us. "Princess? No shit? So it's true. The old king had a little half-blood girl he was hiding away from the rest of us. Well, I'll be damned." The vampire's gaze went to my tiara and made a slow, appraising descent down my body.

Corry's body went rigid next to mine as the other vampire spent a little too long taking me in, but his smile remained locked in place, never wavering. "That's right. Zeke, this is Ruby Renada Baxter, daughter of Thomas Knight and blood heir to the throne. Ruby, this is Zeke Stone of the Salem Coven."

"Salem Coven?" I said. "I thought Salem was known for its witches."

He shrugged. "They once were, but as you might imagine, the fiasco a few centuries back made their kind a bit uneasy to settle in the area. Now it's home to the SC. Our numbers may be small, but we're loyal to the Elders and whoever they deem worthy of the throne." He rubbed his chin in thought. "Though I hear Boston's gathering support for some progeny of Thomas Knight that just came out of nowhere. Rumor is he's gunning for the crown. Not sure how he plans on taking it but keep on your toes there, Princess."

"Um, thanks. I will." If someone on our side knew about the shit Eros and I had to physically beat out of that Boston Coven vamp a week ago, news of Dagon Knight's nefarious campaign for the throne was spreading like wildfire.

"Bleeding hell, is that Deathwish's scent on you?" Zeke's nostrils flared. "Didn't think any woman would be crazy enough to take him as a mate. Hats off to you, Your Highness. If you've survived that crazy fuck, maybe you can handle the weight of the crown after all. Though not everyone is going to be thrilled with the idea of him as king."

At a loss for words, Corry thankfully spoke. "Nothing's decided yet, so watch what you say, Zeke. Wouldn't want to spread more rumors. Especially one revolving around Deathwish. He's known to take tongues who spew shit." Corry's smile had all but evaporated, and there was nothing but serious violence brewing in his blue gaze. It was rare seeing the youngblood like this, but fuck me, it was sexy.

Zeke's brow broke into a cold sweat, and his Adam's apple bobbed with a swallow. "Right, of course. As much as I'd love to chat, the fight will start soon, so I'll lay down a few rules for you, Princess, since you're a first-timer here. All the fighters are sups, but we've got humans who come and watch these things, so no feeding. If you get into a fight, do it with your fists, not your fangs, and no mesmerizing people. If anyone pulls any supernatural bullshit, we have to round up the humans and mesmerize them all. We've only had it happen once, and the Elders threatened to shut us down. So, for everyone to have fun, please keep your bloodlust suppressed until you get back home to your coven."

I gave him a nod, and he ushered us through the door.

The Warehouse had to have some kind of soundproofed walls because the ruckus inside was ear-splitting. The seats were stacked out in rows that reached the far perimeter of the space, and almost every single chair was filled with excited onlookers, chatting and shouting their speculations for who'd win.

It was easy to tell the supernaturals apart from the humans, not because of the scent—there were too many clashing smells in here to pick anything apart—but by the way half the room turned to stare the moment Corry and I strode in.

I frowned. "Sterling said not to draw attention to ourselves."

"Nothing bad is going to happen, babe," Corry consoled me while scoping out the room, probably for threats. "We might be in BC territory, but The Warehouse is a neutral zone. And tonight, we're in luck. Tons of vamps loyal to us here, not a Boston or Detroit fuckhead in sight."

I tried to let Corry's words ease the growing tension in my belly, but no dice. I was still anxious as fuck.

I needed to find Eros and Vincent so I could put a stop to this whole thing before it started.

"When's the fight supposed to start?"

Corry glanced at his cell. "Fifteen, twenty minutes tops."

That was enough time. It had to be. "You get our seats. I'm going to go to the bathroom."

For a second, Corry looked like he was going to insist on accompanying me. Sterling wouldn't want him leaving me alone. "I'll be fast, I promise." Before he could object, I was off, pushing my way through the crowd toward a sign in the back that read "locker rooms."

It was a safe bet that Eros and Vincent would be getting ready in the locker rooms, but even without the sign, I could feel my mark growing warmer with every step that brought me closer to my claimed mate.

A heavy-set mammoth of a man in a blue polo with "security" stamped across his chest blocked my way to the back. By his scent, he wasn't a vampire, but he wasn't entirely human either. Maybe a shifter.

"Where do you think you're going, girly?" The male puffed out his chest, trying to intimidate me. Instead, I was just annoyed.

"I need to see Feral and Deathwish."

"Fighters only," he snorted.

I narrowed my eyes at the audacious fuck who stood in my way. "I'm Deathwish's girl." Pulling the mate card felt weird, but I did carry his mark. By all rights, I was his mate. If only this guy was a vampire, then he'd be able to scent as much, and I'd already be inside.

"Right," he said with a mocking cackle. "And I'm engaged to Lady Gaga."

Propping my hands on my hips, I shot him a sour glare. "Don't make me ask twice. Deathwish won't be happy to hear you refused to let his mate see him before his big fight."

My threat did not land like I hoped it would. A seedy grin spread across the security guard's face, his eyes roving down the length of my body. "You wouldn't be the first chick who's made up lies to see the fighters. They get down on their knees for me and ask *real* nicely." The creep grabbed his crouch and adjusted his hard-on, licking his lips. "So how bad you want in, baby? I'll take you to the back if you agree to show me your appreciation for breaking the rules. With a mouth like that, I bet you give real good head."

The naïve human inside me was repulsed, but Thomas Knight's daughter was in the driver's seat now. Before I even realized what was happening, I had my hand wrapped around his throat. Slamming him against the wall with all my strength, I felt his lungs empty. His eyes bugged out, but I wasn't sure if it was because of his lack of airflow or his surprise by my impressive show of strength. Probably both.

The whole place went quiet as, once again, all eyes were on me. Whoops. So much for lying low.

Oh well. Now that everyone knew the princess was in the building, now was the time to let them know I wasn't to be fucked with. "I want in bad enough to pop off the head of anyone stupid enough to stand in my way."

I let out a dry laugh at the male's horrified expression. "Oh, what's the matter, *'baby?'* Not the kind of head you had in mind?"

"Damn, doll. I don't think I've ever been more turned on in my life," a familiar, guttural voice sounded. I jerked my attention away from the shifter—whose cheeks were turning blue—to see Eros standing in the locker room doorway, lounging against the cement wall with his arms folded over his bare chest.

"Eros!" I dropped the security guard and threw myself into my mate's arms. He held me close, his nose in my hair, breathing me in.

"Fucking hell, you're so sexy. Look at you, dressed to slay, wearing my hoodie, your hand wrapped around the windpipe of a lesser being. I could just fuck you right here and now." His voice was all grated and husky, making me shiver with dark delight in his arms.

"That's not the kind of show everyone came to see, Eros." But dang, he made it sound appealing. "Can we talk for a second?"

Holding me back in his arms, his brown eyes burned with concern, and his smile fell away. He probably already knew that I was going to ask him to drop the bet, but he nodded and pulled me into the locker room, out of everyone's line of sight.

"Nosey fucks," he grumbled, stalking down the hall and into a room filled with lockers, a shower, and a counter lined with sinks.

It was now that I noticed he was wearing nothing but a towel.

Holy Mother. I'd seen him naked before, but this look of his had to be my favorite. His tattooed skin, taut over his bulging muscles, and that tapered waist with the deep V between his hips, wrapped up in a fluffy white towel.

His body was the pinnacle of female fantasy.

Don't get distracted, Ruby. You're here on a mission.

"So what brings my sweet little doll back here? The fight starts in fifteen minutes. That's not a lot of time. If you came for a taste of the other night..."

He knew that's not why I'd come. He was trying to distract me, and it was almost working.

He took a step toward me and then another. My mark was almost on fire. He was so close. My whole body flushed, growing hot and sweaty, and his burning gaze wasn't helping. Those brown eyes bore into me, stripping me bare. I backed up until he had me cornered against the lockers.

With my spine flat against the cool metal, he placed a hand on either side of my head, caging me in.

When he dipped to kiss me, I finally found my words. "You have to call off the bet!"

His lips froze just millimeters away from mine. His brows furrowed. "Why?"

"Because you might lose. The coven can't afford to lose you, especially not now with all this Dagon Knight and Boston Coven bullshit."

"I'm not calling off the bet. Feral needs to be taken down a few notches, and I have every intention of beating his ass."

"But if you don't win?"

The vampire's expression darkened. "I will win."

"But if you don't?"

"I am a man of my word. If I don't, I leave the coven. It won't be forever. I'll talk this out with Feral if I have to because I don't plan on leaving you behind. You're my mate. No matter what happens, I'll be back for you."

My chest tightened, filling with a tingling sensation that made my head go light. "Really? You mean it?"

"I mean it. I could never let you go, not after I've had a taste of you. You're a drug, baby doll. An addiction. Feral thinks that leaving the coven will be enough to keep me away from you. He's never been more wrong. When your father turned me, I was robbed of any chance of an afterlife. With you, I've got a second chance at eternal happiness. You'd think I'd throw that away on a stupid bet?"

Closing my eyes for a moment, I exhaled in relief. "I'm glad to hear that. I just wish you'd call it off completely."

His hands clenched into fists on the locker beside my head. "I can't. That bastard needs to be brought down a few levels. I need to do this, understand?"

I gave him a jerk of a nod and opened my eyes. "I understand. I don't like it. But I understand."

"Good." His brown orbs blazed, banked with evident hunger as little red flecks stained his irises. "Now, how about a quickie for good luck?" He pressed his hips forward, the towel providing very little padding against the rock-hard erection that jabbed my leg.

My breath caught in my chest, and heat bloomed in my belly.

He wanted to take me *here*, in the locker room? It wasn't exactly a private space. And where was Vincent? He couldn't be far off. What if he walked in on us?

At that thought, my panties were soaking on the next breath. Damn, why did I have to be so messed up?

"On one condition."

The depraved prince arched a blond brow, the piercing there glinting in the fluorescent lights of the locker room. "Which is?"

"You tell me the truth. Did you murder Vincent's father?"

CHAPTER SIXTY-SEVEN
WHAT'S HIS

E ros' eyes turned into deadly slits, sharp enough to kill. "If you're asking me if I murdered Feral's father in cold blood, the answer is no. I didn't."

I breathed out a sigh, relaxing against the locker. "I knew you weren't a murderer."

The vampire canted his head, jaw ticking. "Murder is when you kill a man, and Feral's father wasn't anything of the sort, baby doll." His voice dropped an octave, and his demeanor turned dark and violent. I gaped up at him in wide-eyed awe as he loomed over me, leaving no space between us. He kissed my jawline, then my ear, whispering, "He was a monster, Ruby. And I *butchered* him like the animal he was."

Shuddering, I raised my hands to slam them down over his chest to push him away, but he caught my wrists, keeping my palms flushed with his reaper tattoo. "What's the matter, doll? Scared of me now?" He clicked his tongue with a shake of his head. "This shouldn't come as a surprise to you. Not after you saw what I did to Allister. What you helped me do."

"That's different!"

His lip peeled back into a sneer. "Oh yeah? How?"

"He was going to hurt me, hurt the coven. He was evil!"

"Exactly! That's what I've always done. I hunt down feral supernaturals, and I put them in the fucking ground so they can't hurt anyone ever again. Feral calls me a monster. Maybe that's true. But I use my abilities to hunt creatures bigger than myself. My job has always been to take down the bigger beast. Other than in the ring, I've never hurt a human in my life." His hands began to shake against my wrists, and a vein jumped in his brow. An emotion I'd never seen before roiled behind his red-brown eyes like a miasma. When he spoke next, his voice was strained. "Even when I was turned into one of them, I've only hurt—*really hurt*—bastards who've had it coming."

"But Vincent said—"

"Let me guess," Eros spat, cutting me short with a twisted grin that was void of all warmth and humor. "He said his father was a 'good man.' What a load of steaming shit. Of course, a son holds his father on a pedestal. Seeing Feral so blind to the obvious, I'm almost glad I've never had one myself. He's got a skewed perspective, Ruby. Feral only saw his father in his home realm when he was surrounded by his own kind. Here in the human realm, he was a predator. He hunted humans and used their energy for fuel."

"I thought he was a diplomat."

"Is that what he told Feral?" Eros let out an empty laugh. "His dad was a hunter. Their kind preys on human pain and uses it for fuel. They take that energy to turn bigger, stronger. They can even take on whole new forms, which allows them to reap more fear and grow even more powerful. Their kind has no business being in the human realm. Hell, even having a dead one here makes me nervous. And Feral lost a ton of his powers when he was turned. But that's how dangerous they are, Ruby."

He let go of one of my wrists to cup my cheek. With the other, he raised my hand to his lips to kiss my knuckle. "That's why I can't drop the bet. He shouldn't be king, let alone your mate. If I win this fight, he'll have to give up his pursuit of the throne and leave you alone."

All this new information settled at the bottom of my gut like sediment.

This was a lot to unpack.

It surprised me that the first discernible emotion I felt was pity. I felt bad for Vincent. I believed Eros when he said Vincent's father had been a monster that needed to be put down. But I also believed Feral was one hundred percent sure his dad had been a good man. He had loved his parent, and losing him couldn't have been easy. It made sense that Vincent needed to hold on to something that brought him close to his dad, and his hatred for the man who killed him was probably the easiest for Vincent to cling to.

I wondered if there was a future where Eros and Vincent could ever be friends. Well, maybe "friends" was pushing it. I'd settle for a world where they weren't trying to beat each other to death on the regular.

Maybe if I could manage what Sterling had asked me to do, to break through to Vincent, I could be the bridge between them.

Then there was all that other stuff about Feral's race. I could press Eros into telling me more, but like Corry had said earlier, it would mean more if the truth came from the lips of The Feral King himself. Or maybe I would just figure it out myself. The pieces were coming together. In the throne room, he'd said that he had a secondary form. Maybe before he became a vampire, he could shift into other things. But perhaps that was one of the powers he'd lost when he'd died. He had a high metabolism and needed to feed more than other vampires. And whatever he was, he used human pain as an additional fuel source.

Vincent fed on pain.

It was a hard and scary fact to unload, but it explained his demeanor toward me. It wasn't that he was cruel for shits and giggles.

It was in his nature.

I hadn't realized that my fingers had trailed down to Eros' beard and were mindlessly winding the wiry blond hairs until he let out a low purr. "Do you understand now why I'm trying to keep you away from him? He's dangerous."

"He says the same thing about you."

The purr turned to a hell-deep growl, and he shoved me back against the locker, his eyes scorching with fire. "All this talk about Feral. Remember, doll, it's my mark burned into your flesh for all eternity."

I gasped, biting my lip to strangle the noise as his hands gripped my hips, possessive and firm. "It's my scent that warns all other males you belong to me."

His fingers wedged between my thighs, curling up to stroke that place he already had mapped and claimed. "It's my seed that has found a home between your thighs."

He applied pressure through my jeans, right over the place that had me moaning. He brought his lips down over mine in a bruising kiss that sent a rush of heat sinking through my body to meet the place where his hand still gripped the juncture of my thighs.

He broke the kiss, smirking at me. "That's right. He can't make your pussy purr like I can. Now take off your jeans. I'm gonna bury my dick so deep in you, you'll feel me for a week. Do you like the thought of that, baby doll? Sitting in my cum while you watch me beat the shit out of Vincent Feral? Every vamp and shifter in the audience will scent what I've done to you. They'll know where I've been and what I've left behind."

An involuntary whimper slipped past my lips, making his smirk curve into a manic grin. "I think my fuck doll loves it when she drips with my spunk. It sends a message that this pussy is mine." He squeezed me again, applying just enough pressure that hit just the right spot, even through the thick material of my jeans.

I swear to Satan and all that's unholy that this guy could find my clitoris even if he was stranded in the Siberian wilderness with only a compass made out of animal bones.

I couldn't get out of my clothes fast enough. Kicking off my boots, I stripped out of my jeans, opting to leave the Deathwish hoodie on. Pointing to his towel, I licked my lips provocatively. "Drop it."

The grin that stretched his pierced lips was all sex. He hooked a thumb beneath the towel but made no move to unravel it. "If you want this, baby, turn around."

Heat spread through me like wildfire, and I slowly pivoted so that I was facing the lockers with my bare ass at Eros' mercy.

"Now bend over and spread those cheeks, doll. Show me what's mine."

Chapter Sixty-Eight
CONFRONTATION

Glancing over my shoulder, my heart rate skyrocketed when I caught Eros pull his towel off and discard it on the tiled floor. He was all sinewy muscle, smooth skin, and that cock. It was thick and obscene with how a bead of pre-cum pebbled at the top. He fisted his girth, and this time, when his hand moved, I caught the silvery scar of my mating mark on his palm.

My throat squeezed as I watched him give one pump to his dick, then he paused with an arched brow. "What did I just say? Spread that cunt for me, like the good little fuck doll you are."

I reached around to grab my ass cheeks, parting them. With my spine arched and my face resting against the cool steel of the locker, my center was on complete display.

"Look at you." He stepped forward, his husky purr wrapping around me like a touch, a primer for what was to come. Still gripping his cock, his free hand cupped the swell of my ass cheek. "So submissive for me when I know just how wild the fire inside you burns. You know how hard that gets me?"

"I have a feeling I'm about to know in a second." I swallowed.

He pressed close to me, his warmth and heady scent encompassing me like a security blanket. Cloves, smoke, steel. His spicy aroma had become something of an aphrodisiac for me.

Draping his body over mine, his mouth found my neck. I didn't panic when his lips brushed over the place Sterling told me was his and his alone. When Eros kissed me, my muscles eased. If he bit me, he'd probably do it on my shoulder over his mark. In any case, I doubt he'd bite. The minutes were ticking down. There wasn't time for foreplay or feeding or anything else, for that matter. That suited me just fine. The frantic urgency of it all, my stilted breathing, the thrashing of my heart, the rush of his breath over my nape. It all made me so damn wet.

A gasp stumbled out of me when his cock slid through my folds. He didn't penetrate me, not yet. His shaft glided against me, my juices coating his shaft with a few slow thrusts of his hips.

"You don't even know how many times I've thought about you since our night together," he gritted in my ear, his lips on my neck. "You left your panties with me that night. I've jacked off in them so many damn times, thinking about the way you clenched around me when you claimed me as your mate."

His words ignited my hunger like oil on flame. When he moved to slide his cock back over my labia, I angled my core and bucked my hips against his pelvis, spearing myself on him.

His fingers bit into the flesh of my hips, and I felt him jerk against me. "*Fuck!*"

I peered over my shoulder in wicked glee, seeing his mouth stretch into an O, the cords in his neck pulling tight.

Eros was all raw masculinity with his Viking-esque looks. There was just something about his blond hair shaved short on the sides and long on top, his piercings, and his reaper tattoo that made my womanhood weep. But that erotic expression he wore when he was balls deep inside me, with his brows scrunched together and his jaw clenched, was the icing on the cake.

The pinch of the stretch was as pleasant as it was painful, his hips pumping forward as he slowly eased himself out and then back in. "Goddamn. You feel so good."

I knew he wanted to take it slow, to bide his time and tease this thing out. But the match was scheduled to start in the next few minutes, and the countdown sent my mind into a frenzy.

This wasn't Sterling, whose lovemaking was slow and erotic and beautiful.

This was Deathwish, who lived up to his name in every way.

I wanted him to take me hard and fast, so I began slamming my hips back into him, setting a new pace that had him groaning in pleasure.

"Fuck, baby," he wheezed on a growl. "The world isn't ending. Slow the hell down unless you want me painting your insides in the next fucking second."

"Good. Fuck your mate like you mean it. I want the whole place to know what we've done."

The dirty talk had its desired effect. Something inside Eros snapped. His eyes, which had been only red around the rims, blew up into red disks. His fangs dropped, and a predatory growl tore from his chest. He pounded me hard into the lockers as if he was intent on cleaving me in half.

Between the brutal pound of his hips making the metal doors on the lockers rattle loudly and my lover's animalistic grunting, I wasn't surprised that we drew attention. Movement in the hallway caught my gaze.

My heart damn near gave out when my gray eyes locked with green ones.

Vincent Feral stood in the locker room's doorway, watching me get fucked from behind by his greatest rival.

He was dressed in nothing but black gym shorts, with cloth wraps around his knuckles. He'd been off lifting weights or something because his whole body was covered in a thin sheen of sweat that made his dark hair cling to his brow.

"Goddamn, baby," Eros said on a splintered moan, having not noticed our audience. "You're clenching around me so hard, I'm coming—*arrrrgh!*"

The green pools of Vincent's eyes stained crimson.

The look on his face sent a fist smashing through my chest to squeeze my heart until I thought it might explode.

I was still angry at him for telling Sharpe to insert the IUD without consulting me. But this wasn't how I wanted to get back at him. This wasn't revenge.

But that's exactly how it looked.

His fists clenched, and there was that dark, smothering energy rolling off his body that made me choke and gasp. Eros still hadn't noticed him. He was too busy spilling himself inside me.

For one terrifying moment, I thought Feral might try to kill Eros right here while he was still inside me. The murder in his malignant scowl was enough to make me think maybe he wouldn't wait until they got to the ring. But before I could warn Eros, Vincent stormed out of the locker room. There was an eruption of cheers from the crowd that became muffled when the door slammed shut behind him.

Eros, completely oblivious to what had just happened, pulled out of me with a grunt and patted my butt like I was some kind of dog.

Honestly, I kind of felt like a bitch right about now.

A hollow sensation settled in my gut as I pulled my jeans and shoes back on. I shouldn't have felt bad for fucking Eros. He was "officially" my mate, after all. But the way Feral had looked at me, I felt slimy. Like I had betrayed him. Which was stupid. We weren't even together.

He probably thought this had all been a ploy to get back at him. That had not been my intention at all.

I stumbled back out into the main warehouse, ignoring Eros as he called out for me.

Vincent was already in the ring at the center of the warehouse. He stood next to a man with a shaved head who had the 'SC' scar branded into his skull, just like Zeke. He was probably the ref, by my guess.

The Feral King refused to look at me as I left from the back. That cut deeper than any glare he could have given me.

The match would start any second, and I knew once it did, it was going to be a brutal one.

I was such a fucking idiot.

I'd gone back there to reason with the prince I thought might actually listen to me. Instead, all I had to show for my efforts was a cunt full of cum and a belly full of shame.

Vincent was more furious than ever, and he was not about to go easy on his brother.

I had just made this whole thing worse.

Stupid, stupid, stupid.

Needing a moment to gather myself and clean up before I found my way back to Corry, I ducked into the restroom.

I first cleaned away the excess of Eros' cum on my thighs with a wad of toilet paper in the stall, then I moved to the mirror to smooth down my ponytail and readjusted my fang tiara.

As ready as I was going to be, I turned to leave the bathroom when the door slammed open, and a woman stood in my way, blocking my exit.

"There you are, you fucking bitch!"

Super.

Just what I needed.

Blowing out an aggravated sigh, I whirled to face Lexi. As obnoxious as it was to have her show up here, right before the fight, it was fitting. Tonight was a night for settling beef.

And Vincent and Eros weren't the only two about to throw fists.

Chapter Sixty-Nine
QUEEN PSYCHOPATH

"I can't believe you fucked him!" Lexi spat, her dark eyes beady and blazing like little caverns filled with hellfire.

"Yeeeah." I folded my arms over my chest, glaring at her. "You're gonna have to specify." Obviously, I knew she was probably talking about Eros, but oddly, I got a lot of satisfaction from rubbing the fact in her face that I was getting more dick than the coven's resident succubus.

Her face contorted with rage, taking on a look that packed enough punch to make a grown man piss himself. "You greedy bitch! You reek so much it smells like you just took a fucking shower in that psycho's cum!" She lunged for me, moving so fast I barely had time to dodge. I side-stepped her, and she smashed into the sink, sending large chunks of porcelain clattering to the floor. Water spewed from the broken pipes, making the floor wet and slick.

We were causing a tremendous commotion, though I doubted anyone heard us. An announcement came over the speakers, introducing the fighters. Even over the gushing water, I could pick out bits and pieces of the announcer's voice.

"After twelve wins in a row, defeating Jackhammer, Rip Tire, even the savage Ajax, he's knocked all of them out cold. With a fist that can shatter diamonds, it's our dethroned royal... weighing in at six foot three... two hundred and twenty pounds... The Feral King!"

There was a deafening roar of cheers at Vincent's intro.

Lexi and I had swapped places with her against the shattered sink and my back to the door. Now that she no longer barred my exit, I could leave and slip into my seat next to Corry to watch the fight. As much as I wanted to catch the fight the moment it started, I had to settle this shit with Lexi. She didn't respect me. She was dangerous kept unchecked, and I needed to prove to her I was strong. Stronger than her.

I just hoped that it was true.

"Hide your women and your knives!" the announcer roared with the crowd so loud it almost drowned him out. "It's the beast that dethroned our Feral King. Weighing in at six feet and two hundred pounds, you must have one to mess with him... Deathwish!"

There were more cheers and hollering, this time with a few boos mixed in from the audience.

"Deathwish is coming off a thirteen-win streak, with twelve knock-outs. Rumor has it the Knight household keeps this animal caged in the basement, letting him out for tonight only to defend his throne. This rivalry has been going on for over a decade, and we're all on the edge of our seats to see how this one turns out!"

The announcer's voice faded into the background when Lexi began to morph right before my eyes. Thick, twisting horns sprouted from her skull—their color matching her black hair—and her manicured nails grew into vicious, painted claws. My heart skipped a beat, seeing just how sharp and deadly they were. They could seriously hurt me, and I realized that was exactly Lexi's intention.

"What the hell is your problem? You seriously can't be that pissed that I slept with Eros? You don't even like him. I haven't touched Vincent. Shouldn't that make you happy?"

"*Happy?*" Her voice was shrill as a harpy's and her talons just as sharp. "He dumped me, saying he shouldn't be messing around with me now that he intends on making you his mate and queen! Then you go screw the murderer who killed his father!"

She swiped a claw at me, and she was so close now I felt the hiss of air fanning over me, millimeters away from slicing my flesh.

Damn it, her words had disoriented me. I stumbled on the slick, water-logged floor and tumbled backward into the toilet stall. She was inside with me on the next breath, looming in the doorway.

She had me cornered.

"Stupid, worthless, mortal cunt! You ruined everything! You seduced and tricked him into caring about you. Then when you stole his heart from me, you tossed him aside like he was nothing."

What was she talking about? I didn't tell him to dump her... Okay, so I kind of did. But that was the deal. I was going to be his blood whore on the condition that he never touched Lexi again. In the aftermath of our fight, I'd called the deal off.

But Feral had sworn off Lexi anyway.

Totally lost, I fumbled with this new information. Lexi was pissed off not because I slept with Eros per se but because Feral had dumped her. And with me having mated Eros, she thought I was going to pick him as king. Meaning all her hopes of Vincent making her his queen and mate just went out the window.

That meant that even though I called off the arrangement, Vincent still held up his end of the bargain. Sort of. He may not have come clean about what he was or how my father died, but he went through with dumping Lexi.

He'd given up his blood whore even though he had received nothing in return.

Why?

He needed blood, often. There were mortal blood donors that worked for the coven, but how was he going to get a steady supply of vampire blood? Why was he putting his health at risk when he was getting nothing out of this?

Was this his weird, cryptic way of apologizing for what had happened between us in the throne room? The gesture had been one I never would have expected Feral to make. And that just drove the knife of guilt lodged in my gut even deeper.

I knew Vincent didn't expect me to be monogamous to him, not when I was trying to select a mate on the Elders' orders. It was the fact that I had chosen this night to sleep with his rival. It had been the worst timing, and the fact that he had dumped his blood whore just made it all the worse.

I felt bad, horrible even. But I didn't need Lexi's help driving the guilt deeper. I would make all my apologies to Vincent, not this bitch.

"I never stole his heart from you. You never had it. You're just salty that now, whether or not I choose him as king, you know he's loyal to me. He won't be tossing me aside to put you on my throne."

"How dare you! I've been his companion for an entire decade. For ten years, I've kept him sated with my blood and my body. Then you crawl out of your pathetic human suburbian shit-hole, and after only a week, you take his heart and then toss it aside like it's nothing!" She scraped her talons down the stall door in a rage, the scraping of nails on metal making me squirm.

"I knew the Elders had gone senile when they decided to make you queen. The fact that we'll have a mortal on the throne will be trouble enough for our coven, let alone having such a stupid one! You can't even select the proper prince. You pick the savage who will have that pathetic hole between your legs worn out within the year. In his bed, he'll be the end of you. And on the throne, he'll be the end of us all. I can't let you do that."

The succubus took a step forward, her eyes wild with demented joy. "I'm going to make you bleed, little mortal. In a building full of vampires, that will not be good for you. I've heard your blood is real sweet, like candy. It's not virgin's blood anymore, but it will still drive all the younger vampires out there into a mad frenzy, so long as we spill enough of it."

Lexi froze in her tracks for a second, a maleficent grin slashing her lips. It was almost like she was imagining the fucked fantasy she envisioned as the future. "They'll be bringing you home in pieces. Then everything will be back to how it was. Prince Feral will take his place as the rightful king and heir to the vampire throne, and I will become his queen and sit beside him on the council. A mate worthy of a male like King Feral!"

She punched a clawed hand toward me, their needle-sharp tips glinting in the fluorescents of the restroom. The demoness moved with mind-boggling speed, but I was ready for her. Using the toilet as a launch point, I leaped onto the top of the stall. When her claws met nothing but air, she lost balance and caught herself on the rim of the toilet.

I dropped to the floor behind her, grabbed a fistful of her hair, and kicked at the back of her knees to force her into a kneeling position. She let out a blood-curdling shriek, but the gush of water and the roar of the audience beyond the restroom drowned her out.

Keeping one fist in her hair, I seized her arm and twisted it behind her back. She let out a pained scream, and I bent her over the toilet, some of her black tresses falling in the water.

"Listen to me, bitch, and listen closely. I messed up with Feral. I can admit that, even to you. But you know something? He messed up, too. He's not perfect so try bringing down that pedestal a few notches. We both have daddy issues. Part of him hates me, and part of me hates him. Between us is pain, and that's okay because he feeds on pain, and I get off on it. What a perfectly fucked-up match we make. And do you want to know a little secret? I plan on making *all of them* my mates. So am I a greedy bitch? Yup. And I'm making my peace with that. I'm going to be the vampire queen, and no one is going to make me feel shitty for the things I want. And you know what I want? I want to claim the throne without having to have a man to sit beside me to get it. It's my fucking birthright. So keep your hands off Feral. He's mine. Got it?"

"Fucking bitch! I'll kill you!" She thrashed against me, struggling, a lethal bundle of black hair, gnashing fangs, and pointed horns.

An idea occurred to me—albeit a juvenile one—that I'd seen a million times on TV. Without giving myself another second to talk myself out of it, I dunked her head in the toilet and kicked the lever with my boot. I held her head there as the bowl refilled with water, just long enough for her to struggle against me in a battle for air. Her gurgled scream made me chuckle in wicked delight. Wrenching her out of the bowl, I pulled her head back so that she was forced to look up at me through her mass of sopping hair.

"Well, if you're serious about wanting to kill me, I guess I should just drown you right here and now. As queen, I was hoping to put an end to the whole murder thing. It's kind of a cliché anyway. But you know what they say, fight fire with fire. Maybe I just need to kill you to let people know I mean business."

When Lexi said nothing, I moved to give her another swirlie, but she screamed, sagging in my arms in defeat. "Alright! Stop! I yield!"

"Are you sure?" I smiled sweetly, stroking her wet hair. "Aw, I was hoping you'd give me a reason to drag you down to Deathwish's den, where we could have some fun. Have you heard about it?"

Lexi was already a pale woman, but she turned sheet white. "Rumors..."

I arched down, my grin turned crazed. "They're all true."

"Y–you psychopath!"

I tutted, shaking my head. "That's not the proper way to address me, Alexandra."

I used her full name, which I knew because of Sterling, admonishing her as if I was the ancient vampire and she was the lesser being.

Her eyes went wide, regarding me now like I was an entirely different person. In a way, I felt like a different person. Slowly that monster inside me was emerging, bit by bit. So far, I had a handle on my control, and as long as I could keep it that way, I was a lethal weapon.

Resentment sparked in her eyes, but behind that—if I wasn't mistaken—there was the faintest glimmer of respect. "Y–yes, Princess."

"Great." I released her and left the stall, washing my hands off in the remains of the destroyed sink. "Now clean yourself up and get back home. I don't think Sterling will be happy to know you've stepped on Boston Coven turf without his permission."

I adjusted my crown in the mirror before marching out of the restroom, the cheers from the crowd making me feel triumphant as fuck.

CHAPTER SEVENTY
MONSTER

T he fight had already started, and by the look of my two guys in the ring, I'd been in the restroom with Lexi longer than I thought.

If the amount of blood was any indication, Eros was winning. Vincent had a busted lip and a black eye. Flecks of inky blood dotted his chest, but he hadn't broken a sweat. Meanwhile, perspiration poured down Eros' temple, streaking his neck and pectorals. The sheen of sweat made the reaper on his chest shine. Normally, the sight of the tattoo made my thighs quiver in female appreciation.

Now, the sight of it made my knees wobble in dread.

Eros had worked up quite the sweat beating on his opponent. His chest heaved. Strands of hair had come undone from his man bun, spilling over his face. His nostrils flared, and his eyes honed in on Vincent, who stood in the middle of the ring, unmoving as Deathwish circled him.

My stomach flipped when Eros jumped forward and swung a fist at his brother. Vincent ducked and had a perfect opening to land a hit in his gut, but he didn't. He just dodged the blow and pivoted away.

Why wasn't he attacking Eros? That didn't make any sense.

Scanning the crowd, I found Corry standing right beside the ring, his fingers hooked into the cage surrounding the mat. "Come on, Vin! Do something! What the fuck, bro?"

Making my way to Corry's side, my head went light. Being this close to the action, my senses went into overdrive to process it all. The smells, the roar of the crowd at my back, the booming voice of the announcer over the speakers. This sort of proximity to the fight had to be exhilarating for some, but it just made me nauseous.

The tang of my guys' sweat and the bitter bite of their blood stung my nose. I could see the hatred for one another burning in their eyes, and I couldn't shake the feeling that I was just making everything worse by being here.

I wanted to be what brought them together, not what broke them apart.

"Jesus, there you are!" The youngblood's gaze dropped to my soaking jeans, his brown brows cocking. "What the hell? Why are you wet? You reek of Eros. I'd expect your panties to be drenched, but you look like you just waded through a freaking swamp, Red."

"I had to take care of some business in the restroom. What's going on? Why isn't Vincent attacking?"

Corry gave a shake of his head. "Not positive... My best guess is that he was waiting for you to get here so you could see him wail on Deathwish."

"What? Why would he do that?"

"Look at him, babe. Vin's pissed. I know he's always angry, but this isn't our usually grumpy asshole. Even I can feel the dangerous energy. Fuck..." He rubbed the back of his neck with his palm. "It almost hurts to stand here. Notice how everyone is in their seats? Usually, there's a crowd of people gathered around the cage, but our Feral King is putting off some seriously lethal vibes tonight. Whatever went down between you and Eros a few minutes ago, I think it made Vin snap."

My throat convulsed. I could sense exactly what Corry was talking about with Feral's energy. I'd never seen Vincent fight before, but I knew by the tension that choked the air, this wasn't normal.

This was bad, really bad.

Vincent Feral was as tense as stone, his muscles pulsing, every tendon in his body as taut as steel cables. It was as if his monstrous instincts were lurking just beneath the surface, ready to explode any second, and the only thing he was waiting for was me.

Even the announcer seemed worried by The Feral King's imposing demeanor. I could tell by the way he stopped talking, leaving the ring to speak to other Salem vampires that gathered on the other side of the caged-in ring.

They put their heads together, whispering, casting their worried glances at Feral.

They knew he was about to try something. And whatever stunt he was about to pull, all these humans had no business being here for it.

"I have to stop them." I moved to crawl onto the platform to get closer to the cage, but Corry caught my wrist, holding me back. "Red, no. You'll just make it worse.

Whatever that other side of him is, it's not safe. You can't reason with it. And Eros won't back down either. All we can do is watch and hope they control themselves enough to keep from killing one another."

I opened my mouth to argue, but all words froze in my throat when my eyes locked with Vincent's. His bloody lips pulled into a vicious smirk. An invisible hand clawed down my back, sending little shooting branches of ice through my whole body.

"Good. She's here. Now I can kill you."

Eros' eyes turned to slits. "What?"

I crawled up onto the platform, kicking off Corry as he tried to pull me back down. Clinging to the cage, I pressed my face up against the mesh. "Vincent, listen. I'm sorry. I'm so sorry. We can talk this out. You don't need to do this!"

I tried to pour all the guilt and regret that tangled my insides like barbed wire into my apology. But I knew it didn't matter what I said or how I said it. He was already beyond reason, lost to the monster inside him.

Feral's lips peeled back into a gruesome snarl, his fangs coated all in black. His veins bulged, and his muscles seemed to grow bigger as his whole body expanded.

Then his eyes turned not green, not red, but obsidian black.

That's when I felt it. My every nerve was in agony, like something was trying to pull my whole skeleton from my body.

Whatever that side of Vincent was, it wasn't vampire. It fed on pain.

It dawned on me that he was using the pain I felt from my guilt to gain strength, to grow bigger. Then he mouthed something to me that made the blood in my body crystallize. "*Watch this, Princess.*"

Since he was facing me, Feral's back was turned to Eros, who quickly came up behind him. Eros threw a blow that probably would have been fatal to any mortal man. Apparently, he was looking to end this and fast. There was no panic traceable on his face, but by his grave expression, he knew he had to end the fight now before Feral was too far gone to whatever monster lurked inside him.

It was too late.

The vampire-hybrid was already too big, having grown larger than a normal man ever should. He was tall before. Now he had to be at least eight feet in height. His ink-filled veins, his coal-black eyes, and a bone-chilling sensation smothered the whole warehouse. It was too much. The crowd murmured, and a rush of panicked voices signaled the first stage of total and complete hysteria.

A handful of Salem coven members came up to the cage, ready to step in and halt the fight.

But just as Eros' fist was about to smash into the back of Vincent's skull, his blow met nothing but smoke. The Feral King burst into a cloud of dark smoke, and from the plume, a raven emerged and flew behind Eros.

Vincent morphed into a man again. Eros, disoriented, didn't have time to react as Feral grabbed his hair and slammed him face-first against the cage where I stood.

Pure chaos broke out among the crowd. Humans screamed and bolted upright from their seats. People bolted, pushing and shoving at one another to get to the exit.

The veins and the black eyes could have been excused as makeup. But growing huge in one breath and turning into a literal fucking bird in the next couldn't be brushed off as stage magic. And there was no faking the violence that oozed off this dark creature like a gas leak.

It was all too real.

The Feral King had come completely unhinged.

"Holy *shit!*" By Corry's reaction, he'd never seen Feral's raven form before.

But I had. It had to be the same one I'd seen outside of Sterling's tower on the night of my heat cycle.

"He's never done that before!" Corry's hands were in his hair, his eyes as wide as dinner plates. "Shit, babe. I gotta go help the other vamps round up the humans. They have to be mesmerized. If any of them escape, we're gonna have a colossal mess on our hands."

Like that, Corry was gone, leaving me alone with Feral and Vincent.

Even though the warehouse had erupted into a total state of chaos, Vincent didn't stop beating on Eros. He pulled his opponent back from the cage, whose face was already swelling from the blunt trauma, and held him up by his hair for me to see.

Vincent was so tall by this point, Eros' feet didn't touch the ground. With the way he dangled, the muscular male looked pretty helpless in the monster's grip.

Eros tried his hardest to escape, snarling and thrashing, his hands pulling at Vincent's claws.

Feral slammed him into the cage again. The whole fence rattled. Everything in me trembled. "Vincent, stop!"

I clung to the fence as Feral's monster mashed Eros into the fence again and again. The meshed metal cut into Eros' face, pulverizing his flesh. Inches away from the gruesome beating, my own mate's blood showered me.

Thick gobs of black and clumps of skin stuck to the mesh.

It was horrific.

Feral had completely lost control and was killing his brother, intent on smashing him to death right in front of my face.

"Stop it! Please! Somebody stop him!" I cried and screamed, shaking the fence. I couldn't get to them. The ref and all the other Salem Coven vamps—along with every other supernatural—were too busy rounding up the humans.

Vincent was going to kill Eros, and I was completely helpless to stop it.

The monster that had consumed my dark knight held Eros back, about to crush him against the barrier for what had to be the dozenth time, but he paused when his victim sputtered.

Blood spewed from Eros' mouth as he choked out a few broken words. "D–don't l–let her watch. If you're go–nna k–kill me. D–don't let her watch."

Feral's cavernous laugh stretched down to my heart, and it completely shattered seeing the utter lack of mercy in his hell-dark eyes.

"Don't let her watch?" His voice was unearthly, two-toned like two people were speaking instead of one. "The first time I killed you, there was no family, no friends who cared whether you lived or died. Now you have a mate to watch as the life drains from your eyes."

He threw Eros against the fence again with such brutal force that Eros went completely limp. He was barely more than a beaten, swollen mass of flesh and bone. A pool of black covered the mat, oozing through the mesh fence.

"Stop, please! *Please!*" My cries had gone shrill and ragged. No one was stopping to help.

No one noticed.

The mark on my shoulder was burning so hot I screamed. It hurt so damn fucking much. Because of our mating bond, it was almost like I was on the receiving end of Vincent Feral's brutality.

And he was just using that pain as fuel to do even more damage.

Eros was about to die, and no one was here to stop it. Except for me.

I had to intervene, had to calm Vincent's monster.

With my pulse hammering hard in my ear, I scanned the cage and found the door.

Running to it, I flung myself inside and slammed the door shut behind me, locking myself in with the monster.

CHAPTER SEVENTY-ONE

DANCE WITH THE BEAST

T he moment I entered the ring, the monster lumbered around, turning to face me.

He was so large, his shadow swallowed me whole.

His nostrils flexed, and his mouth contorted into a predatorial grin. He dropped Eros to the ground like a sack of potatoes. Seeing his lifeless form lie there, tears burned my vision.

What in the actual bloody fuck was I doing? I didn't even know what Feral was, but whatever hellish beast had come out to play tonight, it was stronger than me by a landslide.

I was growing stronger by the day, but there was no way I could take on Feral like this. He was as big as a tank, and if he could turn Eros into a pulp with just a few blows, what could he do to me?

Run! My human instincts screamed inside my head. Get the fuck out!

I held my ground.

If I left, Feral would finish off Eros for good.

That wasn't an option. I made a promise to Sterling. I told him I would bring both of them back safe, and damn it, I was going to keep that promise.

With the monster's attention on me, I had to think fast.

I could try to fight him. But even then, what chance did I have of taking him down? Zip. Zero. None.

In the muscle department, Feral could probably wrestle Godzilla and win.

Once again, I was at battle with myself.

My human side wanted to run. But there was that other part of me... The one that scared me sometimes. She was trying to claw her way to the surface.

Oh, God.

The prospect of letting my instincts out to play and lose control right alongside Feral was a scary thought.

But I needed to learn to trust that side of me. I couldn't keep her caged within me forever. I had to trust that she would protect her mate, and if that meant going head to head with Feral in a fight... Bring it the fuck on.

Closing my eyes, I breathed out a steady sigh.

I gave into that part of me, letting my monster out into the open.

The first thing that hit me was the scent.

It was different now that I had shoved my humanity to the periphery of my consciousness.

I could scent a male, a dangerous and lethal one. The unadulterated testosterone wrapped around me like a choker, giving me a wickedly dangerous idea.

This man, this creature, he was an unmarked monster, worthy of mating me.

I purred my approval, releasing the same pheromone that I had the night I mated the silver-haired prince. The female aroma permeated the ring, and I could see the male's eyes change.

They returned to that familiar crimson shade, his pupils blowing up.

"That's right, big boy." I smirked, licking my lips. "When's the last time you had a female of your caliber? I'm guessing never, considering you don't carry a mark."

The virile male rattled a low, seductive growl that made my insides molten. The sizable bulge between his thighs twitched, and his fangs flashed, showing me he thirsted for my blood just as much as he thirsted for my body.

"Brave female," he rasped. "Thinking you can take a male like me between your thighs."

I chuckled a purr, stalking around the perimeter of the ring, enjoying the way his eyes followed me like I was the only woman to exist in the entire world.

This was the hunt, the mating dance. The last time I had done this, it had been with a full-blooded vampire.

Feral was some wild, monstrous half-blood. He was so huge, his gym shorts were almost busting at the seams, and by the mass of the piece that hung between his thighs, it was no friend to womankind.

But my options were limited here, and if anyone could handle The Feral King, it was me.

"Believe me." I bit my lips as they took on an impish, taunting smile. "I can take way more than you can dish out. But I welcome you to come over here and try to prove me wrong."

Another vicious growl tore from him, making my bones rattle. He stomped toward me, his tremendous strides eating the distance between us.

"I will make you mine, woman. I'll cover you in so many of my marks, no other male will dare look at you again."

I shivered with dark delight at his devilish threat. His claws snatched for me, and I danced out of his reach. He was bigger than me, but in this form, he was far slower.

He snarled his frustration, whirling to grab me again. "I will have you so full of my cum, so satisfied you will never stray to one of my brothers again. Mark me, woman. You will submit to the superior male."

Rolling my eyes, a brittle laugh slipped from me. "Submit? I don't fucking think so. Maybe to Eros, but you don't deserve my submission."

The monster reached to snatch me yet again, and I timed my jump perfectly. Dodging Vincent's outstretched claws, I leaped onto his arm and scrambled up onto his back.

He released a primal roar as he swung his massive arms, trying to pluck me off his back, but I was too quick for him.

"Stupid male. It's you who will submit to me." I slammed my fangs into his shoulder, his heady blood gushing into my mouth. At first, he fought my bite. But no matter how much he tried to shake me off, I clung fast to him.

Unlatching my jaw from him for just a second, I slammed my fangs down on his throat. He swayed dangerously, and I bit him again and again.

He finally collapsed to his knees. The whole ring quaked dangerously beneath the weight. The moment he hit the ground, I pulled my fangs from him and brought my mouth to his ear.

"Yield to me," I whispered in a voice so soft I took even myself by surprise, "and I will make you my claimed mate. You will not be my king. You will be my mate. And while you will never have the honor of wearing my father's crown, I will give you a child, Vincent Feral. A blood heir."

My words hit their mark. Vincent convulsed violently as if he was having a seizure. He was fighting his monster for control. To help him regain himself, I stroked his hair and purred into his ear. "Yield for me, baby."

A low whine of a purr reverberated from his throat, followed by fateful words that I couldn't believe were coming from his lips. "I yield to you, my queen. My mate. My monster."

"That's right, I am yours." I held onto him tight even as his body shrunk back to its normal size.

Vincent had regained his vampire self. We both lay there on the mat, in Eros' blood, breathing heavily.

After several tense moments, he turned to look at me, his eyes green once again. "Did you mean what you said?"

"Every word."

His brows pulled together, his gaze filling with shadows. "Even after you saw what I am? You'd still have me?"

"Monster and all."

When he spoke next, his voice had returned to its old, baritone cadence, but it was laced with a new emotion. "Why?"

"Because monsters aren't afraid of other monsters."

The vampire stared at me with a thunderstruck expression. He pulled himself up into a sitting position, wobbling slightly as if he was waking up from a dream.

He put distance between us when his attention swung back to Eros. "Little monster, do you see what I am capable of now? Do you see how dangerous I am?"

"I see. But do you? Don't you get it now? This is why Eros killed your father, Vincent. The father you knew and loved wasn't the same thing as the monster inside him. Just like the part of you I have come to..." My voice shook. "Love." I gulped, waiting with bated breath to see how he would react to my confession.

He turned his face away from me, so I couldn't see his reaction. When he spoke, his voice came out in a tentative whisper. "I understand now. There was a side of him he couldn't control. I never saw it. I haven't seen this side of myself in a long time. Not since becoming a vampire. I thought it had died with the rest of my abilities. But it was triggered tonight. I see what I am truly capable of now, and it horrifies me. Now that I've come to care about you so much, I have no business being with you."

My chest filled with ice. "What are you talking about? Didn't I just prove that I can handle you?"

Vincent shook his head as he got to his feet. I grabbed his arm, but he shook me off. "Maybe this time. But I've never lost it like that before. I was triggered because I saw him with you and... Next time I just might kill him. It's not that I don't want to share you, Ruby. I'm fine with it. It's the fact that my monster isn't. He's territorial, and I know now I can't be around you anymore. Not if it means keeping you safe."

"What? No!" He started to leave the ring, but I beat him to the cage door, spreading my arms wide. "You can't leave me! As your princess, I forbid it."

The look on Feral's face broke my heart into a million pieces.

"Goodbye, Princess." He pushed me out of his way like I weighed little more than a feather.

"What do you mean, goodbye? You're not leaving the coven, are you? Vincent! Vincent! Don't leave me, please!"

My pathetic pleas were wasted.

He was already gone.

Gone.

Did he leave the coven for good? Was he truly giving up his pursuit of the throne? His pursuit of me?

A coldness settled over my soul that made me shiver.

I couldn't process this sort of emotion right now. Eros was still slumped face down in his own blood.

On my hands and knees, I crawled over to him and flipped him over. He was still alive!

Sitting up, I skimmed the warehouse, searching the scattered mass of people. Humans were still fleeing for their lives, wolves herding them like sheepdogs gathering cattle. They were bringing groups to the vampires where they had the humans on their knees in a line, mind-wiping them one by one.

Corry was nowhere to be found.

Eros was too heavy for me to carry by myself. Vincent could have carried him, but... *He left.*

Bitter ash stung my tongue.

Why did this hurt so much?

Why did I give a shit if he left?

Because I was in love with him. Hopelessly. It was a brutal kind of love, but it was one that called to that monster inside me, making her purr like no other could.

A set of shoes came into my view, and I looked up, hoping to see Corry. Instead, I was met with a swallowed face, dark eyes, and greasy hair. My lips curled into a snarl.

"*You.* Stay away from us!"

Sharpe let out a sigh, his dark eyes running over Eros in appraisal. "Princess, I know how you feel about me. But I am the coven's doctor. I need to examine your mate."

I narrowed my eyes. "Why are you even here? Did you come with Lexi?"

His lips slanted with a frown. "No. I've been here. I attend the matches in case things like this happen."

That was weird.

Wouldn't Sterling have mentioned that little detail if it was true?

And why was he making his presence known now, when it was almost too late?

"There isn't the time for you to decide if you can trust me or not, Princess Ruby. Normally our kind can only die by beheading and staking, but he's lost a tremendous amount of blood."

I knew Eros didn't have the luxury of time. As much as I loathed and distrusted Sharpe, this wasn't the time and the place for that.

Nodding, I stood back, allowing the doctor to scoop Eros into his arms. I began to follow them out of the ring, but the doctor stopped me with a sharp glance.

"I'm going to take him to the back. Alone. Give us some privacy, at least for a few minutes."

I gave an uneasy nod and watched them disappear into the back.

Five minutes passed, which felt like an eternity. Then my mark grew steadily colder, and when it dropped to almost freezing, I knew something was wrong.

Very wrong.

I scanned the crowd for Corry, but there were only strangers.

Something in my gut told me I didn't have the time to search for him. Leaving the ring, I practically sprinted to the back to find the locker room completely empty.

The back door was open, swinging on its hinges.

They were gone. What the fuck? Where could they have gone? My thoughts exploded into full panic mode.

Logic told me that Sharpe had taken him back to the coven, where there were more supplies and equipment.

But I wasn't going off facts. I was going off how I felt.

My mark was so cold, as cold as death.

My mate was in danger.

I hadn't the slightest clue where Sharpe was taking Eros, but I was sure as shit that it wasn't to get medical care. The other guys would be furious knowing I left to find Eros alone, especially on Boston Coven territory.

Still, somehow, I knew there wasn't time to get help. Sharpe was using Eros to lure me away from the other vampires.

The good doctor had to be the mole.

And damn it, I was the idiot about to take the bait.

Chapter Seventy-Two
RESCUE

The parking lot was as chaotic as it was inside the warehouse. People were being released once they were mesmerized, and they were all stumbling back to their cars, their faces wearing dazed expressions. It was like an episode of *The Walking Dead*.

I ran through the crowd, making my way to the motorcycles. My throat constricted when my eyes landed on Corry's bike. He was still here. Of course, he was here. He wouldn't have left without me.

I wish I had the luxury of giving him the same courtesy. He wouldn't want me leaving without him. Not to mention Sterling would have a total conniption once he found out I had disobeyed his orders. But there wasn't time to look for an escort. The mating mark on my shoulder was so cold, it burned. I had to clench my teeth to keep myself from screaming. Eros was in serious peril, and this excruciating pain wouldn't go away until he was back with me, safe and sound.

Wrestling the keys out of my hoodie pocket, I slapped myself onto Corry's Ninja, started the engine, and tore out of the parking lot in a spray of gravel and exhaust smoke.

Navigating the streets of Boston should have been impossible, not just because I'd never been to the city before or had next to no driving experience, but because I had no idea where Sharpe had taken Eros. By all rights, I shouldn't have had the slightest clue where to go. Yet, by some insane miracle, I did. It had to be my mating mark on Eros' hand; it was like a tracking device with the receiver buried deep in the fabric of my being.

Corry had mentioned that mated couples could always find one another. At the time, that little fact had made me pretty damn nervous. I didn't like the idea of the depraved Deathwish keeping tabs on me. Now, I was thankful because if we were lucky, it would save Eros' life.

Sharpe couldn't have gotten far with Eros. By my estimation, they hadn't even left the city. With how my mark was throbbing and easing from sharp agony to a dull nuisance, I knew I was getting closer.

My pulse was on the rise as the trail led me out of the densely populated city center of Boston through a residential area to a shady part of town filled with old industrial buildings and factories.

When my mark burned hot like a brand, I stopped the bike alongside the curb outside a huge lot with a factory beside it. Judging by all the broken windows and the graffiti on the brick walls, the place was abandoned. A tall chain-link fence surrounded the lot, with a gate that was cracked open.

I strode over to the gate and peered down at a busted chain with a locked padlock still attached, laying on the ground. The chain that had been holding the gate closed hadn't been removed by bolt cutters. The links had been pried open. Only a vampire could pull off strength like that.

Peering inside the lot, I spotted a black BMW parked in the back beside the factory's roll-up door. I'd seen that car a thousand times parked in the driveway outside my bedroom window whenever Dr. Sharpe made house calls.

I had to hand it to the slick fuck. This was a good place for an ambush. Or at least, that's what I fully expected to be waiting for me inside the factory. This entire area was so isolated, it looked straight out of the apocalypse. No one would hear my screams here. I shivered, folding my arms around myself.

I knew it was stupid coming here alone. But Eros was in danger, and the monster inside me wasn't going to stop and wait for someone to rescue her mate for her.

Slipping through the gap in the chain-link fence, I cringed at the fresh memory of Eros' face mashed into one of these. I knew darkness lurked inside Vincent Feral, but I could have never guessed the extent of fucked-up savagery to which he was capable.

I was scared for Eros, and I was pretty damn terrified of what Sharpe had in store for me. Adding the fact that Vincent just *left* on top of it all was just too much to unload at the moment. How could he just leave me like that? After I pretty much came out with my true feelings, he turned his back and left me. Even after proving I could handle him.

Me. The half-human Vincent had patronized on the reg had made the notorious Feral King submit.

He had been horrified by the destruction the other part of him had caused. I would have thought he'd been aware of his other nature. Then again, Vincent did say he thought that part of him had died when he was turned into a vampire. Now that he knew it had just been dormant, and his jealousy had awoken it, he didn't think it was safe to be around me.

Stupid male.

All the guys needed to understand that I could handle them, no matter what kind of baggage they had. I wanted them, and whatever twisted fetishes, dark pasts, and monstrous appetites any of them could throw my way. I decided right then that if I managed to get out of this place alive, the first thing I'd do would be to hunt Vincent down and tell him how it was going to be.

He was going to be my mate, along with the others. And he was going to let me love him, damn it. Monster and all.

I raised my hand to my tiara, remembering the tracker. Corry would have realized I'd left by now. Would he get here in time?

Would he bring Sterling?

I wished I could wait for them. But there just wasn't time. I could sense Eros inside. He was badly hurt, and there was no reasoning with my instincts. Everything inside pushed me toward my mate.

Scanning the exterior of the building, my attention landed on a door that had been left open. Getting closer, the little hairs on my nape bristled when I picked up

Sharpe's scent. My heart lifted when I detected the soothing aroma of cloves and smoke just beneath Sharpe's.

Pushing my way through, I found myself in a huge room filled with heavy machinery. The place was creepy as hell, with conveyor belts, rusted metal scraps lying around, and huge hooks dangling from the ceiling. Whatever this facility had produced, it had only been abandoned for a hot minute. It smelled stale and vaguely of a dead animal, not to mention all the creaking. The whole building groaned quietly, chains shifting in a windless breeze.

It reminded me of a dark dream, perhaps belonging to some ancient god.

It was spooky as fuck.

"Ruby? Damn it. Please, for the love of blood, tell me that's not you," a familiar voice, though weak and grated, sounded from the center of the room.

With my heart in my throat, I crawled over the equipment to see Eros on the ground. He'd been dumped unceremoniously on a pile of leaves and trash that was now soaked through with blood. He lifted his face, and my stomach cartwheeled, seeing how swollen and angry his flesh still was. His body was trying its best to heal, but something was binding his arms behind his back which just seemed to be hurting him even more. By the sour scent of charred flesh, I ventured a guess that it was silver.

The vampire gave a pained growl the moment he registered me, but I had a feeling it had little to do with his wounds. "*No!* No, you shouldn't have come!"

He looked pissed, enraged that I had come for him. I crumpled to my knees beside him, running my hand through his blond hair, crusted in black blood. "I couldn't leave you to die."

"You had to know this was a trap. You have to run, now!"

My fists clenched into balls on my thighs, and I shook my head. "No, I'm not leaving without you."

A jarring snarl unleashed from deep in Eros' chest, struggling against the cuffs on his wrist, steam from his sizzling flesh coiling up through the air. For a second, I thought his rage was directed at me, but his blazing glare was directed to something behind me.

With my pulse set to warp speed, I turned to see Sharpe stepping out from the shadows. He wasn't alone. At least a dozen men flanked his sides. They were equipped with assault rifles and earpieces, looking like the villain's cronies from some shlocky spy movie. They fanned out, surrounding us with their guns pointed.

"Silver bullets," Sharpe said through a malevolent smile. "If you're wondering if bullets can kill vampires, silver-tipped bullets can, so I'd advise you not to take the advice of your mate, Princess. My employer will be very unhappy if I bring you back dead. However, seeing as he is a powerful necromancer, it won't be too much of a grievance."

A chill skittered down my spine that sunk deep into my bones, all the way down to the marrow. Sharpe's statement had been terrifyingly informative. First, Feral had been right.

Sharpe was the mole working for the Boston Coven.

Second, they were armed with silver, and they didn't seem too bent up about the prospect of murdering us.

Lastly, whoever he was working for was a...necromancer? The fact that magic existed made sense. If vampires could wipe the memory of humans, and people could turn into ravens and wolves, of course, magic existed. But *necromancy?* What a terrifying power that no one should have, especially evil vampire overlords.

Eros spat blood in Sharpe's direction. "Traitor! How can you work for the Boston Coven trash? And since when is their leader a necromancer?"

Sharpe's beady eyes glittered with impish amusement. It made my stomach heave, seeing just how much twisted enjoyment he was getting from this whole situation. "Oh no, Erik isn't a necromancer, and I don't work for him. We serve the same master, however."

"And who is that?" I demanded, rising to my feet.

Sharpe's grin spread wide as if he was about to deliver a long-anticipated punchline to a good joke. "Why, Dagon Knight, of course. The true heir to the throne."

A barbed silence settled over the room, which was shattered a few beats later by Eros' sneer. "Dagon Knight, the true heir to the throne? You're kidding. He's not even supposed to be alive. He was murdered on account of being as crazy as our maker! The Elders would never appoint him to the throne."

"The Elders." A vein bulged in Sharpe's brow, his tone dripping with sardonicism. "The rest of the Elders will acknowledge Dagon Knight as the true king once he's the only living heir."

Eros let out a dark bark of a laugh. "So that's your great plan? You're going to kill us? I might be halfway to Hell already, but what about Feral? And Corry Cross? Even if you manage to murder them and cover it up, what about Sterling? You and your whole trash coven aren't strong enough to face him, let alone the rest of the powerful vampire families supporting us. It would take an entire army, which you don't have. Boston Coven might be the largest den of vampires on the East Coast, but they're not strong enough to take us down, not with every other den on the continent loyal to the Elders behind us."

"You're right. If this blew out into a full war, we would lose in all likelihood. The Elders would never agree to give Dagon the throne unless he was the last option. Therefore, you and your brothers must die. And you're right. We're not strong enough to kill all of you." Sharpe licked his lips, his shit-eating grin making my skin crawl. "But Thomas Knight is."

My heart stopped for a second. I looked down at Eros, who looked just as lost as I felt.

"Didn't you get the memo?" Eros said after he regained himself. "Thomas Knight is dead."

"For now. Once Dagon Knight completes the ritual on devil's night, the night when the land between the deceased and the living is the thinnest, the old king will return to the living world for twenty-four hours."

Bring back Thomas Knight from the dead? No. That couldn't be possible... Could it? The hairs on the back of my neck stood up, and I swallowed thickly, trying to gulp down the swelling lump in my throat. "Even if it was possible to bring him back, a maniacal bastard like yourself has to understand how dangerous that's going to be? Why would you even want to bring him back?" I asked Sharpe, almost too afraid of the answer.

"Haven't you worked it out yet, Princess? Your father never wanted you to be queen. He never named you his heir. *I lied.* He would have let you rot in Quincy. Your father didn't care what happened to you, so long as none of his sons put their hands on you. He didn't even like me going to visit you while you were growing up, and he wouldn't have allowed my house visits if they hadn't been completely necessary."

My jaw dropped to the floor. "That explains why you came up with the idea for me to choose a mate among the princes. You were hoping I would mate them all! That way, when Dagon resurrects my father, he'd be driven into a jealous rage and kill them all."

"Very good." The doctor gave me a greasy smile, almost like he was proud of me for working it out. "Performing a powerful spell to resurrect your possessive father simply so he'll kill all the other prospective heirs is far easier than going to war with the Elders and the covens they govern. This way, the Elders can still appoint a Knight heir to the throne. Bloodshed will be minimal and mostly done on behalf of the dead king."

"That's crazy! Let's say you somehow can bring back the vampire king for twenty-four hours. How can you be so sure he's going to kill his progeny?"

To my surprise, it wasn't Sharpe that answered. "He's right, doll," Eros muttered. "Over the centuries, your father has turned thousands of poor bastards. And only four remain, maybe five by the sound of it. He's never had any qualms about killing his progeny."

"Yes," Sharpe said with a gleeful smile. "He's killed over the pettiest things. Getting bloodstains on his favorite furniture, failing to dust his coffin, making too much noise while he's feeding. He would have murdered all four of your precious princes for daring to carry your name in their mouths. But Corry has kissed you, Eros has stripped you of your virtue, and Vincent speaks of impregnating you."

My body broke out into a cold sweat as the doctor took a step forward, along with his goons, all of their guns still held at the ready. Eros snarled, trying to crawl in front of me to protect me. But judging by the sharp pressure building beneath my mating mark, he was in so much pain, he couldn't even stand.

"Then there is Sterling," Sharpe continued with a snicker. "Your father's mate."

I clenched my fists, my blood turning hot with my ire. "He was never his mate. He was his victim."

"Call it what you will. Your father placed his mating mark on Sterling, and you covered it with your own. Once Thomas Knight has risen, he'll kill you both."

"Which will leave the throne empty, making room for Dagon Knight."

"That's right."

I let out a balk of a brittle laugh. "And you just expect the rest of the Elders to be cool with this psycho plan?"

"Well, it's that, or they go to war with us. The only thing the council wants is minimal bloodshed and the most capable Knight heir on the throne. They do so love their traditions. And once they see what he can do—"

"Fuck you, Sharpe." I'd heard enough. I flipped him off, seething with fury. "You won't get away with this."

The vampire heaved an exasperated sigh as he swept his hand over his greasy hair. "I tire of this. Seize them."

Two of the men closest to us slung their guns over their backs and started forward. They hesitated momentarily when Eros released a guttural roar, a ferocious warning that even had me shaking.

"Touch my mate and lose more than a hand," Eros spat on a violent growl.

This was the Deathwish I had come to know and love. Here he was, bleeding out on the ground, bound in silver with a face that looked like it'd been to battle with a cheese grater, and these guys with guns were still practically shitting themselves.

"He's half-dead, you idiots! He isn't a threat," Sharpe snapped at them. "Grab them!"

The first man approached and got a face full of my fist for his trouble. He stumbled back, his shocked expression freezing into a permanent state as I ripped his head clean off with both my hands. I lobbed the head at the second man, who looked fit to shit his spine as the head made a sickening *thunk* against his chest before falling to his feet.

"It's just one female!" Sharpe bellowed, gesturing for every vampire to move forward. "Surely a dozen men can overpower a little half-blood!"

I slammed my fist into the chest cavity of the second man who dared approach me and tore out his heart. I let it fall to the ground with a *splat* and cackled a laugh. This, *this* was my monster coming out to play. And for once, I wasn't lost to her. We were in this as one, both of my halves coming together to create a lethal weapon.

A third man charged, and I mowed him down with ease, painting the concrete floor in his dark blood. But when the rest got smart and surrounded me in a tight circle, closing in, I was trapped.

There were too many of them.

One of them flanked my side, the butt of his rifle aimed at my head like he was ready to knock me out.

The next series of events unfolded so quickly, I could barely discern what was happening.

A streak of black bolted in through one of the broken windows. It moved so fast it was a blur of feathers and black smoke. In the blink of an eye, a half-naked man stood between the vampires and me, ready to strike.

He drove his fist into the lesser vampire's head with such force, the vampire's skull caved in, and he crumpled to the concrete in a broken heap.

The male twisted his head to shoot me a sideways glance, his green eyes sparkling, raven tattoos glistening beneath a coat of sweat.

My heart squeezed, and if this had been the time and place to cry for joy, I would have.

Vincent Feral had come back for me.

Chapter Seventy-Three

Rain of Silver

Vincent Feral had come back for me.

My chest filled with so much warmth, I thought I might explode with a new sense of hope. With him, maybe we had a shot at making it out of this factory alive.

I wanted to slap Vincent for leaving me like he had. At the same time, I wanted to kiss him for coming back. But there was no time to do either.

Eros' ragged screams of pain brought me crashing down from my temporary euphoric high that Feral's entrance had created. My mate writhed in agony at my feet, his body going stiff, his teeth grinding, the tendons going so taut in his neck I thought they might snap.

It didn't make any sense. Vampires were supposed to have rapid regeneration abilities, so why wasn't he healing?

As Feral's form grew larger right before my eyes, I began to grasp what was happening.

Vincent's muscles bulged, and his bones cracked as they stretched to impossible proportions. When he hulked out like this at the fight, he'd done it by accident. Now, he was morphing into a huge beast-version of himself on purpose, using Eros' pain as fuel.

I hated that Eros had to suffer to fuel this weapon, but in this situation, it was absolutely necessary. And if it wasn't for the fact that Eros had passed out again, he'd probably agree.

Feral was now at least nine, maybe even ten feet tall. He was slabs of muscle on muscle, and he took up so much space the other vampires had to jump back, stunned by the sheer size of the mammoth-sized vampire.

"Shoot him!" Sharpe's shrill voice splintered with fresh panic.

"But Sir," one of them interjected, his gun awkwardly pointed to the floor. "What if we hit the princess? Doesn't Lord Dagon need her for the ritual?"

"If she gets hurt, we can heal her with blood from the hybrid's corpse. Shoot him!"

Vincent didn't waste another damn second. Leveraging the hesitation from the lesser vampires to our advantage, he scooped me up in one arm and tossed me over his shoulder. He did it so fast that his rock-hard muscles knocked the wind from my lungs as I was slung over him like a sack of flour.

I held my breath—or what little I had left—because for one moment there, I thought Vincent was going to leave Eros to his fate. But relief eased the tightness in my chest when Vincent stooped to lift his unconscious rival and hauled him over his other shoulder.

A spray of bullets hailed down on metal, the ear-rattling sound echoing through the whole factory as Vincent hauled ass around a corner just in time. Thankfully, we found ourselves in a hallway large enough to fit Vincent's titan form.

The factory was huge, with a maze of doors and concrete tunnels. We headed deeper into the facility, which was great for getting Sharpe and his men off our tails but not so great for finding an exit. "Fucking shit..." Feral mumbled to himself as he came to yet another dead end.

"Put me down. I can walk now," I told him. He hesitated for a beat, then set me on my feet. A span of awkward silence prevailed as I gawked up at him in awe, my gaze flickering between his, searching.

He didn't look any different, other than the fact that he reminded me of one of those little toy animals you drop in water that blows up overnight. It was still Vincent, with his unkempt jet black hair, his chiseled jawline, strong nose, and raven tattoos.

The last time I saw this tank-like version of him, he hadn't been himself. It was the base instincts of his other race in control, not Feral. But something was different this time.

"Vincent?" I paused in the hallway, and he stopped and turned to look at me.

"What?"

"So it is you in there?"

His brows furrowed with mild irritation. "Who else would it be?"

"Hmm... I don't know. Maybe the mysterious monster who would have mated me in the ring under the noses of everyone if I hadn't subdued him?"

Vincent let out a great snort. "We are the same person, Princess. It's just been hidden away until now. You bring out that side of me." He lumbered closer, his eyes darting down the hall to make sure the coast was clear before looking back at me with a twisted sneer. "Doesn't that scare you?"

I jutted my chin out, lifting my head to meet his glare with one of my own. It didn't matter that he was the size of a truck, Vincent Feral didn't scare me, and he never would.

"I already told you, monsters aren't scared of other monsters. Besides, I made you submit to me, remember?"

Maybe it was a trick of the dark, but if I wasn't mistaken, his lips twitched with the ghost of a smirk. "I don't think I'll ever forget that."

"So why did you come back?"

He squared his shoulders and readjusted Eros in his grip before turning away from me, stomping down the tunnel in search of an escape route. "I shouldn't have ever left you."

"No, you shouldn't have. And you can't ever leave again, not now that we know this Dagon Knight is capable of necromancy." I paused, tamping down on an ugly emotion that tried to unfurl in my belly. "Do you really think he can bring my dad back from the dead?"

Every muscle in Vincent's body clenched. He tilted his face in my direction, his expression hard and filled with shadows. "I don't know. All I know is we have to get you back to the Cape. We can't let them get their hands on you. I don't know what kind of 'ritual' they need you for, but whatever it is, it sounds like you're the key to bringing him back."

"With this new ability—or I guess—your reawakened ability, we have to have some sort of advantage. You seem perfectly in control of your instincts—"

The sound of gunfire cut my words short. Vincent grabbed me and flung us into the nearest room. "Fuck!"

My heart sunk to my feet, seeing he'd found yet another dead end. It was like someone had specifically manufactured this place for a horror movie.

There was no time to double back and find an alternative path. If we went back into the hallway, we'd be shot. We had to find a way out of here.

The room Vincent had thrown us into looked to be some sort of garage, and at the end sat a large roll-up style metal door. It had to be the same one I saw from the outside. That meant this would make for a perfect escape. That is if it wasn't for the fact that the door was completely blocked from the inside with huge shelving units, machinery, and other junk.

Vincent set Eros and me carefully on the floor and frantically started to tear apart the barricade, heaving random pieces of junk over his shoulder.

Since this stuff was too heavy for me to move, all I could do was watch as he dug through the mess, freeing the path to the door piece by piece.

His strength was impressive, seeing him hurl huge chunks of metal that were easily bigger than my whole body as if they were made of balsa wood.

Would he free the entrance in time?

The seconds were counting down, and I felt like every breath leaving my body brought us closer to what could very well be our end.

My heart thundered hard in my chest, making me think of how just over a week ago, my biggest fear was not letting my pulse climb too high. My whole life had been completely flipped on its head. I had been so resistant to my new life at first, now I couldn't imagine living any other way.

I would be the vampire queen. It was my destiny, and I didn't need a king by my side to rule. But I would need all four of my father's progeny by my side, as my mates. Together we would figure out a way to kill this Dagon Knight before he could resurrect my father.

They all made me strong in different ways. I couldn't do it without them.

I could hear heavy footsteps stomping closer.

"Bloody hell, Vincent, hurry!"

"Working on it," he grunted as he lifted an enormous piece of equipment—a forklift—and tossed it aside with a deafening clatter. It was the last item to be removed. The way was now clear. All we had to do was open the door.

Just as Vincent reached to snatch off the padlock holding the roller door shut, Sharpe's men poured into the room.

"Kill him!" the doctor commanded, the two syllables sinking to the bottom of my gut like a thousand-ton anchor.

The room lit up with the light coming from the guns.

Bullets hailed down on us.

Vincent threw himself on top of me and his brother, shielding us with his own body.

"*NOOOO!*" My scream was lost in the chaos.

I laid there on my back beneath my dark knight, staring up into his eyes as he took countless silver bullets to his back. His body jerked violently with every bullet that found its mark.

He opened his mouth to speak, blood gushing from his lips. When he spoke, it was a miracle I heard him at all through the blast of all the rifle fire.

"I was wrong..." he choked out, barely able to cobble words together.

Tears welled in my eyes. "About what?"

"Two things. The first was that day in the corridor when I told you that Thomas Knight's progeny weren't capable of loving you. I was wrong." He shuddered and clenched his jaw, holding out for as long as he could as silver bullets continued to rain down on him, shells clattering to the concrete all around us. "We love you. Even me—" Vincent faltered and winced as he moved to place a bloody kiss on my lips. "*Especially* me."

I tried to blink my tears away, but they were flowing freely now. "Vincent..."

"The second thing that I was wrong about is you." His eyes blazed with a fire that warmed my whole being, burning hot and bright. He cupped my cheeks, streaking my skin in his blood. "You, My Queen, will bring the world to its knees. Your enemies will fall before you in terror, your allies will kneel in piety, and your mates will bow down to you in fucking unholy worship."

On the same breath, he raised a hulking arm and smashed his fist through the door, knocking it clean off its hinges. He raised his body to shield me from the bullets. "Now, run."

"I–I can't leave you!"

He was shaking, struggling to even hold himself up with his arms. "For fuck's sake, *RUN!*"

I don't know how I found my feet, but I did. I sprinted out of the garage and ran as fast as my feet could carry me.

I couldn't stop myself from casting one last glance over my shoulder.

I shouldn't have looked.

Vincent Feral was lying lifeless on the ground.

Dead.

Gone.

Even in death, he was the constant protector. A knight through and through. Not only had he used the last breath in his lungs to help me escape, but he had curled himself around Eros to protect him from getting shot.

I was numb all over.

My legs pumped, carrying my body forward as I ran, but I couldn't feel anything.

Vincent was dead. If it had been normal bullets, he would have survived, but they were silver.

And even though Vincent had saved Eros from the initial gunfire, Sharpe would probably finish him off next.

All I wanted to do was curl up into a ball and recede inside myself. But I couldn't. Vincent had sacrificed his life to earn me a few precious extra seconds. I couldn't waste them. I wouldn't let his sacrifice be in vain.

My boots slapped hard against the gravel lot as I ran faster than I ever had in my life.

The second I made it to where I'd left my bike parked on the street, I reached for my keys. My hands were tremoring so badly, I dropped the keys as I pulled them from my hoodie pocket. "Shit!"

Picking them up, I threw myself onto the bike and had a total panic attack when the bike wouldn't start.

Oh, God. It wasn't starting! Someone had tampered with it while I was inside.

Abandoning the vehicle, I opted to make a run for it. What else was there to do? I still wore the tiara. It had to be how Vincent had tracked me, meaning Sterling and Corry couldn't be too far away.

I almost didn't want them to come. I couldn't survive losing anyone else.

No, I couldn't think about that right now. I had to do what Vincent told me.

Run.

So that's what I did. I ran so hard my lungs burned, and my feet ached. It was so cold that my breath froze in clouds in front of me, and tears crusted my cheeks.

I ran until my body screamed, but the pain couldn't compare to the agony of leaving my heart in pieces, nestled between the bodies of the two men I was never supposed to fall in love with.

Chapter Seventy-Four

REVELATIONS AND A SORDID PROMISE

I ran so fast, my mind was in a whirlwind, and my lungs heaved in pain as I took in a huge gulp of the frigid night air.

The only illumination of the deserted road splicing through this industrial area came from a handful of street lamps. Most of them had burnt out, leaving only a few flickering light bulbs, their ominous glow bathing everything in orange.

This whole place was freaky. It had to belong to the Boston Coven. It was the perfect place to lure and hunt down prey, with no civilization around to hear their screams.

Little did Sharpe and the rest of his coven know I wasn't prey. I was the predator here. At least, that's what the monster inside me was sure of. She wanted to kill, maim, and make them suffer.

But the rest of me... All I felt was nothingness.

They'd broken me. I had run from that factory in pieces, and I would have to figure out how to put myself back together so I could make Sharpe pay for what they'd done. What he'd taken from me.

Sharpe had said this plot of theirs was all to avoid a full-out war. But the second Vin had died, they'd sealed their fate.

They didn't want a war, but that's exactly what they were going to get.

I would make them suffer. Before, I had feared the monstrous nature that I knew I had inherited from the old vampire king. Now, I wanted to unleash it in full force on my enemies, and I would leave a fucking crater where the Boston Coven once stood so that no one would forget that even though human blood coursed through my veins, so did Thomas Knight's.

Hell, I'd probably make dear old dad proud. I never wanted to stoop to his level of cruelty, but seeing Vincent and Eros laying there on the concrete in a pool of blood... It twisted my insides into painful knots, squeezing another round of fresh tears from me.

My heart had been ripped out, and the only thing I could fill it with was the satisfaction I'd ultimately get by avenging them.

As much as I wanted to turn around and tear off Sharpe's head, tonight was not the night to make him pay.

I needed Corry and Sterling. Where in the bloody hell were they? I knew they were coming for me. I could feel it. My mark on Sterling's throat was getting closer. He had definitely left the Cape, and thank fuck for the tiara. Otherwise, they wouldn't know where to find me.

They'd want me to find a safe place to hide until they reached me. I swept my gaze over the industrial area, and when I spotted an alley, I ducked into it. Running at breakneck speed, I almost collided with the man that rounded the corner at the other end.

Screeching to a halt, everything in me cringed, seeing who it was.

"*You.* You murdered Vincent! You're a fucking traitor!" Seeing Sharpe standing in front of me with a look on his face that was all disgust and pity, my insides heaved.

I screamed my fury, releasing my agony in a piercing wail that split the night. Somewhere far off, dogs began to howl.

"How?" I demanded, my tone fraught with anger and grief. "How could you do something like this? You butchered him." My legs wouldn't hold me for a second longer. They shook, and I felt my knees hit the wet, filthy cement of the alley.

Sharpe took a step forward, looking down his nose at me like I was nothing but trash. "Look at you. Ruby Renada Baxter. How you've grown. No matter how hard we tried to keep you sheltered, you ended up just like your mother after all. She was fierce and wild, just like you. Until those she loved were hurt, that is. Then she'd do exactly what you are doing now. She'd crumble into a helpless heap and cry like the pathetic human she was."

I looked up at him through my tangle of red hair, blinking in confusion. "My mother was never fierce or wild. She was scared of me. She hid behind her crucifix and locked doors."

The doctor's mouth split into a manic grin, his eyes completely devoid of anything that could be classified as good or merciful. "Stupid girl. You still think that mortal was your mother? She was just a woman the coven paid to shelter you. We compensated very well. She had to be, considering how frightened of you she was."

A chill pulsated through me, filling my body with ice. What was he talking about? My mother wasn't actually my mother? If not her, who?

What was even real anymore? Had everything I'd known been a lie?

Sharpe took a step closer until he was standing over me. He canted his head, his lip peeling as he regarded me like I was just a piece of gum stuck to his shoe. "For a moment there, I thought you might truly make a half-decent queen. But look at you. Take your mates from you, and you're reduced to a shaking, blubbering disgrace. It was a shame what had to be done back there. It was almost moving, hearing Feral admit his feelings for you. You have a way of wrapping the hearts of hopeless males around your finger, don't you?"

He chuckled, his serpent's tongue flicking out to lick his lips. "I had hoped you would take a liking to all the princes so that the old king would be tempted to kill them upon his resurrection. But I didn't think they would be quite so taken with you in return. Corry, yes. Eros and Vincent were a surprise. But the biggest shock of all was when you managed to steal the heart of the jaded Sterling."

"You keep their names out of your mouth, asshole!"

Sharpe stooped to a crouching position, getting to eye level with me. It was something an adult would do with a child, something he had done with me when I was a child.

Sharpe still saw me as that child. It would be his downfall. He couldn't even begin to fathom the sort of strength I possessed. Hell, I was barely coming to terms with it myself. But I did know that I had every ability to make this fucker hurt.

I moved so fast, he didn't have time to react. Plucking my tiara from my head, I mustered all my strength to drive the silver teeth of it deep into his eye socket. He reared back, his vocal cords fraying as he screamed bloody murder. His skin smoked around the silver as if he was being branded.

Standing to my full height, I shoved the tiara into my hoodie pocket, and for one oh-so-satisfying moment, I watched him squirm at my feet.

I would have torn his head off right there if it hadn't been for the other Boston vampires who surrounded me, dragging me down the alley toward a black van parked out on the street.

They'd caught me. But this wasn't over. Fuck no. These idiots were all about underestimating me. It would be the last thing they ever did.

I hoped they were taking me back to their den. I would tear it down from the inside with my own two hands.

I would make them scream.

I would bathe in their blood.

I'd dance on their ashes.

One of the vampires opened the back door to the van, and it took another two to toss me in, right between the bodies of Eros and Vincent.

A chill swallowed me.

I clamped my eyes closed, trying to hold my shit together.

Keep it together, Ruby. If you're going to be a vampire queen, you have to be okay with people dying. Hell, they were already dead. My attempt to console myself only seemed to drive the sharp knife of grief deeper into the hole where my heart had been.

A numb paralysis spread through my limbs, slowly taking over my entire being.

At least I was able to fend off another wave of tears until the van's doors slammed shut behind me, leaving me alone with the bodies of my lovers.

"Why? Why did you do that for me?" I cried out, agony unfurling in my chest as I burrowed next to Feral's limp form. He'd shrunk back to his usual—still very large—self. He was completely crusted in blood, and his shorts were riddled with bullet holes along with much of his flesh.

I skimmed my hand over his chest, my fingers shaking as they grazed the wounds.

"Why did you save me? You were supposed to be my enemy. Things would have been so much easier between us if we had just kept hating one another. Why did we have to bring love into it?"

I gave his chiseled jaw a tearful kiss, then I twisted around to face Eros and kissed him in the same spot.

I tried to recede into myself, to bury myself deep into the darkness inside me. But the coldness that had settled over my body was chased away by warmth.

Body heat.

I opened my eyes to see Eros *breathing*.

He was still alive!

I pressed my nose to his jugular and inhaled the scent of him. The warmth of his blood, the shallow drag of his breath. He was out cold, but there wasn't so much as a single bullet hole in him, and the damage he'd gotten in the fight with Vincent was finally healing.

Curling up beneath his arm, my tears were bitter-sweet. At least one of them had made it. For now. And it would make fighting our way out of the grip of the Boston vampires that much easier.

As I clung to Eros, my thick tears peppered the reaper tattoo on his chest and my gut twisted at the irony. "You survived, you crazy bastard," I said to him, even though he couldn't hear me. I brushed his blond locks from his face and kissed him again on the corner of his mouth, his piercings cold against my lips. "Feral saved you from getting shot. Can you believe that?"

"No, I can't."

My heart nearly jumped right out of me when a voice answered, a voice that wasn't Eros'. I flipped to my other side to see Feral looking at me. He was alive.

Both of them had survived!

The vampire groaned in pain. He was completely crusted in blood, pale as death, and looked like he could barely move.

But he was still alive.

Crawling over to him, I crouched beside him and took his head in my hands, my breath shaking as I stared down at him in disbelief. "How?" It was all I could manage to say. It made sense that Eros was still alive since he'd been shielded from the attack. But how had Feral survived?

Vincent winced, his face contorting. It was as if the simple sound of my voice split his skull in half. "Immune to silver," he rasped. "It's iron I have to worry about."

I blinked, my jaw falling open. "Immune to silver but weak to iron. That sounds like—"

"Fae," he said, finishing the thought for me. "Dark fae, specifically. We're different than the pointy-eared forest folk you might have read about. Though we come from the same world. Dark fae are shapeshifters who feed on the pain and fear of mortals to gain more forms, and with it, more power."

"A dark fae." I tested the words on my tongue, weighing them. Of all the things I had guessed Feral to be, it wasn't a fae. Yet, it made sense in retrospect.

"That's two," he said in a grated whisper that was so weak, I thought his voice might break in half.

I scrunched my brows together as I gawked down at him in confusion. "Two what?"

"There were three conditions you had for becoming my blood whore. While I am immune to silver, I am still very wounded. I need your blood to heal properly. The first was that I vowed to never touch Lexi again. The second was to tell you what I am. And the third—"

"Was to tell me how my father died."

He grunted in agreement.

I closed my eyes, trying to steady my nerves. "I want to know how my father died. But you should know that no matter what, I'll give you my blood. You saved me and Eros. You didn't have to do that for him, but you did. Why?"

"Because you love him. As much as that fucking irritates me—"

"You can have my blood. You can have anything..." I swallowed and reached to touch Vincent's cheek.

He caught my fingertip with his lips and kissed it before taking it into his mouth. I flinched as I felt his fangs descend and puncture my flesh. He suckled on me, his eyes firmly fixed on mine as he fed.

He unleashed a heady growl, the green of his eyes staining crimson.

Since he'd sworn off Lexi and had lost a lot of blood in the factory, he had to be absolutely ravenous.

"You must be starving. You don't need to be gentle. Take what you need from me."

The invitation made his pupils expand, pushing the red in his eyes to thin rings. He grabbed me and flipped me over so that I was pressed flat on my back, sandwiched between the van's metal flooring and his steel-hard pectorals.

Taking a fistful of my hoodie, he ripped it at the neckline to expose my shoulder.

For a beat, I thought he might try biting me over Eros' mark, but instead, he pushed his teeth down into the stretch of flesh sitting below my collarbone.

I bit back a scream. He wasn't being gentle, but I didn't expect that from Vincent Feral.

I bucked against him involuntarily, as if my body was fighting the beast who fed on me even though my brain was all for it.

He kept me pinned beneath him with his body weight and released a soothing purr of a growl to calm me as he fed.

The sound sank through my core and burrowed deep into a place he had yet to claim.

Bloody freaking *hell*. Of all places to be turned on, of all situations. For fuck's sake, I was in the back of a van, being taken to God knows where. Not to mention Eros was still passed out, and the male on top of me was full of bullet holes. Or, he *was*.

As the dark fae fed, his wounds began to knit shut. His body began to push out the bullets still lodged in him, and they fell onto me in thick red gobs of gore-drenched metal.

All I could do was lay beneath him and gaze up at this creature as he feasted on me. I felt like an offering meant for some ancient deity.

He was a feral monster.

And I was the hopeless half-blood who'd fallen into a dark and irrevocable love affair with him.

I parted my legs, reveling in the way he healed, and grew stronger right before my eyes. His regeneration wasn't the only way my blood was affecting him. He was growing hard. His masculine heft throbbed as he began to grind his hips into mine.

This wasn't the time or the place for him to claim me, but I ached so badly for him. I needed him to the point of pain.

My animalistic instincts wanted to take him in his hybrid form, to have him push me to the brink of my limits. I wanted to let that fire that burned between us consume me, and from the ashes, I would be born something new.

His claimed mate.

I was the only female to make The Feral King submit, the only female who'd claimed him as my mate and lived to tell of the depraved tale.

Together, we would be an unholy force of destruction.

"Say that you're mine," he growled into my ear. My own blood dribbled from his chin as he spoke, streaking my throat in red. "Admit what you've known all along, little monster."

He slipped his hand between us and caressed the juncture between my thighs. I shivered in wicked pleasure, earning me a devilish chuckle that made his chest rumble against mine.

"I am yours," I said. "But I belong to you as much as I belong to Eros, Sterling, and Corry. You have to learn how to share, Feral."

He flashed me a sinister smirk. "I'll agree to share. I'll agree to give up my pursuit of the throne. I'll even play nice with Deathwish. But you have to agree to give me a part of you that you won't share with my brothers... At least for now."

"What is it?"

When he spoke next, his baritone cadence was husky and came out in fragments, like the mere thought of it was getting him worked up. "You give me your womb. You wear your father's crown and sit on his throne. You take as many mates as your sweet pussy desires. But when you're ready, I'm the one that gets to breed you."

His words ignited a fire within me. Flames licked my core, and I purred beneath him, nodding my agreement. "Yes, yes, I agree."

He gripped my jaw, forcing me to look at him. "Say it. Say your womb belongs to me."

"It's yours. My womb is yours."

"That's right, little monster, it is mine. And the second we kill these bastards who dare think they can touch our queen, I'm going to mark you."

I moaned beneath him as his teeth nipped the shell of my ear. Then he bit me again, feeding for pleasure this time, rather than necessity.

I don't know how much time passed. The back of this van felt like its own universe in a way where time had no meaning.

After Vincent had his fill of me, he kissed the patch of skin beneath my ear and said something that I had known deep down all along.

"I killed your father."

My brain stalled out for a second, and I jerked my head to meet his hooded gaze. Every inch of my skin erupted in goosebumps, seeing the expression etched into his chiseled features. "How? I thought progeny weren't strong enough to kill their masters."

"Not in a fair fight. But since when do any of us play fair? As you know, I was your father's blood whore. He drank from me every night. One night, he decided it would be '*fun*' to make Sterling suck him off in front of a few of the coven members. It..." Vincent's sanguine orbs blazed with a thinly veiled rage that struck me like a lightning bolt. "It made me get to thinking, wouldn't it be '*fun*' to drink some liquid silver right before Master's nightly feeding session? The stuff doesn't hurt me, after all. And how sad that our poor king didn't have the same kind of immunity."

My eyes widened at Feral's confession, my heart constricting in my chest. Thomas Knight had died from ingesting liquid silver. But it hadn't been by suicide. His blood whore had ingested it, and when the king went to feed...

"Oh, my God. That's—"

His brows flicked up as he quietly appraised my reaction. "Horrible?"

"I was going to say brilliant."

A delicious smile curved his lips that made my heart throb. "Most people wouldn't be impressed to hear about the murder of their father."

"Yeah, well, I'm not like most people. Thomas Knight might have supplied the sperm, but he wasn't a father to me. And apparently, my mom isn't my mom."

I was curious to see Vincent's reaction to this. Did he know that the woman in Quincy was just a glorified babysitter? Did any of the guys know?

Before he could reply, the van came to a stop, and on the next breath, the doors ripped open.

Vincent crouched over me in a defensive position, bristling. He bared his teeth, and he gave a low growl of warning.

I blinked against the blinding light that spilled into the dark van. Two silhouettes stood in front of the doors, their features indiscernible due to the light shining at their backs.

"Well, well," an unfamiliar male voice spoke. "So, you weren't lying when you said you captured her alive. Though I thought you said Feral was dead."

"He's supposed to be," Sharpe's voice answered. "What should we do now, Erik?"

Erik. I'd heard that name before. That was the name of the Boston Coven's leader.

"Call Dagon Knight. Tell him we've got his sister."

THE END OF BOOK 1

Find out what happens next to Ruby and her princes in
Our Sins in Shadows: Coven of Sin Book 2

A Note from the Author

Thank you so much for reading *Our Sins in Blood: Coven of Sin Book 1*! If you enjoyed this story pretty please consider leaving a review. Taking a second to leave a few words or even just a star rating makes a world of difference to indie authors like me because it helps new readers find my work! :) If you're eager to see what happens next to Ruby and her guys, you can grab the next installment of the story in *Our Sins in Shadows: Coven of Sin Book 2*. Feel free to stalk me at any of the links below to stay tuned for release date announcements, news, and general Aiden Pierce shenanigans.

Reader Group:

https://www.facebook.com/groups/190582886541183

Instagram:

https://www.instagram.com/aidenpierceromance/

Goodreads:

https://www.goodreads.com/author/show/20185732.Aiden_Pierce

Website: https://www.authoraidenpierce.com/

Made in the USA
Las Vegas, NV
18 March 2022

45906471R00356